I0726769

Copyright © 2016 Alexandra Allred

Please note this book is intended for mature audiences due to explicit language and graphic sexual content. Reader discretion is advised.

This book is a work of fiction. Names, characters, places, and incidents are the product of the author's imagination and are used fictitiously. Any resemblance of actual events, locales, or persons, living or dead, is coincidental.

All rights reserved. Except as permitted under the U.S. Copyright Act of 1976, no part of this publication may be reproduced, distributed, or transmitted in any form or by any means, including photocopying, recording, or other electronic or mechanical methods, without the prior written permission of the author

Cover Design by: T.M. Franklin
Interior Formatting by: Lindsey Gray Formatting Services

IBSN: 978-1-941398-13-5

DEDICATION

In the last 1960s, while living in Baltimore, Maryland, an effort was made to try to get black Americans to the polls. As many polls were well outside inner-city limits, it was almost impossible for many ot make the trek without transportation. But strong and determined Americans began to organize, recruiting people to serve as drivers, shuttling citizens to the polls so they, too, could cast their ballot. In those very formidable years of my young life, I did not yet understand how brave, how determined, how great my own mother was while she volunteered to drive these people. As wonderful as it was for those people to have their voices heard and be counted, I believe my mother was the true winner.

A delicate and beautiful woman, Karen Jene Watkins Powe showed us all a different kind of strength and courage. She reminded us all of the importance of standing up -- not just for herself but for those around her. Today, those values were instilled in me as I fight on to reveal the truth. We are all equal. We are all special.

Thanks, Mom.

TABLE OF CONTENTS

viii

ACKNOWLEDGMENTS

Without Gina Bates, this book would not be possible. The hilarious, outrageous, gregarious, and often sweet Tina Wolfe is a spin off of this dear friend. From there, more friends fell onto the pages of this book with their spirited, funny, quirky mannerisms, and their triumphs and stumbles. Thank you for sharing the good, the bad, the ugly, and the you-did-not-just-say-that! I love you guys.

CHAPTER ONE

They say you can never go home again. I say, why even try? Hell, you left for a reason. In the end, however, I agreed to come home.

One month, I told Momma. One month. Just until I figured out what I was going to do about my life. I gave my hometown of Granby, Texas, one month.

On paper, it should have been an easy move and an easy decision. Room and board were free. My aunt, Cecilia, set me up to work at *The Recorder*, the town's paper, on a short-term basis. Cici, as I called her, had connections in some way with everyone in town. I knew every road, every face, and every name there about. It would be as easy as slipping into an old pair of shoes. But there was a reason I left in the first place.

Small-town living is often thought of as being quaint, peaceful . . . quiet. Small-town living has a romantic appeal if you live in Maine or Vermont. But small-town living in rural Texas is anything but quaint.

Since I was in the eighth grade, I had counted down the days until I could get out of that godforsaken town. Every cent I'd made from the Beanie Weenie and babysitting had been applied to the dream of escape.

My grades had been less about personal growth or education and more about a ticket out.

So when the day came that I graduated *summa cum laude,* I made that fatal mistake that all small-town kids do. I compiled a list of everyone I loathed and told them all to kiss my ass when I left for college. I had a full academic scholarship with a partial athletic scholarship for volleyball. I was going to Duke University to major in business. I was going to make it big in the corporate world, and one day—I hoped—I was going to wipe the memory of Granby from my mind. I arranged to have Momma and Cici come to me on the holidays because I was never, I repeat *never,* going to go back home again.

I did what I had set out to do. I graduated from Duke in the top ten percent of my class while working full time at Kinko's. I was accepted in the master's program and had some serious talks with my advisor about the steps to take beyond Duke. He had amazing contacts and offered to help me ease my way into the corporate world.

With everything going my way, I took one little detour, following the footsteps of my ancestors. With success and financial independence all but locked up, the ancient spirits of my grandmother, great-grandmother, and great-great-grandmother awakened inside me. I ran right out and got pregnant.

Well, I didn't run. In fact, I'd been too drunk to run.

Once upon a time, I'd been a serious party girl. My roommates, a few friends from work, and fellow classmates used to go out and just get hammered. It was harmless fun, and it became part of a routine. Like most college students, we had our hangouts. We were all serious, dedicated students, committed to our academics. Then there'd been times to let our hair down, among other things.

On that night, however, there was no party time with my girlfriends. I sought peace at the bottom of a vodka bottle. The first and last time. I was upset and wanted to make the hurt go away. Funny how only after did I see the irony there.

Five weeks later, I understood that I'd fulfilled a legacy. However determined I was to succeed, history had something else to say.

I hung on into my first year in the master's program, still working at Kinko's as night manager, until Ella was born. Then everything came apart. I couldn't work the same hours, studying was impossible, bills spiraled out of control, and the father of my child was gone. Even faithful friends suddenly couldn't relate to me.

The home I had made at Duke was no longer home once Ella arrived. I'd lost my academic standing and had to give up my management position at Kinko's, but what really broke me was when my advisor—a man who'd felt more like an uncle than educator—had sat me down and said he was *disappointed* with my recent decisions. I had shown promise, he'd said in a saddened, past-tense manner, as though I was washed up academically. I was twenty-four years old, and the dream was dead. What was left was the very place I had damned to hell and to which I had sworn never to return.

CHAPTER TWO

There was no great fanfare when I came home. Travis Miles saw me at the Town Pump, the local gas station, and just laughed.

"Hell, Thia, I knew you'd be back. Heard you were some highfalutin businesswoman up east. But I knew you'd be back." He cocked his head to the side and eyed my car like an appraiser judging its worth, and then he spied Ella. "Just like all the other girls in this town," he said.

I flipped him off.

I can't figure why it made me so mad to have Travis say what he did. At least I got out for a while; at least I made a go of things, got myself a college education. Travis barely graduated from high school and did nothing more than patch leaky roofs and mix paint. But his words followed me for weeks.

To be likened to the other girls from Granby was like being called trash because that's what most of the girls were.

Even though Momma was happy to have me home, Travis's voice echoed in my brain. Cici told me that she hadn't seen Momma this happy in a long time, but I couldn't celebrate. I had my own room, a built-in babysitter, and a job at *The Recorder,* but again, no sense of relief.

The fact is that I was so preoccupied with Travis's comparison of me to the other female folk of Granby that I had become obsessed with the term "trash."

You can't live in the South, particularly Texas, and not hear that word a dozen times over in just one day. The way a body might walk, talk, dress, or smile could put you on the trash-o-meter. How you wore your makeup, touched another person, or named your baby were indicative of your trashiness.

"Trash is trash."

That was what Cici always said. You could throw it, bag it, and haul it to the dump. You could even pick through another man's trash yet be clean and fresh as baby's breath. It was how you carried yourself. That was what distinguished household garbage from human trash. I always thought she said it because she had an awful crush on Bubba Peters, but as I would come to learn, there was indeed a different kind of human trash, and my Cici didn't always have all the answers on the human condition.

I can't speak for people of color. How or what they choose to call each other is their own business. Some things tend to be more of a cultural thing. But for me, for my family, I can tell you there are two different kinds of trash. There's trash and there's white trash. Lest you think there is no difference, I offer my hometown as testimony to the recurrence and/or revival of white trashiness to the likes that leave even me ashamed. On another level, it offered me some sense of relief. As I would come to learn, a town doesn't make a trashy town—the people do.

The easiest distinction is this. Trash know they're trash. They'll laugh about it, sing songs about being a redneck, and embrace their lot in life by doing things like putting ceramic statues on their lawns and reaching for toothpicks rather than after-dinner mints. If you're higher-end trash, you might just have flavored toothpicks. Trash tends to be happier than you'd think. Block parties are cool until someone gets too drunk and pulls a knife or hits someone else, but there's no exclusion. Come one. Come all. That's just how it is.

White trash folks, on the other hand, have no idea how trashy they are. They think they're high-end. Period. They look down on other folks and operate under the misconception that the darker the skin, the dumber the person—or at least, the more prone to violence. It doesn't matter that almost every year about Thanksgiving time, Old Man Vargus—a good-for-nothing, out of work white man who still drones on about fighting in Vietnam—beat the ever-living snot out of his wife. I knew folks in town who acted as though it wasn't the same as black men or Mexican men getting drunk and beating their women.

While I tended to think of Granby as a redneck town, we had a healthy mix of black and Mexicans. A little over two hundred miles from the Mexican border, Granby was one of those in-between towns. And like most small towns, we had our own history.

Once upon a time, Granby had been a sugar refinery town where blacks were granted land but could only farm certain portions. Most farming permits had been allocated to white farmers, leaving blacks to work the refinery and get paid squat for their efforts. It was supposed to suit everyone just fine, but when the farming community had folded, unable to compete with bigger industry up North, the refinery suddenly looked better to everyone. The whites got paid more, and the blacks got laid off.

During the 1950s, there had been lynchings and terrible stories about young black men getting the crap beat out of them for simply looking at a white woman or talking out of turn. By the mid-1950s, stories had circulated of black-on-white crimes.

Funny thing, I could never find any news stories to back up such claims, and I wish I could say that it was these injustices that set me to pondering my family, white folks in the South, and in general, who we really were. It wasn't. After some time, it wasn't even Travis Miles's comparison of me to other women because I'd gotten myself pregnant. I guess I was as set in my ways as anyone else. I was kind of resigned. A better word would be defeated.

I was back and I didn't want to be. I resented having to come back and found myself looking down on other people. I was so fired up about not being like the other trashy women in my town that I guess I needed something to shake me up.

Hell, I lived in a town where everyone knew Marla Dodson was stealing from the register at the video store, but no one dared stop her because she was married to Clyde Dodson, who got kicked in the head by a horse seven years back and hadn't been right since. I'd personally heard people exclaim, "Dammit, I got me a four dollar charge on this here video, and I didn't even rent the damned thing!" They'd go and pay the bill anyway because we all figured that poor Clyde had himself some pretty hefty doctor bills.

From time to time, goats got loose and could be seen running downtown. Everyone knew that Jared Durham was a drunk, but he continued to get cases sent to his law firm because his sister, Jessie, worked at the courthouse. Monica Tyree smoked dope, but no one did anything about it, much less talked about it because her daddy was Pastor Tyree. There didn't seem to be much that could shake this old tree.

Then came the word that turned it all 'round for me and made me rethink everything I thought I ever knew.

Niglet.

Niglet, like piglet, but it was used in reference to a little black baby. And even more curious, it was used in a way that was meant to be a compliment.

Niglet.

I don't mind telling you it was a word that rolled around in my head for the rest of the day, all that night, and into the next day until I determined that I did not like it. More than that, I detested it. And that was a big moment, for I don't believe I'd ever detested any word before.

In the South, words are just that. We don't hold much stock in words. Spit in a man's face, shoot his horse, puncture his tires—that's something else entirely. But a word for a black baby was nothing to get all stirred up about. So, even though I knew I hated the word more than any other word I thought I'd heard, I didn't say much about it. I just kept to my work.

Niglet.

If I didn't think on it, I was fine, but it was like a hangnail. It started to fester, just getting worse in my mind, and I set to thinking about the very people who had used it and who had been there when it was used.

To set this up, you had to picture *The Recorder*. It was the town's only paper, with a circulation of five thousand—not that we had as many as five thousand living in Granby. We were surrounded by four small, dried-up towns, each sporting a few hundred residents, who also received *The Recorder*. We were in the flood plains, though we'd not had a flood since I can't remember when. As a result, the main street in Granby was built up so that the steps onto the sidewalks were a good three feet from the street. We still weren't wheelchair friendly, though one of three large signs greeting your drive into town touted us as the FRIENDLY CITY. The second bragged about our football team going to nationals three decades ago, and the grand finale is, YOUR HOUSE IS OUR ROYAL FLUSH. That sign belonged to Shelby Harrelson. She owned a thriving porta potty business, rented out to all the construction sites from here to Mexico, and was easily the richest woman in town. I'd always thought it spoke volumes that our city was in the toilet business.

Another three miles and you were right in the middle of downtown Granby and its two gas stations, Subway, Sonic drive-in, a few antique shops, a small grocery store, and *The Recorder* office. One street over was the county courthouse, the bank, and a few lawyer offices—all things I could see perfectly from my desk situated next to a large bay window. I had the bird's eye view, so to speak, of my town.

While there were four of us in the office, only two of us ran the paper. My job description was typesetter, writer, sometimes editor, and bill collector. When I wasn't collecting or reporting, LeAnn Ricks did. Vicky Jackson answered phones, and Tammi Whatley, wife of the owner, did nothing.

It just so happened the day Tasha had walked in with her baby latched firmly around her hip, she'd walked into a snake pit.

CHAPTER THREE

"Hey, girl," Tasha called out when she saw me, drawling out the girl part.

"Hey, girl," I said with a smile. It was the standard salutation.

I'd known Tasha since grade school. She was naturally lean with thin, toned arms and a bootylicious backside that got her into considerable trouble. Thus, the baby on her hip. As always, her grin was wide and gorgeous. Her teeth were set off beautifully against her cocoa-colored skin, and I was jealous. Her eyes were wide set, looking even larger because of the careful eyeliner she'd applied.

"What'chu want?" I asked, flexing my fingers at her baby, the universal sign for *Hand him over!* She smiled and handed Darion to me. I smelled his baby powder-fresh body and rubbed my cheek back and forth over his fuzzy head. He was plump and heavy, a doughy mound of cuteness that I loved to hug.

"Girl, James is fixin' to graduate from school, and we are havin' a party!" She beamed.

Her baby daddy was James Otis, a classically nice guy who

everyone in town just loved. A one-time hometown hero until he broke his back at the regional playoffs against the Mexia Wildcats, James was the one everyone knew would make it to the NFL, take care of his momma, and put Granby on the map. He was a terrible student but a charismatic, dominating personality, on the field and off. Teachers in Texas tend to become blind with such a fellow.

I could remember it like it was yesterday. I'd been at the game. Hell, everyone had been at that game. We'd heard it clear up in the stands, above the roar of the crowd, when he'd made that spectacular catch. James took a hit so hard, we'd all gasped as if on cue. Just like that, it was over. It was the last catch he'd ever make. For months, he'd been laid up in the hospital up in Waco. When he'd been allowed to come home, it was to a hero's welcome with a parade, signs, and loud cheers all around. Then . . . nothing. Six years had passed, and no one gave James much thought anymore. But he was one of our few success stories. He'd finished school, worked the local gas station, the Town Pump, and went nights to a local community college.

"Is that right? James Otis is gettin' his associate's?" LeAnn clasped her hands together.

I looked at Darion's perfect face and Tasha nodded happily.

"That's right, and we're having a party." She tossed her head, her big hoop earrings skimming her shoulders. On anyone else, those earrings would have been too much, but on Tasha, they looked perfect.

"What's his major, honey?" Tammi asked her, and I could feel my fingers tighten around little Darion. "I mean—" She gave a sweet smile, as if Tasha were too stupid to know what she had meant by that. "What was his area of study?"

"He's gettin' a technical degree in technology computers," Tasha told us, still beaming, still unfazed by what was to come, but I knew. I had to sit and listen to these cows talk all the time, and I could tell what was coming.

"Now, is that a bachelor's or an associate's?" Tammi asked, continuing her assault. "I ask because, you know, my Ryan is at Texas Tech . . ."

Tammi droned on, and my mind wandered off. Lord, but I'd heard this so many times I thought I might vomit. Yes, yes. The all-mighty, all-glorified, spoon-fed, pain-in-the-ass Ryan Whatley had gotten himself a scholarship to Texas Tech. Whoop-dee.

Tasha's smile faded, and I jumped in, standing to hand Darion back. He kicked his legs excitedly, looking thrilled to be alive. He pursed his little lips together and began ooh-ing and ohh-ing.

"He's getting an associate's," I said and turned to Tasha. "Am I invited? I better be or this announcement will cost you double!"

Even while Tasha was telling me how she wanted the announcement to read, we could both hear the remarks being made on the other side of the office, and I felt my face burn a little. Everyone knew that the Otis family didn't have two nickels to rub together, but the office cows would sit back in judgment of him because he didn't go to a big university. Somehow, I managed to get down all the words and promised Tasha it would run, but all the while, I was wishing they would just hush.

I would say I was annoyed but forgiving of how the ladies acted because it was just the way things were. It's not something I'm proud to say. It didn't matter if you were a female of ten years or eighty; there were rules for females in a cluster. If the majority of the group trashed another person, particularly a female, you let it slide. Little girls learn early on that if you want to be part of the group and ensure your chances of not getting trashed, it's better to be in on the group side.

Boys never have to worry about this because most boys don't bother having any kinds of conversations that involve the community or members thereof. They don't care if it isn't right there in their faces, directly impacting them. So when they're older and just happen into a conversation in which someone they know and like is being trashed, and they speak up, they don't realize that defending the poor soul is social suicide. Again, this kind of thing is not the same among boys.

"That's assuming that that baby even belongs to James. You know," Vicky said, emphasizing her statement with a nod and pointed stare.

After Tasha left, I nestled in my corner, watching the world, as Granby knew it, pass by and listened to Vicky, Tammi, and LeAnn talk. They would spend another few minutes talking about Tasha Williams and how she toted that baby of hers around, acting as though the only daddy could be James Otis when we all remembered good and well how there had been some questions as to the baby's daddy. To their way of thinking, the issue had never been resolved.

Cardinal chick rule number one: Don't defend those who aren't there. If you don't like what's being said, don't be a part of what's being said.

Vicky Jackson was one to talk. Her husband was Tom Jackson, owner of Jackson's Appliance, on the backside of the courthouse. He fixed everything electronic, from outdated answering machines to dishwashers and treadmills, but he did more than that and everyone knew it. How Vicky could pretend not to notice that Ms. Miranda McGhee had more broken appliances than any other woman on earth, I do not know. Everyone in town knew what was going on, yet the more obvious it got, the blinder Vicky got. So I thought it funny that she should sit there on her high horse, judging Tasha for a mistake—not that Darion was a mistake.

I don't mind saying it. I judged Vicky. I stared at her over-teased, backcombed hair, where she tried in quiet desperation to make her pie-faced head look as if her hair had some life. It didn't. Her hair was too light or her eyebrows were too dark. I couldn't decide which.

She came from an era when face powder was critical to the complete makeover, and no one had told her that natural was in, so she always looked slightly ill. In her late fifties, age had not been kind. Her body had settled into a doughy mass, nothing like Darion's, but fleshy with loose skin, which she'd tried to encase in tight clothing. Either that or she refused to accept that she was now two sizes larger than a year ago.

"But he's a cute little niglet," Vicky said, and everything inside me seized up.

LeAnn chuckled then turned to include me. "Don't you think, Thia?"

I should have spoken up. I should have been indignant. I should have demanded they explain what a niglet was—some sort of half-human, half-animal as they seemed to imply. I should have pointed out the hypocrisy of these women who never missed a sermon, who claimed to have read and revered the Holy Bible and the word of God—the same God who created all children, black, brown, or white, to love and be loved. I should have pointed out that they missed the finer points of those teachings. Or, maybe I should have just taken pity on them for their horrible thoughts. It would have been so easy to threaten to tell Pastor

Tyree about their nasty indiscretions. That would have been great. That would have fixed them but good.

Instead, I rose from my desk and went outside. It was close to lunch, and I wanted a sandwich from Subway.

I looked up and down Main Street, resigned to what I saw. This was it. This was my hometown. To the right—the Town Pump and Doc's Veterinary Clinic. I saw people off in the distance. I didn't know their faces or their names, but I recognized them. To my left, two blocks down, past Luther's Garage, I saw Amber Hirsh and Lisa Gary strut along, pushing a stroller and shaking what God gave them.

I knew Amber and knew of Lisa. Neither was good. There was no telling if they were ever good girls, but boredom and the disease of little expectation had rotted them both to where all one could expect was when the next would be expecting.

Amber Hirsh was winning that race. Word around town was it was Cody Kyle's baby. If that were true, it'd be a fine looking baby—most likely thick blonde hair, blue eyes, and creamy skin, just like the parents. That kid would also have the brain capacity of a hamster.

Fortunately for Amber, she was too stupid to know how stupid she was and that her little offspring would qualify for disability by taking an IQ test. Unfortunately for the town of Granby, Cody Kyle was said to have fathered two other little kids. At the age of seventeen, he was doing what he could to boost the town's population. It was like watching goats breed.

Cody was an okay kid overall, but beyond intelligence, he lacked motivation. Talk to him and you'd find he had no grand plan. He had no desire or ability to go to college, no passion for anything, cared about nothing and nobody. He didn't read the news, couldn't discuss anything of consequence, but loved playing video games and partying. It was hard to be mad at a kid like Cody because he generated such a buzz of non-importance about himself that you couldn't muster enough energy to care. He was just there.

By all accounts, Amber was different from folks around these parts. Her daddy was Dr. Randy Hirsh, the town vet, who was never out of work, believe it or not. They lived on a fifty-acre ranch, in a super nice house with an in-ground pool, a Jacuzzi, and a heated and air-conditioned ten-stall barn. Amber could have gone to any school she wanted, despite her intellectual deficiencies. She had the best clothes, the nicest car. Whatever she wanted, her daddy got her. The sad thing was she didn't have a clue what she wanted from life.

She rebelled against everything, which was bullshit. When you've got a great life and you rebel against that, you're just stupid. For one thing, she claimed to not like animals. The first time I'd heard that, I knew my suspicions about her were correct. She disliked the very thing that made her father happy and put the clothes on her back.

Cici once told me there is something off about a person who claims to believe in God and read the Bible but not like animals. And Amber lived as you would expect for a person who professed not to like animals. She was all about Amber. She was all about material things, and she couldn't give a rat's ass who was hurt in the process of her day.

Lisa Gary was even worse. The mere sight of her pissed me off so much, she set my teeth on edge.

Lisa had a baby some eight months ago, and she strutted around town as if she suddenly had importance because she was someone's momma. I saw it all for what it was—an act. She didn't know what the hell she wanted to do with herself, and having a baby was, she figured, the easiest way to get her own daddy off her back.

Hut Langford was the daddy. Not surprising, he was fresh from his second prison stint for running guns, another six months of his life gone, which about broke his momma's heart. He could be real funny and charming, but he was not the kind of guy you shared tidbits with. It wasn't a coincidence that there had been a rash of break-ins and stolen guns about the same time Hut had entertained his gunrunning career.

When word had first traveled the town that she was pregnant, Lisa had cried all the time. As more and more folks had consoled her, asking her what she was going to do, I could see that she was having a good time with all the attention. She'd enjoyed her pregnancy, not because she had some great love of the life that grew in her belly, but because she loved all the special treatment her belly brought. That baby had kept her from having to mess with the two things she had had no intention of doing—college or work. After graduation, she'd spent her days with Amber, and now that Amber was pregnant, the population of losers was growing.

Lisa popped a cigarette in her mouth, careful to pop her hip and strike a pose while she lit it. She was the Paris Hilton of Granby. Talk about trash. With her cigarette poking out from her mouth, she leaned over to check the baby and blew death-smoke in the kid's face, damaging whatever functioning brain cells there were in its little head.

A sharp whistle caught my attention, and I looked across the street to find Officer Tina Wolfe pointing at me.

I grinned.

Tina Wolfe was the one breath of fresh air in this hellhole. I did a quick peek to the left and right and hustled across the street. It was a blatant jaywalking offense, and Officer Wolfe could not have cared less.

CHAPTER FOUR

"What the hell are you doin' here?" Officer Tina Wolfe called out as she stood with her partner on the opposite side of the street. Her sly, lopsided smile was contagious. "Get on over here and grab a bite with us," she demanded in that way no one could refuse.

Chuckling at the part order, part promise for a good time, I readily agreed to lunch with Granby's notorious duo.

Tina Wolfe and I had known each other in high school, and we couldn't have been further apart. She'd been wild and unruly. I would have sworn that she'd turn out to be nothing more than a teenage statistic—either dead or in jail.

Tina and her brothers were famous for the parties they threw when their parents were out of town. Jack Wolfe Sr. was a big investor in the circuit rodeos and traveled quite a bit with his wife, leaving his children to run the ranch. True as it was that the kids were capable ranch hands, they were also wild kids with an even wilder streak for trouble. As wild as the Wolfe kids were, no one liked to make too much of it because the Wolfes were also good friends to the school district, local businesses, and the policemen's association, if you know what I mean. So, the general rule of thinking was, as long as no one got killed, how bad could it be? That all changed when Tina's little brother, Jake, was killed when the kids were out on the back pasture, doing doughnuts in the truck. The driver, an unlicensed fifteen-year-old, too drunk to spell his own name, flipped the truck and came crashing down on top of Jake. He was decapitated.

Tina had short hair, frosted at the tips, and spiked out. She was loud, abrasive, and about the most honest woman in the entire town. She could be shocking, but you couldn't be mad at her because she was so real.

She'd once been under investigation when it had been discovered she'd falsified documents at the station house. A fellow officer had been injured while she, the acting senior officer, had been in charge. Fearful she'd be reprimanded, she hadn't exactly told the entire story.

It was during the Olympics, and they were holding their own couch-hurdling event. Officer Davis, all six feet three inches of him, forgot about the low overhang near the doorway, launched over the back of the couch, and promptly knocked himself unconscious. He required six stitches in his forehead. Tina stated in her report that Officer Davis was injured while subduing an irate couch. She hoped that anyone reading the report would believe she had misspelled coach. That way, she reasoned, she wasn't lying. Unfortunately, the chief was a stickler and wanted to know who the irate couch was.

Tina had her own unique way of policing. She once stopped an old man for speeding, but because it was raining, she didn't want to get her hair wet and made him come to her car for a ticket. Once she realized he was about a hundred years old, she simply gave him a warning. Another time she locked herself inside a citizen's house when she responded to a disturbance call and discovered the disturbance was a snake. Terrified of snakes, she refused to leave the house until more help came. No one dared call her a sissy. She was fast to throw her stick, or even a flashlight, at someone who pissed her off.

The chief reprimanded her when a series of complaints were lodged against her. Tina was known to park outside Paradise Park, a trailer park on the outskirts of town that was predominantly Mexican, and wait for someone to fire up a car. It was, she calculated, simply a matter of time before a broken tailgate passed by, which allowed her to pull the driver over, and low and behold, find he didn't have auto insurance.

While the complaints lodged had claimed racial discrimination, Tina had been more practical about it. It hadn't been racial; it was just the way it was. She'd had a quota to fill, Mexicans tended not to get auto insurance, and so it stood to reason that that had been as good a place as any to stake out.

We were munching on chips and catching up on old times, including complaints against certain police officers, when Officer Rosa Fox, perhaps the only officer in Granby who could tolerate Wolfe on a daily basis, spoke up.

"Bullshit," Fox said, shaking her head at me. "She don't like Mexicans, so she seeks us out. It's why she got me. She saw me and thought, 'Now, how can I drive her crazy? I know! I'll be her partner.' "

Tina barked out a laugh, giving me a friendly shove toward the doorway of Los Pepes, a Mexican restaurant. It didn't matter if I wanted lunch or not. We were going to eat. Officers Fox and Wolfe were on lunch break.

"We have an understanding," Tina said, after we placed our orders. "I don't much care for Mexicans, and she don't like whites. So we figure we even things up pretty good."

"They spit in her food here." Rosa smiled at me while she dipped a chip into her own little bowl of salsa. "It's why they give me my own bowl. They don't spit in mine. Just the bitchy gringo."

Wolfe and Fox had become Granby's own superstars. Their names alone had caused enough of a sensation that even other departments were aware of the two attractive female officers. They'd become known as Wolfie and Foxie. But it had been the story of the waterbed that had shot them to celebrity status.

It was Rosa Fox's first official call—a domestic dispute. A woman had bitten off her lover's ear during a spat. Since the assailant was a woman, the chief sent out Wolfe and Fox. Rosa, just twenty-two years old, hoped her partner would take the lead. At just five foot three and barely a buck o' five, Rosa hadn't been hired on for her brawling abilities. She was a crack shot with an assault rifle and scored top in her class for procedure and protocol. The thinking had been that she might be able to teach Wolfe a thing or two about proper police etiquette. She was also bilingual. She was opposite of Wolfe in every way—long black hair, black eyes, calm, quiet, and composed. But standing at the doorway of the domestic, Rosa balked.

"Go on." Tina laughed. "Let's see you bring this one in."

Together they peered into the bedroom of one Wanda Tuckett.

More than two hundred and fifty pounds of pissed-off nakedness, Wanda had dared them to take her in. "I ain't goin' anywheres!"

"She's like a giant marshmallow," Tina said with a chuckle.

"Git her outta my house," a man yelled behind them, still holding the side of his head and demanding justice. "The crazy bitch just bit my ear off. Bit it off and she won't give it back!"

"Ma'am, I need for you to—"

"You can come on in here and git it if you want it so bad! C'mon and git it! I dares you! You think you can git it?"

Rosa took a step into the room. "Ma'am, I need for you to give me the ear. Let's try to be—"

"Don't come anywheres near me, you Mexican bitch!"

Tina seemed giddy with delight as she gave Fox a quick poke to the ribs. To Rosa's horror, her partnered offered her up. "Go on, get the ear. I'll wait here."

Wanda rose up on her knees, spread out her arms, and exposed herself for all to see which took effort as she was on a waterbed. Instinctually, Rosa stepped back. The woman was enormous. Her body moved up and down as waves beneath the sheets lapped back and forth in the bed's frame.

Tina didn't even try to suppress her grin.

The man behind them continued screaming even after the ambulance arrived. For a moment, Tina turned to be sure he was well taken care of.

Wanda continued to shout profanities, threatening the officers and daring anyone to touch her.

"We're going to need that ear if you can get it, Wolfie," Frankie Larson said to Tina, pointing in the direction of Wanda's right hand. He had worked the EMS ever since Tina Wolfe was hired on.

"You want the ear? You want it?" Wanda screamed, becoming more incensed.

"Ma'am, if I could get you to get off the bed, step down . . ." Rosa put her hands out, showing her good faith as she stepped into the room, but Wanda wasn't listening.

"Then you can have it!" Wanda yelled, heaving the ear across the room.

It landed hard against Tina's chest, making the sound a tomato slice would against a wall, and Fox's eyes widened as she watched the ear slide down her partner's chest and onto the floor.

"Oh, it's on!" Tina called out. She leapt across the room and knocked Wanda hard against the waterbed. The force drove the water against the other side of the frame, and as would later be recounted in the break room by Rosa, the naked Wanda Tuckett and Officer Tina Wolfe were catapulted off the bed and flipped mid-launch. When they landed hard on the ground, the naked Wanda was perched atop Tina.

"Oh, God! She's naked, and she's sitting on me!" Tina screeched. The sight paralyzed Rosa. "Shit, Fox! Get her off! Get her off!" In that moment, all Rosa could see were great mounds of white flesh moving over Wolfe. She saw how Wolfe struggled, with her arms flapping in one direction while her legs kicked out, hoping to find traction. There was none to be found. Wolfe was hopelessly pinned by the overabundance of a naked Wanda blanket.

Rosa's approach was awkward as she tapped Wanda on her back. "Um, ma'am," she said, clearing her throat.

Wanda turned, swinging a mighty arm and knocking Rosa back.

"Hell, Fox, stop playing with her and save Wolfie!" Larson yelled from the doorway as he watched the assault.

Rosa had gotten to her feet once more and lunged onto the bed in an attempt to bring Wanda's arm behind her back in a proper arm lock. Wanda's bare breasts had swung about as Tina shielded herself.

Although I've heard the story many times before from Momma and other friends who kept in touch while I was away, I was elated to hear it from the women themselves. As Rosa explained how she eventually wrestled Wanda off Tina, Tina gobbled a chip loaded with salsa and shrugged.

As they argued, Wolfe and Fox also wrestled over the chips basket and salsa bowl. Wolfe was content to keep the basket in front of her, not sharing with us, salting each individual chip over the basket, while Fox kept trying to slide the basket toward us. Fox pulled the chips basket back again, slapping Wolfe's hand when she tried to hold it, and Wolfe scowled.

"It was terrible. I still have giant boob dreams," Wolfe said.

"You?" Rosa laughed. "I still have dreams of that doughy, white skin." She shuddered. "After I freed my partner, which is something that we learn in the academy and that any good cop would do." Rosa leaned across the table and glared over the salsa bowls.

Tina simply shrugged.

Rosa rolled her eyes and threw a hand up in front of Tina's face. "I wrestled that fat lard for what? Ten minutes! And you know what?! She just watched. I jump in, wrestle Wanda off her, essentially saving her life, and she just watched. Yes, after being freed from her blubber prison, my faithful partner leaned against the wall and laughed while I wrestled that walrus."

"It was all part of your training." Tina grinned. "I keep telling her that, but it never sinks in. It was all for you, partner."

"It's why I hate white people," Rosa said.

"Well, I feel safe," I muttered, choosing Rosa's salsa bowl for a little chip dip. "So, what about black people?" I could see Tina and Rosa look at each other, puzzled by this question. "Well, you don't like Mexicans," I said, pointing to Tina, "although you are one." I wiggled my finger back toward Rosa. "And you don't like whites but—" I swung a finger back to Tina "—you're one, therefore, you figure you're even. But what about blacks?"

"Oh, see, we're still even there." Rosa snorted. "Don't like 'em, neither one of us."

I raised my eyebrows.

Rosa took her time, chewing and then swallowing her chip. "But not cause they're black. We don't like Asians, Arabs, you name it. We don't like nobody."

I heard myself laugh in disbelief. "Except, you like Mexicans," I pointed to her. "And you like whites," I swirled a finger in a wide arc toward Tina.

"Not really." Tina took a pull from her ice tea and picked through her chips, deciding on more salt. "Whites are generally your serial killers, rapists, and pedophiles. And, in this town, insurance scammers and dopers."

"And Mexicans are abusers, drunks, and thieves," Rosa said.

"Wow. You do realize that I work for the paper? I am the press." I put my hand to my chest, realizing how this story would sound should it ever make print. It would be the headline that roared across the nation. RACIST COPS WHO HATE EVERYONE. EVEN THEIR OWN KIND.

Tina threw a chip at me. "Oh, whatever! You're just an uptight college snob who tried to escape her small-town ties, got knocked up, and came running home to lick her wounds. Whatever you write is just you being bitter and trying to stir up some controversy like in the big city."

My mouth fell open.

"What? I'm just sayin'." Tina's eyes widened, and she cocked her head to the side.

"You ain't gonna get some big story out of this town," Rosa said with a shrug. "This is just your standard issue hellhole."

"Yeah, this is where dreams come to die. Welcome home," Tina said and raised her drink for a toast.

Rosa joined her and then smiled as our food was brought out to us. She spoke to the waiter in Spanish and Tina scowled.

"Did he spit in my food?"

CHAPTER FIVE

His name was Teddy, but for some reason, everyone just called him Bubba—Bubba, the trash man. You could set your clock by him. Six o'clock every Wednesday, there he'd be, making the slow drive along the streets of our small town, scouring all the trash set out. By God, if there was something that could be rebuilt, nailed up, sanded down, spit shined, or repainted, it would land in the back of his pickup truck. Whatever was on the menu for Thursday morning's trash pickup was on Bubba's Wednesday night treasure run.

All these years later, I realized that Cici was right. Bubba, a.k.a. Mr. Peters, was about the classiest man in town. It was the rest of us who were trash, and it got me to thinking. It was obvious why he steered clear of us all. What we set out at the curb was probably the best thing we had going for us.

Because it was a Wednesday night, Cici would be there, too. I knew that she'd be waiting to see Bubba come rumbling around in his old Chevy, picking through trash. We'd picked on Cici a lot over the years, but never about Bubba.

We teased her something awful when she showed up with fire-red hair from a bad dye job she let Arlene's teenage daughter do. Why anyone in her right mind would let Debbie Myers touch her hair was beyond me. She was one of those teenage girls who thought big boobs and tight T-shirts kept the rest of us from noticing all the fat flowing over the top of her jeans. And she picked her nose. I'd seen it. But Cici loved Arlene. They went way back, so Cici treated Debbie like her own.

My aunt Cici was the kind of woman who, when in doubt, became the loudest, most brazen woman in the room. No sooner did everyone see the botched job that Debbie did on Cici's head than Cici herself gawked into the mirror and burst out laughing.

"By damn, they'll see me coming now, won't they? Thanks, Debbie. I needed a shocker! Everyone's become too damned complacent around me. This'll rock 'em back!" With that, she pretended to shake her short, reddened locks, rose to her feet like the Queen Mother, and burst out the door of Arlene's beauty shop, hollering, "Look out world, here I come!"

She might have gotten into her car and sobbed at the sight of her hair or maybe she celebrated the new look. There was just no telling with Cici. However she'd felt, she'd never bothered to set the color straight. Shit happened. She'd dealt with it. Even when she'd been called tomater melon or tampon head. Nothing. But she had no humor about Bubba. Bubba had always been, since I could remember, off limits.

By the time I pulled into the driveway, Momma, Cici, and sweet little Ella were already perched in place.

"Well, hi. Are you all waiting for me?" I feigned breathlessness. Ella's legs were kicking in her port-a-swing, and I hoped that meant she recognized my voice.

Momma got up from her seat, a tall glass of iced tea already in hand, and greeted me at the stoop. "How was your day, baby?"

She brushed the bangs from my face, and I resisted the urge to duck away from her hand. It wasn't that I didn't love her, but it was difficult to be back, on that same stoop where I had plotted my escape. But Momma was so happy to have me back. The unwitting warden.

I shrugged and turned the question around. "How was yours? How's my baby?" I leaned in, plucking at Ella's pink booty-covered toes. She was talking—I knew she was—but I still hadn't heard a thing.

I couldn't wait to get Ella out of her swing and hug her. I couldn't wait to get her smell all over me and feel how she melted against my chest. And I couldn't wait to embrace that feeling I'd never imagined I could own—some crazy, undying maternal love for a person who so recently joined this earth. She obliged, fitting perfectly against me and finding the crook of my neck with her sweet, precious face.

There was the familiar rumbling. Without a word, I found my spot against the brick on the porch. With bikes and chairs and lawn furniture perched or hooked all over the outside of his truck, Bubba rolled into sight. His own design, the truck consisted of three walls, covered in pegboards, and lined with dozens and dozens of hooks and loops of rope. This allowed for the larger, bulkier items to sit in the bed of the truck while lighter items hung in every open spot available like ornaments.

Four houses down, Bubba stopped at the Riley place. As if on cue, I swear, Ella turned her head, and I entertained the notion that Cici had talked so much about Bubba that Ella had wanted to see the man. He was a pleasant distraction from the small talk about work. Beyond the news that James Otis had earned his associate's, I didn't have anything to share. We settled back and placed our bets.

"He'll take the bench, leave the stove," Momma wagered, and I turned to look at her.

"You think he'll pass up that stove?" I laughed.

"Nope. No stove. You watch. The bench, those picture things, whatever those are there on the ground, and that little stool thing, there. He'll take those, leave the stove."

"Momma, you know he loves appliances. Look at his truck. He's got nothing inside the bed yet. He'll take the stove." I was quite sure of myself.

"A dollar says no stove."

"You're on. And you'll see; he'll manhandle that stove like it was a toy. Two minutes, he'll have it in the back."

"Would you two please shut up," Cici said in a low growl.

I shrugged, settling back on the cement step to watch Bubba.

He was a good-looking man if you could get over the fact that he picked through garbage. He was tall and wiry, with long, stringy arms that might fool another that he was of a weaker disposition. Too many of us in Granby, however, had seen him wrap those pipe cleaners around an old stove or dishwasher and heft it up off the ground to be fooled. He was strong like a steel trap. He had some kind of freakish recoil mechanism. I swear, he might be able to lift a truck off a body with his bare hands. That alone landed him a kind of sexiness.

His hair was thick, coarse, and unruly. Even under his ball cap, wisps of hair flew every which way. The hint of a beard outlined his jaw, making his features all the more chiseled. He had a nice profile with a straight nose. It helped that, even from Momma's stoop, I knew what pretty eyes he had—a warm chestnut with crow's feet that made him look like he was smiling even when he wasn't. Crow's feet on Bubba were attractive. Crow's feet on Cici made her frantic. Just another factoid that isn't right about men and women.

"Yes," Momma's voice drawled as Bubba studied over the Riley's trash pile. "Oh, look. What potential that bench has . . . that's right. Closer. Closer," Momma said as Bubba seemed to pause over the stove.

"You want the stove," I whispered in a singsong manner. "The stove, the stove . . . *take the stove.*"

"Hush," Cici hissed and leaned back in the porch swing, watching him.

"Aha." I nodded my head as Bubba Peters moved to the oven, opening the door and examining it. "Get ready to pay." No sooner had I said it than he shut the door, hefted the bench, and stepped back to his truck. *Momma was right. No stove.*

She stuck out her hand. "One dollar."

"Yeah, yeah," I said, nuzzling Ella for a moment. "I'll add it to the growing bill I owe you."

The truck rumbled toward us. Though she never moved, never made a noise, and never changed her demeanor, I could feel the change in Cici as Bubba drew nearer. It was hard to resist the urge to watch her. I'd never seen her this way before. She was Aunt Cecilia. Thick-skinned. Independent. Yet here she was, mooning over some man.

I changed my position on the stoop, twisting Ella around in my arms, facing her outward so I could see Cici clearly. She looked radiant. I swear, she was blushing. There was no way Bubba could see her clearly from the road, but she was blushing. By the time he got to our house, he'd slowed enough to put a hand out the window, offered a slow motion wave like a windshield wiper, and kept on going. We all remained motionless until he'd passed the Bryers' house, two doors down.

Momma turned, a ridiculous grin on her face, raised her eyebrows at Cici, and asked, "Okay, who wants dinner?"

"That sounds good." Cici stood up, contented by the evening's events. Together, they moved through the front door, and I felt my jaw fall open.

Ella gave a little kick, which brought me back, and I followed Momma and Cici into the house.

"That's it?" I asked.

"What?" Momma didn't even look over her shoulder while she pulled out plates, and Cici busied herself with the flatware.

"What, 'what?' " I looked at the two women I knew and loved. "That! That was *it?* We sit on the porch for Mr. Peters to happen by, he waves, and we all go in?"

They both shrugged.

It didn't matter how long I had been away. Some things never changed. Day-to-day attitudes, generational prejudices, and sitting on the front porch watching Mr. Peters go by with another person's trash.

"I mean . . . it's kind of anticlimactic, isn't it?"

"Mr. Peters looked like he had a good haul this evening, didn't he?" Momma asked, opening the oven. There was a singsong tone to her voice and I knew she was trying to be nonchalant.

The aroma brought back waves of memories of Momma's cooking, my father, and my childhood. Escalloped potatoes were warming in the oven, and in the crock-pot, a roast had been cooked to perfection.

Daddy had bought that crock-pot for Momma almost twenty years ago. It was one of the few kitchen items she had held on to and one I had a special affection for. Momma lifted the lid to the crock-pot, letting out yummy steam—indeed, this was a roast that had cooked all day.

"I'm not at all surprised he didn't take that stove. Sandy Riley finally threw that thing out. It's been sitting on her back porch for I don't know how long." Cici stood, paused long enough to give Ella a small kiss, the smile from the porch still gracing her face, and fluttered on by. She had that same tone to her voice Momma had, and I had to smile. The two sisters were trying to be as cool as a summer's breeze. Not a care in the world. Only we were in Granby, Texas. There was no breeze and they were not cool.

"He was looking good, too, don't you think?" Momma said, setting out three large plates to dump the potatoes on. A small bowl was set aside to cool for Ella.

"Hmmm? Oh, yes. He did. Real healthy."

"Okay, okay . . . please. Stop. I can't take it anymore." I shook my head at them, pushing Ella into Cici's arms while I took over setting the table. "Have you ever talked to the guy? Have you ever actually had a conversation with him?"

"Who? Me?" Cici's hand flew to her chest.

"It doesn't leave this house, Cici. You have the hots for Mr. Peters." She looked appalled. I turned, putting a hand on my hip and smiled. "Here. Let's say it together. I have the hots for Bubba."

"Thia!

"You know, I don't ever recall seein' Ms. Sandy get a new stove," Cici said, eyebrows raised. She would now pretend I wasn't even in the room.

"You know, I believe you're right," Momma said.

"But that stove's been sittin' on her back porch for, oh, I don't know how long." Cici stepped back, examining the dinner table. She gave it a nod of final approval. "Poor thing. You know, I don't think she's got herself a stove at all."

"Maybe she got herself a microwave," Momma said as she set the roast on the table.

"Well, that breaks my heart. Imagine doing all your cooking by microwave only." Cici poked out her lower lip and nudged me to sit and fold my hands in my lap.

Ella had already been placed in her high chair, sitting prettily next to Momma.

Momma smiled at her. "Fold your hands, Lily," she whispered.

My head shot up. *Lily?*

Momma winked. "It's a name we came up with together. She likes it." And with another shrug, Momma blessed the food with Lily banging away at her tray.

After my "amen," I started to ask about Lily but was cut off by Cici.

"Thia, why don't you go over to Ms. Sandy's after dinner? Take Ella to show her off as your excuse, but you let me know if she has a stove or not, won't you?"

"I'm not going to barge into her house just to see if she has a stove."
I laughed. "For one thing, she's insane, *and* she hates people. It's good
that a woman like that doesn't have some large appliance that could cook
a human."

"Thia!"

"Well, I'm not going."

■ ■ ■

I adjusted Ella on my hip as I reached for the doorbell. I had the dubious
assignment of finding out if Ms. Riley had a stove or not. What I was
supposed to do once I got that information was a little unclear to me, but
I'd been assigned this task. Once Cici *and* Momma made up their minds,
any kind of whining was just wasted breath. Ms. Riley must have been
standing right at the door because the moment I raised my hand to ring
the bell, the heavy wood door was jerked open.

"Why, Theresa Franks. Is that you?" She stepped out, smiling.

Ms. Riley was the same Ms. Riley I'd always known. Over-permed,
short, brown hair—a home job if you ever saw one—pale, clear skin. No
makeup. Youthful for her years. As she spoke to me, commenting on my
hair, I had to wonder how old she was. She was getting on up in there in
years, but she remembered me well enough.

"I thought certain you'd be the one what never came back," she
said, slapping her hip with a giggle. "Oh, I remember watching you,
missy. Climbing into your window in the middle of the night. Oh, I saw,
all right. Never did tell your momma what I'd seen. Figured she had
enough of her own troubles since your daddy left, and as long as you
were always coming back, that's a good thing, right? Oh, but I'd get a
tickle outta watching you outfox your momma. And Cici." She stepped
back and invited me into the house.

There was an urge to whisper, "I'm in," but I was distracted by the
fact that Ms. Riley had been taking notations of my late-night escapades.

Ella squirmed in my arms, a cue for Ms. Riley to reach out.

"Let's have a look," she said, taking Ella. Ella didn't bat an eyelash,
leaning into Ms. Riley's grasp.

"Lily. Isn't that her name?" Ms. Riley asked without looking at me.
She was coo-ing and ooh-ing over Ella.

"Ella," I said, correcting her.

"Oh. I thought I'd heard your momma calling her Lily."

"You did. Momma thinks she can rename my kid." I rolled my eyes, and Ms. Riley laughed.

"Well, I can just imagine that. She never liked you doin' things without her say-so. I guess that's why I figured you'd never come back. Once you broke free . . ."

I groaned. I never thought I'd be back either.

With deep regret, I remembered the time I mouthed off to Mr. Baxter, the high school principal. He'd been harping about the importance of a solid education when I'd been caught—again—sneaking back onto school grounds after ditching class. I'd been a smartass. I'd been a kid too big for her britches in too small a town, and I'd thought my you-know-what just couldn't stink. So when he was droning on about education, I'd said something to the fact that his education had not gotten him too far off as he was right here in the middle of Where-The-Hell-Am-I, USA. I'd said once I graduated, I was gone, never to be back.

Right when you're busy being a smug little know-it-all shit, life comes and smacks you square between the eyes, and suddenly, that place you couldn't exit fast enough is the one place open to you.

I cut her off. I wasn't all that pleased about my mission and wanted to get it over with. "Gee, Ms. Riley, I am thirsty. You got some water?"

"Why, sure, come on back." She coo-ed into Ella's sweet little face. "So, who's her daddy anyways?"

I ignored the question about Ella's daddy and settled my eyes on the gun propped against the vacant enclave where a stove had once sat. My eyebrows shot up, and for a moment, I was completely unconcerned about the missing stove. "Expecting company?"

"Oh . . ." She waved a hand at me, still cradling Ella against her chest. "It's them squirrels."

I nodded, trying to imagine Ms. Riley blasting away at some squirrels because they were messing with her pecan trees. If there was anything I would remember about Ms. Riley, it was her love of her pecan trees. She had her own miniature orchard that she was immensely proud of. She loved her pecans and hated the squirrels that stole them.

I also knew a thing or two about rifles. My daddy had been a hunter. Hell, for all I knew, he was still one today, but that's neither here nor there. I had my fill of memories of watching him clean his rifles, talking about this one and that, how to care for them, cautioning me against touching them. The day he disappeared, he'd cleaned out all his things, but he'd left two guns—a .30-06 rifle he'd used for elk hunting and a little .22 pistol that Momma kept under her bed.

Why in the blue blazes Ms. Riley needed a .30-06 rifle to go squirrel hunting—in the middle of a neighborhood, no less—I couldn't imagine, and it was hard to suppress a grin of astonishment.

"Ms. Riley, I don't mind sayin' . . . if you were to hit a squirrel with that rifle you're using . . . hell, there'll be nothing left of it."

"That is the plan, Theresa. And it ain't any squirrel. It's that fat, gray one with the scrawny tail."

I squinted out the window. "They're all fat and gray!"

"No, no." She shook her head adamantly. "They're brown. Everyone thinks all squirrels are gray but they aren't. They are a brown with flecks of black and white and gray in their fur, but they're brown."

Okay.

"But this one. The fat one . . . he's all gray, and I know it's him cause of his scrawny tail. He's the one that's eating up all my pecans. He's taking more than his share."

As her voice rose, I instinctively stepped forward to retrieve Ella, smiling as I did so as not to look like I wanted to take my kid and bolt from the crazy house. I remembered that she had always had a thing about squirrels but hadn't recalled that she was arming herself, propping powerful rifles against the walls in case of a rush of squirrel action in the yard.

I nodded back toward the space where a stove once sat. "Your stove broke?" I asked innocently, refocused on my task.

She shrugged. "I got tired of it," she said and looked out the window again with a sigh. " 'Sides, I don't really need one. I have this little toaster oven." She pointed to a small oven on her counter, sandwiched between a large cow cookie jar, the kind that mooed when you opened the lid, and a three-piece flour/sugar/tea cow pottery set. "You can make really good pecan pies in this. Ever'thing else is microwavable, you know. You got a microwave?"

I nodded again. "Yup. They're pretty handy."

"So, want some water?" Ms. Riley stepped away from the window.

"You know, I'm okay, but it's been fun seeing your kitchen again. I remember all these cows from when I was a kid. I love it." I tried to smile with sincerity.

When I got home, Cici and Momma pounced.

"Well?" Cici demanded. I sighed.

"No. No stove. And she doesn't seem too shook up about it," I said, placing Ella on the floor to play with her toys. Cici and Momma followed me, wanting details.

It's funny, but when I came back to Granby, the one thing I hadn't worried about was any sort of violence. I dreaded having to face people again, getting sucked into the mundane and inane things like, oh, does or doesn't Ms. Riley have a stove in her cow kitchen, but I'd never worried about whether a crazy old woman with failing eyesight was shooting wildly at gray, not brown, squirrels stealing her pecans with a rifle meant to bring down thousand-pound animals. What if from her side of the street, Ella looked like a fat little squirrel stuffing her cheeks with pecans? Besides, I didn't know what the hell she was talking about because every damned squirrel I'd ever seen was gray.

"Momma." I sighed. "We got way bigger problems than how, or even *if,* Ms. Riley's gonna cook a turkey."

CHAPTER SIX

On the corner of Bellows and Main sat three of the dumbest human beings in the world—Roland Wyck, Milford East, and Willie Strictland. They couldn't rustle up a good idea between them, yet there they were, procreating and populating our world with more dumb people.

Roland Wyck was David Wyck's boy and possibly had the most potential of the lot. But because of his youth, he was also the most easily influenced. At twenty years old, with not a thought in his brain, yet one pregnant girlfriend, I didn't see much hope for him. It was too bad, too, because he was cute. I imagined all the girls in school were crazy for him. He had a young, strong body, shown off by his greasy muscle shirt. His muscles were long, lean, and well defined. His sandy blonde hair was long on top, short on the sides, giving him a more youthful, tousled look.

Beside him was his polar opposite. What Milford East lacked in mental faculties and common grace, he made up for in girth. Everyone called him Ford for short. Apparently, Ford sounds way tougher than Milford, but it never stood to reason why a guy who did everything big would shorten his own name. He was oversized, rude, obnoxious, and far too stupid to realize how annoying he was. He drank two-liter bottles of Dr. Pepper rather than the normal twenty-ounce drink and doubled his supersized meals because he claimed to be so big. He was the kind of guy who, when you said, "I'm gonna run down to the store," would say, "Are you sure? Wouldn't it be faster if you drove?" That kind of guy. He was big, bad Milford East.

How Linda White couldn't see this, I never knew. None of us did.

In grade school, Linda White had been my buddy. We had been closer than two peas in a pod. By high school, we'd strayed a bit. I'd been looking for trouble, anything to appease the boredom, and she'd been looking for a man.

In the South, there were women who still believed that the thing to do was find a good man who would protect them, give them babies, and pay their way. While women around the world had discovered the joys and satisfactions of combining family and work, of being able to take care of themselves, women in rural small-town, USA, still cottoned to the idea of being saddled with a baby at the age of seventeen.

I guessed what hurt the most was, as observant as I'd been about this, I wasn't much better. Hell, I wasn't any better. I made it all the way to twenty-three before I got pregnant. There were still a few *buts* that allowed me to hold my head up, in my opinion. I had an education, I could pay my own way, and Ella was perfect.

Linda had a different story to tell. The same age as me, and she had five kids. She'd had Richard when she was just seventeen years old— three months shy of graduating high school and she'd dropped out. When she'd been pregnant with Kaleigh, she'd gone back for her GED. At twenty-one, she'd had Brandon and Bradley.

Momma sent me a letter when I was at Duke telling me about Linda's little girl named Kimberly. I was studying for exams, stressing over what I was going to do with my life and fearful that I might be pregnant. I was late. This was something of a concern since you could set a clock by my period. In fact, you could set a clock by everything I did in my life with my careful calculations. I thought I had the world. Then crap hit the fan, as it's apt to do when you're secure in life.

Though we were worlds apart, I realized I was a lot closer to Linda's situation than I ever imagined. I thought I had a handle on things. He was an adjunct professor who often came into Kinko's late at night. It started innocently, chatting it up while waiting for his class materials to be printed. We had everything in common, from musical taste to political interests to pleasurable reading, so it seemed a natural progression when we landed in bed . . . together. Six months later, I was wondering if I was pregnant, studying Latin, and he was gone. I had a handle on nothing.

Momma's letter had come with the news of Linda's fifth baby. Five babies by the age of twenty-three. *Holy shit.* What had she been thinking? I happened to know she'd wanted to be a veterinarian. When we were kids, we'd pretended to fix up animals all the time. We'd even had a pretend price list for services rendered.

But the most painful part was who the father of the children was. When she was pregnant with the twins, Ford did "the right thing" and married Linda. While Linda thought she'd been made an honest woman, the rest of the town mourned the loss of her soul. Ford continued to knock her up and brag about his expanding family; after all, he was a big man who needed a big family. Just a few weeks later, it was confirmed that I was pregnant, but I knew I had nothing in common with Linda. She was certifiably brain dead with five babies at such a young age. She was a party of six wherever she went. She was overwrought with responsibilities, and it showed in her kids. They were dirty, unkempt, and had zero manners. They were miniature Fords who made people cringe as they approached.

Unlike most of the people in town, I didn't dislike Ford so much as I just felt sorry for him—for the whole lot of them. The East family was a family to pity. Now, while I saw the kids, Ford, and the East home, I wasn't in any rush to see Linda. To be honest, I was afraid. There was no way to pretend to be happy for her. It was easier to avoid her. However sad I was for her, for her loss of own self, I was even more disgusted by her choice of a man.

Whatever Ford was—or wasn't, Willie Strictland took the grand prize for King Jackass. In looks, he was somewhere in the middle of Ford and Wyck—okay on the eyes, hard on the ears. He hee-hawed, knee-slapped, and guffawed his way through life. In his small-minded little world, because he'd once had sex, it afforded him the right to loudly comment about women and what he might do with one if he had her naked and to himself. Never mind that the only women known to lie with him had all been so stinking drunk they didn't know what they were doing. Only because ours can sometimes be a merciful God, he'd not gotten anyone pregnant.

The truth of their situation was most people took their cars to the neighboring town, some forty miles away, to get auto repairs because those three idiots couldn't be relied upon. Somehow, Griffin's Garage stayed in business and kept them employed, although most days, that consisted of little more than them sitting on tiers of tires and deciding the most doable of the female population as they passed by.

It was of great concern to me to learn that Willie Strictland would do me. I'd seen what that trio called *doable* and wasn't sure where that put me.

Standing on Main Street, I paused before a large bay window and peered at my reflection. The truth was, I'd ridden the just-had-a-baby train as long as I could since it was obvious the twenty pounds I'd earned while growing a baby didn't plan on going anywhere. In fact, there was talk amongst the fat cells, and happy as they were, they were thinking about expanding. If I wasn't careful, my doability could be in danger.

"Theresa Franks! Thia!"

I cringed. Almost five years away from Granby, but that was a voice I knew well. I turned, trying to fix the smile on my face.

"Miranda," I said.

Unwittingly, I'd stopped in front of Miranda McGhee's store, Blink of an I. She hadn't changed since school. She had been a short, thick girl and was now a short, thick, fire hydrant of a woman. She had an expensive haircut, obtained every six or eight weeks when she went into Houston to get inventory for the store. Other than that, everything she wore was cheap. She had oversized, faux rhinestones in her ears, on her fingers, and around her neck, all accenting her "Mexican peasant" dress—a term that had to make you think, and I said as much with a smile.

"Well, you know what it means." She laughed. "It's just an expression."

I nodded with a bigger grin, looking myself over. "I guess that would make me Granby peasant." I was wearing faded jeans, an oversized G.H.S. (Granby High School) T-shirt with a large bobcat-swiping out, claws extracted.

"Oh, girl, don't worry about that." She waved a hand at me. "Come on in here. I don't care what you look like, just glad to see ya." She pulled me in, offering a hug. "I swear, everyone's always worried how they look around me," she said as she dragged me into her store.

Blink of an I was very much like its owner—overdressed, cheap, loud, and busy. It was loaded with Mexican pottery and sculptures, bright turquoise and rose-colored patterns on pillows, quilts, throws, and housecoats. There were a healthy number of wind catchers and door wreaths with feathers or pinecone patterns. In the far corner of the store were oak and wrought iron pieces of tables, side tables, chairs, stools, and coat racks. If you were into Mexican, Southwest, or Western motif, this was the store to shop. In the center of the area, surrounding the cash register, was a glass case that included jewelry, belt buckles, and wallets with the same motif. Yet, I had to give her credit where credit was due. Miranda made it work.

Miranda spread her arms out, giving a little whirl. "Well?" She grinned at me, eyebrows raised, making her impossible to resist.

I smiled back. "I love it," I heard myself saying.

I did kind of like it. I'm not that into Southwest style; probably because it was all I knew growing up, but it had a comfortable feel to it. It was better than a kitchen full of cows, for certain.

"How'd you come up with the name?" I asked, walking around, picking things up and inspecting the price tags.

"Just like how the idea of getting this store came to me." She was proud as a peacock.

"How in the world did you afford this?" I asked. "I mean, you've got some really nice stuff here!"

"I've got an investor." Miranda giggled. Behind the counter, she leaned on her elbows and gave a mock whisper. "A *private* investor." Again, her eyebrows shot up, and I found myself smiling with her, sharing her joy in her secret, though I had no idea why.

"Ahh," I said, not caring to find out more about this private investor.

I heard rumors about Miranda McGhee and how she spent her time with private investors. What was fact or fiction, I didn't care. Had I been of the mind, I might have said something about my lack of interest in the rumor mill, but you can't live in Granby and not care about what feeds the beast.

"I saw you talking to Roland Wyck."

I shook my head. "Well, I wouldn't say I was talking . . ." I turned over a small sculpture. A bucking bronco. *Kind of cool. Forty-nine ninety-five. Too rich for my blood.* "I walked by while Ford and Willie ran their mouths."

She rolled her eyes. "I guess that would figure. Wyck don't say much. But I tell ya this, he's more quiet than usual. He's mortified is what he is."

A Wyck mortified? I looked up. "I didn't know he knew how." It was hard to imagine.

I ran my hand along a felt cowboy hat with a leather and turquoise band. *Very nice.* It was one hundred and twelve dollars and ninety-five cents—too much, but there was something about it I liked. It reminded me of my daddy. Maybe it was the feel of the hat or the smell of the leather. I ran my fingers along the brim, reminded of a picture I thought I knew. Vaguely, I remembered a photo of my father leaning against a post, one leg crossed in front of the other, looking really cool, every bit the cowboy.

"Oh, it's nothing Roland did. It was his sister, that little whore."

Again, I stopped to look at Miranda.

Miranda and Angela Wyck had gone at it since grade school, and it was a curious thing.

Angela was, for lack of a better term, a little shit. She'd always been a little shit. Yet she'd always had the best guys. From Johnny Vargo and Matt Lewis in elementary school to Doug Carson in high school, she'd never been without a guy. All super cute, all sweet as could be, and every last one of them treated like dirt by Angela. It made a body wonder how a venomous, man-hating piece of trash like Angie Wyck could get cute guys. Then I realized it was that they were dumb.

If there's one thing you should know about the South, it's that we've got some cute boys—dumb as dirt, but cute. With gals like Angela, dumb just doesn't matter. How he fills out his pants, how large his arms, how ripped his abs, and how he looks in his cowboy hat or baseball cap mean everything. The fact that he can hold a job is just a bonus.

"Angela's got herself in some big trouble this time," Miranda said and continued with her story. "Big trouble." She looked around as though someone might hear us.

Not a soul stirred and I wondered how often Miranda actually got a customer. I might have been the first person in her shop all week, and I'd been dragged in.

"You know she's been on workman's comp," she said in a stage whisper.

I shook my head. "I didn't know."

"She's been walking around, well,"—she laughed at her own choice of words—"*hobbling* along. Which, by the way, didn't fool anyone. She's been moving around, acting like she threw her back out. She'd been working up there at the state hospital, don't cha know, cleaning the floors. She was on night shift, which is when I guess she got her idea. She and this other loser threw soapy water on the floor, and she said she slipped on it, threw her back out and has been on workman's comp ever since."

I was all too familiar with the antics of the Wyck family. Last year, when a big storm blew through Granby, lots of roofs were torn up. Momma had written to me, telling me all about the damage done to our roof. We had trees in the streets and everything. Fortunately, Momma had just upped the insurance with State Farm. I'd never said a word about it, but I thought she'd been a bit smitten with Mr. Lewis, our friendly, State Farm insurance guy. Why else would she up and get more coverage? Turns out it had been a good move. No one, but no one, could have seen that storm coming.

Momma had always been an upstanding citizen and never given anyone cause to question anything she did. So Mr. Lewis had been quick about an appraisal and had given Momma five thousand dollars for damages. It had been a sum of money grand enough to cause a sensation, and it'd about tore Angela and her buffalo of a mother, Missy, apart.

Those two buffoons climbed up on to their roofs and began tearing up some of the tiles with crowbars so that they, too, could claim storm damage.

All the while, Ms. Caston watched them. She knew exactly what they were up to, and she called up Mr. Lewis to tell him what the idiot Wyck women were doing.

Sure enough, he came on out, sat across the street watching, and even took a picture with his new digital camera. One day later, when they came into his office making claims about the storm damage, he just showed them the picture, and they shut up real fast. Two days later, he dropped them, saying they were a liability or something to that effect. No one knows for sure what was said after that but there was talk of insurance fraud.

When Angela had worked at the Crispy Chicken Shack right out of high school, she was supposed to have been cleaning the kitchen when she'd spilled soapy water all over the floor, slipped, and hurt her hip. She'd gotten paid leave for the rest of the summer, and while sitting on the back of Jim Tuckett's pick-up getting loaded, had bragged about how she'd gotten free physical therapy and pay. Because of her, Darwin Chubbs had had to buy thick rubber mats for his kitchen. It had been a pain in the ass because you had to wash the floor while standing on the mats so that no one slipped. I knew since I'd worked two summers following Angela's costly slip. The irony had been that Mitch Bates had tripped over the two-inch thick mat, fallen into the counter, and busted out his two front teeth. He'd never collected on any kind of workman's comp out of pride and dignity. Darwin had paid for Mitch's dental bill, and everyone blamed Angela Wyck for the damned mats.

"I guess she figured it worked before, why not again. Can you imagine that?" Miranda laughed incredulously. "She went and did it again. It worked at first. Then I guess someone around here talked to the right somebody out there. They had an official investigation and everything. The woman that worked night shift with Angela got scared and fessed up. Ratted Angela out, sayin' it was her idea and everything. Don't you know that Angela is sweatin' bullets right now."

In truth, I wasn't surprised at all. Those Wyck women would do anything for a fast and easy, if not illegal, buck.

"I bet you thought you left all the excitement behind when you came back home," Miranda said. "Hey," she nodded at the cowboy hat, "you like that?"

I hadn't realized that I had been holding on to the cowboy hat while Miranda spoke. "I do." I nodded at the hat then put it back and shoved my hands in my pockets. "But I can't afford it. Not now, anyway."

"I can make you a deal." She leaned forward and smiled at me.

"Let me think on it," I said and headed for the door.

Outside, it was the same old Main Street, with the same idiots sitting on tires and the same cars parked outside *The Recorder*. Ignoring the heat, I stepped off the curb and headed back to work, not knowing how exciting small-town living could be. It was the kind of excitement I could have done without.

CHAPTER SEVEN

Small towns thrive on drama. You hear about people being so bored that they make things up, but the way to truly know if you're in a small, Southern town is there's no need to make anything up. Someone's always doing something they oughtn't, and as a result, one-upping someone else.

You hear what Sam so-and-so did? Well, that ain't nothing. Guess what Jack so-and-so did?

I wasn't the least bit surprised, after learning that Angela Wyck was scamming insurance companies and cringing from the law, to step into *The Recorder* and hear the latest and even bigger news: Cody Kyle had been busted for hauling a suitcase full of guns across the state line. When the police had stopped and questioned Cody about where he was going, to whom he'd intended to sell the guns, and where he'd gotten his money, Cody had panicked and said that the money had come from Dr. Randy Hirsh.

For a moment, I just sat, slack-jawed, as LeAnn and Vicky went on and on about how Amber was a fool for taking up with the likes of Cody

Kyle and how Cody had been influenced by Hut Langford. I was having the same crazy spinning feeling I'd had when I'd been sent to see if Ms. Riley had a stove only to discover that she was armed to the teeth and prepared to blow out neighbors' windows if it meant the death of a fat, gray squirrel with a scrawny tail. All I could think was, *Where in the hell am I?*

I listened as the conversation somehow, insanely, turned to the fact that perhaps gunrunning wasn't such a bad thing, given the present state of affairs in this nation. It had gotten so that a decent person couldn't get a gun if he or she wanted. There was talk of terrorism and gun laws and how and why a law-abiding person had to wait to get an assault rifle when we all knew good and well that wasn't put in the Constitution.

The truth of it was those women couldn't stand to think of one of their own being on the bad side of the law. It was easier to think of Cody providing some patriotic duty—a notion made even more absurd by the fact that Cody Kyle didn't have a political thought in his pea brain. He had all the brainpower of a guinea pig.

I put my elbows on my desk and cradled my head in my hands just as Vicky Jackson came out with the deal breaker.

"Well, I don't know. Maybe in some small way, Hut and Cody are doing us all a service by moving those guns. Leastways, a person wouldn't have to go through all the red tape to protect his home and fight terrorism."

That's it!

Not only was she defending a gunrunner, someone who would happily sell a gun to a terrorist if he thought he could make a buck, but she was also buying into one of the stupidest political campaigns of all time! I couldn't hold my tongue any longer.

" 'Help fight terrorism: Vote Republican.' That's about the dumbest slogan that ever hit this country, but the Republicans relied on dumb-ass hicks to eat it up. Vote for the Republicans or we'll all die from a terrorist attack. I mean . . ." I rolled my eyes and pushed back from the desk. "It's embarrassing is what it is."

"Well, now, listen to you." Vicky turned to face me. She threw a hand on her hip, and I knew I was in for a tongue-lashing. Albeit, not a particularly insightful tongue-lashing, but a tongue-lashing all the same. "You go off to the big city with all the big-city, liberal newspapers and damned hippie, peace-loving tree huggers and come back a new woman, is that it, Theresa Franks?"

I exhaled. *Here it comes.* The full name meant a long one.

"You know well and good that this nation has gone soft, and we have to get back to our conservative roots to set things straight again. You know that the damned Yankee Democrats are the ones who let sex and cuss words on TV and the likes of . . . of . . . of all the half-dressed teenage whores in Hollywood and—"

"Anyone with any damned sense has figured that out without going to the big city, Vicky." Shelby Harrelson breezed in, letting the door slam behind her for added oomph.

Hallelujah! I smiled. I could see Vicky tense up.

It was no secret that Ms. Shelby and Vicky went around and around with each other. LeAnn Ricks, Vicky Jackson, and Tammi Whatley all liked to think of themselves as the sophisticated, cultured group among a bunch of heathens, but Shelby Harrelson posed a problem. She had three times their money, traveled everywhere, and had even been written up in some magazines and a business book as an "innovative entrepreneur." She got their goat but good.

She winked at me as she perched on the edge of my desk. "I made my money in toilets, girls, so I learned long ago to say it like it is. I know shit when I see it, and I know shit when I hear it."

The queen of the porta potty business, the mistress of the business slogan, "In our business, a flush is better than a house," was about to speak. I held my breath and it was bated.

"I think we've long passed that notion of thinking that a Democrat or a Republican can stop terrorism. It was an idiotic notion then and it's an idiotic notion now, but little missy Theresa's got something. Those fellas in Washington that come up with the slogan, 'Fight terrorism, vote Republican,' just counted on small-minded Americans to lap it up. Hell, not me. I been Republican damned near all my life, but that second Bush stopped that. I'm in the business of shit, and that stink was too much for even me. Now, I pity this country for all the cleanup we've got to do after a man with no horse sense and shit for brains screwed everything up!"

Mouths fell open.

"Cody Kyle's been a little shit all his life, but this time he got caught doing it, and even then, he didn't have the decency to own up to his mistakes like a man. No, he has to drag poor Doc Hirsh into it. A man, by the way, who had only given Cody money so that he could pay off his truck and start settling into the idea of supporting his daughter."

Even as Shelby leveled some logic on us, I could see Vicky fuming. I thought about tapping on the keyboard the newest and even bigger headline than Cody Kyle being arrested—SHELBY HARRELSON STANDS IN THE MIDDLE OF *THE RECORDER*, IN FRONT OF VICKY JACKSON, LEANN RICKS, AND TAMMI WHATLEY, AND SPEAKS ILL OF REPUBLICANS. Now *that* was a headline.

"Just what is it you came in here for?" Tammi placed a well-manicured hand on her hip, tossing her chin toward the door. Translation: get out.

Before Shelby could answer, Ryan Whatley stepped inside, and the mood changed.

"Oh!" Tammi clasped her hands together and rushed her son.

"Ladies." He gave a big smile, wrapping his arms around his mother while trying to keep his balance at the same time.

"Ryan! What are you doing here?"

"You knew I was coming." He laughed. "Should I turn around and come back later?"

The others coo-ed.

"Land sakes, Ryan. We're just shocked." LeAnn moved in, sidestepping Tammi, and giving big hugs.

"Well, just look at you!" Vicky clapped her hands. "Look at him!" she said to the rest of us. "Look at you." She focused the full wattage of her grin in his direction.

He smiled, pushing his hands in his jeans pockets. When he tried to look away, he caught me sitting to the right of the office and he dipped his head a little. "Thia." He winked at me.

Ryan was a couple years younger than I was, but I knew him pretty well. I liked him enough. He was always nice to me, and we had an understanding between us. It was the way things were in most small towns—the teenagers and young adults against the full-fledged adults.

Now, as a new momma, I realized how ridiculous the notion was that the adults wouldn't, or didn't, know all the hell the young ones raised, but I was pretty sure that the adults didn't know just how *much* hell was raised, or who exactly was raising it. You could have your own ideas, or hear rumors, but it wasn't quite the same as knowing, for example, that sweet, darling, honor-student Ryan once paid Valerie Matthews twenty bucks to give him a blowjob. Or that Ryan did both the Matthew girls in the same night—in the same house—while their daddy was out hunting with Ryan's daddy.

But I knew.

Just like I knew it was Ryan who had broken into the school gymnasium five years ago and peed all over the coach's locker after he'd benched over half the team for drinking at an underage party. I knew plenty about Mr. Ryan Whatley. And he knew I did.

In return, he knew plenty about me that wasn't worth dredging up. Suffice to say, my momma would be plenty embarrassed by my behavior. My actions could be seriously questioned, and I was a little bit sorry, but I'd been so busy trying to rebel against small-town living that it had never occurred to me those same actions would follow me forever. While I could take solace in knowing that my antics in the science lab had become legend, it was one reason why I'd never wanted to take root in Granby. I didn't need Ella to know certain things about her own mother. Thus, the polite nod.

You don't tell. I don't tell.

"Ryan," I said back, offering a wink of my own that he missed as he was swarmed once again by his mother.

"Baby, does Daddy know you're home?" she asked, preening his hair and brushing imaginary things from his shoulders and collar.

He shrugged a little, embarrassed by the public smothering. "I came here first," he said.

"Let me ask you." Shelby moved toward him with a little sniff, and I felt a smile tug at my lips again. "What do you think when you hear the words, 'Vote Republican, fight terrorism'?" Shelby crossed her arms.

Tammi whirled around, her mouth a perfect *O* shape, but Ryan answered too quickly, first with a laugh. "It's ridiculous," he quipped.

"Ryan!"

"What? Ma? You can't be serious?" He gave an exaggerated shrug, raising his hands up in protest. "You don't buy that stuff?"

"Buy it? Oh, honey, she's selling it."

"Shelby Harrelson! We don't need you walking in here to stir up trouble." Vicky Jackson stepped forward, ever protective of Tammi, but Shelby was in her element and wasn't going to be intimidated by this trio.

She was well aware of what they thought of her. They placed value in community, church, and business by income. Even though she was the wealthiest woman in town, they had decided that Shelby Harrelson was simply new money, and because it was earned through a porta potty business, hers was dirty money. They deemed her an outcast. Shelby couldn't have cared less. This was a game to her.

"I'm not stirring anything. I just came in here to place an ad. Next thing I know, we're talking politics." She sighed and sidled over to my desk. "I do want to place an ad," she said, winking at me once her back was to the group.

Ryan turned toward his mother. "We were talking about this at school—"

"Shush!" Tammi scolded him.

"What can I do ya for?" I asked Shelby, ignoring the hushed tones behind her. I could hear Vicky and Tammi muttering to Ryan, peeved that he had taken Shelby's side.

"Want to take out an ad. Reward offered. Someone stole my damned porta potties out on Highway 543." Shelby sighed.

"Did you call the police?" I was already taking notes.

"Of course, not that it'll do a damned bit of good. I'm taking matters into my own hands now, and as you know, money talks." There was a snort. She ignored it. "This is the second time I've had this happen, so I figured I'd offer a reward. Someone knows what's going on and will cough up info for some dough."

It was probably a high school prank, but I could see some of the construction workers doing this as well. There was construction going along three different highways in the area, all part of the new Department of Texas Transportation plan. It was some whoop-de-doo expansion plan that was costing the taxpayers millions. I'd missed all the debates about it, not that I would have cared anyway. All I knew was there was construction everywhere, and it wasn't uncommon for the road workers to set up their own porta potties along the roads.

Swiping porta potties always seemed like a harmless kind of crime—if you could even call it that—but seeing as Shelby was standing before me offering a reward, she most certainly was. It was her business, and she had no humor about losing her potties.

"You might want to check out that party for James Otis. I hear they've invited half the town. I'll bet you'll find some of your porta potties out there," LeAnn said, her tone snippy.

Again, Shelby did not bat an eyelash. "Then they'd be outright fools since they invited me. I think I'd recognize my own porta potties, thank you very much."

"James Otis is having a party?" Ryan's eyebrows shot up.

Tammi looked mortified by his interest.

Vicky and LeAnn were still trying to figure how it was that Shelby Harrelson was invited to a party that they were not.

"He's graduating. Tasha was in here the other day," I told him.

"No kidding." Ryan nodded. "That's cool."

"Honey, don't you need to go see Daddy, tell him that you're here?"

"When's it gonna be?" Ryan asked, leaning into my view.

"I swear I didn't even get a chance to go to the store. What do you want for dinner, sugar?" Tammi was swallowing Ryan right before our eyes.

"This Friday. It's going to be a grand affair." Shelby made big hand gestures. "Don't you know he's the first in his family to graduate from college?"

"Oh, please!" Vicky sneered. "College? It's a two-year tech school."

"It's an associate's degree, Ryan," LeAnn tried to explain oh, so patiently.

"It's a big deal, nonetheless. More than I ever did," Shelby said. There was a moment of silence as the terrible trio decided how to tackle that one.

"It's one more degree than I got," Ryan said with a chuckle.

"Oh my God, it's not even the same." Tammi turned back toward her friends, rallying their support for mock laughter and surprise.

"Where did you go, Vicky? I've forgotten." Shelby placed a hand delicately against her chest, eyebrows raised.

Vicky flushed. "You know damned well I didn't go anywhere." Vicky placed her hands on her hips.

"Oh, yes. Of course." Shelby turned back to me, ready to write out her reward ad.

Vicky wasn't done, sputtering in her own defense. "I could have. I just didn't have the money, but I had the grades."

"Well, now, Vicky, I'd say you just fell into something. Why don't you?" Shelby winked at me again.

"Why don't I what?" Vicky asked incredulously.

"Go back to school. You've got the money now. And apparently," Shelby's eyes gazed around the office and over both Tammi and LeAnn, "the time."

"Don't be—"

"Just think how good you'd feel once you got a degree. You wouldn't have to start big. Why not a two-year degree? You know, make something of yourself."

Vicky reeled. She attempted to cover with a laugh. "Make something of myself?"

"Well, I mean something beyond working clerical in an office. No offense, hon." Shelby reached across my desk and patted my arm.

I couldn't stop the giggles. "None taken."

"You could earn yourself a business associate's, become a dental hygienist or . . . a vet tech!"

Ryan laughed loudly. I put my head down, not daring to show my open-mouthed smile. All I could hear was the bell over the door as Ryan was escorted out onto the street.

"Was it something I said?" Shelby looked around the room.

I refused to answer. Though I was loving it, I did not want to get involved.

"I think you know very well what you said." LeAnn scowled.

"It was just an idea, is all." Switching gears, she spelled out the ad and how she wanted it to run, offering a reward to anyone who might have information about her six missing porta potties. As she stood, she spoke to no one in particular, "I'm excited about James Otis's party. Will I see you there?"

I wouldn't miss it.

"It'll be a party no one will soon forget." These were Shelby's fateful words.

CHAPTER EIGHT

Paradise Park used to be an old haunt of Tina Wolfe's until the chief called her in due to an increasing number of complaints against her. In her defense, it really was the perfect place to park, sit, and wait for a perp just begging for a ticket.

"Look," she whined to the chief when she'd been called in. "The way I see it, this is good police work. That's all." She'd shrugged. She hadn't appeared the least bit remorseful for staking out a known Hispanic neighborhood to write out tickets. "It was not about race. Hell, I couldn't care less about that. They could be purple for all I care. It's just good, smart police work!"

"Then you're not denying the charges?" Chief Teague almost laughed.

A large, heavyset black man, he'd been something of a controversy himself when he'd come onto the once all-white force two years prior. The very last place he had ever thought he would be was in the middle of nowhere, ticketing punks who flew Confederate flags from their antennas, but life and politics had a sense of humor.

As much as he'd love to say it was just the South, he knew it was everywhere. Police chiefs of color got their posts because of job quotas or affirmative action. It was that simple. He watched several African-American police officers who were unqualified, ill prepared, and unable to lead large departments make chief. The resulting effect was embittered fellow officers—not something you wanted in the often-dangerous field of police work—and actual danger to the community the department was sworn to protect.

For Teague, it was a dreaded question mark over his head, and he hadn't liked it. He hadn't liked it one bit. So when an opening for chief in the small town of Granby, Texas, was made public, Teague knew he wanted it. With a small town, he could immerse himself in the community. Though his wife had protested, fearful of how a small town would respond to a black chief, Teague was confident in his leadership abilities. It would all be fine.

For the most part, he'd been right. There had been some remarks made, but he'd been a welcome sight. For far too long, the Granby Police Department had battled the reputation of white cops hauling in poor blacks on trumped-up charges. It hadn't been but a few years since a nearby town made national news when it was discovered that dozens of innocent citizens had been arrested on drug charges when their only crime had been poverty and skin color.

Teague set out to change things by hiring Rosa Fox, a bilingual female cop. Fox was an expert marksman, a dynamo with paperwork, pleasant with citizens, and easy on the eyes. But her greatest quality was her ability to work with Tina Wolfe.

Also easy on the eyes, Wolfe was anything but pleasant with the public. Hell, he hadn't been in office more than one week before Officer Wolfe had shot Joe Wilson's goat.

Wolfe had responded to a domestic dispute out at the Wilson property and while standing on the porch, talking things over with Ms. Wilson, one of their billy goats jumped onto the hood of Wolfe's cruiser. By Wilson's account, she pulled out her weapon and shot the animal.

Wolfe told a different story, saying she tried to reason with the goat, coaxing it off her cruiser, but when it charged at her, head down in an aggressive manner, she shot in self-defense. Because—and only because—Sarah Wilson was still pissed at her husband and despised the goat that kept eating her blankets on the clothesline did she concur with Officer Wolfe's story.

Teague, however, was fully aware of Wolfe's temperament. Having heard the stories, he hadn't put goat killing past her, but staking out Hispanics for tickets would not fly.

"You cannot sit outside Paradise Park, lying in wait," Teague said.

"Why not?" Wolfe asked.

Teague rubbed his eyes with a meaty hand. "You're killin' me, Wolfie. You know that, right?"

"Chief, I don't see the problem. Statistically, who's most likely going to drive around here without insurance?" She spread her arms out wide and leaned back in her chair.

"It's called *racial profiling*," he said, pointing a finger at her. He leveled both elbows on the edge of his desk, scooting in closer, and studied Wolfe's face for a moment.

He'd decided long ago, she was a woman to be reckoned with. On the surface, she could fool a person, and perhaps that was one of the things that made her such a good cop. Men would, and often *did*, underestimate her because of her soft appearance. Large, brown eyes with a healthy rose to her cheeks, her hair was cut short and spiked with gel around her pretty face. She was lean and muscular in a feminine way and busty enough to show in her otherwise formless uniform.

She was the most entertaining police officer on the force and the single most difficult to reprimand, partially because she was like an overgrown kid, refusing to see where she made her mistake. She could set her jaw in such a way that Teague knew he was talking to himself. She was infuriating. One minute she was screaming about a damned snake and refusing to take a call, the next, she was covering a buddy, ready to take a bullet. She was a bundle of contradictions, but there was one thing he knew. She was loyal as hell. She'd tell you exactly what was on her mind, not giving a second thought to political correctness or hurt feelings. But she'd run into a burning building or crawl over broken glass for a fellow officer. It was hard to find a cop like that these days.

As annoyed as he was, he tried not to smile.

"Oh hell!" Wolfe threw her hands up into the air. "It's science. You know and I know that half the folks in Paradise Park do not have insurance. I've deduced and concluded." She gave an exaggerated wave again. "Therefore, I write tickets. We all win."

"Tina," he said, lowering his voice. "This is not up for discussion. Stop sitting outside the trailer park, profiling Hispanics."

"I'm not . . ." She snapped her mouth shut and rolled her eyes. "Fine. No more police work to make sure that certain people have their auto insurance so as to protect the citizens of this fine city that I took an oath to protect." She started to stand.

"Another thing," he said, flipping through papers attached to a small manila folder. "Please tell me, because I'm so curious, why you would throw a flashlight at Pastor Tyree?"

Wolfe froze and her mouth dropped open. "What's that?" She pointed at the folder. "Are you looking at my file? You pulled my file?" Her eyebrows shot up and her face flushed.

"Yeah," he said. "I'm getting complaints, Wolfie! So, yeah, I pulled your file. I had to!"

"I can't believe this!" She paced for a moment and slapped her side.

He watched as her hand fell on her pistol—old police officer's habit.

"Okay . . . okay. Yes, I threw my damned flashlight. I'm working the parade, which I hate, by the way. It's two hundred freakin' degrees outside, but I'm working this damned parade, directing all the idiots down Main Street. You know, it's not rocket science. Everyone starts on Hyden Street, turns down Main, turns again at Abilene. Pretty easy. But this idiot . . . who was it? I think it was David Wyck. He's driving along and not turning. I wave at him, you know, waving him on to turn, and the idiot almost runs me over. So, yeah, I yelled at him and threw my flashlight at the side of the truck."

Teague kept reading the file as she spoke.

"I suppose next you're gonna ask about the good pastor's organ player and reputed God-fearing woman falling off the back end of the trailer?"

In answer to Wolfe's question, Teague smiled at her.

"It's not my fault that Carol Dickson's fat ass couldn't fit on a bale of hay."

True enough, Carol Dickson was one of the largest women Teague had ever laid eyes on.

"I'm sorry that she hurt herself. I promise not to scare fat women . . ."

Teague felt the shake starting—the laugh was coming. He stifled it with a short cough.

"... throw flashlights, shoot goats, racially profile no-insurance-havin' people, or make Fox crawl under any more trucks." Wolfe's tone was flat as she went through the list. She rolled her eyes again as if punctuating the end.

Teague opened his mouth to question that last statement when his phone rang. He held out a finger, telling her to stay put. "Hi, baby. I'm in the middle of . . ."

He looked at Wolfe, who smiled and blew him a kiss, walking out the door while he tried to decipher what his wife was saying, something about a stray goat.

▌ ▌ ▌

Officers Wolfe and Fox were on patrol when the call came in—domestic disturbance off Highway 543, out by the water tower.

Rosa Fox sighed.

"I hate goin' out there," Wolfe grumbled to Fox before responding into the radio. "This is Wolfie. We're southbound on five forty three, headed that way."

"Roger that," dispatch responded and Wolfe clicked off.

"You're just worried someone will recognize you as that bigot cop who hands out tickets to poor migrant workers," Fox said, intentionally laying on a bit of a Mexican accent. She turned her head, smirking out the window.

"Don't start with me, partner. I've got a bullet with your name on it. I'll just claim self-defense."

Fox laughed.

"Everyone knows how hot-blooded you are," Wolfe said with a chuckle.

"Mercifully, I'm not of Irish decent and don't possess the need to get rip-roaringly drunk by ten a.m. every third day of my life so"—Fox shrugged—"it all evens out."

Wolfe squinted her eyes at Fox. "I hope that is not some reference to my ancestry."

Fox smiled.

"Because it's every other, and I don't tie it on until at least *two* p.m."

"Good to know," Fox said and laughed. "If I need backup, I'll make sure I call before noon."

" 'Course holiday schedules are different."

Still smiling, Fox looked out the window.

She knew the truth behind Wolfe's parking outside Paradise Park. It really wasn't about skin color. It was about the neighborhood. It was about the domestic calls, the abuse, the voiceless children. It was particularly bad in Paradise Park. There were always too many family members involved. Too many people crowding in, wanting to tell, or rather, shout, their own version of the story, and that made the police anxious.

The address dispatched seemed vaguely familiar, though Fox couldn't quite place it. Whether it was a domestic, a disturbance, a party, it hardly mattered. Late night calls to the Paradise Park area were never good, and they rode in silence for a moment, both readying themselves for whatever was to come.

As they turned onto Del Rio, it all came back.

A fight between two brothers had taken place on Del Rio several years ago. Officer Brian Watson had tried to break them apart when—big surprise—family members intervened. The one brother had lunged, knife in hand, at the other and had stabbed Watson instead. Everyone had panicked, run back to his or her home, and left Watson dying on the ground. A twelve-year-old girl had stayed with the officer while her grandmother called for an ambulance.

Though it was before her time on the force, Fox remembered the story well. *Hernandez.* That was the name. The one brother was eventually caught and convicted. And in Texas, you kill a cop, you can kiss your ass goodbye. The other brother, if memory served, was still around. He was pretty screwed up.

"Oh, goodie."

As the patrol lights swung around the corner, the beam crossed over a large figure.

Wolfe said, "You remember the story of Hernandez? That's him. He's one bad dude."

In unison, they stepped out of each side of the cruiser. Each officer poised, hand on her gun holster, the other hand outstretched.

"Hey, man. What's going on?" Fox kept her voice calm, reassuring. She had hoped the Spanish accent would help their cause, but Hernandez appeared agitated. And armed.

Both women locked eyes on the weapon in his right hand—a hunting knife. Wolfe sidestepped her open car door, moving to Hernandez's right. Without a word, Fox flanked his left.

She continued to talk, this time in Spanish. *"Why don't you put that knife down? Why don't you tell me what's going on? Maybe I can help. We're here to help you. You're scaring people with that knife, and you don't want to do that, do you?"*

She saw Wolfe from her peripheral, moving slowly. Deliberately.

Hernandez said something back and Wolfe stopped. As long as he was talking, she knew Wolfe would not advance, and Fox hoped to talk some sense into him. Maybe this could go down peacefully—something Fox dearly wanted.

While she spoke, Fox took stock of the situation. The address wasn't his. So far, the neighborhood appeared to be quiet. No family, no parties, no fights. It was unclear who had called in, but for the moment, it was unimportant.

Fox took a step forward while Hernandez spoke. It was a step too far, and his voice rose. Fox froze.

"Easy, man," Wolfe's voice was reassuring.

"He doesn't speak English," Fox told her partner.

"Fabulous. Does he understand *drop the fucking knife before I blow your brains out?"* Wolfe said.

Nothing happened.

No one moved.

"That would be a no," Fox deadpanned, though her humor was fleeting. She tried again in Spanish with no results. "Shit, Wolfie. This guy's not gonna stand down."

"Tell him that we need for him to drop the knife. Tell him there is no need for any violence, but we need to talk to him without the knife."

Fox translated.

Hernandez made a low growling noise and shifted his attention toward Wolfe. He said something and Wolfe drew her weapon.

It didn't matter what he said. They both heard his voice, and neither of them was a rookie. This guy was not going to go peaceably.

Fox spoke in rapid Spanish.

There was a pause and then the sound of Wolfe cocking her pistol. For such a small sound, it was incredibly powerful. The sound echoed through the housing compound, and Fox could feel herself begin to shake. Not because she was afraid and not because she didn't think Wolfe could do it, but because she knew she could and would.

Wolfe leveled the barrel at his left shoulder, and Fox held her breath. "Tell him I don't want to do this, but I will."

Fox's voice was low but her words were true enough that Hernandez darted his eyes between the police officers. Two long seconds ticked off before he made his decision, turned his hand over, opened it and let the weapon fall to the ground.

"Good choice." Wolfe exhaled loudly.

Again, Fox spoke, telling him to lie down on the ground, hands behind his head.

For a moment, it appeared as though Hernandez would comply. He crouched, putting a hand down on the ground in a three-point stance, but then he stopped.

Fox and Wolfe exchanged glances. No one moved. Fox began to repeat the commands when Hernandez rose like a giant bear, turned, and fled.

"Shit!" Fox darted forward. She'd been about ten feet closer to the subject, already poised to move forward, but Wolfe had been caught flat-footed, and she shoved the pistol back to its holster and began running.

The chase was on.

Hernandez ran around the long white trailer and vanished into the shadows. Blindly, Fox followed with Wolfe close behind, around the house and toward a small, square porch. In a flash, Fox was up and over the three steps to the porch and flinging a screen door open. She heard Wolfe charge into the back of the house only three steps back and head through the kitchen. It was like a slide show while her brain processed information. Porch. Click. Kitchen. Click. Dark hallway. Click. Hernandez coming out of the shadows headed straight for her. Click.

They went down so hard that it seemed to rock the entire house. Hernandez raised an arm as though he were going to throw a punch. Fox tensed, readying herself for the blow to land.

Wolfe's body flew into her line of sight as she dove onto his back, driving him forward and they both pitched into the wall of the narrow hallway.

Fox scrambled beneath them, clearing out and preparing to kick the shit out of this big boy as Wolfe distracted him, but Hernandez regained his balance and stood up, Wolfe still riding his back.

They staggered backward, landing in the kitchen. For a moment, Fox could not find Wolfe and it was slide show snippets again. Light. Click. Kitchen. Click. Wolfe, as her back was slammed against the counter by Hernandez. She saw her partner's eyes squeeze shut.

Wolfe cried out in pain, falling off Hernandez's back as he stepped forward. There was a shout before he slammed a fist into her face.

Fox was behind him, and she drew her gun and barked out commands in Spanish, but he reeled, threw something at her, and knocked her back. He was too large, or the kitchen was too small.

Wolfe was up again, grabbing at Hernandez, who loomed over Fox. She missed his arm but managed to get a handful of fabric and pulled. The material pulled away and exposed a tattoo on his large, powerful arm.

Horrendous Hernandez surrounded large, blood red boxing gloves.

There it was. That nagging feeling that there was more Fox knew about the Hernandez brother. He was a professional boxer. He annihilated his opponents. He was a one-punch wonder with a thirst for violence, and this evening, he also happened to be strung out on drugs.

Fox, still straddled on the floor between his legs, and Wolfe, slack-jawed and still holding part of his shirt in her hand, exchanged glances.

A plethora of curse words came to mind. Some really, really good ones.

Instead, Wolfe spoke. "I'm sure this could be a lot worse, I just don't know how . . ."

CHAPTER NINE

I sat there, watching the party change from fun to frantic in less than an hour. Funny how small-town parties can do that.

Most of the residents in this neighborhood were third and fourth generation Granbyites. Poor, with a high school education, if that. Mostly black. Mostly senior citizens. But as was part of the sad movement all over the nation, grown kids had come back to roost. James Otis was back. Melvin Sparks was back. Lucia Jacobs and Terrell Whitehead were back. I felt a little less embarrassed. With this group, I didn't have to explain anything. I didn't have to worry about how dressed up I was or wasn't. People had gathered to celebrate Otis and to have a party.

Georgie Clemmons and his boys—his sons and grandsons—had hooked a huge stereo system to the back of his old horse trailer and parked it on the edge of the empty lot, sitting adjacent to Mrs. Otis's backyard. Lights had been strung up surrounding the yard. Enough food to feed a small army was set out along two tables I just knew came from Mrs. Otis's church. More food was lined along the open tailgates of two pickups, which had been strategically parked beside the tables. From fried chicken to Jell-O dishes, Budweiser to water, if it could be consumed, it was here.

I'd been to my share of parties at Duke, alcohol included, and they were just different. As I watched people I'd gone to high school with, it brought me back to the whole redneck thing. My old friends at Duke would have died before they'd have attended a party like this one.

I chatted with Mrs. Otis, gave congratulatory hugs to James and Tasha, and talked with Terrell and Lucia. It was strange how different things were, though everyone was the same. It was as though time had stood still while I'd been away.

I'd arrived with the idea that I would leave pretty early. In fact, I'd promised Momma that I would, but I'd been paralyzed when the impromptu karaoke began. Melvin Sparks had been drunk enough to regret what he'd done for the rest of his life. We'd all see to that. And Kylie Myers would wish she'd been able to claim drunkenness after she'd destroyed Stevie Wonder's "Superstitious." I, like everyone else, had to laugh while she'd belted every single note out of tune.

People in the South don't laugh quietly. We let it rip. Loud laughter, hoots, and hollers filled the air. No neighbors complained because they were all there. I kind of forgot how much I hadn't wanted to come home and how ugly Tammi Whatley and LeAnn Ricks could be as I stood there with all my old school mates. There was no black, no white, and no differences. We were all neighbors, playing dominos and chicken foot. For a moment, it was pretty nice, and I had no regrets about coming home. Then the fight began.

Brian Wessen started it, goading Jeff Hanson about his ex-girlfriend—a girl who made the rounds easily enough but had ended with Oscar Ruiz. Her reputation was such that even as she stood there, listening to Brian makes remarks about her, she just laughed.

"Shut up!" Her protests were playful and carefree. She was a ho and she knew it, and she was drunk enough to not pretend otherwise.

At first, it was funny, but then . . . you could feel it. Less smiling, more teasing until there was no backing down. I hoped someone would stop it. I looked around, thinking James, certainly Tasha . . .

Instead, Tasha joined in, teasing Jeff mercilessly about his choice in women.

Then came the stinging yet most predictable statement: *Oscar is the* real *man.*

There was the chorus of *oooh* noises, and that was it. Before I knew what was happening, a circle was formed. The rules were laid out while Oscar and Jeff circled each other and guests chose sides. You could tap out at any moment, otherwise, the circle of men wouldn't let you out. It was anything goes. Ready, set . . .

Jeff took the first swing, and just like that, guests were jumping onto the back of pickups for a better view or adding to the wall of men who encircled the fight.

Oscar ducked and swung back, landing a vicious blow. Although I hadn't seen the actual hit, I heard that sickening thud—knuckles meeting face.

Mrs. Otis and a few of the older women scooped up platters of food to carry inside, lest they get destroyed by a fight that may spill over to the rest of the yard.

We wouldn't want the food to get ruined. Never mind Jeff's face.

Another dull, but loud, thud noise, followed by a chorus of cheers, and it was time to go. I started for the house, thinking I would help Mrs. Otis for a second and then scoot out. It was all coming back to me why I didn't like these gatherings. They were always fun at first, but a fight was most often guaranteed. I knew that fights broke out all over the world when young men gathered, but for the South, in small Texas towns, it was par for the course.

I turned to get out and crashed into Ryan Whatley.

"Ryan?" He was one of the last people I'd expected to see. He caught me, his hands cupping my elbows, and held me for a moment. His mother would croak if she . . . "Your mother would croak if she saw you, Mr. Texas Tech, at a party like this." I couldn't let it slide.

"Well, now, we'll have to make sure she doesn't find out then, won't we?"

There was a loud crack and another roar of cheers. Someone was beating the crap out of someone. I had a feeling that Jeff Hanson would have a date with an ice bag later on.

The calls of the crowd caused Ryan to jump. He wanted a better view. He licked his lips and tried to ease tactfully away from me. I'm sure he wanted to say something more about not mentioning his presence to the ladies at work, but he couldn't contain himself and hurried over to the circle.

"What is it with guys?" I heard Tasha's voice as she moved next to me, holding Darion on her hip. He lunged when he saw me and I caught him and snatched him from her grip.

"I don't know," I said to Darion's big, expressive eyes. He grinned a toothless grin at me. "What is it with you boys? Well, you won't do that, will you? No. No. Oh, no." I made my eyes bigger each time, which drew a giggle, and I suddenly missed Ella. No sound—not the ocean, wind chimes, a summer breeze, an orchestra—was as beautiful and complete as the deep, satisfied giggle from a baby.

"He better not!" Tasha was angry, her eyes never moving from the fight. There were more thuds, but I didn't bother to look.

"Darion," I looked into his perfect brown eyes. "You need to tell your daddy that you don't like that."

Another giggle.

Perfection.

"Oh, he wouldn't dare. He knows what he'd have to look forward to. Me!" Tasha said with great authority. "Just because these damned fools want to knock their teeth out, don't mean James do. He's done with all that, Thia. I mean it. He's a changed man. He loves Darion and me like crazy. He's a changed man, uh huh."

"Does he love you? Does he love you?" I teased Darion. I turned back to Tasha. "I know, Tasha. I can see it in him."

It was the truth, too. James was a different guy, and we all had Tasha and Darion to thank for that. Once upon a time, he'd been a wild man. Parties and fights. That was what James Otis had been all about. But Tasha had scooped up the broken pieces after his football career was over. I was sure that it was Tasha who had encouraged him to go to school for his associate's degree. While she liked to say it was all him, I couldn't help but think of that saying, "Behind every good man . . ." there was Tasha.

Finally, she had enough and marched off muttering that she would have James put a stop to this fool nonsense.

Happy to stay a while longer holding Darion, I eased over to the back porch and took a seat, with Darion facing me. I sang, "Darion, Darion, went to town . . ." as I bobbled him on my knee. "Darion, Darion, he fell downnnn." I separated my legs, letting his bottom fall through.

He squealed with delight as I caught him and propped him back up again for round two then round three and four and five . . .

■ ■ ■

Chief Teague was frantic. *Where the hell are they?*

"Anything?" he hollered at Francis. "Can you tell me anything, dammit?" He yelled into the radio at dispatch while he flew down the highway.

"No, Chief! I keep radioing. I get nothing. Nothing!"

He could hear the fear rising up in Francis's voice. He didn't like it. He didn't like it one bit. The normally mundane, almost zombie-like Francis Nickels was afraid.

Dammit. He was, too.

Where are they? What the hell could they be doing? He couldn't decide which idea to latch on to—they were out doing something stupid that would get them written up and get him an earful from the city council leaders or something had gone wrong. Something had gone terribly wrong.

Carter Teague was a calm man. It was something he prided himself on. Never jump to conclusions. Assume the first reports are always wrong. No need to get into a panic. Most of the time, alarms were false. But this—he hadn't experienced this before.

A terrifying 911 call had been placed. Francis had been so shaken, it had been difficult to report back to Teague. He'd had to ask her three times what she was saying.

"It's terrible, Chief. Someone called, screaming. I don't know who yet. A young man. Maybe a woman. I can't . . . I just don't know. It was terrible. The screaming."

"What is it?" Teague had been sleeping. Early to bed, early to rise, but with the last sentence, he was up, dressing, but dammit, he needed Francis to be clearer. He needed details.

"They . . . the person, I mean, was screaming."

"Screaming what? Help me out here, Francis, I—"

"That James Otis is dead. He's dead, Chief. James Otis is dead."

When I got home, Ella was already asleep in her crib next to my bed. But I couldn't stand it, and I picked her up and put her in bed with me. I knew I wasn't supposed to sleep with her. There was always that danger that I might roll over and squash her.

When Ella was born, I had placed her still swaddled in her blanket next to me. I'd insisted that she sleep next to me, not wanting to leave her in the nursery. Despite assurances, I'd been afraid she'd be mixed up with the other babies. So I'd asked that she stay in my room with me. I'd needed to know that she was still breathing, that everything was fine.

Each time the nurse came in and saw us together in bed she chuckled. "No, no, no," she said, reminding me that I must not sleep with her because I might roll on top of her.

I know it's happened before, but the possibility of it happening with me was nonexistent. I didn't sleep while she was with me. I just watched her face and memorized every inch of her perfectly formed eyes, nose, mouth, cheeks, and forehead.

Over a year later, the fascination hadn't worn off. In fact, I felt more enthralled than ever. Maybe it was because it seemed like I spent less time with Ella since moving home. Maybe it was because Ella, newly named Lily, seemed to be attaching herself to Momma. Maybe, after holding Darion, I just realized how lucky I was to be a momma as well. Darion was the best thing that ever happened to James Otis. I guessed the same could be said for me and Ella.

I stroked the side of Ella's face while she slept. Her bottom lip was scrumptiously thick, so kissable. Her cheeks were so large it was hard not to grin in the dark. The silhouette of her body next to mine was therapeutic. In my waking hours, I cursed myself for coming back, tail tucked between my legs. I cringed each time I saw a former teacher, the parent of an old friend, and worse, my old friends. But at night, alone with Ella, all my anxieties slipped away. She was the reason I was back, and she was perfect. So how could it be wrong?

I ran a finger along her lips, nose, and earlobes.

I made her promises.

As I lay with Ella, I thought about how differently laughter sounds at night than during the day. I could still hear the echo of laughter when

Keisha Williams shoved cake against Terrell Whitehead's chest. It felt good—no, great—watching Mrs. Otis playing chicken foot with her neighbors and watching everyone laugh while Kylie Myers butchered a song. It felt warm and right to see Mr. Owens, swinging his walking cane around and pretending to dance with all the young women. The strings of Christmas lights and the summer smells of food and dried grass, mixed with laughter, all felt right. Once upon a time, I'd taken all that for granted, even resented it, thinking everyone small-minded and simple.

Granby was a different place now. This was a safe, small community where I could raise my baby, and I would, I'd decided. At least, until we could branch out on our own. Being here, living with Momma, we were safe and happy. Darion had reminded me of that.

I wanted to promise Ella success in her life. I wanted to promise her success in my life. But I thought I'd start smaller, striving for more attainable goals. I promised to take her for walks and arrange play dates with Darion and Tasha.

I remember thinking how lucky I was to have friends and family and a place for my baby. I remember that I fell asleep happier than I'd been for a very long time. Funny how quickly things can change and everything you thought you knew, never was.

CHAPTER TEN

They fell into the bedroom, all three connected by fists and chokeholds, but nothing seemed to faze Hernandez.

What is he on? Crack? PCP? Whatever it was, he appeared to feel nothing, and the chokehold he had on Fox was killing her. It didn't matter what they hit him with; he was a human freight train, oblivious to pain.

Fox couldn't breathe. She couldn't feel the floor underneath her any longer. He was slamming her against the wall when she could make out Wolfe getting back to her feet.

She charged down the hallway, a woman possessed, and leapt onto the entanglement of Fox and Hernandez. Together, they spun through an open door and onto the bed of Marilyn and Joseph Phitzier.

However clumsy, Wolfe's tackle freed Fox from the madman's grip, and Fox gasped for air. She watched as the elderly couple bounced and shifted with the force of the trio's landing, but never woke.

How do you sleep through World War III taking place in your house? "Hey!" Fox shouted, hoping to wake the dead. *Shit, were they dead? Maybe they were dead. Wouldn't that be . . .*

Somehow, Wolfe landed in front of Hernandez. Fox, again, was behind them and saw everything in a brief and insane instant. She saw Wolfe's eyes flash back and forth from Hernandez's hand to her partner's face and instantly understood what Wolfe was thinking as she reached for her handcuffs.

Grab his arm and cuff him to the heavy bedposts.

But he saw it coming and backhanded her across the face, catching more of her neck than face. It spun her violently to the side, knocking the cuffs from her hand. Her gun had been lost long ago. Both Wolfe and Fox were in for the fight of their lives. Literally. Hernandez wasn't going in peacefully, and he was determined to prove it. He also wasn't going to just walk away.

He lunged for the cuffs and Wolfe dove, swiping a hand across the floor and sweeping the cuffs under the bed. Again, Fox understood what Wolfe was doing. It was better that she get rid of them than let him turn the cuffs into some sort of weapon.

Behind him, Fox had her baton out and used it like a riding crop, beating a steady rhythm against Hernandez's back. Still, no amount of pounding seemed to slow him, and Fox knew they were running out of time.

"Hey! Hey!" She tried kicking against the bedpost, hoping the vibrations would stir Sleeping Beauty and her prince. "Hey!" Fox yelled again. As much as she hated to admit it, she and Wolfe could have used the help of a ninety year old with nimble phone-dialing fingers.

Fox struck again. And again.

Hernandez was on top of Wolfe. She was on her back, facing the monster, trying to grab hold of his neck, face, arms, anything. He swatted her hands away like gnats and clutched her throat. His strong hands closed up on Wolfe's neck, and he throttled her, banging the back of her head against the floor. As she cried out, cursing, Fox felt a desperate rage of her own.

Wolfe managed to wiggle around and gouged an eye, causing him to rear back, sitting on his haunches, still hovering over her. Her hands went to her neck as she clawed desperately at her throat, trying to get just one good solid breath.

The man wiped at his eye and roared. Enraged, he came down on her, slamming a powerful fist into her sternum, and Fox heard the sound of something snap.

Wolfe made a noise as if all the air had been forcibly ripped from her. That was it. Game over. She was done, and Fox saw red.

Standing behind the crouching Hernandez, Fox reared back and slammed her steel-tipped boot into his testicles. As she did, she unleashed her own battle cry, calling on all the power and strength she owned, hoping that she could slam those puppies clear up his throat—forever lodging them in his neck. She held nothing back. She was terrified already, but she'd seen the hit Wolfe had just taken, and she prayed that her partner would be okay. All her fears and anger were unleashed in that one kick.

He fell over, sliding off Wolfe's body. Fox could not afford to hesitate. She couldn't look at her partner but focused every bit of her attention on slamming a knee into the small of Hernandez's back and driving him into the floor, face first. She shoved his head against the side of a dresser, grabbed the back of his head by a fistful of hair, slammed it again for good measure, and reached for her cuffs.

One, two.

As soon as the ring snapped tight on his wrist, she lunged over his body for the alarm clock perched on the edge of a side table. Grabbing the cord, she bound his ankles before he began to move again. As he did, she grabbed another handful of hair and performed another textbook head slam. "Shut up!" she screamed, perhaps a bit more hysterical than she'd have preferred.

Hernandez was still.

The fight was over.

Fox fell off him and leaned over Wolfe. "Tina. Tina, talk to me, Tina. C'mon, Wolfie. Talk to me, please." Fox tried to control her voice.

Wolfe wheezed, and Fox could see that Wolfe was trying to get just one good lungful. Wolfe squeezed her eyes shut and continued to fight for air.

Fox knew the pain had to be incredible as she pleaded with Wolfe to be okay. "C'mon, Wolfie. Talk to me, baby!" As she spoke, Fox searched Wolfe's face, trying to understand her partner's injuries.

There were scrapes and the beginnings of a bruised cheek but no blood. Still, Wolfe couldn't seem to catch her breath as Fox fumbled with the buttons before finally tugging the uniform shirt free. As she peeled the shirt back, surveying any damage, Hernandez began to complain.

"Shut up!" Fox yelled at him again.

At long last, the Phitziers woke up.

"What's going on here?" Mr. Phitzier sat up, swinging a leg out from under his covers while Mrs. Phitzier gathered her covers under her chin.

"Police business," Fox declared. "Please, call—no, oh, geez, Wolfie . . ."

The breastplate to Tina Wolfe's chest protector was caved in. While the vest had protected Wolfe from Hernandez's punishing punch, the force had snapped the plate, pushing it into Wolfe's sternum.

Had she not worn the vest . . . Fox didn't even want to think about that.

"By damn!" Mr. Phitzier exclaimed. "By damn." He started to climb out of the bed but stopped at the sight of Hernandez cuffed and bound on the floor.

"Help me up," Wolfe wheezed.

"Are you sure?" Fox raised her eyebrows, secretly relieved to hear Tina talk.

Wolfe nodded.

"What in the blue blazes is going on here?" Mr. Phitzier demanded again.

Mrs. Phitzier began to make noises about calling the police.

"We *are* the police, ma'am," Fox said then turned back to Wolfe. "You sure you're okay?"

Again, Wolfe nodded, and Fox took an arm, easing her onto her feet. Through gritted teeth, she rose, turned, and kicked Hernandez.

He yowled.

"Good. Asshole!" Wolfe winced with pain.

"Get out of here!" Mrs. Phitzier ordered the women. "All of you; get out. I'm calling the police."

"It's okay, we're—" Fox couldn't understand how the uniforms and badges weren't giving them away.

"Forget it," Wolfe waved an arm, finally standing on her own. "Can you hop, asshole?" Wolfe turned to Fox. "Ask him if he can hop, 'cause

I'm not carrying him."

He could and he did. By the time he'd reached the cruiser, he was crying foul.

Fox was more concerned about her partner. "You sure we shouldn't call for help? Geez, Wolfie, you look bad."

"Shit, Rosa. After all that? You'd call for backup now? Hell with that. We're taking in this son of a bitch by ourselves, thank you."

By the time they reached the station, Wolfe was in obvious pain, and in an uncharacteristic move, she asked Fox to book the prisoner while she found a seat.

Also battered and bruised, Fox took Hernandez to booking, the next room over. This wasn't Dallas or Austin. When you were a cop in Granby, you did everything—the fingerprinting, mug shots, and booking. You did the paperwork and phone calls. That also meant you took down doped-up professional boxers when need be.

Wolfe eased into the chair at her desk as Fox wrestled with the now whining Hernandez.

He wasn't so Horrendous when he's served his own nuts.

"Son of a bitch, that hurt," Wolfe said and exhaled in her chair. She stretched out a strong, lean leg. It was an injury she was sure would hurt worse tomorrow. She ached, and all her movements were in slow motion. Even removing her shirt was difficult. She gingerly unbuttoned her uniform and eased out of the vest. As she pulled at the Velcro strips, she cursed under her breath and gritted her teeth. The slightest tugging sensation against her body caused electric shocks across her chest and ribs. She blew in and out, in and out, closed her eyes, and readied herself to remove the vest. She winced as Douglas Fitz walked in the door. Using her legs, she swerved around in the chair and grinned at him.

"Dougie!" Wolfe managed a loud salutation to a fellow officer. Despite their pain, both Fox and Wolfe knew that hauling in that monster would make for a great story.

They had laughed, just thinking about the fact that the old couple had slept through the entire fight, in their own bedroom, no less. But Wolfe would have to wait for Fox to share the story.

"Where've you been?" He moved in quickly. "You look like hell."

"Thanks. We've been through hell."

Doug Fitz was a good guy. He was a Northerner and didn't always swing with the way they did things around here, but a good guy. He'd been there the night she wrote up the false report when Hatch smacked his skull on the ceiling. While he hadn't participated in the Squad Room Olympics, he'd never ratted anyone out either.

As Hatch lay on the floor bleeding, Dougie just said, "I didn't see anything. I was never here," and stepped over Hatch's writhing body to go out on early patrol. In fact, that might have been his only true fault. He was far too serious, and Tina Wolfe had taken it upon herself long ago to loosen him up.

During the required CPR certification, which Wolfe declared to be bullshit since the one time she'd ever had to perform it, the woman up and died anyway, Wolfe had partnered up with Fitz. When it was her turn to blow into the dummy Annie's mouth, she did obscene things to Annie.

Fitz never cracked.

It was when she was supposed to be doing the chest compressions while he did the breathing, she did other obscene things that finally caused a laugh. He had humor; he just suppressed it.

"We've been trying to contact—" He looked around the room. "Where's Fox?"

"Booking. We brought in a deranged boxer. Here, help me with this," she said, trying to sit upright.

Without knowing what was being asked of him, he stepped forward, hands out. "What are we . . . Damn, looks like you caught something." He pointed to the caved plate to her vest.

She nodded. "Yeah, a fist."

"A fist? Someone punched you with their *fist* and did that?" His eyebrows shot up. "You okay?" He looked back toward Booking.

They could hear Fox yelling at Hernandez to shut up and stop being a baby, that they were almost done, and he could find himself a nice comfy cot to sleep on.

"She need help?" He gestured a thumb toward the other room.

"Me first. Help me get this damned thing off. God, I can barely move."

Beneath her vest, she wore a thin, cotton undershirt, and Fitz turned a bright red when it registered.

"He bruised my boobies. Wanna see?"

"Shit, Wolfie! Don't say things like that. Geez." He turned his back, putting her vest on a desk and keeping his back turned while she inspected the damage.

"Nope, they're still good. Sure you don't want to peek? Many a man has killed for this opportunity!" She was feeling better every minute that Fitz blushed. For the first time, she looked around the squad room. She'd been in so much pain, so uncomfortable with the breastplate digging into her chest that she hadn't been able to focus on much else. "Hey. Where is everyone?"

"Oh, dammit!" He jumped and reached for his radio. It was on and flush to his mouth in a millisecond. "Chief, Wolfie and Fox are at the station house. Okay. I repeat, okay."

"Well, I wouldn't say okay—"

"Roger that. I'll deal with them later." Teague's voice on the radio overlapped hers, and Wolfe leaned forward.

Something's wrong.

"C'mon out here. The Larson farm, backside. You know where." His voice clicked off.

"What's up?"

There were all kinds of clambering and clanking noises in the back, all signs that Hernandez's sorry ass had been thrown in the clinker.

Fox reappeared just as Officer Fitz clued Wolfe in. "It's bad, Wolfie. James Otis, you know, they had a party out at his place. Sometime tonight, he was found dead. Looks like maybe a hate crime."

"A hate crime?" Fox asked.

Fitz turned around to see her for the first time. "Shit, what did you two do, wrestle a bull?"

"Just about," Fox said.

Her hair, typically in a tight French braid that lay flush against her head, was loose and tousled. So much so that she'd given up on it, removed the scrunchie that held it, and created a new ponytail. Her uniform shirt was torn in two places with blood on her right shoulder. She might have wondered whose blood that was, but she and Wolfe were too fixated on what had happened to James Otis.

Wolfe had known James far better than Fox, but everything Fox had ever heard about the kid had been positive. He'd been in some trouble a few years back but had turned himself around. He'd been one of the rare ones who was respectful of the police, didn't want trouble with the law, and was even less interested in making some kind of tough-guy show in front of his buddies. Lastly, he'd been a new father and had taken on the role with a certain pride. It was nice to see. She'd liked him just fine.

"What did you say?" Fox redirected him again. "James Otis is dead?"

"Yeah, and the chief wants us out there. I'm here for the tire kit. We've got some fresh tire—"

"Whoa, slow down. Give more details. Where is he? Who found him? How do you know he's dead?" Wolfe eased out of the chair, and they could see the look of pain sweep across her face.

Despite her protests, Fox knew Wolfe would have to see a doctor about her injuries, and she would complain every step of the way.

"Looks like he was dragged to death behind a truck."

"Oh sweet Jesus."

"Pretty much decapitated."

"Oh no," Wolfe groaned. "What about his little girlfriend? What's her name? Tasha . . . Tasha Williams? Dang." Wolfe shook her head.

Talking over his shoulder, Fitz collected all the equipment they needed to take moldings. They were a small-time operation but still had what they needed to gather evidence.

"Francis took the 911. Someone screaming that James was dead then hung up before she could get much else. But the caller did say he was out at Larson's farm, on the back road. Just kept screaming that James was dead."

He pulled out two large, hard-shelled briefcases from a locked cabinet and passed one off to Fox. He didn't even bother with Wolfe, who stood hunched over and wincing.

"Tried to call you in but you didn't respond. Chief called in me, Hatch, and Shea Griffin." He was loaded down with extra flashlights and dragging a generator from room to room, yelling out the information as he moved through the small station house.

"Shea Griffin?" Fox and Wolfe simultaneously asked, surprised.

Chief Teague hated Griffin.

"We need manpower and didn't know where you were," he yelled back, slamming doors. "All we know is there was a party out at his place—Otis's, that is. Some kind of fight broke out. Next thing we know, he's dragged behind some kind of truck, head damned near ripped off. Dead. That's it. Now, c'mon, let's go. Chief's waiting."

"Uh . . ." Fox pointed a finger toward the cells where Horrendous Hernandez sat, whimpering.

"I'll stay," Wolfe said. "I'm not much good right now. You go." She nodded to her partner.

"Sure?"

"Yeah, just keep me posted." As they headed out the door, Wolfe called after them. "I mean it, I want to know everything!"

When the door slammed shut behind them, she eased back into her chair and cursed. Another noise came from the cells, and Wolfe scowled. "Oh, shut up, ya goathead!"

Tina Wolfe hated goats, she hated stupidshit punks like the one in the other room, and she hated being hurt. Everyone knew that. More than anything, however, Wolfe hated being helpless.

CHAPTER ELEVEN

It was all anyone talked about over the weekend and into the following week. As much as I wanted to get away from it, it was impossible. Working at *The Recorder*, we gathered and printed just about everything we could, but we were low man on the media totem pole. And every news agency worth their salt was in Granby.

A black man dragged to death—nearly decapitated on the night of his graduation party.

There were all kinds of theories. Rogue Ku Klux Klansmen who hated to see a young black man become successful had lured him away and dragged him to his death. That was bad enough, but I could do without the agencies that sensationalized his death, reporting how James begged his captors to release him, talking about his baby.

How could they know that?

I remembered crying with fury the first time I had read that. They'd had no call to mimic James's voice.

Everyone who'd attended the party had been interviewed and re-interviewed. I wished so much that I could've been of help, but the truth was I had seen very little of James. We'd talked when I'd first gotten there, and I'd seen him playing around during the party with other guests, but I'd never seen any kind of confrontation, and I'd never seen how the party had ended. I hadn't even known who won the fight, not that I cared, until the following day when people had been talking about the entire party.

Oscar pummeled Jeff. James and another stopped the fight. According to everyone who was there for the fight, Jeff sat down on the tailgate to Eddie Mann's truck and got doctored by Lisa Gary, which was apparently something to see because she's supposed to be Hut Langford's girl. More people focused on that than anything else.

What no one seemed to know was when, or why, James Otis left his own party.

During my second interview with Chief Teague, I'd been asked to compile a list of everyone I could think of who'd attended the party. Certain the police would be cross-referencing all the lists and checking everyone out, I was sure I'd offered no more information in that regard than anyone else.

I tried to focus on other town news. I suppose I was in denial. I couldn't bear thinking about James being killed, much less how much this was hurting Mrs. Otis, Tasha, and little Darion. I was sick about it, but sickened all the more by listening to the office chatter.

LeAnn Ricks was leaning over the front counter, watching the news trucks roam up and down Main Street when Tammi hurried into *The Recorder*. Her cheeks were flushed, her eyes dancing with excitement.

"You will not guess . . ." She panted as she shrugged out of her sweater. It was over ninety degrees outside but she wore a sweater because she didn't like the way her arms looked.

They're called p-u-s-h-u-p-s, *Ms. Whatley.*

I frowned and looked back at my desk, sure I didn't want to hear whatever it was she thought was so exciting.

"Chief Teague has called for a press conference at noon at the convention center." She huffed, puffed, and wagged a finger at me.

I saw the motion out of the corner of my eye but pretended to be lost in thought.

Tammi cleared her throat. "Thia. Theresa!"

I was forced to look up.

"You need to be there, so get whatever you need, pen, paper, tape recorder . . ." She was pacing, thrilled with all the hubbub. "Noon. Don't forget now. He's got more information he says he wants to share with the public. I've heard through my own little *private* grapevine that the FBI will be coming here, may already be here, investigating as well."

"No!" LeAnn and Vicky were the perfect audience, both wide-eyed, mouths agape, perched on the edge of their seats, and looking in need of a bib at any moment.

"Indeedy. And you'll never guess who they've been talking to . . . Shelby Harrelson!"

There was a chorus of gasps—happy gasps.

"About what?" LeAnn clapped her hands together.

"It seems—" she whispered.

Walking in front of the bay window was Shea Griffin, strutting like a peacock. His head had swelled so damned much I wasn't sure he'd make it through the doorjamb when Tammi rapped on the window and beckoned Griffin inside, and I'm sure Vicky heard me groan out loud.

Shea Griffin owned the Griffin Garage and employed the dumbest humans on Earth, but Griffin wasn't too far off himself. He was a volunteer cop. You know the kind, nowhere near the fitness level to be a real cop, so he played pretend wannabe cop. He walked around with a badge in his wallet and drove an old police car he'd bought at an auction.

When I'd come back to Granby, his car was the first I'd seen, and I'd slowed, thinking I was about to get busted for going twenty miles over the speed limit. As I'd slowed, I'd been shocked to see Mr. Griffin, until I'd realized the idiot was just playing policeman. Still, he'd had the gall to point a finger at me, warning me to slow down.

Until the death of James Otis, the Granby Police Department never had any real call for Griffin. But with all officers needed to interview and gather information, Griffin was asked to patrol the streets and respond to non-emergency situations. He was puffed up like a damned Macy's Day Parade float. Maybe that was what bothered me most. He was having his dream come true at the expense of James's life.

His impressive belly made it through the doorway first. As he stepped in, all business, he adjusted his belt. "Ladies," he boomed in a deeper-than-usual voice.

"Why, Shea Griffin." LeAnn pulled out her butter-won't-melt-in-my-mouth voice. "We were just talking about you."

"All good, I hope."

There was a chorus of chuckles and series of mindless nods.

"What about?" he wondered, still smiling, though it looked a little forced. He had to know he was a bit of a joke around town.

"Tammi just heard that the police have been talking to Shelby Harrelson," Vicky blurted out. "What's that about?"

"You busy gettin' the scoop on the other papers?" Shea joked and licked his lips.

I leaned back in my chair and watched him. *He doesn't know a thing, and it's killing him.* He was only asked to patrol the streets, still cut out of the police loop.

"Yes, Shea, what's that about?" LeAnn asked.

"Ladies, I am not at liberty to discuss these things." He spread his hands out, palms up toward the ceiling. "You know that."

"Of course," Tammi said. "But why do you . . ."

"Uh-uh." Shea clucked his tongue. "Can't talk about it. Those are the rules. However, should you hear anything . . ." he said as Ryan Whatley stepped inside the office.

"Hi, baby," Tammi said, flitting across the room.

Ryan froze like a deer caught in headlights as he looked at each of us. "What's going on?" he asked, looking embarrassed to have his mother drape herself over his shoulders. He was a good enough son that he would never say anything, but the rest of us could see how uncomfortable her undying, obsessive love made him. He squirmed in the most polite manner and then gave me a head nod.

"Hey." I smiled, suffering with him.

"Shea here was just telling us how he couldn't tell us how Shelby Harrelson is involved with the murder case," LeAnn announced, and Shea jumped.

"Well, now, I didn't—"

"Oh, now, don't be modest. It's the truth, isn't it? You know something about the case and her involvement. You just can't tell us *civilians*," Tammi gushed, that last word having the greatest effect. You could actually see Shea Griffin puff up.

"What does Ms. Harrelson have to do with the . . . with any of this?" Ryan asked, confused.

"That's what we were trying to get Shea to tell us." Tammi clapped her hands together. "According to my source, the police have been talking to Shelby Harrelson and talking *specifically* about this case. Maybe she knows something or saw something. No one knows . . ."

The statement hung there as she stared at Shea Griffin, who was careful not to look as amazed by this news as everyone else.

"What could she know?" Ryan asked.

"With Shelby Harrelson," someone laughed, "there is just no tellin'."

"Isn't that the truth?"

"And nothing I could hear about Shelby Harrelson would surprise me in the least bit," Tammi said, and Ryan scowled.

"I don't get it." Ryan shook his head. "She's real nice. I like Ms. Harrelson. She—"

"Oh, stop it!" Tammi gave him a playful push—enough to rock him back against the door.

He looked a little surprised and raised his eyebrows at me.

I shrugged.

These women had had it in for Shelby Harrelson ever since she'd had a huge party out at her place about five years ago. She'd invited a U.S. Representative, and hadn't invited the wondrous Ms. Tammi Whatley. Ever since then, it had been war. Any talk of Shelby Harrelson having traveled or met celebrity-type people drove Tammi, LeAnn, and Vicky over a wall.

"Well, she's not in any trouble, is she?" Ryan looked to Shea Griffin.

Griffin just shrugged.

He doesn't have the slightest clue.

I studied Ryan's face for a moment. It was entirely possible that Ryan had been away long enough that he either didn't know, or had forgotten, what a complete farce Griffin was as a police officer.

"Honey, I wouldn't worry about her," LeAnn told Ryan. "She's got high friends in high places." She made an ooh-la-la gesture with her hands while the others chuckled.

Ryan wasn't impressed.

"I'm sure it's something else," I said, not wanting to sit by while they tried to trash Shelby Harrelson. "I bet it's just, you know, routine questions like . . . they've done to everyone else." I started to say "like us" but bit my tongue. For all I knew, Tammi had no idea that Ryan had talked to the police, the same as everyone else who attended the party.

He seemed to be relieved. "I just don't get how she could be involved in all this," Ryan said. He shrugged and leaned into his mother, whispering in her ear.

She giggled and patted his arm. "Why sure, honey bunch." She sashayed behind the counter to get her purse, but pulled the bills out of his reach at the last second in an attempt to make her point. "Don't be gettin' upset over the likes of Shelby. We should all be held accountable for our own actions. Sometimes it's a little embarrassing but that's the way it goes in a small town. Everyone knows everyone else's business at one time or another." She gave me a quick little look.

Was that for me? I felt myself cringe.

CHAPTER TWELVE

The battle lines had been drawn between Ms. Riley and the fat, gray squirrel with the scrawny tail. Apparently the fat, gray squirrel had been gathering and consuming far more than his share of pecans, and Ms. Riley had called in the big guns—Momma and Ella/Lily. Together, they'd gathered three buckets and a Scooby Doo lunchbox filled with Ms. Riley's pecans. Love her pecans as she did, she'd decided she'd rather we have the nuts than her formidable nut-gathering opponent.

"He comes when I'm sleeping or not lookin'," she'd said with disgust.

The bonus for Ms. Riley, Momma had later reported, was the shrill screaming Ella had done each time she found a pecan. The squeals had been so high-pitched and so offensive as Ella had tossed the small pecans into her Scooby Doo lunch box that Ms. Riley just howled with delight, sure that all living creatures had fled the territory.

Ms. Riley had surveyed the trees, hands on hips, and declared, "Not a one. I don't see a damned squirrel anywhere, not a one." She had chuckled as Ella screamed and clapped her hands.

"She really think those squirrels aren't coming back?" I asked, sitting on the front stoop, cracking open pecans.

"No, but I think she likes those small victories," Momma said.

The only sound I could hear was the periodic cracking of shells as the four of us sat out on the front porch. Cici had come over. It was Wednesday evening, after all. Ella, not to be confused with Lily—though I wondered how Ella was adjusting to the fact that she was called two different names—plunged her hand into the pecan bucket, always pleased to be able to get that one specific nut at the bottom of the barrel. It was a game in which only she knew the rules. It seemed to entertain her mightily.

Except for the occasional giggle, ours was a somber household. Truth was, I just couldn't stop thinking about James, so anything I could do, from shelling pecans and talking about Ms. Riley to wondering about the whole climate change situation, was a load off my brain. I guess we were all trying not to think about him. He wasn't the kind of fellow you could forget, though, and again, I suppose that was a good thing. It wasn't that I wanted to forget him. I just wanted this . . . the reality of his death and how he might have died, not to exist. It was a feeling that cast a shadow on everything and everyone.

Dragged to death.

A hate crime.

It just couldn't be.

When I'd been at Duke, however, I'd told my fair share of stories of how people from my own town had spoken about blacks and Hispanics. Hell, I'd heard the way Hispanics and blacks had spoken about each other. I'd heard crap that Latino girls had said, standing in line behind me, thinking that I couldn't understand Spanish. I'd understood enough to know when something ugly had been said about me. Because I was white, and because Ella had darker hair, because she looked like she could be part Latina, I'd heard the remarks, the low whispers.

You could make fun of, or pass judgment over Bible-thumpers, someone who was snooty, or even on welfare, but there was always a different edge when it became about skin color. Maybe because deep down we all knew that attitudes could change, financial situations could change, but skin color is a done deal. Right there, the whole subject is put in another category. That's when the trash tries to justify.

Well, there's black and there's niggers. There's Hispanic and there's spics. There's white and there's . . .

I'd never heard that last one.

I cracked open a few more nuts, listening to the sounds of Ella and shells, and wondered if I'd ever been referred to as a cracker. I didn't think so, and oddly, I didn't care. It wasn't the same.

"I heard it was supposed to rain this weekend." Cici's voice interrupted this last thought pattern, and I was grateful. It wasn't taking me anywhere. "Lord knows, we could use it."

"Though, not for James's funeral," I declared.

More silence.

"You going?" Cici asked after a while.

"Yes," was all I said.

Sitting there, busying our hands while our brains hummed and buzzed with sadness, I had a flashback to when I was a kid, after Daddy had left. Momma hadn't known what to say. Cici hadn't known what to say. I hadn't known what to say. So there we'd sat on the porch shucking corn. Tons of it. There had been some big affair in town and Cici had brought danged near a truckload of corn for us to shuck. There had been breaks in the silence when someone commented about a certain shape of a corn or how long the stalk was. It had been enough to let us share with each other but not have to talk.

Now I was grateful for the pecans. So much so that when Danny Archer rode by on his bike, throwing the evening paper on our driveway, no one moved. He waved to us and we all waved back. No one spoke.

God knows what the headlines read.

I'd left LeAnn pecking away at the computer after Shea Griffin's visit. She'd been so hell-bent on *The Recorder* scooping the other papers, there was no telling what she'd printed.

The rumbling of Bubba Peters's truck redirected our attention, and we all watched with great interest as he came around the corner, his truck packed with curbside goodies. He slowed by the Tillmans' place and continued to cruise by Ms. Riley's when she burst out of the house, waving her arms.

"Yoo-hoo! Yoo-hoo. Mr. Peters!" she called out, picking her way down her front steps.

"What does she want?" Cici abandoned shelling pecans and eased off the porch swing.

"Apparently, she wants Bubba." Momma winked at me.

Cici huffed. "She's always pestering him." She stepped forward, taking the step next to me.

Ms. Riley hustled over to his window, and I had to admit, she did appear to have more of a sassy step than usual. She wore a floral print skirt that swooshed a little more than needed. There was no breeze. That was all hip action.

"Maybe she has more appliances she needs moved," Momma said. "Or maybe she's decided she's gettin' to be too old to stare at him from her front porch." There was no missing the small giggle in her voice, though Cici did her best to ignore her.

"I just want to know what's so important that she had to come running down her front walk like that." Cici bore holes in the woman across the street, and while there was no way I could see Mr. Peters having any interest in Ms. Riley, steam would soon be coming out of Cici's head.

I saw Mr. Peters nodding his head while Ms. Riley flitted about.

"Cici," Momma said. "Why don't you just ask Bubba out?"

"Don't be stupid." Cici scowled.

"You've been mooning over that man long enough. I swear, you aren't scared of a thing. You'll talk to anyone about anything, but . . . I just don't get it. When it comes to Bubba, you're acting like we're kids again."

Ms. Riley gave a little wave and started back toward her house, and Mr. Peters rumbled forward.

Momma laughed, remembering something. "Do you remember how we used to call—oh, what was that boy's name?" she asked.

"Bruce Howard," Cici recalled, and Momma slapped her knee, hooting.

"Bruce Howard! That's it. Thia, you wouldn't believe the phone calls we used to make. And those were in the days when you could call without worry of caller ID." As Momma spoke, we all watched Mr. Peters's truck ease down the street, looming closer.

"We'd disguise our voices and . . ."

Mr. Peters's truck pulled into our driveway.

I felt Cici go rigid next to me. Momma's mouth snapped shut.

Bubba Peters was under an excruciating microscope. Every inch of his person was being measured and analyzed. I would have felt sorry for him, having to make his way toward us, if I weren't so busy scrutinizing the way he walked, the fold of his jeans, his shoulders, and the tilt of his hat. I wanted to poke Cici, remind her to breathe, but didn't dare move.

As he got closer, he grinned and removed his hat.

"Ms. Franks." He nodded to Momma. "Ms. Radosa." He smiled at Cici, and then to me he bobbed his head once more. "Good to see you back, Ms. Thia. We missed you around here. It's been boring, to say the least."

I smiled back, a little uncertain as to what that was supposed to mean, and I found myself straining to recall if I'd ever pulled a prank on him. Not that I could remember, but then I'd been trying so hard to forget some of the awful things I'd done. Seems I was untrained in the art of recollecting anything embarrassing or humiliating. I gave a quick smile and continued with my pecan cracking.

"Ms. Riley said I needed to come over here and get some pecans from you all. In fact"—he scratched his head and looked embarrassed—"she was pretty insistent about it."

"Well, pecans are healthy," Momma said.

Both Cici and I looked at her.

"I s'pose so." Mr. Peters smiled then looked down the street for a moment.

Ms. Riley was standing at her front door and waved when she saw all heads turn her way.

How odd.

"You do much cooking, Bubba?" Momma asked.

"I get by." Embarrassed, Mr. Peters shoved his hands in his pockets, smiling handsomely at us.

I squinted up at him again. *My goodness, he's a gorgeous man.* Funny, I hadn't noticed it before. He was just always Bubba, the trash guy. Now, standing in front of a group of women, he seemed like a shy teenager.

He shuffled his feet a little.

"Thia, why don't you go inside and get Bub—*Mr. Peters* a bag for his pecans." As I stood, she said, "You should taste Cici's pecan pie. To die for. You'd love it."

"Oh, well—" Cici sounded as if she might deny the claim, but Momma kept talking as if Cici wasn't there.

"What do you plan on doing with these pecans, Bubba? You have recipes?

"Well, I don't know. I hadn't planned on . . . I'm just doing what I'm told." He grinned.

"Ah, the mark of a good man." Momma laughed softly.

As my hand reached the screen door, I looked over my shoulder at her. This had Momma-stink all over it.

"Well, Cici, you should have Bubba over to your place and show him all your pecan recipes."

I groaned. I'm sure Cici's innards just turned to liquid. *All your pecan recipes?*

"Oh, well . . ." Mr. Peters said.

"I don't really have any pecan . . ." Cici managed to croak out. She tried to laugh but it was painful.

I knew she was dying. I went inside, unable to listen any longer.

When I returned, Momma was laughing with Bubba. Someone had said something to ease the tension, but I knew Momma wasn't done.

"Here you go, Mr. Peters." I handed a bag to him.

"Oh, no, let's have Lily do that." Momma rose from her throne of a swing seat and pushed Ella toward a large bucket.

"You mean Ella," I was not at all amused by this continued manipulation by my mother.

"Oh, pooh." Momma waved a hand at me and directed Ella toward the bucket. "Right there, sweetie. Put your little hands in there and fill up this bag for Grandmamma. Can you do that?"

Ella clapped her hands, looking around at everyone.

"Good girl, Lily. Fill it up," Momma instructed Ella.

"*El-la,*" I said.

Mr. Peters scratched his head. "I'm confused. Is her name Ella or Lily?"

"Well, now, that's an excellent question, Mr. Peters. And who would know the answer to that? Hmmm, let's see. Would it be the person who gave birth to the child and gave that child the legal name that is on said child's birth certificate? Or"—I waved a hand toward Momma, who was ignoring us all and purposefully encouraging Ella, saying *Lily* as much as possible—"would it be a deeply troubled person who is in denial and can't accept the fact that she can't always have control over everything?"

"Uh." Mr. Peters seemed uncertain as to how to respond to that.

"Wonderful, Lily! Oh, that's my big girl," Momma said.

Ella cooed and then spilled pecans all over the porch.

"Momma." I sighed. "It's Ella, and you know it's Ella."

"Faster, Lily, faster." Momma clapped, causing Ella to squeal more and more.

"How long does this go on?" I leaned forward, asking Cici.

"Forever." Cici buried her head in her hands.

"Ella," I said again, more to myself than anyone else.

"It will never stop." Cici cupped her hands around her mouth.

"You know, I just had a thought," Momma said. "Why don't we have you over here for dinner one evening, Bubba? That way, we can show you all the clever ways you can use these pecans."

"Just when you thought it couldn't get worse," I mumbled.

Cici laughed—or choked on her tongue. At this point, I wasn't sure anymore.

"That'd be real nice." Mr. Peters nodded his head.

Without looking, I knew Cici was torn between joy and fear.

"Lookie there! What a good girl you are," Momma said to Ella once she'd filled the bag.

"Yea!" Ella applauded herself.

"How about this evening? You're here. We'd love to have you, wouldn't we, Cici?"

"Well . . ." He looked almost terrified.

"Please, we'd love it, and you'd be a nice distraction from all this terrible business with James Otis."

To that, she couldn't have been more right. It appeared that Mr. Peters was inclined to agree.

His facial expression changed, and he gave a nod. "Sure. Why not?"

"Wonderful. Lily, let's go in and wash up. We've got company tonight!"

"It's Ella! Do you want me to get out the birth certificate? It's *Ella!*"

"Thia, be a dear and clean up all the pecans." Momma never heard a word I said.

"I'm sorry, Bubba," Cici said. "I'd like to tell you that this isn't how things typically are but . . ."

"Lileee! Lileee!" Ella clapped her hands, following Momma as she stood to walk into the house. My mouth fell open.

"Please, call me Teddy."

"Teddy." The soft tone of Cici's voice said it all—she was flustered, but happy.

"Lileee! Lileee!"

"Mom, gosh dammit!" I yelled over my shoulder.

"Wonderful!" Momma's voice trailed off into the house.

As I stooped down to pick up Ella's spilled pecans, something caught my attention. Ms. Riley still standing at her front door, smiling.

"At least you won't be bored," Cici said, attempting humor as Mr. Peters held the door open for her and they stepped inside. I believe it was the first time Mr. Peters had ever been inside our home.

"How about that," Momma whispered, bending down next to me, and I jumped. Momma was like a ninja when potential gossip was afoot. She looked pleased as punch.

"Yeah, how about *that*," I said, nodding toward Ms. Riley's house. "Why do I get the feeling that you two are in cahoots?"

Momma paused and looked across the street. She gave a little wave, topped off with a thumbs-up motion, and I groaned.

"Geez, Momma. Please, promise me that you won't get in my business like that."

"I wouldn't dream of it." Momma put her hand to her chest as if to offer an I-cross-my-heart. "Cici just needed a little boost in the self-esteem and love department. I wouldn't interfere with you that way. I know better."

I opened my mouth to say thanks but snapped it shut.

Ella tottered down the hallway already half-naked and stripping her diaper off. "Lilleee! Lileee! Lileee!"

CHAPTER THIRTEEN

She'd seen it. She'd seen who was with James Otis the night he died. Hell, it had been just minutes before he died, and she had seen who was in that truck, but how could she tell anyone? She hadn't been where she was supposed to be.

Then again, why should she care? She didn't know him personally. She was sorry about James Otis, but it's not as if she really knew him. Other people, however, were a different story. As sorry as she was about James, there didn't seem to be any reason to get herself in trouble trying to save people who, in her opinion, weren't worth saving.

She was tempted to write an anonymous note and mail it to the police. Maybe if she just wrote it down, didn't even mention who she was or where she'd been standing, it would be enough to make people understand what had happened. She could use gloves and print everything out. She was certain it would stump that Chief Teague, but the FBI were said to be in town. She just couldn't risk being caught. She watched enough television to see all the amazing little gadgets and gizmos they had to catch criminals.

Criminals.

She hesitated over that word.

That's what she was. If she was caught, she would be charged and could go to prison.

Nope. She couldn't risk it. She wouldn't risk it. She was sorry about James. She would go to his funeral and pray over his body, but that was it. She wasn't going down for this. She wasn't going to have her life ruined because of others she couldn't even stand to begin with. Whatever happened would happen, and there was nothing she could do about it.

▌▌▌

The funny thing about Tammi Whatley, if you didn't know any better you'd think she was the queen of all gossip, the root where the grapevine began. She breezed through town, acting as if she were the ultimate source of information, when in reality, she was one peg down and merely regurgitating what she was told. Jessie Durham was the main source.

Tammi choosing the role of Supreme Being was fine because it kept Jessie out of trouble. As county clerk, she didn't want it known that she was giving out information about the good citizens of Granby . . . or the not-so-good citizens. That was what this was all about, after all, Tammi Whatley sucked up to her and pretended to care about her because she was vying for information. As if Jessie didn't know that.

What a fat cow Tammi is.

Because she was married to the owner of *The Recorder*, Tammi took it upon herself to gather information and spread whatever stories she knew, even those loosely based in fact, around town.

When the story had broken about Marla Dodson stealing money from clients at the video store, Tammi had gone on and on about how she knew people, that she had *connections*. The truth was, she'd waddled into Jessie's office and sucked down half her candy jar while Jessie had told her the story.

Tammi Whatley had a way about her. She got people to talk. Jessie had to give her that. It was frustrating and interesting at the same time. If you took a poll around town and asked who the most mean-spirited gossip was, hands down, the number one answer would be Tammi Whatley. Yet people still talked to her, confided things in her, shared personal stories and secrets with her, knowing full well that they were telling the town mouthpiece. When she was talking to you, though, she pulled you in, made you believe she was on your side and that yours was a secret to be shared. She didn't giggle; she cackled. Yet it was infectious. In her own mean, tough-talking kind of way, she was fun to be around. So when she poked her head in the doorway of Jessie's office, it wasn't such a bad thing. Jessie had to admit she enjoyed talking to her. It was fun to tell her stories and watch Tammi as she gasped, gleefully clapped her hands, cackled, and ranted. She was expressive and entertaining.

And maybe there was a part of Jessie that sold out to Tammi just to keep her off the scent of her brother, Jared. While Jessie was pretty sure most people knew Jared had a drinking problem, Tammi left him alone. It was an unspoken rule—he was off limits. In exchange, Jessie was never short of information. Almost every penalty, ticket, or trial passed through her hands. In fact, the docket for the next two months had enough information to keep Tammi very happy.

David Wyck's piece of trash daughter and his wife were facing insurance fraud charges. Angela Wyck bought a brand new plasma television and a four-wheeler then filed the paperwork to declare bankruptcy. She turned right around to sell the four-wheeler to Milford East. Milford used a cashier's check which left a paper trial for the credit card company investigator to follow. When she was instructed to pay back the credit card company, she claimed the money was gone, and then, wouldn't you know it, someone stole Ford's new four-wheeler.

While everyone was pretty sure the Wyck family was involved, it was just speculation. Ford had declared war against Angela. What no one else knew was that Angela made a hefty payment to the insurance company, trying to once again make good on her bankruptcy claim.

Now, where did Angela Wyck come up with that kind of money?

However tantalizing the information, Tammi, like everyone else, was only focused on what was happening with James Otis's death and the terrible cloud hanging over the town of Granby.

Years ago, there had been the awful lynching death of a black man from another small Texas town. The men involved were known racists, and yes, the torture and death of that black man had been based solely on a man's skin color.

Now, Granby was being called horrible names and the citizens of the town were being scrutinized as racists. What was worse, Granby citizens, those of color, were now questioning their own neighbors. People who had once partied together, attended festivals together, picnicked and played together were whispering behind closed doors.

Tammi didn't care that Mrs. Vargus had finally filed charges against her husband, Johnny, after all these years of him beating the shit out of her. Cody Kyle was still in lock up for possession of illegal arms, and Jessie also knew a little something about Miranda McGhee that Tammi would drool over, but it all had to wait. Tammi was only interested in the ongoing Otis investigation and whether any charges had been officially filed against anyone in their county.

All Jessie could tell her was that the police weren't any closer to determining the make and model of the truck used to kill James Otis because it appeared there could be several trucks involved. A new rumor was that the Mexicans working the construction on the local highway could be involved.

One puzzler was the phone call made to Francis at the station house. The call had been made by someone who spoke fluent English, which had had the chief wondering why he or she hadn't come forward. They knew the call made to 911 had been made from James's cell phone, but no fingerprints had been found on his phone.

Jessie had heard that a plant had been placed in Granby—someone pretending to be one of them, but Jessie held back this last bit of information. While Tammi had nosed around for more information about the actual investigation, Jessie had been focused on finding out who the plant was. In a town of four thousand, it couldn't be too hard to weed out a newcomer, but with feds, cameramen, reporters, and incoming family and friends for James's funeral, it hadn't been going that easy either.

Not that it mattered much to Tammi anyway. As soon as she'd heard something about the Mexicans, she was off and running.

▌▌▌

He tried to get back to the property. It was pointless. There were so many police officers, investigators, cameramen, and nosy neighbors milling about, there was no way he could sneak back.

Dammit.

He hadn't realized it at first, what with everything happening the way it had, he'd just tried to act as if things were normal. Then he'd noticed it. His key chain was missing. Well, a *part* of it, anyway. A part that could be traced back to him.

He knew as soon as he saw the missing decorative medal. It could only be one place. Larson's farm. His stomach lurched. He knew that there was no way to get back there and find it without being caught. Still, he had to try. He had to know there was no way. He entertained the notion that people would be lined up along the yellow tape surrounding the area where James's body had been found like they do on television. If that were the case, he could act like a curious person and pace around, and if he was lucky, really lucky, he might be able to find it somewhere in the field.

He wracked his brain to come up with a reasonable response should a homicide detective come knocking on his door and swinging his key chain in front of his face. He could already hear the cop.

"You want to explain how we found this out at Larson's farm?"

Why? Why in the hell had he been out at Larson's farm? There wasn't a reason. None.

Shit. I do not need this.

He had no luck. He'd never had any luck.

When he found the yellow tape running across the street, leading into Larson's back property, it simply confirmed that all hope was lost. People were lined up along the old highway, unable to get onto the actual property.

He climbed out of his truck and sauntered across the road, nodding occasionally to friends and neighbors who recognized him. He worked hard on his expression, struggling with how to respond—concerned, intrigued, just plain nosy. He sidled up to a woman he knew.

"How long they been out here?" he asked, looking out into the field. As near as he could count, there had to be at least fifteen officers fanned out, all in a straight line, searching the grounds.

Shit.

"Since day break, same as yesterday, and the day before that," she said. Her voice sounded excited.

This was big doings around Granby. No one had seen anything like it, much less watched the police department actually doing something.

"What are they doing?" he asked.

They were looking for his key chain. They were just hours, maybe minutes, away from his downfall.

"I'm not sure. They're just looking for anything that'll give 'em clues, I guess. I heard someone say a dog is coming tomorrow, you know, to pick up scents and stuff like that. Someone was saying these dogs are so good, they can pick up scents in the field and then walk through the streets and pick out people they smelled. Can you imagine? A dog could smell out the murderers then go into town and sniff 'em out!"

His heart sank.

He couldn't leave. That would be too obvious. If it was true . . . if dogs were coming to sniff him out. He watched the officers in the field again, recognizing some of Granby's police, but there were others he didn't know. One thing was clear. As much as he wanted this mess to go away, it wasn't. In short, he was screwed.

CHAPTER FOURTEEN

It was a hell of a thing. Hours before we were to bury James Otis, Clyde Dodson up and died. Everyone had been waiting for him to die for the longest time, but he'd chosen the day of James's funeral to do right by Marla. It sounded harsh, but his soul had left us long ago. Ever since he'd been kicked by that young stallion, he'd just been laid up, mindless and vacant. He'd never known how his wife had changed over the last two years, trying to care for him while holding down a job and paying his medical bills. He'd hung on long enough to ruin Marla, ruin their business, her reputation, and possibly, her freedom, then as his final thank you, he up and dies.

I'd gone into work a few hours before the funeral. Truth is, I'd needed a distraction. I'd changed at least three times before I'd decided I just needed to get out of the house. Momma and Ella were going to come after the church service. Momma said she'd see me at the cemetery. I'd been torn about that. Ordinarily, I'd have tried to dissuade Momma from coming at all—there was no need to drag Ella out there—but James Otis was dead, murdered, possibly because he was a black man. It seemed like his family needed all the support they could get—from neighbors of all colors.

I was surprised to find two items on my desk, one being the memo regarding Clyde Dodson's death. I wasn't surprised that he'd died since it was long time coming. I wasn't even surprised that he'd died on this day. Everything had been in complete turmoil since James was killed, after all. What surprised me was reading Clyde's obituary.

I hadn't known the man well. He had always been quiet and polite, he'd tip his hat at women and removed that same hat when he went indoors, which, believe me, was a rarity. Most bubbas think of their hat the same as pants and shirt, a necessity, but Clyde had worn his as God and manufacturers had intended—for a purpose. He'd been a bona fide cowboy, even though he hadn't worn a cowboy hat working outside, day in and day out, no matter the weather, with those horses of his. He had seemed to prefer the ball cap, and that was pretty much what I knew of him.

There was so much more. He dropped out of school at the age of twelve, ran away from home, and worked as a rodeo crewmember until he began training for bull riding. He was a two-time world rodeo champion and had been instrumental in some of the safety gear that was now required for professional bull riders. On the circuit, he learned how to play chess, and at the age of twenty-two, received a rare invitation to the National Chess Championship, which he won. Right before worlds, he walked away. He returned to his roots, where he built his own working ranch while attending night school to earn his GED.

When he was twenty-four, he met Marla Powell and married her just six months later, saying that she was the love of his life. Together, they had one child who was stillborn.

It was common knowledge that he'd been attending community college when Marla had been diagnosed with breast cancer. He quit school and devoted himself to caring for his wife and began taking on more horses to train to cover the rising medical costs. Three months after Marla was medically cleared of all cancer, Clyde was kicked in the head by an unbroken stallion. He was just forty-five when he died.

The obit concluded with the standard list of surviving members, his wife, Marla; parents, John and Betty Dodson; his sister, Arlene; and three nieces, Riley, Samantha, and Ashley.

I read it two more times.

I'd had no idea what an interesting man he'd been. I felt a pang of guilt that I hadn't spoken more to Mr. Dodson and that I had judged Marla for her actions. I had been too young, but I'd never known they had wanted or tried for children.

The other surprising item was another reward advertisement from Shelby Harrelson, complete with a check for accounting. She was still missing her porta potties and as determined as ever that she would get them back.

"You're going, aren't you?" I looked up to see Tina Wolfe with her head poked into the office.

I waved her in and smiled. While I was pleased to see her, it was not a happy smile. "Yeah. Just . . . you know, keeping myself busy until it's time to go." I picked up the note regarding Clyde's death and waved it in the air. "You know that Clyde Dodson died?"

"Yeah, we went out there. It's a sad thing. That Marla. She's been through a lot. Feel sorry for that gal."

"Kind of weird that he'd die right now, you know?"

"Not to me." Tina laughed, pulled a chair in front of my desk, and sprawled out, her heavy boots thudding as she seemed to find her comfy spot. "Nothing's weird right now. Hell, I wouldn't be surprised if it started to snow."

I raised an eyebrow at her and propped my chin in my hand. "Do tell."

"How exactly do you measure weird right now? We got Feds crawling around town and I'm wrestling professional boxers in someone's bedroom. Doc Hirsh says I got a bruised sternum. Lucky that son of a bitch didn't crack it."

"Whoa! Hold up!" I put my hands up, palms out. "Dr. Hirsh?" I smiled in disbelief. "You went to a veterinarian for a checkup?"

"What?" She pretended not to understand, but her smirk said it all.

I laughed out loud. "You went to a vet for medical treatment?"

"Hell, yes. You want good treatment, you go to the best. You know how much more medical schooling vets have over regular people doctors? Not to mention, the bedside manner of most human doctors sucks."

I laughed again and shook my head. "You're right. Man, it's good to be home."

"Ain't it though?" She winked at me. "I don't guess you had this much action up North."

"Not even close," I said, letting my eyes fall on Shelby's reward ad. "Hey, you know anything more about Shelby's missing porta potties?"

"Nada. But I'll do ya another. Did you know that Dr. Hirsh had his medical supply cabinet broken into? That's how I came to see him for my chest."

"Sure, why not?" I shrugged. "Take a police report, get X-rayed next to a cow—all in a day's work."

Tina attempted to aim a fierce scowl at me.

I redirected. "What was taken?"

"Just what you'd expect. Pain killers, anything to get high off. That's about it. Typical stuff. Wouldn't be surprised if it was a stupid teenager."

The outspoken Tina Wolfe seemed uncharacteristically vague as she looked away from me to her fingernails, rubbing her thumb across the top of each one. I didn't press her.

She looked outside and groaned. "Man, but I don't want to do this."

"What's that?"

"I got duty today, working the funeral procession." She leaned up, propped her elbows on her knees, and let her head hang low. She looked miserable but her mood shocked me. Everyone was grieving the passing of James.

"You don't want to do it?" I was surprised and perhaps disappointed.

Tina looked at me as if she sensed my reaction. "No, it's not that. It's not that I don't want to help out. You know I liked the kid. But . . ." She shook her head again. "I just know what's coming."

"Why?" I asked. "What's coming?"

"Bullshit. Lots and lots of bullshit."

I looked at Wolfe, the silence and repetitive blinks giving me away. *I got nothing.*

"Fights. High emotions, family grieving. You watch, there will be fights. Chief's already warned us. We've heard the buzz—"

"The buzz?"

"Crap. Junk talk. You know, people blaming others. One group is sure that another group is responsible, and the stink is going to fly before this day is out. Sorry to say it, but I am dreading what's to come."

"I hadn't heard anything." I looked around my desk, picking through papers, shuffling them back and forth, as if the answer to the question of life was in there waiting to be found. *Please look away, please look away, please look away.*

"Well," she said, raising her eyebrows at me and standing to brush off her dress blues, "heed these words. Steer clear and stay close to an exit."

▮ ▮ ▮

Since my morning talk with Tina, I'd been anxious. I didn't know what to expect but believed her tone. She knew something was going to happen. I thought I was prepared for anything, short of gunfire, of course, but I didn't expect that. What I did expect was a black funeral, and though I'm hesitant to say that out loud, it's different than a white person's funeral. That's the truth.

Sitting in the middle of the First Baptist Church of Granby, a mostly all-black congregation, almost everyone in town, it seemed, had turned out for this day. That wasn't a surprise. I couldn't imagine a person who didn't like James Otis.

His casket was closed, and I was relieved about that. I wasn't sure I was ready to see him not smiling his megawatt smile. *I think I'll miss that the most.*

As Reverend Ward raised his hands to the skies, his voice boomed over the congregation, and his members called back. They were very vocal, shouting *amen* and *hallelujah* every now and then. The church was packed and hot and highly charged with emotion, which just seemed to heighten when Mrs. Blake, a close friend of the Otis family, passed out. Someone else near the front collapsed as well, but Reverend Ward didn't stop. His voice grew louder and more passionate.

I could feel my heart pounding, and tears sprang to my eyes. It was more than mourning James, and I didn't like the feeling. It was something inside the church. It was a power—an energy—that was causing my emotions to go out of whack.

"It's easy to smile," the Reverend's voice boomed in the small church.

"Easy to smile," someone shouted.

"And James Otis always had a smile on his face. Always!" He pounded at his podium. "Did you know that it takes forty-one muscles to frown but just seventeen to smile?"

There were chuckles throughout the church.

"We could all learn from James. He figured out that it was so much easier and nicer to smile. But I'll tell you this about him—he wouldn't settle to just use seventeen muscles."

"No," someone echoed.

"James used more than twenty-five or thirty muscles when he smiled. He used up every facial muscle he had!"

More laughter.

"He was a good man. You might recall . . ." And the Reverend began to tell stories about how James was once a wild child. As he began talking about how James turned his life around with the news that he would be a father, the mood turned again. The loud, sorrowful weeping was unbearable.

I'd been to a few funerals in my time. It's a truth about small towns. Teenagers get bored and reckless. They try to race trains, drag race, and do stupid stunts on dares because there's nothing else to do. I hadn't thought about the statistics of teenage death until I'd gone to Duke. When I'd shared stories about back home, my friends and roommates had always been horrified. When I'd gotten the letter from Momma saying that Jeremy Kessling, three years behind me, had been killed when he wrecked his dirtbike and became entangled in barbed wire, my roommate had been aghast.

"Geez, it's more dangerous to live in a small town than it is the big city!" Most of my urban-raised friends, I'd learned, had never known a friend or schoolmate to die.

Or was it because we all just lived in a closer community and knew each other?

Sitting in the church, I wondered about the cultural differences between blacks and whites, even the way we celebrated life and mourned death. I didn't know what I thought, but when Tasha leapt forward, I had to get out. My eyes flooded with salty tears as I watched her try to embrace a large, cold casket, and I fled. I felt so much emotion about to burst out of my chest and I couldn't face it. I didn't want to deal with all the anger and sadness I felt. I would never again see James's bright smile or handsome face. I would never again hear him laugh. He was such an overgrown kid. I was furious that Darion would have to rely on stories to know about his father and that he'd been robbed of knowing James himself. And I was so sorry for Tasha. It was only two weeks ago that she was bragging about how she'd whipped James into shape. I crawled ungracefully over six or seven people and staggered out of the church, leaving behind the chorus of moaning and sobbing that Tasha set off throughout the congregation.

I stumbled out the door and down the three short steps. I grabbed the stair rail and tried to settle my breathing, my nerves, and my emotions. I couldn't remember the last time my heart had known such heaviness.

Vaguely, I realized there were people some forty feet away, beneath a large oak tree. Cars and pickups were scattered through the small parking lot and across the adjoining grassy area. More cars were parked up and down the highway that ran through town, turning into Main Street.

"Thia!"

I heard the shout and moved toward it. I was numb, moving just to move. The image of Tasha throwing herself against James's casket was burned in my brain.

"Couldn't take it anymore?"

By the time I recognized the voice, it was too late. I stutter-stepped. I couldn't turn back and didn't want to move forward.

Angela Wyck sucked on a cigarette and stood with the idiot humans—Roland Wyck, Linda and Milford East, Lisa Gary, and Amber Hirsh, answering that age-old question, if white trash dress up and go to church, are they still white trash?

You betcha.

"Oh, hey," I greeted the group with little enthusiasm. I suspected they were too stupid to realize my disdain for them.

"Got to be too much, eh?" Ford grinned at me.

I shrugged.

"I told you," Lisa said. "It's not a funeral for whites."

"That's why we're out here," Roland explained as I looked at the cars, searching for someone else I might know and the prime excuse to get out of here.

"I just can't get into all that." Angela took another drag off her cigarette and flicked the ashes against the base of the tree.

"Into what?" I asked.

"Girl, you better stomp that out!" Ford chastised Angela. "We got a burn ban going. We don't need you flickin' ashes around and burnin' us all to pieces."

"Shut up, Ford." She waved her cigarette dangerously close to his face. "I know what I'm doing."

"Into what?" I asked again.

"Oh, girl, you know. All that moaning and groaning. The eye rolling and passing out and screaming, 'Hallelujah.' I can't take it. Creeps me out."

"You know how they do," Ford said.

Linda caught my expression and hit Ford on the shoulder. "Quit it, Ford. That's disrespectful."

"There's no eye rolling or screaming," I said.

"Disrespectful? *I'm* disrespectful?" Ford gave a forced laugh. "I'm not the one rolling around the floor and screaming."

"I'm sure no one is rolling around on the floor." Linda backed me up, but I knew it was just for my benefit.

"They're just in there trying to outdo each other," Lisa said, looking annoyed. "It's ridiculous. You don't act like that at a funeral."

It occurred to me how just easily a person can sit in judgment. I had been sitting in the church moments before with neighbors and friends I had known my entire life, wondering about their behavior at James's funeral myself. We're different, blacks and whites, but not so much more different than the prejudice and the non-prejudice. Like I said before, there's trash and there's white trash.

"How are you supposed to act at a funeral?" I asked, interested in their views.

"Well, not like that." Ford pointed a finger in the direction of the church. "You know what we're sayin', Thia. Don't always have to be so difficult. We're just sayin' it's stupid to be carryin' on that way when someone dies."

"Yeah, you don't have to be jumping up and down and acting like a fool because someone died," Lisa said, agreeing with Ford.

"You're supposed to be respectful. You know, sit still and cry if you want—" Roland's insight begged clarification.

"They *are* crying. *I* was crying," I said.

"Yeah, but you weren't passing out and having fits. You cry quietly, move on. That's life." Ford addressed the group with a final nod, as though the big man had spoken and that was that.

I smiled and shook my head a little.

"You know exactly what we're talking about, but you're trying to be all politically correct and act like there isn't a difference between us. You know it, I know it, and they know it. There is. There just is. And that's okay. But there is a difference. You can see it at funerals or even out in public. You know . . . how they always yell and carry on and have to be the center of attention. They can never just laugh. It has to be real loud. And at the movies, they have to talk back to the movie screen," Ford said.

Roland snickered at this. When we locked eyes, he resembled a bobblehead doll nodding at me. "It's true."

"So where's the brood?" I turned to Linda, changing the subject, and she stared blankly at me for a moment. "The kids," I restated.

"Oh. They're with Ford's mom."

I nodded, and we all stood in silence for a moment.

Mercifully, the church doors opened. Two men in suits stepped out, holding the doors wide, and I knew we were all waiting for James's casket to be carried out to the hearse. His casket emerged, carried by friends and family members.

Except for two men, I knew everyone in attendance, and again I felt washed over by grief and hurt. This was all so wrong. For so many reasons. I wanted desperately to move away from the dumbest people on earth. Once James was placed into the hearse, there was mass exodus from the church. I was looking forward to sitting alone for a moment. I could feel the dam about to burst and wanted to be in private when it did.

"So, you're the big reporter." Ford approached me just as I made a move to step away. "What's the latest with James's murder?" And he made little rabbit ear motions with his fingers when he said the word murder.

People were streaming past us, heading to their cars, ready to follow the hearse and limo that carried Mrs. Otis and her family.

"Nothing." I shrugged my shoulders.

"Do you want . . ."

Linda's question faded when I saw Terrell Whitehead step into Ford's path. Terrell was no match for Ford in size, but unlike fatty Ford, Terrell was well muscled and fit.

"What the hell is that supposed to mean?" Terrell didn't stop until he was standing right in Ford's face.

Ford didn't back down, but I sure did, stepping away and looking around for help. *This is what Tina was talking about, and all it took was an idiot like Milford East to start it.* I was especially sorry I was seen standing next to them all.

"Hey, easy man." Ford attempted a casual laugh, raising his hands up to signify that he didn't want a fight.

"I saw you, man. You did this"—Terrell mimicked the rabbit ear motion—"when you said murder. You think this is *funny?*"

Terrell Whitehead looked like a man on the verge of a breakdown, but it would not be through tears. He was going to beat the shit out of Milford East, and while I would have dearly loved to see such a thing, I didn't want it to be here, because of this, on this day.

"Terrell." I tapped Terrell's shoulder. "Come ride with me."

"No!" He yelled and several other young black men walked over to where we were all standing. "I want to know what he meant by that!"

"I didn't mean anything by it." Ford put his hands up as though he were surrendering. He looked around then took a small step toward his friends.

I could smell his fear.

I'd read that expression before. It's a good phrase, but I'd often wondered if you could actually smell something in the air that could be linked to a human emotion. I'm here to answer that with a resounding yes. You could smell his fear. And it was potent.

Ford backed up against the tree, hands still out, and laughing. "No. You misunderstood, man. Relax. I was asking Thia about the case. Is it murder or an accident? Didn't I, Thia? I was asking because no one knows what's going on." Ford rubbed his chin and licked his lips and looked around at the growing group. "Look. I'm here, ain't I? I liked James the same as you. He was a good guy. I hate that he's gone, and I was just asking—"

"All right, break it up," Officer Tina Wolfe called out.

In seconds, people were backing off as both Fox and Wolfe came through, poking people with their nightsticks.

"Listen up, little sunshines!"

Smack, smack.

As Wolfe moved through the group, she forcibly created her own circle. "This is not the time or place for any nonsense. Terrell, I love ya, buddy, but I'll cuff you and throw you in the back of my car if there's any trouble."

"Me?" He stomped a foot.

"He's going with me." I waved my hand as though I was asking permission, and hoped it would be enough to diffuse the moment.

"Why me?" he asked he asked Wolfe.

"Because I saw you"—she poked at him—"walk over to him"—she poked at Ford—"and start something. I know he's a jerk—"

"Hey!"

"—and I know you're hurting, but do what James would have you do. Now, go with Thia. Thia, you taking him?"

I nodded as soon as Wolfe looked in my direction.

"You others, get going. Respect your friend. He was a great guy. Don't disrespect him this way."

There was mumbling but people dispersed, headed to their respective cars.

"*I'm* a jerk?" Ford asked loudly, planting a meaty hand against his chest. He looked around. "I'm a—"

"Aw, hell, Ford. You're the biggest ass I know. Now shut up and get along, little doggie." Wolfe waved her baton around. "You, too, sunshine." Wolfe turned to Angela who was staring open-mouthed and appalled. "Get your happy ass in gear and . . ." She pulled the cigarette from Angela's hand and stomped on it. "Try not to burn us all down."

Terrell placed a hand on the back of my neck and gave it a little squeeze. It could have been his way of saying thanks for the ride or maybe thanks for being a friend. I wasn't completely sure of the message but understood the gesture.

As we walked off, I heard Fox congratulate her partner.

"Nice going," Fox said. "And nice touch with the happy pants remark."

"That's happy ass."

"Ahh, yes, there is a difference."

"Damned right. Now if we can just keep all these asses happy throughout the day . . ."

"We should be so lucky," Fox said, and I worried what was to come.

CHAPTER FIFTEEN

When the fight broke out at the cemetery, spilled out into the streets, and sent three people to the hospital, Officers Fox and Wolfe were nowhere in sight.

Wolfe and Fox had been leaning against their cruiser, arms folded over their chests, watching as the burial service began out at Myers Cemetery when the call came in.

"Whoa, slow down, Francis. I can hardly understand you." Fox tried, but Francis was almost hysterical.

"... at the funeral ... no one is responding, and she's out there alone!"

"Who? Who? C'mon, Francis," Fox said again, speaking slowly and deliberately into the radio. *This is nothing like the big departments.* She had a grandmother playing radio dispatch and droning on about one of her friends.

"Gail Vargus!" Francis blurted out, and Wolfe was already moving around the driver's side of the car.

"C'mon, Francis. What about Ms. Vargus?"

". . . filed for divorce and he's out there right now, killing her. He's going to kill her."

With a final glance toward the burial service, Fox frowned and clicked her tongue. *I don't like it. I don't like it one bit.* She had a strong sense that as soon as they left, something else was going to happen.

She made eye contact with Chief Teague and Lyle Hatch on the other side of the cemetery. She made the universal *We gotta roll* motion with her hand, and Teague nodded. No doubt, Teague had heard what was going on via his own radio.

"We're on it," Fox said to Francis.

Instead of the typical *roger that* or *ten-four* that Francis liked to say, she pleaded for them to hurry.

Wolfe killed the siren just as they turned off the highway, and they sped silently down FM 33. With their lights flashing and their adrenaline pumping, she worried they might be too late. Both knew that domestic calls were the worst, and both were still hurting from Horrendous Hernandez. Sure enough, Vargus's truck was parked outside the small A-frame home.

Once upon a time, Mrs. Vargus had worked a garden, selling her fruits and vegetables in town. Mr. Vargus had used kids from the local high school's Future Farmers of America organization to help man the seventy-acre farm. As far as anyone knew, Vargus had it worked out so that he'd had to do as little as possible. The cows had mowed the land, and local kids had roped and moved the cattle. The arrangement had suited everyone just fine, as Vargus was rarely seen. Mrs. Vargus had stayed outside as much as she could, working with the kids, and loving the land. Then a few years back, she'd stopped the program with the high school and then had stopped gardening altogether. She'd become as rare a sight as Vargus himself.

That's when the late night calls out to the Vargus place started. The pattern was classic spousal abuse behavior, and it hadn't taken long for stories of abuse, compliments of Francis, to get around town. Still, Vargus appeared unfazed by it all. Not that anyone had the nerve to accuse or ask him directly. In fact, no one would know anything about the Varguses at all were it not for those once a month late-night calls from Mrs. Vargus.

"I got three problems with what's about to happen," Wolfe said, and

Fox smiled.

She knew Wolfe was already anticipating the obstacles as they crept onto the property.

"What's that?" Fox asked, amusement in her voice.

"One, you know and I know that she's not going to press charges. We're going to go in there, guns a-blazing—"

"I'm not going in there guns a-blazing."

"—break up whatever fight they're having, and tell him not to use her face as a punching bag anymore and then—"

"I don't know. She filed for divorce. She just might mean it this time," Fox said. Still, she adjusted her bulletproof vest and readied herself for whatever she might find inside the Vargus home. *God, I hate domestics.*

"Naw. This is Mrs. Vargus. She's been married to that ass for over fifty years. What's she gonna do, divorce him and open her own garden shop?"

"She could." Fox shrugged and picked up the radio, giving Francis a heads-up. "We're here. Hang tight, Francis." Francis mumbled something unintelligible, and Fox sighed and clicked off.

"Number two, Vargus won't go quietly," Wolfe said.

"He won't." Fox agreed. "He never does."

"Well, there's a problem there because my chest still feels like I was trampled by a herd of buffalo. This is bullshit. I should *not* be wrestling around with a domestic when I'm trying to heal."

There was almost a whine to her voice that caused Fox to smile. Officer Tina Wolfe was a badass. She was strong, resilient, and thought of as one of the toughest cops around—men included. But she had no worries about whining when she thought she might be hurt. It didn't stop her from her duties, but she liked to complain about whatever pain was to come her way.

"You're not sure you can take a seventy-something-year-old man?" Needling Wolfe was Fox's only shot at finding humor out here. Truth be known, Vargus was a mean son of a bitch, the kind of man who didn't care who he hurt, and had no qualms about brandishing a gun. It was that kind of bullshit mentality that always got someone—usually the good guys—shot.

"Not when I feel like Helga the Hippo did a tap dance on my chest,"

Wolfe grumbled, and Fox laughed.

"That would be Horrendous Hernandez. I don't think he'd appreciate being called a hippo."

Wolfe eased the cruiser up to the house. There was no need for surprises. They knew Vargus well enough. If he was lying in wait for them, he'd already have seen them.

"We'll ask Horrendous when we get back to the station house," Fox said but Wolfe waved three fingers at Fox.

"Three. He's got that damned goat, and you just know he's here somewheres." Wolfe leaned over her steering wheel, squinting.

Fox climbed out of the cruiser, hand on holster, and focused on the front door. She took a deep breath and got her nerves in check. *Stay focused, stay alert.*

A wooly figure moved slightly beyond the clothesline. The dreaded goat. She started to make a remark. Humor was always their best line of defense. It helped them remain calm and collected, steady under pressure, and—though hard to imagine—better police officers. Don't take anything too seriously or too personally.

A shadow moved across the venetian blinds, followed by a shout, and Fox forgot about the goat. Wolfe was right behind her, hand on holster, signaling for Fox to cover the front while she moved around back. Fox nodded and steadied herself.

She knocked on the door and moved to the side of the door. It wasn't as though she expected he would blast through the door with a shotgun; still, it was a good practice.

No answer.

She knocked again, louder. Knowing Mr. Vargus as she did, it was better to pound on his door with a semi-friendly introduction. *Remember me? Your buddy, your pal.* "Mr. Vargus. It's Officer Rosa Fox. We've met before, Mr. Vargus. I got a call from Ms. Francis. She's pretty upset."

Better to let him believe it was Francis who was upset rather than Mrs. Vargus.

"I ain't done nuthin' " he yelled from behind the door.

"Well, now, I don't know that that's true. May I come in and talk to you?"

"Go away! I ain't done nothing!"

"Mr. Vargus . . . Mr. Vargus? I don't . . . I can't talk through this door. Why don't you let me come inside?"

Silence.

"I can't go back to the station house until I've talked to you. The chief wouldn't like it. I need to—"

"That shit-assed chief ain't my chief," Mr. Vargus sounded as though he spit venom, and Fox squeezed her eyes shut for a moment.

With this weaselly bastard, it didn't help matters that she was Mexican. She should have had Tina go to the front door. Vargus could relate so much better to a *good ol' gal* like Wolfe as opposed to a mere Mexican like Fox. At least, this was the feeling that Fox got from Vargus.

"Just go away!" he said again.

"Can't do it!" She was losing patience. "Is Mrs. Vargus there with you?"

"She call you?"

"No, sir." It was the truth. Francis had called her.

"Well, hell yes, she's here. Right where she's supposed to be . . . and me, too. This is *my* damned house. Been my house for more'n fifty years, and I'll be damned if I'm gonna give it up," he yelled again, and Fox turned her head.

It sounded as if he was moving, coming closer to the door. She was aware of a window not far from the door. He might move toward the window and take a shot at her.

"No one is asking you to leave, Mr. Vargus. I don't know what's going on. I just know I got a call, and I cannot leave until I come inside, talk to you face-to-face, and make sure you're okay. Can we do that? Can we do that, Mr. Vargus?"

There was a pause and then a loud crash toward the back of the house, followed by a string of curse words that only Tina Wolfe could put together so neatly. Fox winced.

"What's that?"

"Mr. Vargus," Fox called out, ignoring whatever the hell Wolfe was doing, "Please let me in. If not, I'm going to have to call reinforcements. You don't want that, Mr. Vargus." In truth, she was getting ready to kick the door open. So far, Mrs. Vargus had not called for help. That could be a good thing, but until she saw that Mrs. Vargus was alive and conscious, she had to assume the worst. She said as much through the door and heard him groan, a sure sign that he would consent to opening the door.

Again, there was a loud crashing noise that sounded like metal on metal. And again, it was followed by loud cursing and yelling.

"What's that?"

"A very good chance your goat is about to be killed, Mr. Vargus. Let me in."

"No one better kill Buzz!" Vargus was agitated. Love for his goat drove him to fling open the door.

The sudden movement surprised Fox, and she took a step back, holding one hand up signaling Vargus and the other tightening on her pistol grip. Eyes locked on Mr. Vargus, she shouted to the back. "You okay?"

"Yeah, sure, hell! I'm just being attacked by a freakin' goat. I hate these things," Wolfe shouted back, sounding closer to the attached garage than the back of the house.

Mr. Vargus stood, empty-handed but menacing. While thin, he was not to be mistaken as frail.

Fox gave him a small nod and motioned for him to back up as she stepped into the house and surveyed the damage.

Broken dishes, a turned-over chair, and a broken lamp lay in the center of the room. In the corner, on a stool near the kitchen's entrance, sat a miserable-looking Gail Vargus. She did look frail . . . and frightened.

"Mrs. Vargus." Fox nodded to her, careful to keep her tone neutral. She backed up enough to keep Mr. Vargus flush to her right at all times. She didn't want him getting too far behind her or out of her reach. If need be, she was prepared to jump on him. "So . . ." She took a deep breath, looking around once more. "What's, uh, what's going on?" She looked at Mrs. Vargus when she asked the question, but the frightened woman did not respond.

"We were just having a conversation," Mr. Vargus said. "And I guess I lost my temper. I didn't hit her." His voice rose, and he gestured a hand toward his meek wife. "You can see that. I didn't hit her, but I got a little mad and threw things around."

Fox nodded, making a show of looking around the room again before slowly shifting her eyes back to Mrs. Vargus, who had not moved or spoken since Fox's arrival. If Fox knew the drill, and she did, Mrs. Vargus would not dare speak. It was part of the entire dance routine between battered couples. The abusive spouse always did the talking and only offered up negative information about himself if he thought he was in trouble. He made these grand admissions as though (1) the police couldn't deduce out the broken items and upset furniture were the result of a fight of some nature, and (2) by making said admissions, everything was okay because, after all, did he not just fess up to the outburst?

Fox was unimpressed by Mr. Vargus's confessions.

Another loud crash preceded Wolfe's grand entrance through the kitchen door. Fox focused on her stony expression as Wolfe, who looked disheveled and insane as she fell into the doorway, still tripping over what appeared to be a clothesline wrapped around her ankles.

"I'll tell you why she's asking for a divorce, Mr. Vargus," Wolfe growled. The rumble in her voice was an *actual* growl. "It's your damned goat. She probably hates your damned goat so damned much she can't see straight. Am I right, Ms. V? Tell me I'm right! God damned son of a bitch just up and rammed me. I'm gonna have a bruise on my damned thighbone. I didn't do a damned thing. Didn't even *look* at him, and he rammed me!"

Mrs. Vargus's mouth fell open as though she might speak.

"I was trying to find out—"

"You didn't shoot him, did you?" Mr. Vargus looked at Wolfe.

"Did you *hear* a gunshot?" Wolfe yelled at him. Her face was red and she was sweating.

"Good, because I heard you shoot goats," Mr. Vargus said, appearing relieved.

"Officer *Wolfe*," Fox said, trying to refocus the group. "Mr. Vargus was just telling me that he was—"

"I should have slit its damned throat," Wolfe said, kicking furiously at the cord still wrapped around her boots.

Vargus went pale. "Did you . . ."

"No," Wolfe snapped at the man. "I didn't slit its throat. But I should have. I swear, Mr. Vargus, that thing is a menace."

"Okay, here's where we are," Fox said, hands out. "Officer Wolfe is going to take Mr. Vargus outside to show him that his goat is alive and kicking." Fox looked at her partner. There was the off chance . . . "He *is* alive and kick—"

"Well, yeah! Shit, what do you take me for?" Wolfe sounded exasperated.

"Fine, then. Wolfie, please escort Mr. Vargus outside to take a better look at Buzz."

" 'Buzz'? My attacker is named *Buzz*?" Wolfe whined, and Fox bit the inside of her cheek and tried not to lose all composure.

Vargus was torn between leaving his wife and checking out Buzz, but Officer Wolfe's ranting left him no choice, and he found himself being pushed through the kitchen and out the back door.

For a moment, Fox didn't move. She listened, as did Mrs. Vargus, to the continued rantings of Wolfe about the goat.

The house was very quiet and Mrs. Vargus appeared tiny.

"How are you, Mrs. Vargus?" Fox asked, taking a small step forward and noticing Mrs. Vargus didn't even make eye contact.

"I'm glad you're here, I suppose." Her voice was high-pitched and breathy. She sounded like a small child in trouble. "Though I don't know what I'll do when you've gone."

Fox squatted down to pick up what looked to be a broken coffee mug.

"He did this?" she asked, and Mrs. Vargus shook her head.

"No. I did that." She studied the mug in Fox's hands. "I'm sorry, too. I really liked that mug."

"Well, it looks like you had a pretty bad fight." Fox looked around the house.

"He's going to kill me." Gail Vargus's voice sounded so small.

Fox steadied her own body, making sure that only her eyes moved. Often times, the movement, however subtle, could stop a person from talking. She remained still, holding the broken coffee mug, where she was.

"Did he tell you he was going to kill you?" Fox asked.

The house was quiet making it easy to hear Wolfe and Vargus arguing outside about his goat. If nothing else, Fox knew that Wolfe would keep Vargus distracted with threats of killing his goat.

"No. But I know he will. It's just a matter of time."

"I don't understand. Did he threaten you in some other way?"

"Hmm, no. Not that I can think of," Mrs. Vargus said.

Fox took another step forward, this time offering her hand to Mrs. Vargus. Mrs. Vargus took it and Fox helped her to her feet. From the feel of her hand, the tension from her body's weight, Fox couldn't believe that Mrs. Vargus weighed more than ninety pounds. She felt heat rise to her cheeks, sickened to think that someone could hit or push this woman around.

"What started this . . ." Again, Fox looked around the room.

"I don't know if you know this. With the way word gets around town, I'd be surprised by who didn't know, but I've asked for a divorce."

Fox nodded. "I did hear that."

"Of course you did. Well, it's true. I did. And Johnny don't like it one bit."

Fox noticed something new each time she looked the room over. "No, it doesn't appear that he does. So . . . what? He came over and you threw your coffee mug at him?" She raised the mug up, but Mrs. Vargus shook her head.

"No. I'd been outdoors, working on the line."

When Wolfe had first staggered into the house, said clothesline trailed in behind her. It had been difficult for Fox not to laugh since clearly Wolfe had wrapped herself in the line—no doubt, while running from a goat.

"I don't know how she managed to get herself tangled up, but we'll have someone take care of that for you," she told the older woman.

"Thank you. I appreciate that." She sighed again and stooped to pick up her lamp. "No, I came inside and found him standing in the kitchen with the papers in his hand. He began yelling at me and telling me that he wasn't going to go anywheres."

"And he threatened you?" Fox asked again, eager to get on with things before Vargus returned and Mrs. Vargus clammed up.

"He told me I wouldn't be able to make it on my own and that I shouldn't have to because I was his wife. And he reminded me that we was married before our families and before the eyes of God. 'In God's house,' he said. He told me that he'd built this house and was never going to leave it and neither was I."

"And you threw the coffee mug at him?" Fox reasoned it out. It was more of a question, trying to understand the sequence of events.

"He told me that he loved me, and I threw the mug at him, yes."

"He told you that he loved you? And you threw the mug at him?" Fox repeated, trying to understand. She rubbed her eyes for a moment. "Mrs. Vargus. I'm trying to help you out here. But you need to give me something I can use. I know that he used to beat you. I know that he's done terrible things to you."

As she spoke, Mrs. Vargus looked pained. She put a finger to her lips and shushed Fox. Fox's eyebrows shot up, but she stopped talking.

"You must not mention any of that."

"Uh, well, okay, but . . . well, he did. And you did call 911 asking for help. I'm here, trying to offer help, but all you've told me is that you broke the coffee mug and . . . These other things?"

Mrs. Vargus nodded. "Yes, I broke those as well. I was trying to hit him."

"In self-defense? You did this in self-defense?"

"Yes, he was trying to hug me," she said, and Fox could feel her face fall.

"He was trying . . ."

At that moment both Wolfe and Vargus walked in.

Vargus heard the last bit of his wife's explanation. He pointed and nodded enthusiastically. "That's right. I was trying to give my wife a hug, and she went nuts, throwing things at me. But I didn't hit back or throw anything back, now did I? Did I, Gail, baby?"

"What is it you would like for me to do?" Fox asked Mrs. Vargus, but she was cowed again by his presence. "Officer Wolfe, would you escort Mr. Vargus out the front door while I—"

"Why? Why do I have to leave since this is my house?" Mr. Vargus looked around, bewildered.

Their hands were tied. Although Mrs. Vargus had called 911, she was not going to be pressing any charges against her husband and had admitted to throwing objects at her husband. In return, Mr. Vargus did not have any interest in pressing charges against her.

"God will see me through." Mrs. Vargus patted Wolfe on the hand.

Both Wolfe and Fox were very unhappy as they pulled out of the Vargus driveway.

"This is how it always is. There is never a happy ending with these domestics. But, hey, let's not worry." Wolfe scoffed. "God will see her through."

Fox frowned, ignoring that last statement. She knew Wolfe was only trying to make her feel better, but she wasn't in the mood to get into another discussion about religion with Wolfe. "But she said he's going to kill her. She was very clear about that."

"What he needs to do is kill that goat."

"Uh, somehow, I doubt that killing a goat is going to solve their marital problems." Fox rolled her eyes.

"Yeah, but if I have to keep coming out here, it'd solve mine. You know, I think that goat peed on me."

CHAPTER SIXTEEN

Rosa Fox was most familiar with Boer goats, but she'd had her fill of all kinds. Raised by her grandparents, she'd grown up on a working ranch, which included goats. She was seven or eight years old when her grandfather read about Angora goats and got the harebrained idea to raise and shear goats, selling the mohair. He then tried pygmy goats and Spanish goats until he'd crossed over to the Boer breed. In turn, Rosa had wrangled, dewormed, fed, and cared for more goats than anyone could ever have imagined and fancied herself a connoisseur of goats. She also believed she'd seen everything there was to see regarding goats.

She now believed she was wrong.

She folded her arms across her chest, leaned back against the cruiser, and laughed out loud. She couldn't remember the last time she'd seen anything so funny, and she wished she had a camera.

If only Grandfather were here to see this! It didn't matter that her partner needed help or was yelling at the top of her lungs. Fox was enjoying the show.

She watched as Chief Teague pulled up and surveyed the chaos in the street. As he parked his cruiser, she waved him over. They didn't speak. What was there to say? They just stood together, side by side, watching something that would be discussed for years to come.

While Chester Kennedy was a certain idiot, Fox had to give him credit for taking the proper precautions for his goats. He'd very carefully and painstakingly boarded up the cattle trailer so the goats inside could not see anything outside because he didn't have just normal Boer or Spanish goats. No. He'd had to go and get himself "fainting" goats.

Chester had decided on the "fainting" goats because they were different, and no one else had anything like that anywhere near where they lived. Nancy, his wife, had been furious when Chester had blown the better part of their savings on a bunch of goats that passed out all the time. There was an undeniable irony about Chester and his fainting goats, as their history held a similar story. Rosa knew the history because as soon as his fainting goats had arrived, Chester had contacted *The Recorder* to do a story on his new herd.

According to the goat history books, a man by the name of Tinsley settled in Marshall County, Tennessee, in the 1880s, bringing with him several goats and a sacred cow. He married a local woman and stayed one harvest season to help a local farmer. Then he sold his goats to a man named Goode and took off, taking his sacred cow with him but leaving the wife behind.

Whether Chester had planned to keep the goats but ditch the wife would never be known because it had been Nancy who left first. From that point on, it had just been Chester and fancy fainting goats.

Chester's goats didn't actually faint. They had a genetic problem with relaxing muscles. When startled or upset, the muscles seized up, and stiff as a stuffed goat stuck in a deep freezer, they would simply keel over. The older goats were more apt to lean on fence posts and trees when possible, where the less experienced fainters just locked up and went over, face first and legs straight into the air. Weighing anywhere from fifty to one hundred and fifty pounds, it was a lot of dead weight.

In the early days of the goats' history, they were used for meat but also for protection of sheep. When wolves or coyotes happened by, the fainting goats would freeze up and fall over, offering themselves up as sacrificial lambs while the real sheep bleated on to safety. The goats came close to extinction by the 1980s, what with all the fainting in front of wild dogs and such, but thanks to the efforts of the Tennessee Wooden Leg Goat Association, they were on their way back, and Granby was chalk full of 'em, all over Main Street.

"Gosh dammit!" Wolfe yelled, trying to capture another goat that passed out at her feet as soon as she made contact. She glanced over her shoulder. "Fox, are you just going to stand there or what?"

It was complete and utter pandemonium.

Bill Parker had gotten greedy when Amber Hirsh had stepped outside the Town Pump and tipped back a cold drink, pushing out what God gave her, and a cosmetic surgeon had perked up eight months ago. He'd tried to see it all and missed the obvious trailer in front of him.

Fox and Wolfe who were sitting at the light between Main and Huber, on their way to the funeral home, watched it all play out in slow motion. The cable popped, the latch gave way, and Chester jumped back, trying to keep the gas nozzle from spilling all over the pavement.

"Well, I'll be damned," Wolfe said as Chester returned the nozzle to the pump's hook and the back gate swung wide.

Sunlight filled the otherwise darkened trailer, and the amazing Tennessee Wooden Goats decided to make a break for it. Bill Parker was out of his truck and making faces of shock and surprise, pulling his ball cap off and rubbing his hair as Fox cranked the wheel. She dodged Lewis something-or-other in his pickup and pulled to the side of the road.

The leader of the fainting goats was surprised or shocked or whatever it takes to make the genetic muscle-locking alarms sound off, and he promptly passed out dangerously close to where some gasoline had spilled to the ground.

Chester, horrified, rushed forward and began to half-lift, half-drag the frozen creature to safety.

The scene was upsetting enough to the other goats that a frenzy of fainting ensued.

"Shit!" Wolfe yelled, climbing out of the car before Fox had stopped. "They're dropping like flies! Look at 'em. They're dropping like flies! What the hell?"

Fox smiled. Wolfe had not read the article and did not know they were simply fainting.

Wolfe was out of the car and adjusting her gun. "Chester? What's going on? Were they hit?"

"Just help me get them back in—"

"I didn't see ya. Shit, Chester, I'm sorry. I never saw ya there!" Bill was standing in the melee of stiff-legged goats scattered about the street. One of the older goats was leaning heavily on the side of the trailer, another against Bill's truck.

"Stop yelling!" Chester yelled. "You're upsetting the goats! You're upsetting the goats!"

"Upsetting the . . . Chester, what's going on?" Wolfe stared down in disbelief at a goat that had fallen against her boot.

"They're just fainting, is all," he told Wolfe, laying his hands on a baby and wrestling it into his arms. "Just help me get them back inside the trailer. They'll calm down when they're back inside the trailer."

"Fainting?" Her voice was one of such shock that Fox couldn't stop the shout of laughter from escaping.

Bill Parker stood helplessly, still running his fingers through his hair, looking perplexed and sorry at the same time. All he needed to do was seize up and fall over. It'd be perfect. Just then three goats unlocked, stood again, and ran down the road.

"Well, hell, Bill, don't just stand there!" Chester nodded toward the street as he tried to shove a stiff goat into the trailer. "Go get 'em before they pass out in the street and get run over!"

Amber Hirsh managed to remain confined in her shirt and wrangled up a small, stiff baby goat. Jay Smith came out from behind the counter of his store to lend a helping hand while Wolfe and Bill Parker ran down the road. No sooner had the three goats laid eyes on Wolfe and Parker than they seized up again, legs in the air. Wolfe and Parker worked together, grabbing two front and two back hooves, and carried the first one back to the trailer.

Adam Emerson and his wife pulled over and began the same strategy as Wolfe and Parker, picking up passed-out goats and carrying them back to the grateful Chester, who began doing a head count as he put them back into his trailer.

One older goat made it as far as the door to the Town Pump when Jay Smith had to run by it to go inside to ring up a customer. The goat locked up and leaned against the building. But given a few minutes to recover, Fox watched the goat travel another twenty feet, and she wondered what it might be thinking.

When the sound of wind causes you to pass out, where do you run?

She gave Teague a nudge with her elbow and pointed her chin in the direction of the runaway goat. As she did, she picked up a rock. "Watch this." She threw the rock in the direction of the goat, just missing her and causing her great surprise and shock.

Down she went.

"Hey, Wolfie! You got one over there," Chief Teague yelled, and the two giggled to themselves. The sight of Wolfie would not soon be forgotten. She was hot, sweaty, frazzled, and handling the very animal she loathed most. While goats were busily passing out up and down Main Street, Granby's finest was on the job protecting the good citizens from these derelict goats.

"*I've* got another? What the hell, Chief? When did this become my job . . . and what the hell are you doing still standing there, Fox?"

Amber captured another small goat, which created a sensation of its own. Bill Parker rushed over to help, abandoning Wolfe.

"I'm directing traffic!" Fox shouted, still leaning against the cruiser. Wolfe's shoulders fell.

"You piece of crap!"

"She's talking to me," Chief Teague said, struggling to keep his voice neutral. Again, he pointed to the goat. "Better hurry before she stands up again."

"You know, wouldn't it be great if criminals had this problem. We could just yell, 'Stop, police. Don't run or I'll frighten you,' and they'd drop like cement blocks?" Fox turned to Teague.

"I can't get that goat by myself," Wolfe yelled, looking around, hoping to get someone's attention. "Shit, what do I care? Yeah, I'll get that damned goat." As she strode toward it, she drew out her pistol. Fox and Teague both pushed away from the cruiser but not before Chester was at a full run across the pump area.

"Oh, God, no! She's my best goat!"

The goat stirred.

"She's a menace to society, Chester," Wolfe yelled back over her shoulder, already taking aim.

The goat rolled up on to its side, ready to stand and make another brave move toward freedom.

"Officer Wolfe!" Chief Teague pushed away from the cruiser and moved toward Wolfe.

"I swear, Chief, I've hauled my last goat!" She put away her weapon as Chester flung himself across the goat.

▌▌▌

Standing next to the cruiser, Fox got one of the worst cases of the giggles she could remember since she was in grade school. Like those early years, there seemed to be nothing she could do about it. Wolfe was making it worse with her wheezing.

"I think I'm allergic to goat hair." She sounded like a cross between a train and horse as she huffed and puffed and brushed herself off.

Fox tried biting the inside of her lip and pinching her forearms as she watched Wolfe stir the short, white hairs into a cloud only to have them resettle on another spot of her dress uniform. Nothing would ever shake the image of her partner wrestling with a fainting goat.

The doors opened and a group of young men carried Clyde Dodson's casket to the hearse.

Wolfe made a gagging noise and hacked as though she might cough up goat fur.

Fox squeezed her eyes shut, trying to lose the image, and prayed for her next breath.

"It's hotter than hell out here," Wolfe said, and Fox nodded helplessly.

A man has died, Rosa. Control yourself!

" 'Course, it's probably not so hot to you because you just stood there," Wolfe said, not letting it drop and prolonging Fox's torture. "I'm not kidding. I feel dizzy." Wolfe continued her tirade of complaints. "I think I'm having hot flashes," she said and began fanning her face with her hand as she wheezed.

As the morning sun rose, the heat had become stifling. It was one of the reasons both Fox and Wolfe hated funeral duties. The full dress uniforms, including the chest protectors, made it feel as though you were trapped inside a sauna. They'd been outside for an inordinately long time, leaving both Fox and Wolfe to wonder what more could be said about Dodson. He was a good guy and all, but come on.

Twice they'd promised themselves that once the funeral was over

123

they would get something cold to drink, but then Wolfe had announced she was no longer talking to Fox when her fits of giggles continued.

"I'm not kidding, Rosa. I'm not talking to you anymore."

Fox made one more attempt to get herself under control before reminding Wolfe, "Just don't lock your knees."

And Wolfe was down.

CHAPTER SEVENTEEN

Jared Durham pulled the blinds in his office so that there were little more than slits for him to hide behind and watch the goings-on outside City Hall and the police station. His office was centrally located between the two, offering him more information than anyone could imagine.

He thought about that for a moment.

Few knew who he was. He took a long pull from his bottle then examined it. It was the good stuff, something that would never be found in town. *Not that I would buy anything here anyway.* He didn't need to be the focus of any more gossip. He was well aware of his reputation—a tired, used-up, old drunk who could only get work when it was sent to him, hand delivered by his sister. He knew what people said. More importantly, he knew who was saying it.

So, it was an interesting situation he now faced. Who to help? How to help? And the irony here was his most recent client had not been sent to him by his sister. Rather, this one came knocking on his door, after hours, when no one was around to see.

He took another drink and pondered his current situation.

Technically, he was still looking the details over and hadn't decided whether to take on another client. He'd given advice: Stay quiet, say nothing until further notice.

The truth was that he was tired. He was tired of the small-town gossip and its small-town problems. Marla Dodson about broke him. Hers was a constant, on-going problem that spread like a brush fire, leaping from one hot spot to another. The disastrous funeral of Clyde; goats littering the streets, an officer being sent to the hospital, Marla's wailing while wearing a court-ordered ankle bracelet, Clyde's cousin, Travis Miles, browbeating him into the corner of the funeral home about the last will and testament.

Hell, there wasn't one.

How could they have known he was going to get kicked in the head? How could they have known that he'd die first and not Marla, who had been undergoing chemotherapy the last time anything had been updated? There was no way Clyde could or would have imagined he'd die before Marla. The only existing will was Marla's last testament, and everything pertaining to Clyde was very vague since it had been assumed everything would go to him.

Like it or not, the ranch and horses, or what was left of them, belonged to Marla. While Travis Miles had been trying to bring his farrier business to life and would have liked nothing more than to own and operate a working horse ranch, he was not going to be able to piss and moan his way onto that property.

Not if Jared had anything to do with it.

He liked Clyde. He would genuinely call himself a friend to Clyde Dodson. Many a night, Clyde had found his way into town, knocked on Jared's door, and settled in for a night of drinking and playing chess. People thought they knew them. They didn't. They thought Jared a drunk and Clyde stupid. They were wrong. They were all wrong.

Love thy neighbor.

Bullshit.

He took another drink and studied the street before him. With the office lights out, he felt hidden and protected.

It was because of those late night, complex, and interesting conversations over the chessboard that Jared knew about Clyde's desires for the future, and his thoughts of his cousin, Travis Miles. He was a taker, and Jared would be damned if he was going to let Travis run over Marla in her time of need.

Jared worked with Marla and convinced her to sign over power of attorney to him. It was what Clyde would have wanted. Moreover, it was what Jared wanted. Marla appeared hell-bent on running her property, the horses, Clyde's good name, and whatever promising business he once had into the ground with her ridiculous penchant for stealing.

What was that all about?

He made sure she had a reasonable allowance, but she was uncontrollable. When caught, she sobbed about her poor, bedridden husband and her medical woes, leaving Jared incensed. Still, he protected her. For Clyde. He bailed her out, assured, and reassured her. For Clyde. In the end, he knew he would walk away with Clyde's property. She didn't deserve it. Travis Miles didn't deserve it. As clients walked in and out of his office, Clyde's wife and property became his main priority. Simply put, it was a matter of keeping Marla from destroying it all.

He was like Clyde in more ways than even Clyde had understood. Jared Durham had attended Southern Methodist University in Dallas, Texas, on an academic scholarship, and had been able to go on to law school. He had been popular, well liked, and connected, keeping his very humble, very unknown, very welfare-driven roots hidden.

He hung out with the socially elite. His roommate, Charles Foster—of the prestigious Foster family, often commented about how blacks had corrupted the social welfare system. It never occurred to Foster that there were far more whites on the welfare ticket, using and abusing it, and popping out just as many babies. And Jared wasn't about to enlighten Foster. Just being seen with, living with, and partying with Foster put Jared in a group he'd only dreamed about. Fraternity houses approached him. He partied with athletes, rich sorority girls, and privileged thirty-something students who had enough money to play student and never get a real job. He lived in a world of pretense and prestige, of power and political leverage, and he never wanted to leave it.

It wasn't meant to be.

Drinking was the quintessential step from kid to young adult in the back woods, the rite of passage for country folk. But at SMU, with the pristine and prestigious, when he'd been at his best, or so he'd thought, he'd drowned in alcohol and failure. Things had gone from endless possibilities to the possibility for all to end. As it happens with small-town folks, when the road turned bumpy, home became the one path to salvation.

He watched and studied his neighbors. Granby had its own self-proclaimed social elite. They always made sure that neighbors were aware of their latest purchases. They name-dropped brand names and places they visited. It was a funny thing. They *did* go places and make big, expensive purchases, but it was a joke to think they were anywhere near the same level as the Fosters.

The middle elite believed themselves to be enlightened while they had no clue. To his knowledge, no one served as a better example than Linda East. Linda was the daughter of Pearl and Mark White—both third generation Granbyites, both from ranching families.

Like their parents, Linda's unplanned pregnancy forced an early wedding. Mark worked long, hard hours and Pearl immersed herself in book drives and local PTA meetings, sang in the church choir, and saw to it that Linda attended all the churches in town, including the synagogue at the edge of town. This was considered a bit racy as the Epsteins, though nice folks, were thought to be a bit suspect. They were Northerners *and* Jews. But Pearl and Linda had ventured in nonetheless.

Before she'd married Milford East, Linda had said she'd been blessed that her mother had exposed her to different cultures. Jared hadn't been able to contain his smirk.

One afternoon with Granby's Jews and she was cultured.

Then there was the common trash of the town or, as they preferred to be called, *rednecks*. They didn't know what was going on in the next state or the next city. They didn't know what was going on overseas and didn't give a damn. They didn't know, nor did they concern themselves with, inequalities, social injustices, discrimination, or anything that didn't directly impact their ignorant little lives. These were the bulk of his clientele.

He watched as His Honorable William McKinley exited the courthouse with some staffers, and he tipped back the rest of the bottle.

There is the biggest joke of the town.

The joke was *on* the town. The same group of people who voted straight ticket, no matter the name on the ballot, yet complained about poor wages, tax hikes, and crappy legal systems put their very enemy in office. They were too dumb to see their own handiwork.

It was no secret the judge didn't like Jared. He had the audacity to talk to Jessie Durham about office politics and rumors of her sending clients to her brother. He'd brought Jared to the bench, asking to smell his breath, and had outright accused him of drunkenness in court. It was just a power play by a man in the same boat as Jared, presiding over trash.

How strange life is.

Jared had dreamed of a breakout case, one that would relieve him of this disgusting little town and his hole in the wall office, and with a light knock on the door, in walked that case, asking for legal advice regarding the James Otis murder.

Over the last week, he'd watched the quiet, subtle line between black and white thicken as the quiet murmuring grew louder about who could have killed James Otis and why. James Otis was well liked throughout the community. He hadn't had any other girlfriends, no scorned women, no gang activities, no evidence of drugs or any other illegal activity. He hadn't owed money and hadn't given anything away. There was no grudge, no scandal, and no day-old or even year-old argument. He'd been a clean-cut kid with a bright future, a loving family, and was liked by one and all.

People magazine had done a feature, "Who Killed James Otis?" The rest of the world was ready for another hate crime and had honed in on Granby, but the residents of this town weren't so sure.

Jared sat back, still staring out the window, watching as the rest of the courthouse emptied and faithful employees filed out to their cars. They didn't know anything.

Teddy "Bubba" Peters drove by, and Jared's eyes adjusted to the truck. Now there was someone who knew everything that went on. Whereas Judge McKinley had fooled his way into office, Peters also had the entire town fooled. Known as "the trash man," Peters was judged rather than judgmental. Never had Jared heard Peters speak ill of anyone, yet he knew everyone's trash. He knew everything.

Jared wiped his mouth, wishing he had more whiskey, yet glad it was gone. He had to be clear minded about this. The Otis case had tremendous potential. The more he thought about it, the more he realized there was nothing to think about. It was the case everyone would talk about. It was the case everyone *was* talking about.

His heart stopped. He jerked forward in his chair, slamming his feet to the floor.

No!

There, in Peters's truck . . . he blinked. If what he'd been told was true, he was looking at a key piece of evidence that would have DNA, among other things, all over it.

He licked his lips.

Again, assuming it's all true.

He rose to his feet then pushed his fingers against the blinds, opening two slots wider so that he could see better. He pressed his nose against the glass, breathing so heavily a ring of fog formed.

If it weren't so damned unbelievably like his luck, it'd be funny. It was so typical that he could have the case of the year—hell, century— dumped in his lap and then have the evidence picked up by the town's resident trash collector.

He needed another drink. He hoped he was wrong. But there it was. Key evidence. His evidence. His slam-freakin'-dunk evidence.

What am I going to do?

The even bigger question was: did he know? Did Peters know what he had? And how was Jared Durham going to get it back?

CHAPTER EIGHTEEN

They came upon the truck rather by accident. It was Teddy "Bubba" Peters's truck to be sure. There was no missing it.

Teddy Peters was inside, and he wasn't alone.

They moved in silently, careful not to tip their hand.

The other person looked to be female. Peters, sitting behind the steering wheel, was turned toward his passenger. The female, sitting closer to the middle of the seat, also faced Peters, with her arm up on the back of the seat.

Wolfe and Fox looked at each other, trying to decide how to play this. Using hand signals and silent nods, they separated, one moving to the driver's side, the other toward the passenger. They saw the two figures move together. They were kissing.

It was with great pleasure that Officer Fox whipped out her night baton and rapped against Peters's window.

Officer Wolfe did the same on the passenger side, pressing her face against to the glass, giving a quiet, "Boo."

Cecilia jumped, causing Peters more distress than anyone else, and

Fox heard Wolfe cackle. She watched her partner fling the door open and lean against the passenger seat.

"Why, Ms. Cici." A big grin swept across Wolfe's face. "Whatever are you doin' here?"

"Tina Wolfe! I swear!" Cici threw a hand against her chest, and Wolfe's grin broadened to full smile capacity.

"You can do whatever you like . . . and wherever apparently, but with everything that's been going on around here, I wouldn't recommend parking," Wolfe said.

"We were just talking." Bubba Peters looked mortified.

"Uh-huh."

"Officer Wolfe," Cecilia hissed, "haven't you got something you need to be doing, like fighting crime or figuring out who killed James Otis?"

"Well, now, that's what we were doing when we stumbled upon a truck, suspiciously parked on the side of the road." Wolfe continued to smile.

"Oh, like you didn't know this was Teddy's truck!" Cecilia said.

Wolfe stepped back, scanning the body of the truck. "What do you think, Fox?" Wolfe looked back through the cab of the truck, checking with her partner.

Fox shrugged, playing it straight; her face held no expression whatsoever.

Wolfe looked at the truck again, exaggerating the way she looked it over, top to bottom. "Why, I think you're right. It is Peters's truck . . . which would make sense since Peters is sitting behind the wheel."

Cecilia groaned.

"What have you got here?" Fox asked, stepping away from the truck and heading toward the back.

"Is there a problem with my load?" Peters looked concerned that this was more than Wolfe and Fox teasing Cici.

"I don't think so," Fox said, spinning a tire on a bike that was affixed to the outside of the truck.

Fox could hear Cecilia whispering to Wolfe. "I swear, Tina. Are things that slow?"

She shrugged. "Naw. We're just joshin'. But seriously, Cici. Making out in a truck? Are things that slow for *you*?"

Peters opened his door, following Fox as she moved toward the back of the truck, peering in at its contents.

"What do you do with all this stuff, Bubba?" Fox looked at everything in the truck. "I swear, you got all kinds of things here."

"Some of it really is just junk," he said, standing next to Fox. "Sometimes you don't know 'til you get it home and work on it. Like this"—he leaned in, hitting the side of what looked to be a microwave—"could have some value. Don't know yet. Got to find out why it was thrown out. Or this . . ." He flicked out his hand toward the back of the truck, pointing out a computer. "Something like that, I fix up and donate to the schools."

"For real?"

"Yeah, when I can get them to work. Some of 'em are too outdated." He thrust his hands in his pockets and shrugged.

"How'd you learn to fix all this?" Fox asked, curious about a man who could fix microwaves and computers but was known throughout the town as *the trash man.*

"Oh, mostly by playing around with things, you know. You kind of pick things up as you go. I guess it helps that my father used to own an appliance shop. I worked there with him sometimes. But I never wanted to go into that kind of business."

Fox leaned into the truck, plucking an old lamp from the pile. It was a figurine of a little Mexican girl, holding a lamb. She inspected it more closely. A baby goat. She laughed out loud at the figure, so sweet, so familiar.

The little girl was plump, wearing a red printed skirt, a white blouse with a scarf around her tiny shoulders, and a white ribbon in her shiny black hair. The hair on the doll was like that of a Barbie doll, falling loosely around the girl's face. While it had obviously been someone's trash, it was in pretty good condition. More than anything, Fox wished she could have it.

"What will you do with this?" Fox held it up for Bubba to see.

"Fix it. If I can," he shrugged, removing it from her hands. As he placed it back inside the bed of the truck, he stopped and looked at Fox. "Do you like it?"

Fox nodded, unable to hide her feelings. It was like one of those Hula dancer dolls that, by all accounts, were pretty tacky. Yet to see such a figure. *And a goat, of all things.* She smiled. "Yeah, I'd love it. You think you could make it work? I'd buy it from you."

"Let's see if I can get it to work first." He smiled and headed back to the cab where Cecilia and Wolfe continued to bicker with each other.

For a moment, Fox took further inventory of the contents in the truck, wondering about what she saw. Her glance returned to the little girl lamp.

". . . do you think about *that*?" Cecilia poked a finger at her friend as Peters climbed back into the truck.

"Lord only knows," Wolfe said, and it was clear that Tina Wolfe had been having far too much fun with Cici, who was now flustered and certainly in no mood to continue what they'd been doing.

"Ha! A lot you would know about that Lord," Cici snapped at Wolfe.

"Excuse me?" Wolfe's eyebrow's shot up.

"I'm just sayin'." Cecilia shrugged her shoulders. "It wouldn't hurt you to step into a church once in a while. You lurk outside the services all the time, but you never . . ."

"Lurk?" Wolfe grinned and she raised her eyebrows at Fox.

Fox groaned.

"I lurk around churches? Is that what I do?"

"Yes, you lurk. Maybe if you'd actually go inside one and listen to what's being said . . ." Cici seemed to be intentionally daring Wolfe as she maintained eye contact.

"Well, now, I am a little confused, Ms. Cecilia. What are you saying here? Would it be that if I went into a church, rather than lurking outside, I would be more or less inclined to make out with a man in his pickup truck parked on the side of the road?"

Cecilia let out an audible squeal.

Fox muffled a laugh with a fist, adding a cough for good measure.

"Or would I want to do that inside the church?" She scratched her head.

"Teddy! Please take me home."

Peters looked to Fox who stepped back and motioned him forward with a hand. He turned the engine over and pulled from the shoulder, leaving a large gap between Wolfe and Fox.

They both stood smiling at each other for a moment.

"She never did answer me." Wolfe sighed.

"Less. You would be less inclined to make out with a man on the side of the road." Fox headed back to their cruiser.

"If I continue lurking outside churches?" Wolfe followed her.

"Inside the church, Wolfie. Inside. It's not such a bad place. You should try it some time."

"Naw. I've seen what going to church does for a person,"

"Aw, geez, here we go again." Looking to the heavens, Fox called out, "Please forgive her! She's a good person. She just sees too much bad!"

"I see good, too." Wolfe snorted as she strapped herself in. "But I also know about a God-fearing man who beats his wife. He doesn't miss church. No way. But he also can't stop himself from drinking and beating his woman. And I know of another God-fearing Christian who beats her kids, and another who cheats insurance companies. She lies and cheats everyone and everything she can, figuring she's entitled to the world. But you think she misses a Sunday service?"

"Here we go . . ."

"Hell, no. She's there. Front row and center. Looking all holy and saying her prayers and asking for forgiveness. Then—bam—she backs out, cheating all the neighbors she just promised God to honor."

"Wolfie, you can't judge God by the actions of others. That's not what it's about. Faith is about what it means to you. It's about what . . ." Fox had been down this path so many times with Wolfie, yet she could honestly say it never tired or frustrated her. She knew Wolfie wanted to believe. In something. Anything. For all her bravado, all her rantings and cussing and yelling at people, Wolfie wanted a belief system.

For that matter, so did Fox. She was raised in the Catholic Church. She had very strong beliefs, and while she never wandered from her faith, she had questions. How could someone from this community drag James Otis to his death? How could someone she knew, someone she'd held a conversation—if not many—with, have done such a thing?

This was the Bible Belt. This was where fist-pounding reverends praised the Lord at top volume, where Sundays and Wednesday evenings were dedicated to faith, where taking the Lord's name in vain was as evil as pledging your allegiance to Satan himself. And it was also where racism bred and festered. It was where hypocrisy reigned supreme. It was a place where an entire group of whites could bitch about Affirmative Action yet admit to not hiring someone because he or she was black. It was a place where a woman like Angela Wyck could and would pretend to throw out her back so that she could get workman's compensation. She had no worries about scamming her fellow Americans but talked about how niggers and spics were taking up all the jobs and doing nothing but using up all the welfare. *Now which is it,* Fox wondered. *Are we taking up all the jobs or using up the welfare?* In the case of that white trash Angela Wyck, she'd managed to do both. She'd take a job, keeping it just long enough to figure out how to fake an injury, thereby taking a good job from another person who might actually want to work, and then she'd milk the system for as long as she didn't get caught. Yet even now, caught ripping up tiles on her roof, facing possible charges, she'd cuss that James Otis's killer hadn't been caught because Chief Teague was an incompetent black. Not that she cared about the Otis kid, him being black. But it gave her license to wave her racist flag.

As for Teague, Fox didn't have much to compare him to. He was her first boss. He'd taken a chance on hiring her. Even though there were other more qualified candidates for her position, he'd wanted someone who was bilingual in Spanish and English, and he'd wanted another female officer. Maybe there were some who had a problem with that decision, but so far, no one had complained about her. At least, not to her face. She'd not given anyone the opportunity, however, making sure that she and Wolfe picked up extra hours, busting her hindquarters so that no one could ever complain.

The truth be told, Wolfe had more complaints against her than anyone on the force, but it was the men—the white men—who were the laziest. She liked Hatch and Doug Fitz, but they weren't exactly motivated. The arrival of federal agents had just made things worse. Hatch and Fitz had both adopted the "what's the point?" attitude, leaving the investigative work to the Feds and Shea Griffin.

"Yada, yada, yada." Wolfe waved her hand at Fox. "I know, I know. Damn, you sound like my mom."

When they pulled up to the station house, Fox put the cruiser in park and climbed out. "I really liked that lamp," she said over the top of the car as Wolfe straightened up, arching her back.

"Are you even listening to me anymore?" Wolfe frowned.

"I stopped listening ten minutes ago." Fox headed into the station. "You didn't see the lamp but it was really . . . cute." She settled for the word *cute*, although the lamp was more sentimental than attractive. It wasn't exactly something you'd decorate your living room with. It just reminded her of simpler times, back home with her grandparents.

Wolfe and Fox stopped at the doorway when they entered the room. Everyone was gathered around the desk where Wolfie usually sat.

They'd been laughing but abruptly stopped when they spotted the female officers. They dispersed, all quickly hiding a laugh. Suddenly, everyone had something to do or somewhere to go.

Fox and Wolfe eyed the office, moving forward. Only the two field agents from the Federal Bureau—two men whom Wolfe had christened as "Yankee, heads-up-their-asses twats"—remained seated and straight-faced.

"Boys," Wolfe said, giving a nod to the agents. "You come up with anything earth shattering?"

While she teased, she still looked around. Fox also scanned the room, searching the faces of the men around her. Clearly, something was up.

"Well, we did come up with something," Agent Sikier deadpanned. "Although it's not surprising."

There was a choke of laughter from the break room.

"It's about what we would have expected."

He held out a photo someone had taken of Officer Tina Wolfe, spread-eagle and facedown in the dirt, outside the church. Beside her, someone had cropped in a picture of one of Chester Kennedy's fainting goats. The caption read, GRANBY FAINTING COP.

CHAPTER NINETEEN

I looked down the street to see the three dumbest human beings perched on the tires at Griffin's Garage. Roland Wyck had his hands between his legs, and he was rocking back and forth while it looked like Milford East was punching Willie Strictland in the stomach.

You couldn't help but stare. These were people who voted, drove, and procreated. They had a voice, however weak, in our government and would be expected to mold and shape the young minds of their offspring.

It was a terrifying, yet fascinating, concept.

Willie Strictland yowled in pain, rolled off to the side, and ran toward the back of the garage. Facing the far wall, he appeared to unzip his fly, and let loose.

Amazing. Right there for everyone to see.

And no one seemed more interested in this more than Roland and Ford.

"Free Willie," Roland yelled, his voice echoing down the strip. "Free Willie's willy!" Both Ford and Roland appeared to find this hysterically funny as they rocked back and forth inside the tire holes.

When Willie was done, he raised his hands in the air, and said something that caused Ford to move in on Roland. Roland ran, almost doubled over, to the back of the garage, doing the same thing Willie had done. Only when he finished did Ford raise his arms in the air, doing some kind of victory dance.

"See something you like?"

I jumped at the voice behind me. There are a number of things I hate to be caught doing. Picking my nose, picking a wedgie, being forced to run out into a street with highlight foils all over my head, and watching the three dumbest human beings in the world.

I turned to find Frankie Larson.

"More like, I was wondering if Granby was ever the testing site for scientific experiments."

"Hey, now." Frankie laughed. "I'm born and bred Granby." He raised his eyebrows and opened his arms to me.

I pretended to study his frame for a moment, rubbing my chin.

In truth, Frankie Larson was a total babe. He hadn't been the high school athlete or bad boy. He'd finished out school, flying under the radar, hiding behind his FFA jacket, and spending time with his prized calves.

I wondered how I'd managed to miss his cuteness. He grinned at me, waiting for my reply, and I glanced back to the three idiots, embarrassed by how long my look had lingered.

By damn, he's cute.

Following his victory dance, Ford had walked to the back of Griffin's Garage and relieved himself as well. No sooner had he turned around, zipping his fly, than the other nimrods let out a whoop, high fived each other, and scampered toward the back of the garage again. Ford threw his arms in the air and looked vaguely like he'd been smacked by a fish, following the other two through the garage. As Roland did his business, he looked over his shoulder and said something to Ford.

Ford yelled, "Aw, man. You jerk!"

And so it went. More howls of laughter. More hoots. More cussing from Ford.

"What do you suppose those idiots are doing?" I asked over my shoulder.

"Having a pee contest," Frankie explained it so casually that you'd think it was an American pastime.

"Excuse me?" I looked at him for a moment.

"A peeing contest." He shrugged.

"You've got to be kidding me." My mouth fell open. *The three dumbest humans have surpassed even themselves. Could it be?*

"Yeah. You can tell that Ford was punching Willie in the bladder, then Roland acted like he was giving up on the contest and he went over to pee, only he didn't really. He made out like he felt so much better. Then Ford went."

I slowly turned to Frankie as he spoke, my mouth still slightly agape, confusion written on my face.

Realizing he knew too much about something so idiotic, he grinned sheepishly. "Um. Okay, uh, Ford thought he won, ran over, relieved himself and then . . . well, you saw. They're accomplishing something great by winning the who-can-hold-it-longest competition." His smile widened.

"Wow." I shook my head. "I don't know what to say. I'm amazed and saddened for you all at the same time."

He laughed out loud. "If this makes you feel any better about me, I did that in high school. All guys have a 'who can hold it the longest' contest. It's a rite of passage."

"Which those idiots have never passed. Or, they just like it so much, they feel the need to do it over and over again." I shook my head again. "Amazing."

"The problem with you is you never had any brothers."

"And this is what I would have had to look forward to? No thanks."

"Well . . ." He poked his chin toward the idiots. "Most of us eventually move on."

Together, we stood a moment longer watching as they wrestled with each other, still laughing about the fact that one had tricked the others into thinking he'd gone potty outside while, in fact, he had not. They were all touching each other, whacking each other, and after each one had handled his penis.

Milford East plopped himself back down on a pile of tires, saying something to the others and still chuckling over his foiled pee-pee contest.

What had Linda White been thinking when she decided to marry Ford East? I would never know.

"So." Frankie nudged us toward the office and away from the three stooges. I think he was ashamed of his own kind and wanted to distract me. "What was it you wanted to talk to me about anyway?"

As we walked back inside *The Recorder*, I didn't expect him to tell me anything I didn't already know. For the sake of the ongoing series of articles about the James Otis case, however, I had to hear Frankie's firsthand account of what he found when he arrived on the scene.

███

Fifteen minutes of fame wasn't too far off the mark with what happened in Granby. With no new leads and no break in the case, most of the press had gone, moving on to bigger and better catastrophes.

He looked around the street, surveying the townspeople. He didn't want to be there. He didn't want to be seen. He needed to leave but he couldn't. Not yet.

He'd been in Granby all his life, knew just about everything there was to know about everyone there. And it disgusted him how everyone hung on to the *People* magazine article, how his neighbors were frothing at the mouth to have their opinions printed in a major news magazine. *Oh, well, I've known James Otis all my life and blah, blah, blah.* Or worse, those who tried to be enlightened with the press, saying that there were racial tensions in the town or that there were no racial tensions in the town. It was a load of crap. All of it. The people doing the most talking were the people who knew the least about what happened or about James Otis.

He needed to leave. He needed to be gone.

He couldn't be happier to see all the outsiders leave. It was one thing to have locals asking questions. Most of it was just small talk or wild speculation that no one thought anything about. There was Shea Griffin, continuing his quest to find the real killer and be some kind of a hero, but he was nothing more than Barney Fife, trying to play big man.

Thia Franks, however, *was* a problem. He hadn't worried about her at first. She'd been visibly upset after James's death and hadn't said much to anyone about anything. She'd covered what she was asked to cover for the paper. Nothing more. Her stories had been flat, uninformative, and unfeeling. Then she'd picked up the story where the mass media dropped off. She'd begun talking to people, following up on police reports, and had twice visited the back field of Larson's farm. He watched as she and Frankie Larson stepped into *The Recorder*. Not only did the farm belong in his family, but Frankie Larson had also been one of the first people on the scene. He'd handled James's body and had been quoted by the press as saying that as an EMS, he knew as soon as he saw the body there was nothing he could do.

So, he had to wonder what more Frankie Larson could have to say about James Otis. And why did Theresa now care so much?

He had to get out of Granby. He'd been here all his life, but it didn't mean he was happy about it. He wondered why Theresa would come back after she'd made it out. He knew about the baby, but that wasn't a reason to come home. When he was little, Granby seemed like the greatest place to live because they could walk to the Town Pump for a cold drink and a candy bar. No one bothered them; everyone knew everyone. But as an adult, it bothered him. He didn't want everyone knowing his business. He didn't . . .

He watched as Frankie sat at Theresa's desk and she made notations on a pad of paper, nodding her head. From time to time, she'd laugh, and he hoped that maybe he'd been wrong. Maybe this was personal. It almost looked as though they were flirting with each other, which suited him just fine. He didn't need any more stories or any more investigations or questions about any of this. He just needed to get out. Granby was changing and not for the better.

As much as he'd hoped the entire thing would go away, the townspeople weren't going to let it. He was hearing more and more about fights. There had been the one at James's funeral, right there in the cemetery when Terrell Whitehead had called Jeff Hanson a bigot. Never mind that Oscar Ruiz had beaten the shit out of Hanson the night of the party, Whitehead called him out as a racist and made it out like Jeff Hanson had something to do with James's death. Someone had heard Jeff make some kind of remark about James and the way he'd handled the fight between him and Ruiz.

Not a week later, he'd heard that Tasha Williams had gotten into it at the grocery store with Ruiz's girlfriend. There were increasing stories about fights, mostly verbal, with the increasing topic of racism. But last week when Chester Kennedy refused to sell one his goats to Diego Amaya, the rift between blacks, Mexicans, and whites could no longer be denied.

Amaya's parents were having their thirtieth wedding anniversary, and Diego had planned some big deal, including a barbeque. Diego had already sent his wife to buy one of Chester's goats, but when Chester learned his goat was to be the main course, he'd refused the sale and tried to give her the money back. Just hours before the party and with no other goat lined up for slaughter, she went crazy, screaming and threatening Chester.

This was a no-brainer. Chester Kennedy loved his stupid, fainting goats. He wasn't on board with anyone slitting their throats and roasting them, but suddenly, Diego and his family were crying foul and acting as though Chester had denied the sale because they were Mexican. Diego was a good guy, but lately, everyone had been on edge. They called the police and tried to file charges against Chester while Diego's old lady ranted on about getting revenge.

Granby was changing, all right, and he needed to get out.

He watched Frankie and Theresa a few more moments, fading back against the wall across the street.

Why can't she just let this drop?

He had to get out before anyone ever found out. He had to get out before it was too late.

CHAPTER TWENTY

Shelby Harrelson pulled up in her navy blue dually, towing a long-bed trailer. Shelby drove as she lived life, braking at the last minute and terrifying those standing along the side of Highway 547.

As a thick cloud of dust encircled her truck and drifted over Officers Fitz and Hatch, she could see Fitz complaining. He was, by her account, wound far too tight to be a country cop.

Shelby flung open a door and hefted herself out of her truck, landing with a hard thud. As she was considerably smaller than the average truck driver, hers was a longer-than-usual drop to the ground. Again, she remained unfazed.

"So, what have you fellas got for me," she called out, tugging at her jeans as she moved forward.

Officer Hatch smiled at her as she marched up to them.

Wranglers, wedge shoes, a southwest style print shirt with brilliant colors of red, turquoise, and purple, and oversized beads around both her neck and wrist. Her hair was pulled up in rhinestone clips, and her lips were a blood red. She was proud to say that even on a routine porta potty rescue mission, she knew how to dress.

"Porta potties," Fitz said, blinking the dust out of his eyes. "We're thinking they might be yours."

"Hot damn. Well, where are they?" Shelby raised her hands, looking around.

Hatch and Fitz were standing at the crust of a small, manmade hill. Not twenty feet away stood a large scraper, a grader, and two dozers. Further down the highway, beyond the construction crew who were sitting—half eating and half watching—was a packer. For months, the crew had been working on this portion of the highway, digging up new roads, pushing the heavy limestone to the sides, and creating deep, rocky hills on the sides of the highway. Beyond the crests of limestone was a fall of three or four feet that ran straight into Granby's native tree line, the mesquite.

"Right there." Fitz pointed down the hill, into the thick of mesquites.

Shelby clambered up the limestone hill and peered into the brush, sighing.

"What is that?" She counted with her fingers. "Five?" She ran a hand through her bangs. "I guess five out of six isn't bad. Well, let's get 'em out and see what kind of shape they're in."

No one moved.

"You don't think I'm going in there?" She laughed.

Again, the police officers did not move but looked back to the johns.

"Look, Ms. Shelby," Hatch said. "We found them, but there's no way we're going in there, gettin' all tore up, and ruining our uniforms. Didn't you . . . don't you have workers who can get 'em out?"

"No. You didn't tell me they were half buried under mesquite, now did you?" While her expression was pleasant, her voice was demanding. She was not a woman to waste time, and she usually got what she wanted. "You said you believed you found them up on Highway 547. So I hustled myself over here, ready to put them on the trailer. You never said word one about mesquite; otherwise, I would have made different preparations." She huffed on that last word.

Both Fitz and Hatch remained flatfooted.

It was just before noon, the Texas sun was in full bloom, and Shelby could feel the sweat begin to roll down the back of her neck and shirt and slide down her face and neck. She hated to sweat. She didn't mind hard work, long hours, or getting her hands dirty. Hell, she'd raised chickens, tended flocks, cleaned houses, worked in warehouses, and picked peaches growing up. A stronger work ethic no other woman ever had, but she hated to sweat when it was from nothing more than the Texas heat. She knew soon her makeup would begin to run, and she fanned herself for a moment while she thought.

"Well, now, tell me this. Who found the porta potties?"

"Roy Herdman," Hatch said, pointing behind him.

Shelby's eyes followed Hatch's finger until she saw Roy, foreman for the crew, leaning against one of the large trucks and taking a smoke. She smiled.

She liked Roy. Like her, he didn't have to get out in the trenches any longer, but he did. He was known to still run the big machines, and he liked standing out among the crew, barking orders, and taking a shovel or machines to do it himself, always showing the young ones how it was done.

Next to Roy was Ed Gilman's boy—she'd forgotten his name, but she knew she didn't like him. He only worked the job because his daddy had called in a favor from Roy. He was chubby, lazy, entitled, and spoiled, representing everything Shelby thought was wrong with today's youth.

Next to him were a string of Mexican laborers she saw from time to time. She also saw a few she knew well, including Luis Rodriguez, Hector Lopez, and Javier Moreno.

"Ah." Shelby smiled. "Now we're in business."

She started with Roy, although she gave a quick wink to Luis and affectionate waves to both Hector and Javier.

"Roy!" she called out.

He took a final drag, pushed away from the truck, and dropped his cigarette, crushing it beneath a dusty boot. "Ms. Shelby," he said, wiping his hands against his shirt before he stuck out his right one. "I figured I'd be seeing you soon. Looks like I get my reward." He grinned.

"Hmm. Unless, it might be that you decided to give your boys a place to relieve themselves."

"Ms. Shelby, I'm disappointed."

"Don't be, Roy. I know you better than that. 'Though, gotta wonder. How did they get out here?" As she asked, she let her eyes wander over the group sitting on the ground, eating an early lunch. "You're Ed Gilman's boy," she said to the sullen-looking young man and he looked up.

"That's right, ma'am. Justin. Justin Gilman."

"Nice to meet you, Justin. You tell your daddy I said hello." Justin nodded. "You have any ideas how my porta potties got out this far?"

"No, ma'am," he answered, going back to his sandwich. He didn't make eye contact with anyone else.

Shelby scanned the crowd then shrugged. "You mind if I borrow a few of your boys to dig out those johns?" Shelby looked back to Roy.

"I don' dig out shit houses," a man said. He looked around to his buddies, receiving a few head nods.

Roy gave a quick nod to Shelby and turned back to his men. "You don't have to if you don't want to—"

"What? We do grunt work?" Another man spat on the ground and eyed Shelby. "She can get her own—"

"No, man, she's cool," Javier Moreno spoke in Spanish. *"She's not like the others. She pays good, treats you with respect. You know, she's okay."*

"Gracias, Javier." Shelby smiled, and Javier's face took on a quick flush of red.

Shelby Harrelson spoke perfect Spanish. More than thirty years ago, she couldn't stand that workers might be saying something she couldn't understand, so she'd studied and studied until she was almost perfect.

"It won't take you all more than thirty minutes to move those things. I'll pay twenty dollars a head, right now."

In a flash, Luis, Hector, Javier, the man in the green flannel shirt—something that was a bit of a wonder to Shelby—and the man who had spoken sharply to her were up, headed back to where the porta potties were. Justin and two other men did not move.

"I'm not gettin' torn up over twenty bucks." Justin shook his head and stretched back against the tire of the scraper. He tipped his ball cap over his eyes and folded his arms against his chest.

"What an ass," Roy muttered, walking alongside Shelby. "Most worthless kid you've ever seen. It pains me every time he shows up in the morning. We'd be better off without him."

"So fire him," Shelby said without hesitation.

"Naw. Can't. I owe this one to Ed."

"Friend or no friend."

As they climbed the small hill, Javier and the others were sliding down the other side. They moved gingerly, looking more like snowboarders as they slid down, careful not to pitch forward into the mesquite trees.

"Ms. Shelby comes to us," Javier said with a laugh, *"because she knows if there's hard work to be done, she needs to find a Latino man. The white man is too soft."*

"I prefer the term Mexican-American," Luis called over his shoulder and in turn, Shelby responded in Spanish, calling down the hill as they worked.

"I understand, Luis. I prefer to be referred to as Norwegian-German-American," Shelby said. *"Now, Officer Fitz here, while his name might sound German, I'm guessing is Irish-American. Look at the pink skin. You boys better hurry up. He's not going to last too much longer out here."*

"I heard my name." Fitz frowned at Shelby but she swatted a hand at him, as though to say it was nothing.

"Roy is German-American. He can take the heat but he's prone to bouts of fits and yelling."

This was met with a chorus of laughs and cheers.

"You havin' fun?" Roy asked. "I don't speak it perfect but I caught enough to know you're making fun, Ms. Shelby." But he smiled.

It was common knowledge that this was why Shelby was so popular with her workers, no matter who they were; young, old, male, female, black, or white—or Mexican-American. She liked to make fun of everyone.

"What do you suppose little Justin Gilman is?" Shelby continued to distract them as they began to pull one of the johns free and slide it up the hill. Once it was within reach, Officer Hatch steadied it by the top and pulled it back. From there, Roy and Fitz moved it over to her trailer.

"I, as a Norwegian-German-American, do not do well in this heat. I think I need snow," she said, thinking out loud.

Together, Javier and Luis wrestled a second john free and began moving it up the hill.

"What do you think, Ms. Shelby?" Javier asked between grunts. *"Who you think killed James Otis?"*

"Not a clue. I still can't believe it." In English, she said, "I hate to think anyone in our community . . . in any community, would do something like that. James Otis was a good kid." She turned back toward Hatch, hoping for a response. As she did, both Fitz and Roy made their way back to the hill, waiting for a second john.

"I know who did it," Luis said, panting and pushing another bulky porta potty up the hill. As it teetered on the top, the men paused to catch their breath. The heat was stifling.

"Oh, shut up!" Hector threw a hand in the air then doubled over, resting both palms on top of his thighs. *"You don' know nothin'. You need to keep your mouth shut, is what you need to do."*

But it was too late. Shelby had heard it.

"You know who did it?" She spoke first in Spanish, then in English.

Everyone stopped, staring at Luis.

"He doesn't know anything. Shut up, Luis!" Javier said, waving everyone off and making the futile show of moving a porta potty by himself.

"I don' know, Ms., but I know," Luis spoke to Shelby in Spanish. *"You know what I mean?"*

"Who was it, Luis?"

"Luis, sonofabitch! Shut up!" Hector stood back up and skittered back down the limestone to help Javier. He wanted no part of Luis's talk.

"What? You know as well as me. You know it's true. Those guys are always saying things and causing trouble. Why can't I say something? Because they're white, I can't say something?" He looked back and forth between Javier and Hector and Ms. Shelby.

"Help me with this," Javier yelled at Hector. *"The faster we get this done, the faster we—"*

"Who? What's he saying?" Fitz moved closer as if proximity would suddenly make him understand Spanish.

"Can't say. It's too fast for me." Roy shrugged. "I think he knows what happened to James Otis."

"He don' know nothing," Javier yelled from down the hill, not looking up from his work. Together, he and Hector wrangled the next

john up the hill. *"He's just talking shit."* He pushed the john toward Roy, causing it to slide forward and skid down the other side toward the truck. No one appeared to care.

Shelby fanned herself with her hands, still looking at Luis.

"You know, if you know something, you need to speak out. You can tell me, Luis. They can't understand you."

"I understood that," Roy said with a smile.

Shelby threw him a look of irritation.

"Luis, please. Keep your mouth shut. It'll bring nothing but trouble." Hector stood, shaking his head at Shelby. *"Ms. Shelby. I know you don' mean no harm. You've always been good to us, but please do not ask more questions. There are some things we just . . . just don' ask no more questions. It would be a favor to us."*

With that, Shelby didn't know what else to say or do. Instead, she stood motionless, watching as Javier and Hector moved another john up the incline.

"So, what's going on?" Fitz asked, looking from Roy and Shelby. "Someone knows something but no one wants to talk? Is that it?" Fitz turned to Hatch. "What if we started hauling people in, had their backgrounds checked." It was for effect and everyone knew it, but Hector bit.

"I knew it! Shut up, Luis. See. You see? You see what you've done." Grunting, he pushed until the fourth john had reached the top of the hill. Still balancing it with one hand, he stood and pointed to Luis. Again, he only spoke in Spanish, careful to keep the police out of the conversation. *"You know what they are doing? They will scare us, threaten to deport us if we don' talk. But what about Garcia? Huh?"*

As she watched Hector, Shelby noticed Roy Herdman take an interest when he heard Garcia's name, and he looked to Shelby for complete translation.

"You know what happened to Garcia?" he asked. Turning to Hector, he tried out his broken Spanish. *"What with Garcia? Tell me? What with Garcia?"*

But Hector shook his head.

"Who's Garcia?" Officer Hatch looked at his partner.

Fitz shrugged.

"One of my workers." Roy had the answer, and the officers made note. "He had some kind of accident. Don't nobody want to give me details. Too bad because he was—or is—a good worker, but he's not much use to me right now. He's all banged up, broken arm, split head." He shook his head. "Somebody did something to Garcia, I damned sure want to know about it."

Javier worked alone, shoving the last john up the hill. Hector stood, sweating and panting, glaring at Luis. Fitz, Hatch, and Herdsman were all looking at Shelby, hoping she might impart new information about Garcia. Luis and Hector were speaking too quickly for Roy Herdsman to decipher anything.

Shelby stood stock-still, staring open mouthed at the porta potty perched on the limestone rocks. Unlike the other johns, the top was gone, allowing everyone to look through the hole into the john. It was covered in blood.

"All I know is, somebody better start talkin'," Officer Fitz said.

CHAPTER TWENTY-ONE

He insisted that she call him *Judge*, for that was what he was. He was in control. He controlled her and possessed her. She belonged to him.

She was young and wild, and he drew in a deep breath, taking in her smells and sounds.

Though she acted as though she didn't like it, she always came when he called.

She was amazing.

She breathed heavily, practically panting, bit her lip, concentrated on him as he spoke to her, and she nodded her head as he whispered. She did everything he told her to do.

He lifted her chin and she whispered, "I've been a naughty girl."

He was spellbound. He could not do without her.

CHAPTER TWENTY-TWO

Jared Durham's head was pounding. He leaned back in his chair, tilting it back so he could examine all the cracks in the ceiling. The drought had been a hard one, cracking most of the foundations in town. And briefly allowing his mind to wander, he wondered just how many homes and buildings were now structurally unsound because of the blasted drought.

We need rain. He sighed.

The voice seeped into his brain again. Rain or no rain, there it was. Her hissing, raspy voice.

He'd looked at his phone but her number had come up as every other number in town did. *County resident.* Yes, wireless had finally come to town, but it had been slow in coming, and caller ID had proven to be useless at this point.

I hate this town.

"I know what you know," the voice said.

At first, he'd just been mildly annoyed to have been interrupted. But she said it again, and his blood ran cold. It wasn't even so much what she said; it was *how* she said it. He could hear her smiling, almost laughing.

"I'm sorry," he'd said, remaining calm. After all, there was a chance she was talking about something else.

"I know what you know. I've been watching. I saw it, too."

"Saw what?" His heart banged against his chest.

"You know!" She laughed. "And I do, too. So I guess we both know." She laughed again, tickled with her own little discovery. "We both know who was with James Otis the night he died."

Shit!

"Who is this?"

"Oh, that'll come soon enough. Yes, sir. But . . . I got to know. You've got me so curious." She was playing with him. "What'chu been following ol' Bubba around for? What's so important about him in all this?"

"What?" Jared managed to laugh.

"Come on, now. I seen you. All sneaky like, following him around. What's he got to do with all this?"

He squeezed his eyes shut, trying to place the voice. He knew he knew it.

"I mean, that is the reason you're pokin' around behind him, ain't it? He know something about all this?"

Man! He hated living in Granby. Everyone knew everyone's business. You couldn't pee off a back porch without someone knowing about it and reporting what color your pee was.

"I've got no idea what you're talking about. Look, I don't have time for this." He managed to control his voice, sounding businesslike. "Who is this? You've had your little joke—"

"Oh, this is no joke, but I think you know that."

There was a silence, each one waiting for the other to say something more, both afraid to say too much.

It was at that precise moment that Jared realized he really wanted a drink. He drank too much. He knew that. He'd get to drinking and drink too much, and the end result would be something embarrassing or stupid. If he was lucky, no one else would know about it, but he'd never had such a clear, in-the-moment recognition that (a) he needed a drink and (b) *dammit,* he needed a drink.

He winced.

"You still there?" She was breathing a little heavily into the phone.

"Yes, I'm still here. I'm just wondering why you won't tell me who you are. And, moreover, why you appear to be following me."

She laughed.

I know that voice.

"I'm sorry. Did I say something funny?"

"So formal and all businesslike."

There was another uncomfortable silence, and for a moment, Jared thought she might have disconnected. He looked at the caller ID bar. *County resident.*

"So, why are you following me?" he asked again.

"Well, it's like I say . . . I know what you know. And seein' as how I'm keeping your secret . . . I thought you and me might, you know, become buddies. I help you, you help me."

"Look, this is insanity. I don't know what you're—"

"You got a client with a big-ass problem, and I'd sure hate to have to go on up to *The Recorder*, you know, and tell what I know." Her voice was more demanding, though still laughing. "I mean, some would say that it's my civic duty, as a citizen of this town. You know, to report what I saw, what I know?" She was challenging him. The way she said it sounded almost like a dare. She did know something.

"But I don't imagine you want that, now do you? So, like I said. You help me, I keep my mouth shut."

It was when she choked out a laugh, that raspy laugh, that he knew who it was. There was no question. He was both relieved to know who he was dealing with and filled with dread. Of all the people in town, *she* had to see who was with James Otis.

▐ ▐ ▐

The thing to do is to watch Theresa Franks.

She appeared to be the only person who cared about the Otis case. Chief Teague was an ass. He was so busy parading around like a damned knight; he didn't know how to lead a case properly. For all his schooling, for all his degrees and promises to this town that he was the right man for the job, he was a joke. A kiss ass. And his bumbling cops weren't much better. All their breaks in the case were handed to them by other people. They hadn't turned up one piece of evidence on their own and had no idea who was involved. Or why.

The mass media had moved on, but the Feds still thought they might come up with something and had left two field agents sniffing around. Another big joke. What Yankees don't ever get is they aren't liked. It has nothing to do with the South and the North, the Civil War, racism, or accents. It's a cultural or perceived cultural thing. Southerners just don't like Northerners. Sending two uptight suits just created contempt. No one was talking to them.

No one was talking to Shea Griffin, either. He'd been sent on more than one make-believe chase. People were having fun at his expense. Travis Miles confessed that, just for the hell of it, he told Griffin that he'd overheard some Mexicans down by the trailer lot talking about dragging someone off. Griffin had made an ass of himself, driving down to the Paradise Park, not telling Teague or anyone else. He'd been so fired up about catching himself some killers, he never once thought about the position he was putting himself into. He'd about got the shit kicked out of him. Then he'd been too embarrassed to tell Teague or the agents what had happened and just laid low for a few days, licking his wounds. Still, to hear Griffin talk, he was sure he was closing in on whoever killed James Otis. No one much liked the way Travis Miles had gone about it, but Griffin was such an ass, it was a story that had everyone snickering and shaking their heads.

Darrel Mifflin had joined in, telling Griffin that he'd heard it was a gang from a neighboring town. A few others had bragged about tipping Griffin off to various rumors so that Griffin continued to run to Teague with new and more preposterous notions about what had happened to James. If the Granby Police Department had disliked Griffin before . . . the man was a complete wannabe moron.

That just left Theresa Franks. Good ol' sweet Thia. Everyone liked Thia, and no one seemed to mind that she was poking around. She was born and raised Granby. She was friends with the deceased, and worked for the paper. It was her right to ask.

CHAPTER TWENTY-THREE

Roland Wyck was sitting on what he affectionately called his throne when the ad caught his eye. He'd been thumbing through the pathetic excuse for news in *The Granby Recorder*—not that he cared so much about local politics or his neighbors, but he liked to read while sitting—when Shelby's reward for missing porta potties practically jumped off the page.

He could only stare.

He felt everything seize up inside him. Just seeing the words *missing* and *porta potties* triggered primal feelings to run, to sweat, to pull up his pants!

The memory of that day and those damned porta potties was something Roland would never forget.

"Woo-hoo!"

Milford East's laughter had filled the air and drowned out, just momentarily, the sounds of screams. He'd tilted his head back and let out a full roar.

"Oh, ho! Yeah!"

With Willie Strictland at the wheel, Milford had perched on the back of his pickup and watched the spectacle behind him. Twice, he'd looked over at Roland, who'd felt sick. This was far more than Roland had bargained for when he'd agreed to go out cruising with his friends.

"Yeah, Wyck! Will you look at that?" He pointed to what was behind him, laughing uproariously.

Roland nodded, trying to smile, but he couldn't.

Behind them, was José Garcia. Roland didn't know Garcia well, but like so many townies, had seen him around. He was sure at some point he'd given a head nod, maybe said hello. Now, trapped inside what might be his own coffin, Garcia was screaming for help and hanging on for dear life, and all Roland could do was watch.

"Aw, shit, don't be such a wuss," Milford yelled. "Woo-hoo!"

Milford and Roland pitched forward as Willie cranked the wheel, making a hard U in the middle of the road and throwing clods of dirt everywhere. Dust showered the truck, blinding everyone, but Willie lurched forward. As he did, Roland could hear the *ka-thud* as the slack in the chain tightened again, spinning Garcia around and dragging him once more. With the sudden jerk came another cry from within, and Roland knew that Garcia was hurt.

Willie roared ahead, and Roland could see them clearly as the truck exited the dust cloud and plowed forward, both Willie and Milford hooting and hollering all the way.

Luis Rodriquez, Hector Lopez, that other Lopez fellow, Javier Moreno, and a few others he had never seen before. They stood there—a dozen witnesses, and no one moved. They were screwed. They knew it, Milford knew it, and Willie knew it.

Roland couldn't believe what was happening but every time he thought to speak out, to say something, Milford shot him a look of irritation. He was shaking his fist, standing in the bed of the truck as if he was surfing, and pointing and laughing at Garcia.

Garcia.

Poor, dumb bastard just wanted a place to squat in privacy. That was how it had all started.

"Yeah," Milford had said. "Let's make a few bucks." He'd laughed. "It'll be fast, easy, and fun."

And at the expense of Shelby Harrelson, who had money to burn. Hell, she wouldn't have even noticed a few of her shit houses missing. It had started just like that. Roland had known how wrong it all was, but he just couldn't speak out. That was how it always was when he was around Milford.

Javier Moreno talked to Willie at some point and told him how Roy Herdsman was such a cheap son of a bitch and that he wouldn't even get a john out there for his road crew. Javier said he was tired of crapping out on the side of the road like a dog, and if Roy wasn't going to get a john, they'd get one. They'd put their money together and wanted to buy themselves a john. And just like that, Willie said he had one to sell, and Milford East was involved once again.

Roland hadn't known word one about it until they were out drinking. It was late, and they'd had too many of everything. Already, Roland had gone off, puked his guts out, and come back for more. It would have to be that way because Ford was pissed at Linda and in no hurry to go home. Whenever Linda and Ford fought, Ford expected his buddies to keep him company.

He'd lost track of time. It was three or four in the morning, and he'd been threatening to leave, just walk home if he had to, when Ford had laid out the plan to steal some of Harrelson's porta potties.

Looking back, it was hard to believe how okay that plan had sounded. Drunk, tired, and fully aware of the fact that Ford would get his way or piss and moan about it for days, it didn't seem that either Willie or Roland had batted an eyelash.

Steal some shit houses? Sure, okay.

Roland wished he could even say it had been fun, but it was all kind of a blur. He remembered creeping onto her property and some of her dogs barking. He remembered worrying about the dogs. Suddenly, there they were. A neat little row of porta potties. And within minutes, they'd silently loaded six on the back of Milford's truck, side by side, the more narrow top side in first. Roland stood between the first two, holding them while Willie held in the last two. Milford had eased them back off the property and down old Highway 547 without anyone noticing.

Only now did he wonder why it had to be six.

Why not just one?

He wasn't sure that Milford knew either. When he got pissed at Linda, there was no telling how his brain worked. Most times, it was pretty funny. They did stupid shit all the time. No harm, no foul. But now it was time to unload the stupid things. It was so typical of Ford to run out, steal not one, but six shithouses, and have everything that could go wrong go wrong so that they would have to hide the potties for fear of being caught. Hiding six port-a-potties in the mesquite bushes of the backwoods of Granby was no easy feat. It was officially time to unload the danged things and get out of the potty business.

Willie roared passed all the men on the side of the road, and Roland saw all their faces, watching in horror—stock-still horror.

What could they do? Call the police?

The chain popped and pulled against the porta potty as it dragged along behind the truck. Heavy grooves dug into the dirt, leaving a deep trail behind them. Dust and debris layered the road, and for a moment, the men were just hazy shadows along the side of the road. Inside the john, Garcia was banging and cursing and yelling.

They'd arranged to meet on Sunday—a time when Roy wouldn't be around. While it wasn't going to be a secret from Roy, there was no need to have him there to complain. Instead, the men had decided to just have it there, already set up when Roy rolled up. They'd take the day to level a nice base and set up the porta potty.

As soon as they pulled up, Milford and Roland hopped off the back of the truck, lowering the john to the ground. Although a chain was still wrapped around it, they tilted it upright so that the men could get a full look at it. It had been quite humorous to watch a group of men circle it, admiring it for what it was.

Roland noticed they'd even brought along a new package of toilet paper. Milford laughed about that. The Mexicans had looked like a group of school kids, excited about a new project. But as soon as they stepped forward and saw Shelby's logo, A FLUSH IS BETTER THAN A FULL HOUSE, Javier had stepped back.

"You buy this from Ms. Harrelson?" he asked, his accent thick but dialect perfect.

"Si, I buy from Ms. Harrelson," Milford mocked him.

Javier shook his head. The jig was up. "Naw, man. You didn't buy this from her. She even know this is gone? She know you got one of hers?" Javier persisted and Roland could see that Milord was getting angry.

Milford and Javier went way back. They tolerated each other, but that was that. Milford had been scamming Spanish-speaking customers for a long time. They didn't know what he was talking about half the time. He'd name parts that didn't even exist, and being the only garage in town, the Mexicans would pay for it. Until Javier and his family moved in, that is, causing two problems. Javier's kid, about Roland's age, was pretty handy with cars and set up his own shop there in Paradise Park. Most of the residents went to him. The second was that any time someone needed electronic work done, something they were set up to do at Griffin's, Javier would come along and play translator. Milford found out pretty quickly that he couldn't jack with Javier.

Roland decided this must be Milford's payback. But again, Javier wasn't buying. He took one look at the porta potty and knew it wasn't a clean deal.

"Are you shittin' me?" Milford laughed. "You're gonna get picky over a shit house?"

"Man, we don' wan' to buy stolen merchandise."

Milford had thrown up his hands and directed his attention to Garcia. Garcia, everyone knew, spoke enough English that he could make his sale. While Javier was shaking his head and having a conversation with a few of the other men, Milford was making fast promises, telling Garcia that he wouldn't find another porta potty so cheap, that Roy would never even have to see it if they put it off the road, further back in the mesquite. He'd told Garcia that if they got any other porta potty, they'd have to lease it because no one was going to sell them a porta potty for just this construction job. And it was for damned sure that no one would want it back after they'd sat on it and did Lord only knew what else inside of it.

Roland smiled. It was Milford at his best, talking fast and confusing the facts.

Garcia appeared to be waffling, since it was no secret that he, like the others, was tired of squatting on the side of the road. Roy Herdsman didn't appear to be in any hurry to supply one.

"So, what's it gonna be?" Milford asked.

"We don' wan your trouble, man," Javier said.

"But I'm not talkin' to you, am I, *amigo*?" Ford yelled, putting his back to Javier and staring down Garcia. The other men began to talk amongst themselves. "Besides"—he shrugged—"by now, Ms. Shelby knows she's got some missing shit houses."

"Aw, man," Javier groaned.

"You don't want trouble out there, do you?" he said, turning to face a few of the men Roland knew to be illegals.

They looked uneasily at Javier. Again, there was more talk among the men, with headshakes. No one wanted any part of the porta potty or Milford East.

"Let's just get out of here," Roland said. He'd had enough, but Milford was far from done.

"Tell you what. You make me an offer." He poked Garcia lightly in the chest.

Garcia turned to his friends, asking something in Spanish.

Milford ran his hands through his hair and wandered over toward Willie, speaking in low tones. Willie nodded, and Milford returned to the men, putting his hand on the back of Garcia, guiding him toward the porta potty.

"Take a look inside. It's clean. Perfect condition. You can stow it down there." He pointed toward the mesquite. "Have it all to your own. No one will ever know about it. Easy as pie."

Javier had thrown up his hands, turning his back to everyone, walking back toward his car. A couple of men had turned as well, ready to follow Javier, when Milford had given Garcia a shove inside the porta potty. Roland had had a sinking feeling.

Before anyone could react, Milford pulled out a cable from his back pocket and clamped it across the door, stretching the hooks from one side of the door to the other. For hauling purposes, four circular bolts had been fitted on to all four corners of the john. With a shout, Milford threw up his hands and Willie, already behind the wheel, revved up the engine.

"Come on!" Milford shouted, shoving Roland forward.

Working on instinct, Roland leapt into the bed of the truck, catching the tailgate and hauling himself over and inside the bed. He couldn't explain it. He went on autopilot when Ford came up with his asinine ideas. Like always, good or mostly bad, Roland just went along with it.

Garcia banged on the inside of the porta potty, and Javier turned on his heel, running back to help when the john flipped on to its back. Willie was flying down the road, the porta potty bouncing along behind.

Briefly, just briefly, Roland laughed. They'd gone some fifty feet when Willie tugged at the wheel, sending the porta potty skittering across the road. It smashed into a nearby tree and made a sickening smacking noise, followed by more shouts from within.

"Shit!" Roland yelled, but Willie jerked forward and Roland fell back inside the bed, losing his balance and hitting his own back against its metal floor. For a few seconds, Roland struggled to roll over and get his balance. All he could hear was both Willie and Milford, hollering at the tops of their lungs as though they were having the times of their lives.

And so it had gone. Willie made three more passes up and down the dirt highway, hauling past the construction equipment and the frozen men until Roland turned, throwing himself against the rear window of the truck and banged hard against it.

"Cut it out! C'mon, Willie! Stop! *Stop!*"

Javier and Hector were screaming and pointing at the porta potty. Only when Willie stopped could Roland hear their voices, and he realized they had been yelling for some time. Like a child following a string, Roland's eyes followed the chain toward the john as the dust finally settled. Suddenly, Roland was aware of Milford's breathing. It was heavy, labored . . . frightened. The joke had gone too far.

As Javier and Hector ran toward their friend and the dust cleared away, Roland could see the damage done to the porta potty. One side was partially caved, the indestructible fiberglass strained beyond its capacity. Seeping out of a hole was something thick and red.

"Oh man," Milford whispered. His voice sounded surprised, and Roland looked at him. He could see that Ford hadn't meant for Garcia to get hurt.

At once, all the men were huddled around the john, tugging at the cable. The hooks were mashed in so that Hector had to pull out his pocketknife and swipe at the cable. The cable sprang back, lashing out wildly. Javier moved in and flung open the damaged door. More bodies. More huddling. Then Garcia emerged with the help of others. He was bloodied and moaning.

Luis Rodriquez began screaming at Roland, Milford, and Willie, throwing his arms up about his head. Roland stood, slack-jawed, while Milford jumped from the truck, moving toward Garcia.

"Man, I was just playin'," he said, but Luis stepped forward.

Milford, big man Milford, puffed instantly, and Roland knew a certain dread. He would not be able to say "sorry" or back down and they were about to get into a brawl. A bad one. Some of these guys, Roland knew, carried switchblades. Willie was out in a flash. He carried a baseball bat Milford kept behind his seat.

"He okay?" Roland asked, staying inside the bed of the truck.

"You bastard!" Hector shouted. The men were gathered too closely for Roland to see clearly. Garcia was bleeding. That was all he needed to know.

Milford's hands were up, as though he was trying to make peace, but he continued to move forward with Willie hot on his tail. Roland knew that Milford relied on his buddies for backup.

Another man stepped forward, also yelling in Spanish, and Milford was talking back, hands still up, still moving forward.

Whatever he said caused Javier to jerk forward, leaping in front of Luis, who reached for his back pocket.

Roland readied himself.

Oh, shit, here we go!

Willie puffed up beside him, taking a batter's stance. He choked up on the bat, making it known to all that he would be swinging at the next head that moved. Slowly, Milford squatted down, unleashing the chain from the porta potty. Willie stood guard.

Hector and Luis spewed profanities while some of the other men helped Garcia toward their cars.

A horn honked, and a shout sounded from one of the cars.

Hector turned, shouted back, and then pointed to Willie and Milford. "This," he said in a low growl, "is not over." Locking eyes with Milford, he gave a twisted smirk. *"Amigo."*

Like some kind of sitcom joke, all the men disappeared in just two vehicles. More dust kicked up as they peeled out, Roland guessed, to find medical help.

He didn't move. He couldn't. He was shocked, horrified, and embarrassed all at the same time. Milford's booming voice broke his trance as he watched Garcia disappear into the distance.

"Frickin' wetback," Milford said, gathering the chain. He hefted it into the back of the truck, letting it crash with tremendous noise, and then stood staring at Roland for a moment.

"What?" Roland asked uneasily.

"What the hell was your problem?"

"What?" Roland asked again, aware that Willie had also turned to stare at him.

"I can't believe you," Milford said. "What's your problem?"

Roland almost laughed. "If I hadn't yelled for Willie to stop . . ."

Both Willie and Milford looked at him as if he smelled bad.

"We were just screwin' around. Damn, Wyck. You're such a puss." Willie seemed all too eager to stand beside Milford.

"It was no big deal," Milford kept talking, speaking to no one in particular, and Roland knew that Milford would easily convince himself that none of this was his fault. "They come over here, don't speak English worth a piss." The pitch in his voice began to rise. "Take our jobs and cause all kinds of . . . shit, what a mess. Damned Mexicans. Shit."

"Well, what are we going to do now?" Roland asked, thrusting a hand forward, motioning toward the banged up john.

"I'll tell ya what we're gonna do. Nothing. That's what we're gonna do. Damned Javier. Son of a bitch. He wanted this thing so damned bad. He can have it." Milford kicked at the porta potty. "Come on, let's roll it over that hill!" He pointed to the thickest mesquite patch.

Limestone, gravel, and dirt had been pushed and cleared from the road enough to form a significant mound on either side. From where they stood, one could not see beyond the mound, making a perfect hiding place for the bloodied, damaged john.

Together, they rolled it over and over until, at last, it slid down the other side of the rocks and disappeared into the brush.

"What about Garcia?" Willie asked, wiping his hands on his jeans.

"What about him? He ain't gonna say squat. He's illegal, Willie. What's he gonna do? Confess that him and the others were out here, working out some kind of a deal for a stolen porta potty behind Roy's back? Nope, they won't say nothing. You watch. They ain't gonna say a word," Milford said as they all headed back to the truck.

Finally, Roland had to ask. "What about the other johns? We can't hold onto 'em, you know."

"I'll tell ya what we're going to do," he said again. "Tonight, we come back here and dump 'em all."

"You crazy?" Willie laughed. "They'll see them all tomorrow when they come back to work."

"I know." Milford chuckled. "Don't you get it? That's the perfect part." He crawled into the driver's seat, revving the engine. "Them guys can't say a thing. They know and you know if they open their mouths and cops come out, somehow someone's gonna need a driver's license or something like that. Those guys live in fear of being busted and sent back. So they can't say one word. You know they'll see 'em lying out there in the trees and won't be saying a thing." He chuckled more deeply. "And they'll just be dying to take a dump in one of 'em, but they won't be able to." He slapped a knee and nudged Willie with an elbow. "That's some funny shit."

CHAPTER TWENTY-FOUR

I'd taken a class at Duke on modern culture—specifically, urban pop culture. I'd been looking for electives and it sounded cool, so why not? It turned into a "why not" class that I'd probably thought about and applied to everyday life more than any other class I'd ever taken.

In part, it was my age. I knew and accepted that. I was a mom, working full-time, playing grown-up, and trying to manage grown-up concepts like bills and insurance. I was also part of a generation that hyper-focused on celebrity status, video games, pop music, and anything techno.

Every day at *The Recorder*, I logged obituary and personal information about senior citizens who'd experienced food rationing, the terror of World War II and the Korean and Vietnam Wars. I listened to older folks talk about the fear that had ripped through the town when an unknown soldier had driven in, hand delivering news about a fallen comrade. While our American troops were in the Middle East, I was with my friends from Duke, sitting around at coffee shops, laughing our asses off, and talking about the latest television show. We didn't go without. If anything, our soldiers were an afterthought. Sure, you felt bad when you heard about someone from the area dying, but did any of it really affect us?

Not really.

Even the most insightful, most impassioned liberal arts student of today never *felt* the war. It didn't touch us. I accepted that as truth when Mr. Wallace told me about being a small boy during World War II, and he played with cardboard cutouts of a tank, a truck, and his little soldier men because all metals and plastics were given to the war effort. When he talked about how he'd forgotten to bring in his cardboard army and it had been destroyed when it had rained, I'd laughed, but the story had stuck with me. There were guys my age fighting a war across the globe, and we were playing with handheld video games and setting new ringtones to our cell phones. While a techno geek might think it cool, the entire thing made me sad.

In class, we'd discussed how pop culture had changed family relations, the concept of marriage and divorce, single-parent homes, body piercing, and public manners. As a newly out-of-wedlock mother, I'd decided I didn't care that much about the dying institution of marriage. My father had decided he'd had enough of paying bills and being responsible and just walked out the door one day. A lot of good having a husband had done for my mom.

Another kick to the institute of marriage was the legalization of abortion. That had been the argument, anyway—pre-marital sex was no longer forbidden because with the option of abortion, it was just party, party, party.

It had been one of the stupidest things I'd ever heard, and I'd figured it was just one idiot's thinking, but then I'd heard it more and more when I'd gotten home. Initially, I'd bristled.

On one particular day, I couldn't hold myself a bit longer when Vicky and Tammi sat at their desks, their middle-aged spread exceeding all possible spreads for the average office chair, talking about how girls today could just go and get themselves an abortion. I pointed out that for decades—nay, centuries—women got abortions, often times with butchers, dying slow and painful and bloody deaths. I pointed out that because this was America, founded on the very principle of freedom—of choice, of liberty, of happiness—religious groups' and individuals' opinions should not rule. Tammi bristled right back, more annoyed that someone had the nerve to talk back to her while she was on her soapbox.

"Well, now, Thia, I don't know what you're gettin' into such a lather about. You did the right thing." She flashed what I suppose she meant to be a maternal smile. I felt the snarl begin to build on the inside. "You went and had your baby."

"And aren't you glad for it, too, Thia? She's just the most beautiful baby," Vicki said. She seemed so proud to have thought of that one.

"All babies are beautiful, Vicki," Saint Tammi corrected her friend. "Just too many aren't given the chance to live."

"Tammi . . ." I smiled sweetly, trying the same tone she used on me. "I know with all your reading that you can't be for making abortion illegal."

She gasped. "You know no such thing! Abortion is dreadful!" She threw a hand to her chest to give the full, pearl-clutching effect.

"I agree," I said. "It's not a pleasant thing."

"It's murder, is what it is!" Vicki pounded a fist into her other hand.

"So, tell me," I turned to Vicki. "Let's say that . . ." I clicked my tongue and tapped at my desk with my pen for a moment, flipping through my mental Rolodex of scenarios. I looked toward LeAnn. "Let's say that LeAnn's daughter is raped."

"Thia!" Tammi and Vicki gasped.

"I know, I know. I'm saying this for effect. See how horrible it seems when you say it out loud. Sorry, LeAnn." I waved both hands at her to indicate that this was not something I *wanted* to say. But she wasn't having any of it and shook her head at me, covering her ears. "Let's say this terrible thing happens." I ignored the terrible fact that I had just asked us to imagine a thirteen-year-old girl being raped. "And she gets pregnant. You gonna have her carry that baby, LeAnn?"

"I'm not having this conversation, Theresa!" LeAnn snapped at me.

I understood and didn't blame her, but I also knew that my point was well made. LeAnn was willing to think about other people's kids getting pregnant but not her own. Wasn't that always the way?

It reminded me of Geri Williams. A member of the Republican Women's Society on campus, Miss Holy, Miss Perfect, but damned if she didn't get herself pregnant and run right off to get an abortion. I was betting she was still anti-choice, never once telling anyone a thing about her past because, she would reason in typical Miss Holy fashion, what happened to her was a dreadful mistake. That was different.

"I'm just saying"—I pleaded my case, purposefully not letting it drop—"there is no way I, or anyone else, would expect you to make your child carry a baby of a pedophile—"

"Thia, I think we can all agree that there are special circumstances." Vicki was the voice of reason.

"Like, if you were to get raped."

Vicki gasped audibly. "Theresa Franks! You're doing this on purpose!"

"You better believe it." I smiled shamelessly. *This is fun.* "Let me ask you, Tammi. Let's say you get raped by a big black guy. No, no. Wait. A big, hairy, coke-snorting black guy knocks you down behind the office. Then—"

"Stop it!"

"It's a horrible thing. Very painful."

"Thia, I'm not kidding. This is in very bad taste," Tammi said. She knew where this was going and didn't want to play along.

I persisted. "You have reoccurring nightmares and live in terror that he will somehow find you again, and then, just when you think it's over and the physical wounds are healing, you learn you're pregnant."

"Ugh."

"What do you do, Tammi? I really, *really* want to know."

"Thia Franks. I should call your momma right now." LeAnn picked up the phone, showing me her menacing dialing finger.

I shrugged. "I already know what she'd do."

"This is in no way funny. Not in the least." Tammi swiveled in her chair, turning her back to me.

"No, it's not. So what will you do? Will you keep and grow this baby inside of you?"

"I am not having this conversation."

"You don't know what the baby will be like, either. Maybe a crack baby. Maybe it'll grow up to be a rapist, too. You know, some people think criminal behavior can be genetic—"

"Thia!"

". . . have yourself a little psycho baby . . ."

"Okay! I know what you're after. I know what you want me to say." Tammi swiveled back at me. She was mad.

"I don't *want* you to say anything. I am curious as to what you'd really do. Real life, not holier-than-thou kind of talk. And before you answer, I can't see you keeping that baby, Ms. Whatley."

"I think we've agreed there are some circumstances in which—" Vicki said again, but it was LeAnn who jumped in this time.

"I can't condone this . . . this scenario."

I laughed. "Who condones rape?" I asked, and she scowled at me.

"I mean, you know, perhaps in the matter where a woman will die as a result of having the baby, perhaps . . ."

I had to give Vicki credit, she was at least *trying* to see another side.

"But otherwise, you think Tammi should go ahead and have her crack baby, even filled with terror that the guy might come back to find her, and constantly be reminded of the horrible rape each time her hand touches her growing belly?"

I could taste victory as they all flustered. Here is the truth that no one wants to hear and no one likes to consider. Rape occurs. Horrible, rotten, wretched things happen. And until it happens to you, don't you freakin' *dare* act as though you know what you'd do or how you'd handle it. No sooner had I put their own names or family members in the equation than they didn't want to play, much less listen. And let's get real. Tammi Whatley would rather throw herself into the path of an oncoming train than carry a black man's baby. I was just sorry for the fictional man I concocted for the scenario. I wouldn't wish that on any hairy, oversized, drug-crazed black man.

"So," I concluded for the group, "it's murder unless it would just be better off for the individual to not have to have the baby." I nodded. *Okay, check. I understand.*

No one said a word and I returned to my work, clicking away at my keyboard and feeling the incredible burning sensation of eye-darts slamming against my skull. I peeked back up to find Tammi Whatley rolling a toothpick around in her mouth and pondered how an uptight, self-righteous Miss Priss, who prided herself on being the upper crust of our quaint little society, justified public usage of a toothpick, and it brought me back to that class at Duke.

We'd talked about people who'd carried impressive looking toothpick cases or even had fourteen-karat gold-covered toothpicks. We'd talked about how people tried to make it something other than what it is—picking teeth in public. We'd had an entire conversation about teeth picking when we discussed today's self-perception—you know, wearing sweats or curlers in public or the teen culture of looking sloppy on purpose. The tooth picker is the copy to that. And as we'd sat in judgment of the tooth picker, we'd analyzed old money versus new money; old values versus pop culture values.

I thought about how Tammi Whatley perceived herself and how she compared to Milford East.

He'd been picking his teeth as well, a toothpick forever stationed in the corner of his mouth, when Officers Fitz and Hatch had approached them. I had known something was about to happen. I'd received a phone call, an unknown caller, letting me know that something was going to happen at Griffin's Garage.

The female caller had sounded strange yet vaguely familiar. Twice, I'd asked who she was, but she'd just laughed, telling me that I needed to take a walk outside. With a camera in my hand, I wandered out my door. And there they were, the police talking to the biggest idiots on earth.

Surely they weren't being arrested for being idiots. Hell, if that was a case, I was going to sprint to the police station and report at least another two dozen people.

Fitz removed his hat and began reading from it as Milford stood, slack-jawed yet toothpicked.

No, these idiots were being arrested for something very specific. I picked up my pace, but when Fitz saw me, he waved me back.

"No, now come on, Thia. Just let me do this, okay? No press."

"Aw, damn. She gotta be here? Shit, I don't know . . . c'mon Fitz!" Milford whined. He was like a huge, dull-witted grizzly bear, slobbering over Fitz.

Fitz wasn't listening, and Hatch had gone straight to work, lining both Roland Wyck and Willie Strictland against the tire tiers. Spread eagled and wide-eyed, all three men claimed their innocence.

Of what?

I took another step forward, but Fitz yelled at me. "I mean it now, Thia. Back off!" He looked past me. "Frankie, get her out of here, will ya?"

I looked over my shoulder to find Frankie Larson staring at me, a slight smile on his lips.

Milford continued to plead innocence behind me.

Frankie walked toward me with a kind of tough-guy walk, and momentarily, I felt myself disarmed. There was something else. I realized belatedly that he'd been watching me.

I smiled back, a little put off. "You spyin' on me?" I half teased.

"Just admiring you work," he said, moving closer.

He looked as though he'd just come from work, still wearing his uniform. Already a big boy, the design of the shirt added to his shoulders, making him look broad and powerful. It was a nice look, I had to admit. His sandy blonde hair and green eyes were highlighted by his tanned skin. He looked sun kissed, strong, and very handsome.

I shrugged my shoulders, feeling like a teenager. I made some stupid gesture with my camera and instantly regretted it. Still, he laughed and gave a nod to Fitz.

"Let's get out of here," he said, putting a hand gently over my shoulders.

"But I . . . what's going on?" I asked. I wasn't ready to abandon my post. Not yet. Not until I knew why big man, Milford East, was getting busted.

"He stole Ms. Shelby's porta potties." Frankie shrugged. "And messed up one of Roy Herdman's guys . . . some Mexican."

My mouth fell open. "No kidding. How do you know?"

"Over the scanner." Frankie gestured a thumb backward, and I was guessing he meant to point to the radio in his truck. "Idiots locked some Mexican in one of the porta potties and dragged him around, broke his arm and collarbone."

I winced and opened the shutter to my trusty little digital, snapping a quick picture of Milford East seated in the back of Fitz's cruiser and cussing. He saw me take the picture and cursed again, complaining to Fitz, who scowled at me.

He straightened up and walked over to us. "What do ya say, Thia? Don't make a stink, and we'll give you something later."

I nodded and tucked the camera under my arm, turning to walk away with Frankie when it hit me. "My God," I gasped. "Do you think that's what happened to James? Do you think they dragged him to death, maybe in a porta potty?"

CHAPTER TWENTY-FIVE

I was a heathen who chose to grocery shop rather than go to church on Sunday. I moved up and down the aisles blissfully while others asked forgiveness for having impure thoughts, which has always been a funny thing to me, because how does one really know if the person giving forgiveness is in the position of giving said forgiveness. What if the forgiver was a raging perv?

We had a lot of Catholics on the outskirts from the Hispanic community, but no in-town Catholics, which was the nice way of saying *white Catholics*. We had Baptists coming out our ears, a smattering of Methodists, some of those non-denominational Bible Churches, and of course, our Jewish sect, the Epsteins.

Catholics or not, I knew enough of my neighbors that I felt uneasy sitting next to them in church, singing hymns and pretending I didn't see one sneak the grocery store's steam cleaner out the back of the store and load it into their car, or see another pick up dollars left on a table meant as a tip for Linda Marie at the Mexican place. Don't you know the Mexican bus boy got blamed for that? I bet John McConnell was forgiven for swiping the tip money while ol' Miguel got another warning from his boss.

Needless to say, I was happier shopping than praying. But on this morning, I was late because of Ms. Riley. She'd been at it again, shooting at that damned squirrel, and Momma had been afraid she'd hit something or someone else beside the squirrel. Before we'd set out, Ella and I had gone over to pick up more pecans, which had set us back enough to be in Lyle's Grocery just in time for the after-church rush.

Somehow, I'd managed to get locked into a dinner date with Frankie Larson.

At my house.

With Momma.

That thought alone made my heart rate quicken, and I could feel my anxiety level rise. I still couldn't figure how it had happened. We'd just been talking, and one thing led to another about people and dinner and Ella. He'd never met Ella, and the next thing I knew, he was coming over for dinner.

I could find out if he really liked me and make my specialty— macaroni and cheese with pork chops and green beans. Instead, I decided to play it safe, and Ella and I planned steak, baked potatoes, and zucchini for dinner.

"Didn't see you in church this mornin'."

I knew that voice, and I looked up to see Tammi Whatley in a sea-green colored dress, with a high collar, down to the calves, and tight enough to make her look like she was a stuffed sausage. She'd looked into her mirror before she set out and obviously decided that her strands of pearls and pearl earrings set inside a circle of diamonds would distract us all from the fact that she couldn't breathe in her dress.

I smiled. "I'm sure I wasn't missed."

"Oh, go on! You know we miss you." Tammi leaned forward and fingered Ella's hair.

Ella looked at her with increasing uncertainty. She was becoming very aware of strangers and closed her eyes so she wouldn't have to see Tammi anymore. I wished I could do the same.

"You need to come. It's important now that you do this for your baby. She needs to know about our Lord and Savior."

"Oh, she knows about Him," I said to her. In fact, it was true that I sometimes said prayers with Ella and sang hymns that I knew and liked while putting her to sleep at night, but I felt that was no one's business but my own. And Ella's.

"Well . . ." Tammi said, and I braced myself.

I knew that tone. I knew from the way she rolled her eyes up toward the ceiling and then closed them that her holiness was about to impart some wisdom upon my humble self.

"This is neither the time nor the place but, well, after your remarks from the other day. You know . . . about being pro-abortion—"

"I'm not pro . . ." I sighed. *Forget it.*

"Well, I'm just saying. Children often follow in the footsteps of their parents. Ella is watching you now, Thia. If you go to church, she's more likely to go to church. And you want to make sure she goes to heaven, don't you?" She turned again toward Ella, talking in a baby voice.

Ella had locked her big baby blues on Tammi, watching with fascination and—I was sure—partial terror. When Tammi looked at her, though, Ella clinched her eyes shut again and turned her little face.

"Tammi, I'm just worried about when she goes to pre-school. That's as far into the future as I go."

"Oh, stop, Theresa! You know what I mean. You need to go to church so, you know, you can *both* go to heaven," Tammi said. There was an edge.

I managed a smile and rubbed the side of my head.

There it was—again. I was a heathen because I didn't go to church. I didn't do things the way Tammi Whatley thought I should, therefore, I was not going to be permitted into the heavenly club of the church-going elite. But liars, cheats, and thieves could all make it because they sat in pews, cracked open the Bible, and bowed their heads in prayer so that neighbors could see the Sunday Christians. A preciously sweet little girl living in a hut, herding livestock every day for her family on the other side of the world, however, would *not* make it to heaven because she didn't know anything about church or Tammi's notion of worship. I clenched my teeth, doing the internal count to ten. It was that or punch her in the face.

"If I remember correctly," I said, shifting gears, "you make one mean apple cobbler. What ingredients should I get? I'm attempting one tonight." I raised my hand, as though confessing. "First time. Help!" I pretended to be fearful, and I watched her expression change.

My diabolical culinary diversion worked, and soon Tammi was scribbling out her recipe, forgetting her sermon.

I leaned into Ella as we moved away. "It's okay, baby. We're almost done."

She smiled and swatted softly at my face. "Lileee."

We doubled back toward the spices to grab the nutmeg, but when I saw the backside of Tammi, I made a "whoops" noise and scooted over to the next aisle where I had a perfect view of the front desk, or as Mr. Lyle would have it called, the *Service Station*. But let's get real. It was a desk with Mrs. Lyle sitting behind it. Most days she sat there, filing her nails, popping her gum, and watching her stories on the little black and white she kept stashed under the counter. Instead, I saw Tasha Williams.

I was happy to see her. I hadn't seen her since the funeral. I'd been too chicken to call on her. I didn't know what to say or how to act. Was it right or wrong to suggest that Ella and Darion play together? Seeing her, though, I was ready to find out.

Shoulders back, head up. I took a deep breath and started down the aisle to make the suggestion.

That was when I, along with everyone else in the store, watched the unraveling of the always-together Tasha Williams. She was trying to buy some things, including diapers and baby food, on the state-issued food stamp card.

I slowed my pace.

Mrs. Lyle was telling her that she'd exceeded her limit and that there was nothing she could do. In return, Tasha was screaming.

I stopped to examine some canned goods on a shelf, hoping to appear distracted and oblivious to what was going on.

Tasha was yelling that it was impossible, that she'd just bought what Darion needed. She was asking and telling at the same time. Darion needed what he needed, and no one was going to tell her otherwise. Mrs. Lyle was unmoved.

I pressed forward, my heart thumping. I cleared my throat when I was right behind Tasha. I noticed Darion for the first time, strapped against her chest. When he saw me, he offered a toothless grin and pitched forward as he always did, hoping I would grab him. Tasha, on the other hand, only looked irritated to see me. I understood. She didn't want to be there. She didn't want to be in this position. She wanted James back. She didn't want to have to be asking for any favors.

"Mrs. Lyle," I said quietly. "I'll cover that." As soon as it left my mouth, I was sorry. I should have motioned discreetly to Mrs. Lyle or taken care of it later, but I hadn't thought it through.

Tasha rocked back on one heel, turning toward me. She cocked her head to one side and set her jaw. "I don't *need* your money, Thia. And I don't *need* you stickin' your nose in my business. This don't concern you, so why don't you carry yourself on over there, check out, and go on home."

"Tasha, I know you're good for the money. Don't sweat it. I'll just—"

"Shit, Thia! I am not playin' with you. Mind your own business." She did one of those head shakes to let me know that we were about to throw down if I didn't get the hell out of her way.

I backed up, embarrassed. "Sorry . . ."

Tasha never heard me. She turned back to Mrs. Lyle, more animated than ever.

I turned tail and headed to the checkout where Mary Alice was scanning and watching at the same time, almost smiling.

Behind her, leaning against the ice machine and chomping on toothpicks were Lisa Gary and Amber Hirsh. Amber said something under her breath to Lisa, causing both to laugh.

"Typical." Mary Alice snorted, scanning my items through.

I looked up for a moment but said nothing.

The truth was, it was exhausting to be fighting against everyone all the time. Heaven, abortion, racial slurs, politics. In college, I'd used my hometown as a model when we debated cultural versus individual. I'd honestly believed that the attitudes were a small-town cultural thing, as if the individual people weren't responsible for their own behavior because it was simply the way they were raised. But standing there, watching Lisa, the whore, and Amber, the slut, judging Tasha, I couldn't buy my own arguments.

"Look at 'er." Lisa sneered. "I wan' what's mines," she said in mock black lingo.

Again, Amber snickered. "Then get a job," Amber said in a mock whisper.

"They do this all the time," Mary Alice told me, shaking her head. "They come in here and demand to use their food stamps for things they ain't entitled to, or they act like they can just buy as much as they want. Like there's no limit because they're entitled to whatever they hell they want. I gotta work for what I need, but no, they can walk in here and demand what they want." She made the final ring and gave me the total. "Look at her," she said, her eyes squinting and nose wrinkling as though she smelled something rotten.

Behind me, I heard Tasha making her case. I didn't have all the facts, but it was clear that Tasha had exceeded her limit but didn't know how. She was listing what she'd purchased, and near tears, asking how she was supposed to take care of Darion.

In front of me, the whore-mongers were talking trash about Tasha. They stood in judgment, wearing their please-look-at-me clothing—one with a bun in the oven from a guy who was going to prison, the other never to overcome her reputation of serving more than McDonald's—and making remarks about Tasha.

I had that feeling you get when you know you're about to say something. You don't know what, but you can feel it bubbling up. I felt a rage building inside of me, listening to the white trash talk junk about my friend. Just as I opened my mouth, I heard Tammi's voice.

"This is exactly why our prices keep going up."

"That's right." Mary Alice nodded and wagged a finger in the air. "That is exactly right!"

"They get theirs for free. Who do you think pays for it? Someone has to pay for it." Tammi continued her rant.

I signed my credit slip, loaded my grocery bags into my basket, and pushed out as quickly as I could. I no longer knew what to do about Tasha, so I just kept my mouth shut.

■ ■ ■

Some people just can't keep their mouths shut. This was made most evident as we sat at the dinner table and the discussion turned to me.

We'd been talking about James Otis, the recent arrest of the three idiots, and our gun-toting, squirrel-stalking neighbor when, somehow, this led to how I'd been as a child and then, regretfully, how I'd been as a pre-teen and teenager.

It was tough enough to live through it. At no point should any family member attempt to relive it for you, much less in front of a hot, new prospect. I could feel my ears burn with embarrassment.

"Oh, Thia, don't looked so pained. You were just like any other girl your age." Momma laughed, passing the dinner rolls around the table. "She was just like any other girl her age."

"Except she was doing the exact opposite of 'I must, I must . . .' " Cici said with a wry smile, and I choked.

"Oh, yes!" Momma burst out laughing, and while still choking, I began wildly waving my fork in the air.

It was the international sign for *please, dear God, don't say another word!*

" 'I must, I must, I must *decrease* my bust!' " Cici and Momma said in unison, cracking up.

I saw Frankie's glance slide sideways. He wasn't going to lock eyes with me, but he wanted to see my reaction. He had an amused look on his face. I put a hand up to my ear. I think it was about to burst into flames.

"I'm sorry." Frankie laughed out loud, still chewing. He shook his head and tried to choke down the food in his mouth.

Poor Frankie. It must have been difficult with that ridiculous grin on his face.

He swallowed hard and turned to me. I died. Right then and there. I actually felt some of my innards begin to shut down.

" 'I must, I must, I must decrease my bust,' " the traitors chanted again.

Ella looked on in agreeable fashion, having no idea that her grandmother and great aunt were single-handedly destroying her mother.

"You did a fabulous job." Frankie smiled at me.

More important organs closed down, including my jaw muscle as my mouth fell open, and I only managed some pathetic squeaking noise.

"Oh, honey, more than you know," Cici burst out laughing, looking at Momma. "Do you remember how she would—"

More fork waving. More international signs. *Stop! No! No more! I surrender. Whatever I have, I'll give you. Just shut up!*

"Ha!" Momma's laugh seemed to explode from her body. "She

would try to beat her chest to stop herself from growing. Ha!"

"And jump off the chair and land on her rear end! Do you remember that? You remember how she was trying to stop her hips from growing? She didn't want to be hippy. Oh, Lordy, that was funny!"

There it was.

The visual.

No first date should be without it—the visual of me pounding my chest and jumping off furniture to land on my bottom, all in an attempt to stunt my own growth. Frankie's grin broadened until I could see his molars.

"Maybe she triggered something and made it grow more," Frankie said, playing along with Momma and Cici.

They howled in appreciation.

"Maybe that's what I did wrong. I did it the old-fashioned way. Maybe Thia woke everything up, got those little hormones of hers working into overdrive. Then bam! The brick house effect!" Cici said.

My left boob burst into flames. I could feel Frankie trying to give me the once-over without being obvious.

"Why would you do that?" he asked, still chuckling.

I shook my head, still at a loss for words.

"Oh, it was the neighborhood boys." Momma waved a hand. "It was the boys, Lily. It's always the boys," she said in a cooing voice to Ella. She fed Ella some mashed potatoes, made a yummy noise, and turned back to Frankie. "She was my little tomboy, playin' all the sports with the boys. They loved her, too. But that one summer, she changed. The boys just didn't know what to make of her, and their mommas were tellin' 'em not to hurt her. But you know Thia. She didn't stop or slow down. She was running them all over, and they couldn't defend themselves. They couldn't touch her and couldn't slow her down, so they just stopped playing with her."

"Poor Thi Thi." Cici patted my leg.

I snarled then recovered. "Well, Frankie. I'm so glad you came over. This was exactly what I had in mind when I made dinner this evening. At first, I thought I might expose myself and urinate in public, but, you know, Milford East and 'em did that, so it seemed a bit redundant. Then I thought, 'No, wait a minute! I could have Frankie come over to my house, and we could talk about my overactive hormones as a youth.' " I took a bite of my roll and shot Momma a look. "After dessert, I'll tell you all about how I got knocked up."

"Oh, Lily, a story about you." Momma clapped her hands together and Ella cooed.

"Lileee!"

Truly, I was on the verge of tears of rage.

Cici gagged on her drink, recovering with a hoot. "That's my girl," Cici said.

Momma knew I'd had enough and turned on her sister. "I'm afraid Thia comes by her hot blood honestly," Momma said to Frankie.

Frankie's eyebrows rose.

"Cici, I heard from somewhere that you were caught in a rather compromising position with Mr. Peters, parked along the side of the road in his pickup truck."

"Oh, hey now," Cici said, waving her fork in the air, and I ignored the international *back off* signal.

I smiled. "You were parking with Bubba Peters? Really? When did this happen?" I had a renewed interest in the conversation. The blinding, devastating heat of the spotlight had been shifted to Cici. *Alas, I can breathe!* "I didn't think roadside parking was your style."

"Life, as you know, presents itself in such a way that doesn't always make sense, but there you have it." Her voice was flat. Almost daring. There was a slight curve to one side of her mouth.

She'd said a mouthful. And happily, I can report that it was not said in a judgmental manner. Cici had a way of putting her finger right on it.

Indeed, life had a way of presenting itself in ways I'd never planned for, but there it was.

CHAPTER TWENTY-SIX

"I'm confused," Frankie said, leaning against his truck.

I'd walked him out, happy to be out of the house and out of the scrutiny of Momma and Cici.

"Okay, let's see if I can help. I'll speak slowly. What is it, my child," I said, working hard not to laugh.

Frankie smiled patiently. He'd had his fill of sarcasm for the evening. "Is it Lily or Ella?"

"Ah, yes. That. Ella. Her name is Ella," I said, leaning on the truck next to him. "I've always loved that name. It sounds stupid to say out loud, but I imagined all the cute nicknames. You know, like Ellie or Elle." I shook my head. "But Momma just had it in her head that I should have chosen a family name like Lily. Lily was my grandmother's name."

"Well, uh . . ." Frankie cleared his throat. "What, uh, does the father have to say? I mean, you know, did the father care or, you know, know about the baby?"

In the moonlight, Frankie looked very handsome. That's not to say he wasn't handsome in the daylight, but standing there, arms folded across his chest, leaning back against his truck, his facial features looked strong. Though he was blonde and green-eyed, he had a certain Latin look to him. Very handsome.

Between his job and working out, he was a fine specimen of a man. But what had caught my attention was his jaw. Sounds weird to say, but watching him chew his food at dinner, the way his jaw muscle clenched, flexing a muscle on the side of his clean shaven face, I found myself attracted to him in a very sensual way. Funny how something like a jaw line could be a turn-on. But in the words of Cici, there it was. He was super yummy.

"Yes." I smiled though I was not happy. "Ella's biological father knows about her and couldn't care less. By now, he knows she's been born and has made no effort to contact either one of us, which suits me just fine."

Frankie nodded as though he was processing the information.

"I made a mistake with him," I said, ready to say things I hadn't before. It was important to me that he not think I was some kind of floozy. "I thought he was someone he wasn't. An even bigger mistake was I didn't think he was what he was, if that makes any sense."

It didn't, and Frankie rolled his body toward me in a sideways lean against the truck. He was big and strong and handsome and very, very close. His eyes were kind, and I felt myself getting sucked in, wanting to believe in Frankie. His arms were still crossed, his fingers hidden beneath the opposite arm, and his thumbs poked out.

"How so?" he asked, a slow, sweet smile spreading across his lips. My heart thumped a little harder, and I cursed myself for seeing where this was going and not putting an immediate stop to it.

"I thought he was single, caring, and in love with me." Frankie leaned in, and I could feel myself fight for composure. The air seemed so thin. "He was none of those things."

"He was a damned fool, as far as I can see," Frankie said. He let his head drop, left shoulder still affixed to the truck, and his lips grazed over mine. As he did this, his eyes locked on mine.

Damned if I wasn't just as hot-blooded as my aunt Cici, ready to make out on the side of the road, but headlights prevented anything further from happening. As the lights shone on us, Frankie pulled back a little.

"Well." He sighed. "I guess I oughta be headin' out. Maybe I'll swing by your work tomorrow, see if you're free for lunch."

The lights cut out, and we heard a door slam. Bubba Peters stepped into view and ducked his head, looking shy.

"Sorry 'bout that. Didn't mean to interrupt nothing." He touched his hat at the sight of me and went on up the walk toward the house. Neither one of us spoke another word but grinned at each other until Mr. Peters was in the house.

"All right, then," Frankie said and moved toward the truck's door.

I nodded. "If I hurry, maybe I'll be able to tell a few raging-hormone-Cici stories." I rubbed my hands together with a cackle. I almost didn't mind the fact that I'd missed a deeper kiss from Frankie Larson. I had bigger fish to fry, and I headed back to the house with mischievous glee. *Oh boy, oh boy!*

■ ■ ■

Bubba Peters's damned dog had all but given him a heart attack.

He felt his heart still slamming against his chest. It had been so quiet when he'd walked up to the garage; he hadn't expected the Rottweiler to be right there, waiting in the dark for him. Just as he was about to reach for the door, the dog had lunged. Damned thing hadn't made a noise. It had been out of the corner of his eye that he'd seen the movement and jumped. The dog had come within inches of his face, but, mercifully, the heavy chain stopped the dog from getting any closer.

He fell back, staring into the darkness. He could make out the outline of the dog. Powerful, large, with flashes of long, white fangs.

With the dog barking, he needed to move more quickly. Peters, he knew, was out for the evening, but he couldn't risk neighbors hearing the dog. He moved to the side of the garage and broke the glass out of a small window with the flashlight he carried in his back pocket. He crawled in easily enough but had no idea how he was going to get it out of the garage with Cujo standing guard.

He scanned the garage filled with all the junk and throwaways that Granby had to offer, looking for that one piece of evidence. If he got a hold of that, perhaps he could erase the connection to James's death. And maybe, just maybe, he could finally get the hell out of Granby.

Frankie wasn't just cute. He was dangerous and distracting cute, and I changed my mind about a lunch date.

I'd meant to tell Frankie that while Ella's father was a mistake, I was eternally grateful for Ella, and it was hard to hate the man for that alone. So, while he'd been a cheat and a snake, he'd given me something beautiful. I'd also meant to tell Frankie all that and more, but when he'd moved closer, I'd been instantly flustered.

As I lay awake, I pondered what Frankie Larson knew of me. In high school, I was wild. Now he knew that I beat my chest to stunt my growth, that I was hormonally, if not genetically, hot-blooded, and I'd come back home after having a baby out of wedlock—maybe not the best knowledge base to start with.

He needed to know that I was funny, smart, and compassionate. He needed to know that Ella and I were a team, and I was not the kind of mom who married and put her husband first. If there was an emergency situation, he'd have to take care of himself because I'd be focused on Ella. He needed to know that coming home was hard, but I did it for Ella. And he needed to know that while I'd already had an issue with trust because of my father, it had only worsened with Ella's father. For all those reasons, the last thing I needed to do was hook up with Frankie—at least, not until he knew the real me, not the high school me, or the rumored me.

At ten minutes 'til noon, I'd worked myself into a lather and headed out the door, telling LeAnn Ricks that should Frankie stop in, I'd gone shopping.

Cici had said it. Life had a way of presenting itself. I hadn't thought about my father since I'd left for Duke until I walked into Miranda's place, saw that hat, and couldn't help but think of him.

When I was young, rebellious, and hadn't a clue, I'd blamed Momma for Daddy leaving. She'd always had to have her way. Everything had to be just so. I'd assumed she'd driven him out, but that was bull. He'd left because he'd quit. He'd left because he didn't want to play the role of father and husband anymore. And where had it gotten him? Dead, three years later. Killed in a car accident that wouldn't have ever happened had he been home. Maybe he was destined to die in a car accident. Who knows? We'd gotten the phone call, and I hadn't cared that much. At least, that's how I'd handled it at the time. I'd finished my work, talked with friends and co-workers, and hurried out to see him— Mr. No Name.

I decided long ago that his was a name not worth mentioning. Momma didn't know it. Aunt Cici didn't know it. I wrote it down, along with how we met and some facts I knew about him, sealed it in an envelope, and decided if or when Ella wanted to know, she had that right. Otherwise, I never said his name—not in hate and not in hurt.

I'd been drunk and lonely and he was there. Freud would say that I went looking for a father figure, I'm sure. An authority figure. A man who, ironically enough, was already a father to two children, and like my own father, had abandoned them to have an affair with me.

My father had abandoned me. Ella's had abandoned her. I'd convinced myself that I didn't have any feelings toward my father one way or the other, but with Ella, I wondered how she'd feel when she was older and without a father. Darion had known and loved his daddy. Tasha would never be the same. How might Ella have felt about her own father if she'd been given the chance to meet him? At least my father had been there for most of my life, physically speaking. Ella wouldn't even have that.

So life and all its ponder-worthy questions were what led me to Miranda's store, asking about one dark tan, buckskin Stetson with a leather and turquoise band for one hundred twelve dollars and ninety-five cents. It offered a good, strong memory of my father.

"Oh, girl! I knew you'd be back." Miranda winked at me.

"Well, I couldn't stop thinking about it," I said and I turned it over in my hand, inspecting every angle of it and taking in the delicious leathery smell. "Do I remember right? You said you'd make me a deal."

She guffawed. "You know it. But, girl, you should see what we just got in." The collective *we* must have been, I decided, Miranda and her private investor. "Wait here." She waved at me and dashed off toward the back of the store.

While Miranda whooshed around the store in her full, vibrant peasant skirt, I began playing with the band of the hat. The inlay of the beadwork was gorgeous. I looked at it intently, wondering how it was done, to see if I could do such a thing, which was absurd since at no time in my life had I ever wanted or attempted to do beadwork. Hell, I couldn't even string popcorn. But I fiddled with it and managed to knock off a few beads that held the band in place.

"Oh, crap!" I whispered, diving to the floor to scoop them up. As I did, I heard Miranda hustling back just as the small bell tinkled over front door. I reached for another bead, pinching my fingers to retrieve it from between two shelves.

"What the hell do you think you're doing, Miranda?" Tom Jackson's voice boomed as he spoke in the small store. He didn't see me, and I stayed frozen in place. He was angry. Very angry.

"Well." She gave a strangled laugh. "What are you talking about?"

"You know good and well what I'm talkin' about. I just come from Jared Durham's office. You talked to him about me and Vicky? You talked about my marriage? Dammit, Miranda! You've got no right to—"

"Tom."

I saw Miranda look in my direction, but Tom would not be silenced.

"What the hell were you trying to prove? I told you I would—"

"*Tom.* Honey, listen. Now is not the time to be talking about this. I just went in with a few questions, you know, about my store. About this as an investment for you." She seemed to be grasping at straws, throwing more looks my way.

I rose slowly, dusting off the hat, and tried to look like I'd not heard a thing. *A miracle! Here I was this entire time but completely immersed with finding the beads.*

"Got 'em!" I said loud and proud, producing the beads. "I'm sorry, Miranda. I was messing with the beads and knocked some off . . ." I stepped forward to show her. "Hey, Tom." I waved to him. It was that spastic kind of a wave that a five-year-old does when he runs up to his best buddy.

He flushed.

"Did you want to see the other . . ." She raised another hat in her hand.

"No. I like this one," I told her. "It reminds me of someone I used to know."

"Forty percent off." She shrugged.

She wanted me out of the store, and I was happy to oblige. It was the fastest purchase in Granby history. Tom stood in the corner, stewing, until I left. Only when I waved goodbye did he manage a civil response.

Once outside, I took a deep breath and put the hat on. It was strange to think of someone my own age, with Tom Jackson. Then again, there would be those who might have something to say about me being with Mr. No Name. I turned toward the bay window to check my reflection. I liked the way it looked on me. I fussed with it a little more with growing satisfaction. Inside the store, Tom Jackson and Miranda McGhee were going at it.

Wouldn't you know the first person I saw when I got back to the office was Vicky Jackson, letting me know I'd missed Frankie Larson and that I didn't know a damned thing about men?

CHAPTER TWENTY-SEVEN

The Judge touched her again in a way that made her jump, and it pleased him. She'd gone through the stages of their relationship. If, in fact, that's what it could be called. She'd been his whore, his confidant, his toy. She was his secret life, and he craved her, desired her, needed her. When they were in public, however, he looked at her in such a way that no one knew their secret. He was polished. He was a professional. But he felt his power slipping away. She was resisting. She was trying to break free and he would not have that.

She was a nothing.

There was no escaping him. They both knew this. He had a fever for her.

Still, he could feel the shift. Once, she had feared him. Briefly, he believed, she had desired him. She had gotten off on his power and control. Lately, she shrank from his touch. She'd become robotic. It was unfortunate but was of no consequence, however, because there was no way out. He owned her.

When she'd begun a new relationship, when her life had changed, she had hoped that would be the end her time with him but she had been wrong. Very wrong. She had come to him with the news, to tell him that it was over, and she'd hoped he would appreciate and understand this. But for him, it changed nothing.

"I hope you understand," she said.

He moved closer and said, "We just have to be more careful." He saw the disbelief in her eyes, and it excited him. He saw the feeling of hopelessness in her eyes. He saw how the realization washed over her that she would forever be linked to him.

It could be argued she should have seen this coming, but she apparently thought she owned some kind of power. Now, she knew. He saw it in her eyes, and it aroused him. She was his.

He bent down, hovered over her, and breathed on her neck. He felt her shudder. His blood thickened. She turned her head, not allowing herself to be kissed and it amused him. She still clung to some hope of power or resistance.

He watched her as she squeezed her eyes shut but lifted her chin, exposing her neck to him. She offered herself because she knew she had no choice, and he groaned with pleasure.

"This has to stop," she pleaded, but he ate it up. He loved it. He loved how her voice trembled. He loved how she pushed against him in one moment and offered herself in the other. She was conflicted. She was imprisoned. She was helpless. She was property. She was his.

Leaning against her, his right elbow pressed against the door, he used his left hand to capture her face, cupping his hand under her chin, and turned her toward him. He pulled back for a moment to see the fear and worry in her young, sweet eyes, and he devoured her.

Her life was no longer her own.

CHAPTER TWENTY-EIGHT

"Yep," Officer Wolfe said and rocked back on her heels, studying the window. "A clear case of breaking and entering."

Both officers stared at the window to Bubba Peters's garage.

"But, what did they take?" Fox asked. *Why would anyone break into Bubba Peters's garage?*

Peters shrugged. "I know what you're thinking," he said. "Why would anyone take something from me? I don't know. But I don't like the fact that they thought they could do this." He pointed a finger to his broken window. "But more than that, I don't like what happened to Brutus."

Wolfe looked over to where Brutus was typically chained. His doghouse was vacant. A bloodstain, an almost perfect circle, colored the ground where he'd been hit. She nodded even as her face blanched. A little known fact about Tina Wolfe was that she was an avid dog lover, and Fox knew this was hard for Wolfe to see.

"How's he doing?" Wolfe asked, drawing her eyebrows together.

"Still don't know. Doc's still watching him. Cracked skull. He's damned lucky to be alive from what Doc says. Been a smaller dog, he'd be dead."

"He'll be okay, Bubba," Wolfe said with an uncharacteristically sympathetic tone. "Doc Hirsh is the best around these parts. He's seen worse than this." She looked back at the bloodstain and frowned. "He'll be fine."

Not ten minutes after she'd uttered those words, Wolfe had called in to Doc Hirsh's. Brutus had died.

Fox watched her partner closely. Wolfie appeared to be lost in thought and Fox knew enough not to speak.

Every cop had a personal thing. For Fox, it was children. She could talk to drunks, druggies, and hookers—whatever. She'd dealt with wife beaters, rapists, even murderers. It was her job. She'd had to. She could remain levelheaded until it came to children, then it became emotional. That's how it was with most cops.

Fitz, on the other hand, could have a regular sit-down chat with a rapist or murderer. He could ask how and why they did this or that. *Oh, hey, you wanna drink or something?* It was just regular, everyday chat. But he couldn't abide by a drunk. Maybe it was because he couldn't get that rapport going, couldn't swing with the buddy-buddy routine that Fitz had so finely tuned. Whatever it was, everyone knew not to let Fitz work with the drunks.

For Wolfie, it was animals—specifically, dogs. She could handle just about anything else. Anything.

Fox could clearly remember the time they'd been called out to old lady Gifford's house. Her son had been trying to reach her for days and couldn't get her to pick up. He'd been living out in Houston at the time and needed the police to do a check. Sure enough, Fox and Wolfe had found her—dead in her chair, her fingers and toes partially eaten from the four cats that lived with her. It wasn't unusual for pets to do what they had to when they were starving. Digits were usually the first thing to be gnawed on. Wolfe had been all business about it.

Later, Fox had been struck by how upset Wolfe had been for the pets. Fox had found it odd. . Having only worked with her for a couple of months at that point, she'd thought of Wolfe as one of the most hard ass cops she'd ever come across.

The big surprise was when she'd learned that Wolfe owned two dogs—two teacup poodles—Ginger and Pop. Fox had laughed out loud, having decided Wolfe would be more of a pit bull/Doberman kind of gal.

Teacup poodles? Never.

Together, Wolfe and Fox set out to pay Chester Kennedy a visit. He had called multiple times about goat-napping and no amount of rock, paper, scissors could get them out of the call. Fitz and Hatch were already on another call.

"You okay?" Fox finally asked, as they made their way up Kennedy's front drive.

Wolfe nodded. "I'll be better once we figure out why someone would have done something like that. For one thing, what could Bubba have had in his garage that was worth breaking into, stealing it, and killing his dog?"

Fox had no idea.

"Have you noticed, ever since James Otis's death, this place has gone to hell?" Wolfe asked as Fox put the car in park. "I mean, *everyone* has gone nuts. You notice that?"

Fox opened her mouth to speak but stopped when she saw Chester Kennedy fly out his front door and charge down the walk toward them. He had a gun in his hand and was yelling.

"Out of the pan and into the fire," Fox muttered, opening the door. Her motion was fluid. Right hand on her holster, left hand out. While Chester posed no serious threat with his rifle dangling at his side, he *was* armed. "Mr. Kennedy, sir, please stop where you are and put the weapon down."

He stopped, suddenly confused.

"Mr. Kennedy, you can't come running outta your house like a shit house rat, waving guns and talking crazy," Wolfe yelled and he frowned.

"Nice," Fox said sideways to her partner as Wolfe stepped out from behind the door.

"They killed another one of my goats!" he yelled back, on the verge of tears. His shoulders sagged. "Why would they do this? Why would they kill my goats?"

Fox watched Chester carefully as Wolfe walked up, her left hand out, palm up, motioning silently for the gun. Her right hand poised over her holster. He obliged without argument, offering her the rifle.

When Wolfe took the rifle and passed it back to Fox without ever turning around, both officers took a deep breath. Wolfe patted Chester's back, getting the details while Fox secured the rifle out of his reach.

"Okay, so tell me, slowly, what's going on?"

Chester Kennedy exploded with information. He gave the time and place, complete with how he'd started his day and what he ate, and wasn't it strange, he'd thought, that the dogs were barking when he was eating his toast. Normally, it would have been oatmeal, but the kettle was broken and he didn't want to bother with a pan of water. It had been toast when he heard the ruckus and decided it was coyotes. He hadn't hurried because, figuring it to be coyotes, the dogs would take care of things. Sure enough, the dogs had quieted down. So, when he'd gone out to feed, he was surprised to find two missing goats and one slaughtered. It was done by human hands, by God, because he knew the difference between coyote, wild dog, and people.

As he talked, they walked out to the pasture. The herd, huddled together, bleated upon seeing Chester, and moved forward. But the scent of Wolfe and Fox set off a sequence of fainting or heavy tree and post leaning.

Chester was unmoved by the hysteria of passing out, opened the gate, and headed toward the back. As they followed, Fox sensed Wolfe's tension and she smiled. She knew Wolfie was afraid of being attacked by something horned.

"Relax," Fox said. "They'll pass out before they ever get to you."

Chester talked on, giving a full description of what he'd found once he got out to the back pasture. It was then that he'd realized two others were missing.

"My females. One's pregnant. And that ain't right. I paid for those, but it's more than that, officers. I . . . well, they're like my babies." He looked down at the ground as though he were embarrassed. "Biscuit. That's the one who's pregnant. I've had her since she was born. I just want her back. I don't want those Mexicans eating her." He stopped for a moment, giving Fox a sideways glance. "That's who's done this, ya know. It's that crazy Mexican lady."

"Whoa! Names. I need names, not name-calling," Wolfe said and winked at Fox. "Thought he was talking about you for a minute, didn't ya?"

Fox remained stone-faced while Chester was temporarily confused.

"Diego Amaya," he blurted out. "He's the one. Well, not *him*. His wife. I don't know her name and don't care to. But it's that Amaya woman what's done all this."

"How's that?" Fox asked patiently. They knew the story, but it was worth hearing again. Perhaps something would be different or offer more light.

"It's her that's done this. I wouldn't sell her my goats cuz she was gonna eat 'em, and she went nuts, killing and stealing my goats." As he spoke, his voice rose.

"Well, now, we don't know anything for certain just yet," Wolfe said, still looking around. A certain older goat, leaning on a tree, was looking at her, and Fox could see that it distracted Wolfe. "Do you have a picture of Biscuit?"

"Yeah, sure." Chester's face lit up. "I got 'em in the house. You know, I've got a website coming up to sell my goats. I'm going on the Internet," he said with unabashed pride. "I've got pictures of all the goats." He hustled off, headed back to the house, leaving Fox staring slack-jawed at Wolfe.

"A picture?" A smile crept to her lips.

"What?" Wolfe asked, rolled her eyes at Fox. "Dang it, I hate it out here. Those damned things give me the creeps. They got those yellow eyes. I think they're evil," she grumbled, hurrying to get out of the pasture.

Fox laughed out loud.

While Wolfe followed Chester Kennedy into his house, Fox headed straight to the cruiser. She knew what was to come for her partner—the full tour of the inside of Chester's personal tribute to fainting goats. *Pass.* Instead, she delighted herself in radioing the station house. As predicted, Francis picked up.

"Dispatch."

"Frannie, Foxie," Fox spoke into her radio, already smiling.

"Officer Fox," Francis replied, pretending some modicum of professionalism. Whenever Teague lectured the house, this was one of his pet peeves. He was big city, toe the line, Mr. Professional. He'd done everything by the book then he came to a small town where citizens tended to address officers by their first names. Hell, most went to school together. If it wasn't first names, it was nicknames.

Had Tina Wolfe not been an officer, Teague might have stood a chance at professionalism. But Wolfe was contagious. She had more complaints than any other cop on the Granby force. Perhaps, Granby history. She was crass, rude, belligerent, a rule breaker. And she had the habit of putting an "ie" on the end of everyone's name or just shortening it. Fox had to remind herself that Officer Hatch's name was actually Hatcherson. Officer Doug Fitz was Dougie. Chief Teague was Chief T, Teagie, C.T. Man—it really just depended upon her mood. Thus, she easily became Wolfie.

It hadn't taken long before Fox found herself doing the same.

"Dougie around?" Fox asked.

"Hold on," Francis said.

There was a click, a pause, and then Doug Fitz's voice.

"Officer Fitz." Fitz sounded official, and Fox knew somewhere Chief Teague lurked.

"Dougie? Yeah, listen. I need you to get ready to run a missing person when we get back. Wolfie's inside right now, getting an updated photo."

"Oh, shit." His voice dropped, and she knew she had his full attention. "Who is it?" In a town like Granby, there was every reason to believe that Doug Fitz would know the person or family involved.

"Yeah. Chester Kennedy's printing it off right now. We'll run it by in, what? Ten minutes." She smiled to herself.

"Chester Kennedy?"

"Uh huh, that's right. Wolfie requested the photo and we'll be running through all the proper channels, you know, within what? How far you reckon a goat travels, what with the periodic fainting spells?"

"Oh, ho!" She heard him let out a howl, and her smile split wide open. It would take another two minutes before everyone at the station house knew Wolfie had requested an updated photo of a missing goat.

She watched as her partner exited Chester Kennedy's house. He stopped at the doorway and waved what was probably more pictures of goats while Wolfie gave a backhanded wave as she stepped off the front porch and made her way, scowling, back to the cruiser. Fox signed off with Fitz and regained her composure.

"I think we need to pay a visit out to Paradise Park," Wolfe said once she was seated and strapped herself in.

"Got a hot lead?" Fox asked, starting up the engine.

Again, Wolfe scowled. "You got something you want to say?" She turned toward Fox, putting her back to the door.

"Nope." Fox shook her head, smiling. "Where to? Diego Amaya's?"

"That'd be my bet."

It was a bad bet. As soon as they turned into Paradise Park, tensions rose. The fourth house in the complex was the Moreno house, surrounded by cars. It had been turned into a working garage, but that was coming to an end since Shea Griffin used every spare moment to pester Chief Teague about José Moreno illegally operating a chop shop on his front lawn.

Somewhere in the swarm of men and cars was José Moreno. Both women knew he needed to be dealt with at some point, but this wasn't the time. All heads swerved and conversation stopped as the men watched the squad car cruise by.

"Uh-oh," Wolfe groaned.

Fox saw the men fall in step behind the car in the rearview. She drove on until they reached the end of the road, which opened up like a large teardrop.

The Amaya residence, a long double-wide, stretched across the entire cul-de-sac. Tires lying flat on the ground served as oversized flowerpots. Three oversized butterflies were affixed to the side of the trailer near the door. The butterflies and the door were all a brilliant turquoise. Low flying aircraft could find the door without trouble. The banister aside the three small steps that led to the front door was painted white, but the steps were also turquoise, no doubt because there'd been just enough turquoise left to paint the steps.

Why not?

While neither Fox nor Wolfe was particularly wild about the décor, the trailer was clean, well-kept, and neither could recall ever having a problem at this residence. Fox knew she'd have remembered that door.

"We got a fan club," Wolfe mumbled when they reached the Amaya driveway.

"We're in, we're out," Fox said.

She hated this. She hated this more than Wolfie could ever know. She, Officer Rosa Fox, was viewed as a flat out traitor for partnering up with a known bigot, or so they thought.

Ironically, Wolfe was what this world needed more of—a straight shooter. She said what she thought and made jokes about everyone. If she was a bigot, she was an equal opportunity bigot. She thought like a cop, plain and simple. White male: serial killer, serial rapist, child molester. Black male: drugs, assault and battery. Hispanic male: domestic disputes, alcohol, petty theft. She thought in terms of statistics and labeled people, however wrong, as such. It wasn't personal.

Fox knew Wolfe wasn't well liked by the Hispanic residents of Paradise Park, who felt Wolfe gave out pissant tickets just to cause problems. Fox was also well aware just how this looked—Chester Kennedy, a white guy, double-crossed Lidya Amaya and no one cared. No one cared that he had taken her money and then, just hours before the big birthday, refused sale of one of his goats. No one cared until one of his goats is killed, and then the police were all over it, banging on the door of a Latino.

Fox watched Wolfe ease out, turning to give the men down the street a head nod—an acknowledgement of, "Yeah, I see you. Now go on back to what you were doing."

No one said word.

Fox stepped out as well without acknowledging anyone and headed straight toward the Amaya's door. Wolfe, she knew, had her back covered.

Fox skipped the steps and hopped on to the platform of a porch, ringing the doorbell.

Lidya Amaya opened it and squinted. "Que?" She was blunt. Two little heads poked out from behind her legs, looking Fox up and down.

"She's a police woman." Fox heard the children whisper in amazement to each other.

Children were always amazed to see a female officer, but in this neighborhood, a Hispanic female officer was even more fascinating. She tried to smile at them but Lidya shifted, blocking her view.

"What do you want?" she asked in Spanish. *"Where were you when Arno Rodriquez was beating the shit out his wife? Or when Maria Avila had her house broken in to? Three times the Avilas have been robbed, but no one comes. Where were you when Hector had his car tires slashed? And how many times does that Milford East get to come here and make threats about José Moreno's garage business? Because Shea Griffin pretends to be police, no one cares. But one man gets a goat stolen or whatever happened to it and you come here to me. Why?*

Because I'm a loud Mexican woman who stood up to him?"

Fox said nothing for a moment. She knew Lidya spoke the truth. The residents of Paradise Park quite often *were* an afterthought. They were given leftovers for jobs, customer service, and police assistance. She tried to convince herself otherwise, but she knew the police were much faster to respond to the Highlands—a place where people such as the Whatleys, Jacksons, and Hirshes lived.

Residents of Paradise Park weren't without fault, however. Many made no effort to speak English. They didn't try to integrate, befriend outside their immediate community, or—because many were illegals—comply with the law. This was a huge problem and the reason every negative stereotype she knew of lived on.

It was frustrating for Fox. She saw the best and worst in all people. She was no longer surprised by what people did or said. Whether she liked it or not, she understood how Wolfe saw statistics rather than people. The probability of one person committing a crime was higher than another based on neighborhood, clothes, and ethnic background.

The probability was great that Lidya Amaya did goatnap and/or kill a few of Chester's prized animals. Lidya was tired of feeling screwed over and family—and all that comes with that, like planning a birthday celebration—was important, so it was likely she'd taken the law into her own hands.

"You know that Milford East tortured poor José Garcia. You know what I heard? I heard that Milford East and his friends, who are they? Roland Wyck and Willie Strictland? I hear that they laughed the entire time. They tricked our men into what happened. They lie and cheat and steal and try to kill our men, but you do nothing. I hear that Milford and his friends, they are out. They are out of jail soon. They get out, do their work, make their money, and laugh at us because they know that no one will stop them. And I am supposed to not care? Is that it? I am not supposed to worry that next time it could be my husband?"

Fox forced her face to remain blank. She hadn't heard that East and his cronies were being released on bail. She was disappointed but had nothing to offer in the way of comfort. Worse was what Fox saw in Lidya's expression. She was disgusted with Rosa Fox. She wanted and expected Rosa Fox to do something for her family and neighbors. Officer Fox wanted Lidya Amaya to do something for her neighbors and family, make them understand the importance of speaking English, obeying the laws, and integrating without giving up their own identity and culture.

Is that even possible? She sighed.

"And you," Lidya said to her, not yet done. *"Do you protect us? No! What your mother say? Is this how she raised you?"*

Fox stiffened. *"I was raised by my grandfather. He was a goat farmer."* She looked toward the back of the house. *"Let's talk about Chester Kennedy's goats."*

CHAPTER TWENTY-NINE

When in doubt, ask.

Such a simple thought.

My eyes had strayed toward Blink of an I. I wondered if Miranda was inside working. Or was she with Tom Jackson? Vicky's voice still buzzed in my head, all high and mighty about slutty, but very pregnant, Amber Hirsh and her baby's daddy, Cody Kyle. Not particularly newsworthy, but great gossip and one hell of an opportunity to reaffirm one's greatness over another.

I wonder how Vicky feels about Tom privately investing in Miss Miranda McGhee? Ho boy.

I'd begun to think about Modern Culture class at Duke again. Snobbery. It was a great topic, though I'd never thought so at the time.

Tammi Whatley and Vicky Jackson, however, reminded me, as they were two living, breathing examples of people who presumed superiority over others, even at the expense of others, to make themselves feel better. I was sure I was the victim of it even more than I realized. Ironic that I could be put on edge by women with over-teased, hair sprayed heads, bad clothing, and too much makeup. Thus, the cycle of snobbery continued to spin.

I judged them as well; I admit it. I knew and understood the process but didn't much care for it. The only way around that was to get away from them.

No sooner had I stepped out the front door of *The Recorder* than I heard the idiots had gotten out on bail.

Scratch that.

I walked out the front door, looked to the left, and saw them—Milford East, Roland Wyck, and Willie Strictland all standing at their post. I was dumbfounded.

Instead of being embarrassed, withdrawn, or resolute, they were more obnoxious than ever. Ford towered over the other two, arms draped over each guy, and all three faced the street. Across the street, there were three high school girls. I *knew* I knew them, but I couldn't place their names. They were sixteen at best, wearing low-slung jeans, bamboo flip flops, high ponytails, and over-stretched, undersized T-shirts that, in theory, could look good on young, hip bodies yet never worked on today's modern, over-sugared, french-fried teenyboppers.

Do they even own *a mirror?*

"Girrrl," Willie drew his wolf call out a good six syllables. "Come on over here and let me have a better look. C'mon. I'm so lonely. I ain't seen anything pretty all day."

The girls grinned, turning to each other, doing the teenage girl huddle.

I looked back at the idiots.

Ford, husband to my childhood friend, Linda, and father of five, stood gawking and grinning at teenage girls. It was a train wreck. I couldn't believe it, couldn't look away, and couldn't call out to stop it. I just stood, slack-jawed and staring.

"A-wooo," Willie howled.

The girls' giggling was all the encouragement he needed. Eventually, that cool, subtle calling of a buffalo in heat was too much for the girls and they sashayed across the street.

"Those boys just don't know when to stop."

I jumped a little and spun to find Linda East standing behind me. I was embarrassed and ashamed for her. My mouth fell open but nothing came to mind.

Her voice was meek. "They think they're being funny."

Behind me, I could hear the idiot brigade making noises, flirting with children. I was disgusted and didn't bother turning back. I didn't want to see anymore. I forced a smile at Linda.

"What have you been up to?" I failed to sound normal, but she was too distracted to notice. Or care.

"Just trying to keep Ford out of trouble."

I repressed the knee-jerk responses that came to mind and just shrugged, trying another smile.

"Actually," she said, ignoring whatever was going on down the street between her husband and three young girls. "I came to see you. You know, um, you know computers, don't you? Like websites and such?"

"Enough to get around," I answered.

"I, uh." She laughed nervously, running a hand through her bangs. "Wow, this sounds so bad. I kinda need some help but didn't really know who to ask." She laughed again. "It's not something you go around askin'," she babbled.

"What?" I tried a smile, mostly to help her from babbling. "Just ask."

"How do you . . . I mean . . ." She managed a smile.

There was a whoop and an unnaturally loud burst of laughter from down the way. It, too, sounded forced. Ford wanted everyone in town to see that he hadn't a care in the world. He was a big man.

Big man, good times! Woo-hoo, look at me!

"Can you put, or help me figure out how to put, parental controls on my computer? You know, for like porn sites and stuff."

"Porn?" The burst of laughter caught in my throat. She wasn't smiling. She made some vague reference to the children, all far too young to know anything about computers, and we both knew it.

Another booming laugh. Ford was living vicariously through Roland and Willie, doing everything possible short of touching the girls himself.

"So, what? You want to block out all porn access?" I asked, already nodding to myself. *It will be a freaking pleasure.* "Sure, I could do that. It's easy. Put a password protection on it, he'll . . . no one will ever get through it. At least, not in your house, not on your computer." Anyone who knew anything about computers would have a way around it, but I was willing to bet that Ford's working knowledge of computers was limited to licking his lips and jabbing at keys with one finger at a time.

"Where are the kids?" I asked, looking around.

"With Momma. I wanted to talk to you alone and . . . I was, you know, hoping this could be like old times, Thia. Between you and me. I don't need people knowing about this."

I waved a hand at her. I wouldn't breathe a word.

We stopped in at the Town Pump for a cold drink. Ever since I could remember, the Town Pump had the coldest cokes in town. They kept their fridge colder than anywhere else did, and it was a place where you could get a real honest-to-goodness glass coke bottle that was, hands down, the best. We both grabbed one, and as we pushed through the doors and headed back outside, I traveled back in time—the heat pressing against us, the sounds and smells of downtown Granby and my once best buddy by my side. With an extra cold bottle of coke in hand, there wasn't a thing we couldn't face. It felt very right.

"How long has he been doing that?" I asked suddenly enough to startle her, and I wondered if she had been having that same feeling.

She jerked the bottle away from her mouth and tried to swallow without choking. She cleared her throat, and we took a few more steps before she answered. "He didn't always. Just . . . I think, when I got pregnant with Richard. But it was magazines then. We didn't have a computer or nothing."

More walking, more drinking. Several times, we stopped and inspected our bottles, the conversation slowly bringing out more details.

"Honestly, I don't know how long it's been going on. I mean, I didn't get on the computer for the longest time. Then, one day, a while back, I came home early from something . . ." She seemed lost in thought, stepping back to the very day she found out. ". . . kids were in Sunday school, and I never—I mean, I never—get time alone with Ford. So I sneaked off. I know that's so bad, but I just wanted some time alone." She took another pull from her drink and studied it a moment longer. "He'd stayed home, you know. He don't usually go to church. Not unless it's a wedding or a funeral." At first, she laughed at this and then frowned. "I'm sorry I said that. Thia, I'm not thinkin' straight."

I made shrugging gestures and don't-worry-about-it noises.

"I guess I'm still kind of shocked, you know." She seemed to drift off again, then she shook her head, her eyes focused, and she joined me in the present once more. "How's Tasha doing?"

"Not so good, I don't think," I said solemnly. The trouble was, there was a time when I could tell Linda anything—absolutely anything. As much as the sweet memories were flooding back, and as easy as I felt standing next to her, I was conscious of the fact that this was a person I no longer knew.

If I'd told her ten years ago she'd be the mother of five kids with an overbearing, obnoxious husband who nobody liked, she would have laughed at me. In high school, Linda had been on the path to everything excellent. She'd been pretty, popular, smart, kind, and organized. Everything had a plan. Now, she lived in a gravity machine of utter chaos, spinning in midair, and Ford was at the controls. Simply put, her life sucked. In a weird way, I knew that Tasha was better off than Linda.

"You know, Ford didn't have anything to do with that," she said. She caught my glance and nodded as if to reassure me. "I know it, Thia. He didn't. Right here." She pointed to her car, parked in the back of *The Recorder*.

I laughed. "You've got to be kidding me," I said, staring at a 1973 Mercury. "The bat mobile?" I ran my hand over the copper colored car, and more memories came back. It was the car we had cruised around in during high school. It was the car that we challenged the Langford boys to a drag race in. And for the record, won. James Otis had been in this car. Hell, *everyone* had been in this car. I beamed at her.

She looked embarrassed. "I know, can't believe I still have it." She shrugged.

"Wow, this was . . . *is* a great car," I said, and she looked up, surprised at my reaction. "I mean it. I can't believe you still have it."

"Milford keeps it running in tip top shape." There was an edge to her voice. "I had a Camaro, but it got wrecked."

Somewhere in the back of my mind, I was sure I'd heard about that. *Maybe Momma had written.* The idiot had entertained the notion of being a drag racer, and Ford had cracked up the car.

The afternoon slipped away from me. I'd gone to her house, put on the parental controls, and none too soon. I'd seen what websites Ford had been viewing, and I'd used excellent restraint in saying nothing. In exchange, I'd asked that she never mention that I'd been the one to put the controls on the computer.

Teenage sluts doing barn animals. Well, I'll be damned. It was hard to imagine that I knew someone who would look at that kind of thing. It made me sad and sick at the same time. I felt less sorry for Linda and more . . . mad. *Why does she stay with someone like that?* Can a guy look at teenage girls engaging in barnyard animal sex and be respectful to his own wife and daughters? Can he effectively raise his own sons? I knew that Linda already knew the answer and just pretended there was nothing she could do.

She denied her shitty life and focused on the positives, telling me repeatedly that while Ford did drag around the Mexican, he never intentionally harmed anyone, and had nothing to do with James Otis. She was so sure, she'd put the house up for his bail.

I'd opened my mouth to point out the obvious—he'd dragged José Garcia to his near death; it stood to reason that he'd dragged James Otis to his. Instead, I'd bummed a ride back into town, given her a hug, and set off for the courthouse. If anyone knew what was going on around here, it'd be Jessie Durham. And Jessie Durham loved to dish the dirt.

She looked like her brother, which for a female, wasn't such a great thing. She was short, thick, and busty. She reminded me of a pigeon. She had small eyes that darted about while she talked, and she tilted her head from side to side—a characteristic I was sure she was completely unaware of.

I updated her on the latest at *The Recorder*, told her about Momma, Aunt Cici, and her new love. We had a good giggle over the latest report that Mavis Clarette had the fire department come out after Charles threw his hip out while they were making whoopee. It was fun to know that ol' Mavis was still getting action at seventy-two.

"More than I'm gettin'." Jessie huffed, and we snickered a little more.

On a less funny note, Gail Vargus was back in the courthouse, refiling her divorce papers. How much more was Mrs. Vargus supposed to take? Johnny Vargus had been abusing her in one form or another for years, but it was hard to imagine what their future apart held.

Jessie also told me that Sandy Harris, our vigilant postal carrier, got bit on the ass one too many times by Lester James's dog and filed suit against Lester. This was a long time coming as far as I was concerned. Over the years, Lester's dogs had bitten or scared the crap out of little kids on bikes, walkers, and poor Sandy Harris more times than anyone could count.

On the flip side of the canine news, it had been confirmed that someone had killed Teddy "Bubba" Peters's dog while breaking into his garage. Why would anyone want to break into his garage? For what purpose?

It was a natural segue into other questions that I hoped Jessie could answer. When in doubt, ask.

Who wanted James Otis dead? Were there any more clues from the crime scene? Was the crime racially motivated? Was there a connection to the Garcia attack and James Otis? Was there a connection to the Garcia attack, the Otis attack, and the Peters's break-in? But like everyone else in town, Jessie could only speculate. As for the bigger question—who was the woman calling me and offering tips about Milford East and his buddies getting arrested? I kept that to myself. At least for the time being.

CHAPTER THIRTY

As Jared Durham brought the bottle to his lips, he watched his sister. The look of disapproval was clear as he took a long pull anyway.

"I've got a freaking goat lawsuit. Tom Jackson is crawling down my throat. Claims Miranda's forcing him against his will. No one forced him to unzip in the first place. But there it is. He's screwed in every sense." He shook his head, flipping absentmindedly through a stack of papers on his desk, and swallowed another long pull from the bottle. "Marla Dodson's case is coming up, and I still don't have justification for what she did. *Shit*. She stole videos. Freakin' nut. As much as I'd like to help her, there's just so much magic I can perform. And Travis is doing his damnedest to undermine her character. He don't give a damn about Clyde's wishes." He looked at her, shoved his chin in the air, and dared her to stop him from drinking.

"But that's not the end of it. Do you know that little tramp Amber Hirsh came in here and all but accused me of not doing my job and threatened to report me to the bar if I don't get Cody Kyle off for gun trafficking, which is completely insane since he was caught red-handed. Unbelievable! What am I supposed to do about that? These people act like I'm supposed to just make evidence disappear."

Yet, that's exactly what he'd been doing.

Jessie folded her arms across her chest, and he slouched in his chair at the intensity of her stare, swallowed up behind his oversized desk.

"Let me take care of her," Jessie said.

"Fine!" He threw up a hand, not wanting to deal with it any longer and happy to have any help.

"We've got much bigger problems than Amber Hirsh," Jessie said. "Theresa Franks is asking a lot of questions."

"I know." He sighed then took another drink. "Too many." He almost laughed. "You know, everyone else has gone away, given it up. Hell, even Tasha Williams doesn't ask any more questions. No one cares—not that no one *cares*. Everyone liked that Otis kid from what I understand. But . . ." He shrugged his shoulders and looked back at his sister. "No one cares to turn over any more rocks around here."

"No one but Thia." Jessie pulled up one of the client chairs and slid up to the other side of Jared's desk. She slumped down into the soft, leathery seat.

"Some rinky-dink newspaper that no one ever heard of, cares about, even reads, and she's gotta play the next Barbara Walters."

They stared at each other for a moment, and it occurred to Jared how long she'd been taking care of him. Moreover, he loved that she took care of him. She was all he had. In many ways, the two of them sitting together, alone, conspiring, nicely recapped their lives together. The two Amigos. Them against the world.

Some of the loneliest times of his life were when he'd been away at school. He'd gotten drunk and called home, talked just a little too loudly, a little too fast, a little too happily, but it had all been an act.

He'd come back home, acting the part of dutiful brother, prodigal son. The truth was he needed Jessie, just like their dearly departed mother had. Jessie was the link he needed to succeed. He had tried to pretend that he had all the connections, had all the moves, but he was drowning in his own bottle and couldn't save himself. It was Jessie who had all the connections. It was Jessie who knew everyone in town. She had people come to her for help and information. Jared and their mother had been different. They didn't like people knowing their business and for good reason. Jessie didn't have any secrets. Instead, she protected the secrets of Jared and their mother. Their teachers would never know all the times their mother had been a no-show at parent/teacher night or student functions because she was facedown drunk in bed.

No one would know that even to her death, Mother required a certain amount of alcohol to stay alive. Ultimately, she was too far gone to stop drinking. If she went dry for one day, her body would have life-threatening withdrawals and seizures. It was Jessie who'd medicated her daily with vodka.

And being the good son that Jared was, he followed in his mother's footsteps. He hated Granby. He hated the town, the people, the lifestyle. He wanted out. He knew that Judge McKinley was no fan of his and ironically, stood in serious judgment of his lifestyle. So he dealt with his demons in private—except, of course, when he needed help from his sister.

"Shelby Harrelson came in here just this afternoon." He sighed. "She wants to sue Milford, Willie, and Roland for destruction of property and theft of her outhouses. She says she wants to make an example of them. Milford don't have a pot to pee in, but she wants to make an example of him."

Jared leaned over, placing his elbows on the desk and then placing his head in his hands. He sighed again. "The thing is, I know for a fact that Ford and Roland and Willie didn't kill James. They mighta done what they did to that Mexican fella, but they didn't kill James."

"How do you know that?" Jessie asked, and Jared jerked his head up.

He couldn't tell her how or what he knew. Instead, he just shook his head at her. "He . . . someone came into my office, Jess. He told me what happened. And all I can tell you is . . ." He shook his head, still cradled in his hands. "Ford and 'em are innocent. As absurd as that statement is."

He rocked back, hitting the back of his chair and stared at the ceiling for a moment. "She's closer to the truth than she realizes," Jared said. He didn't need to say Theresa's name. "Everything is connected. Everything in this godforsaken town is connected. Now I've just got to figure out what to do about it."

▮▮▮

"Pastor," the man's voice whispered.

Monica drew her knees to her chest and smiled to herself. *Ah, the secrets of the world come daily. Sinners, criers, do-gooders, victims, and predators.*

"What can you tell me? There's nothing." The man sounded desperate. "I know what I'm doing is wrong, but . . . but I can't stop myself. It's a sickness. I can't stop myself, and as much as I want to, part of me doesn't. God help me." He was despondent.

Monica closed her eyes. *I know that voice.* She strained to listen. Not that it much mattered. She would see who it was soon enough, but this was part of the game—listening and figuring out ahead of time who was confiding in the great Pastor Tyree.

It was funny how people came to her father. They all came to him because he was the greatest secret keeper in the world. He listened. He didn't judge. He could and did greet them all in public, never revealing what he knew. He treated everyone equally, keeping their depraved, putrid secrets while blessing them with God's love.

What a crock.

She curled up against the wall, a secret haven behind her father's bench. She was invisible, listening to yet another perv reveal his latest lusting.

They came to Pastor Tyree, begging for help. They listened to his advice, nodded their heads eagerly, all the while just wanting to hear that they were still loved. Once they were out the door, most returned to their old ways. They didn't want forgiveness, nor did they hope to change their ways. They just wanted permission.

Don't we all?

As a child, she'd heard her share of confessions. All innocent fun. More often than not, she had no idea what she was hearing, and she'd spent more time covering her mouth, stifling giggles. For a brief period in her pre-teens, she'd stopped listening, worried what God would think of her. By her rebellious teens, however, her curiosity had been piqued. She'd wanted to know what her neighbors were doing—and to whom— perhaps to appease her own guilt.

More than hearing the confessions themselves, Monica loved to see the people on the streets and in stores, pretending that they were so clean. But she knew. Mrs. Whatley in her loveless, highly dysfunctional marriage; Tom Jackson bopping Miranda McGhee; Lisa Gary binging and purging; Johnny Vargus beating his wife; Debbie Myers mailing a note to Vicky Jackson, telling her about her husband's infidelities. It was typical, small-town drama, but it was fun to know the players involved. Two key public officials had skeletons in their closets. One had a penchant for young girls, another for young boys. They were goodies to be sure, but since James Otis's death, things had heated up. It played out like a reality show. Only this was interactive entertainment, and she would use it to her advantage because she, too, had demons.

That was the rub. Her father, the great pastor, had known about her problems and had not held her hand. He hadn't forgiven. He hadn't given permission or offered worthless, pathetic, but well-intended advice. He'd turned on her. He'd judged. He had presumed to know what it was like to live her life, walk in her shoes. He'd sent her away, allowing her to come back only when she had changed her ways. Yet, day after day, he'd accepted, consoled, tolerated, even condoned what others had done.

She listened to her father promise to forgive others, yet he never fully forgave her. She watched as her father hugged and consoled sinners and wanderers. They were lost sheep. They were wayward. She was an embarrassment.

Her drug use had started out as recreational until college had opened her eyes to new drugs, new usages. One world destroyed another, and before she knew it, she'd been under the constant scrutiny of her father once again. Curiosity had lured her back to her listening post. She'd wanted to know what her father had to say to others while he'd been berating and chastising her. She'd expected the same heavy hand. Tough love, he'd called it. But it hadn't been the same at all. Things about Travis Miles, Johnny Vargus, Tom Jackson, William McKinley, Amber Hirsh, and Angela Wyck that had knocked her socks off hadn't raised an eyebrow with Pastor Tyree. His own flesh and blood had smoked some dope and gotten busted, and he'd sent her away, claiming she'd dishonored him.

Judge not, lest ye be judged.

What was the difference between a wayward sheep and a lost sheep? How could a disgraced lamb ever return?

Judge not, lest ye be judged.

It was a saying that went through her head a lot. As well as the opinion that her father seemed to misinterpret the Bible . . . a lot. Everything was for the church, for God, for father.

Since her mother's death, Pastor Tyree practically lived in the church, devoting his time, energy, love, body, and soul to the church. Monica managed high school, the household, her homework, and various duties at the church for her father. He was her biological father, but he served as a father to his flock. He was quick to forgive them so that they would come back. She said that once to his face and he balked, but she spoke the truth. No pastor wants a flock filled with criminals and deviants, so he washed away their sins. Wasn't that what religion was about—return business? Yet he turned her out.

"Everything is connected," she'd whispered into the phone.

She'd called Theresa Franks at *The Recorder* and left hints. It delighted Monica to no end. The tease was on. Each time, Theresa begged to know who was calling but followed her leads blindly and faithfully.

Ahh, the faith of the new flock.

The more Pastor Tyree agonized over his congregation, wishing and blessing their problems away, the more Monica kept Theresa guessing. As much as her father wanted the sins to die away, she wanted them on the front page.

Judge not, lest ye be judged.

"If only the dog could talk," she'd teased Theresa.

"What? What dog?" Theresa had asked and Monica had giggled. "What does that mean? Who is this?" When Theresa had demanded answers, Monica had hung up. She couldn't chance that Theresa had figured out who she was, or possibly put a tap on the phone to trace the calls.

CHAPTER THIRTY-ONE

Joseph Epstein was the author. I secretly wondered if he was any relation to the Epsteins here in Granby, but it's not the kind of thing you can do, walk up to the only Jewish fella in town and ask if he's any relation to a famous Jewish person. Last time I checked, there were a whole lot of Jewish folks with a whole lot of different names. This Epstein, however, had written a book, *Snobbery: The American Version,* which was an introspective look at how we judge others. The "footholds of snobbery," as he put it, could be anything from food and fashion to schools and shopping. Some books you just muddled through for the grade, but this was one of those books that stuck with me, and one of the few that I kept on my bookshelf even after I was done with college.

I often wondered how Epstein would have viewed a small town like Granby. He was from the big city, yet he nailed it. He succinctly tagged how people want and need to one-up each other—that need to know that their church or their car or their school is better than someone else's.

Now that I had a kid, I could see that parents were the worst. They bragged about their kids, making sure everyone knew and appreciated how much smarter or better behaved their kid was. Ella was just entering nursery school age, and already, comparisons were being drawn. I refused to get pulled into that game, but Momma was already there. She always had some story to tell about how she and Ella—or Lily—were in the park or at the store, and so-and-so's kid was acting up, but not Lily. Oh no, she was perfect. While Momma wasn't too far off the mark on that one, I tried to refrain from judging other, less-than-perfect children.

Instead, I leaned back against my chair, propped my feet up on the windowsill, and stared out into the street. I had full view, a rarity when Tammi was in the office since she swore that when I opened the blinds fully, it created a flurry of dust particles that aggravated her sensitive sinus cavities. This afternoon, however, the Texas Republican Women's meeting was in full swing at the church, so I had the office to myself.

I thought about how to run the next story. No one denied the Griffin garage idiots' role in the porta potty theft. They were arguing charges that they assaulted anyone, however. It didn't appear that charges would stick since the Garcia fellow had all but disappeared and the other workers were pretending not to know anything. I had inside information that Milford East was a raging pervert, but because of Linda, I couldn't say a word. Most worrisome was the fact that there appeared to be a real link to James Otis. What were the odds that both Garcia and James were dragged?

I was lost in my own world, trying to make the connection between child pornography online and the death of James Otis when Ryan Whatley came in, causing the bell over the door to tinkle. I jumped in my chair.

"Hey," he said, halfway in, halfway out of the doorway. He looked around for a moment then back to me. "You chase everyone out?"

"They're at a Republican Women's meeting," I answered, and he laughed.

"You *did* chase 'em out." He stepped the rest of the way in and sidled up to my desk. "She say when they'd be back?"

Tammi Whatley said a lot of things. She talked *ad nauseam* about the mission of the Republican Women's organization, how they were going to help Granby, what they were going to do, and somewhere in there, I'm sure she mentioned when they would be back. I wasn't listening, but I didn't tell her son that.

Instead, I smiled and shrugged. "Lots of things need fixin' around here. Could be a while before they get back."

"With Tammi Whatley at the helm, God help us all." He smiled, took a seat by my desk, and seemed to study my face for a few minutes.

It was a mystery how Ryan Whatley was Tammi's son. He was her polar opposite. As a kid, he had been kind of a punk. He was a rich kid who wasn't shy about showing off new toys, but he grew up. In high school, he'd branched out, made new friends, and had been well liked.

She was uptight, pretentious, judgmental, and obvious. Every statement she made, every gesture she gave, everything that she purchased—it was all for effect. Since Charles Whatley owned the paper, Tammi theorized they were the most influential couple in town. They had one of the biggest homes, prettiest landscaping, and nicest cars. She had the best kid. The most organized, levelheaded, and successful kid. The joke in town was that when Ryan graduated from Texas Tech, we'd all get a degree because the townsfolk had been with him every step of the way. We knew what classes he took, how he did, who he dated, what his electives were, and what recreational sports he played. We knew too much.

To *know* Ryan rather than knowing *of* him, however, wasn't the same thing. He was quiet, humble, funny, and sincere—the classic guy next door. He no longer had a snobby bone in his body, and to his credit, he was loyal. While he was often embarrassed by his mother's behavior, he never spoke against her. He was polite and courteous, and he mastered the art of keeping a healthy distance from his mother's comments so no one really blamed him for her words or little acts of unkindness.

Though it pained me to admit it, Tammi was right. He was a great kid.

When the phone rang, I lifted a finger, signaling him to hold on, and spoke into the phone, "*Recorder*, Theresa Franks speaking."

"Everything is connected."

I snapped to, jerking up in my chair and allowing my feet to slam down to the floor.

I know this voice.

It was driving me crazy. After the last phone call, I went through the phone book, read each female name, and tried to recall what she sounded like. I ruled out senior citizens, those with accents, and close friends.

Ryan cocked his head as if to ask if everything was okay.

"What is?" I wouldn't ask the obvious. Her voice was so familiar. I knew it would come to me. Any moment, I was sure, the light bulb would go off. I knew the voice. I *knew* I knew the voice. "What's connected?"

She chuckled. "If only the dog could talk."

"What dog?" I was almost pleading and I was frustrated. *Dammit!* I knew almost every person in town, but I knew I'd had more than a casual "hello" conversation with this person. "What does that mean?"

Again, she just giggled. It was almost childlike.

I couldn't stand myself, but I had to ask. "Who is this?"

The only answer was a click.

"Man!" I threw my head back against the back of my chair, covering my face. "Argh! I can't believe this!"

"What? What is it?" Ryan knocked impatiently on the desk, trying to get my attention.

"Geez. This . . . this person, this woman keeps calling me and giving me little tips or bits of riddles about this case." I was sure I knew the voice.

Ryan looked confused. "What? You mean about James?" he asked.

"Yeah, like telling me that everything is connected, that I needed to know about Milford East, and just now, that it's too bad the dog couldn't talk. Dog?" I tossed my hands out in an exaggerated, frustrated motion. "What dog?"

Ryan poked his bottom lip out and scowled for a moment. "You don't know who that was?" he asked, and I shook my head.

Not a clue. I was about to say I knew the voice but let it go. It was driving me crazy.

"Was there a dog out there at . . . you know, the night that that happened?" Ryan asked the same questions I had, trying to decipher that clue.

"No. No, I mean, the only dog I can think about is Bubba Peters's." Again, Ryan looked confused. "You know, his garage was broken into and his dog, um, Brutus, was killed."

"I didn't know that," Ryan said.

"He's the only dog that comes to mind." I met Ryan's gaze, and we stared at each other as if the answers would appear on our faces. I had nothing and shrugged. "If only the dog could talk." I couldn't decide how that piece fit in the puzzle.

Somewhere in the background, sirens screamed.

"Man." Ryan laughed, though it seemed forced. "This town isn't what it used to be. To think I used to be bored out of my mind here. Now"—he motioned outside to the sounds of sirens—"it's one thing after another."

"How much longer you gonna be around?" I asked.

"Well, I wasn't going to go back for another couple of weeks, but I'm thinking about going in a couple of days."

I nodded. It was part of growing up, I knew. We spent our teenage years rebelling against the consistency of small-town living, yet when Granby got turned on its head, it didn't feel right.

"Yeah, I guess if I could leave, I would, too," I said.

"Naw, not you," he teased, relaxing a little more. "You're our ace reporter. Mom's been keeping me up on all your work. You're quite the go-getter, Thia. Probably the best reporter this little town's ever known."

Only later would I wonder if that meant I'd received praise from Tammi at the Whatley dinner table.

I nodded absentmindedly, still wondering about the dog. And that voice.

The phone rang again.

"*Recorder*," I said. I wasn't feeling friendly and Ryan stood to leave, starting to give me a little wave. It was Momma. No doubt another Lily story . . .

"Ms. Riley shot Bubba!" Momma yelled into the phone.

"What?" I jumped to my feet and then looked up at Ryan in disbelief. "Ms. Riley shot Bubba Peters."

CHAPTER THIRTY-TWO

"So, let me get this straight," Officer Wolfe said, sticking out a hip, and leaning her clipboard against it. "Was Ms. Riley shootin' at the squirrel or the nut?" The corner of her mouth twitched, and she seemed to be fighting the urge to grin.

"Tina Wolfe!" Cecilia snapped. "If you think for one minute—" She bit her lip to hold back the tears. "This isn't the least bit funny!" she cried, the blood still on her hands, shirt, and face now smeared where she continued to wipe her eyes and nose. What appeared to be a bloody murder scene was, in reality, just a flesh wound. Bubba was going to be just fine.

"He's been grazed. That's all," Fox said, kneeling next to Bubba, and throwing cautionary glances toward Wolfe. Cici was almost hysterical, and as usual, Wolfe didn't know when to stop. "He's going to hurt for a while but—"

"Aw, hell," Wolfe said. "He'll be back to picking through people's trash in no time."

"Shut up, Tina! I'm not kidding. This could have been a tragedy."

Cici covered her face with her bloodied hands.

Fox made a jabbing motion for Wolfe to put a comforting arm around Cici, and for a moment, Wolfe shook her head and crossed her arms. While Bubba was loaded into the ambulance to be taken to the hospital, Fox made continued hugging motions at Wolfe until Wolfe rolled her eyes and awkwardly gave a pat, pat, pat to Cici's shoulder.

"Oh, Cici, lighten up. He's lucky. Coulda been a lot worse. That's the way to look at it. Hell, this is nothing. He's going to be fine."

"I just don't think you should stand around making jokes when a man's been shot," Cici scolded, and Wolfe shrugged.

Fox looked across the street and saw Hatch and Fitz speaking to a visibly upset Ms. Riley. The woman wasn't dealing with a full deck as it was. Shooting Bubba Peters could send her over the edge, and Wolfe seemed almost giddy at the thought of it all.

Fox watched as Hatch nodded and patted Ms. Riley on the shoulders. They'd confiscated her gun and given her a ticket for illegal discharge of a firearm in the city limits, but it was a wrist slap. Everyone knew Ms. Riley didn't have a menacing bone in her brittle little body. She just had it bad for squirrels. But Fox also knew there would be a hysterically funny report from Fitz and Hatch regarding Ms. Riley and the squirrel shooting and she couldn't wait. They only needed to tie things up with Cici and Bubba's truck. While Wolfe continued to give harder than necessary pats to Cici's backside, Fox motioned to the truck.

"Why don't you be useful and drive Bubba's truck back to his place," Wolfe said to Cici. "We'll follow, bring you back."

Cici sniffed.

"We'll take you on up to the hospital if you'd like," Wolfe mumbled, and Cici looked at her.

Wolfe's voice sounded so sweet that it caused Fox to look up. Fox knew Wolfe. Fox knew that voice.

"You could crawl onto his gurney, and you guys could make out."

Cici narrowed her eyes and put her hands on her hips. "You know what I heard, Tina? I heard that you've been reprimanded and might have to take sensitivity classes." She smirked when she saw Wolfe's face grow serious. "I'm thinkin' just one more phone call to Chief Teague might be the one vote to put it over the edge."

Fox laughed.

"Aw, now, Cici. You don't need to be goin' off and doing something like that. I was just kidding." She shrugged and motioned Cecilia to follow her to Bubba Peters's truck. Wolfe peered into the truck, nodding to herself. "Keys are still in the ignition. You up for taking it over?" Cici nodded and climbed into the cab.

Fox laughed again as an unusually somber Wolfe gave a pat to the side of the truck and headed back toward Fox but then stopped.

Wolfe's head cocked to the side, and she looked around the scene once more. "Well, now that's curious," she said. "You say he was shot over there, by the tree?" Wolfe asked over her shoulder.

Cici poked her head out of the truck. "Yeah, why?"

"Probably nothing. There's blood here in the truck."

"Well," Cici opened the door and hopped out. She stood on her tiptoes next to Wolfe and peered over into the bed of the truck. "He probably cut himself," she said. "He's always moving glass and metal things. He just probably—"

On the inside wall of the bed, flush against the wall, was a white, fiberglass, saucer-shaped object, covered with blood.

"Hey, Foxie! Uh, you wanna come here for a second?" It was the tone of Wolfe's voice that made Fox move.

Wolfe found something.

The sun was in full bloom, just the kind of day Wolfe quite vocally hated. Between their three-inch-wide standard issue belt, the chest protectors, and the navy-blue uniform soaking up the sun's rays, Wolfe figured they endured three times the heat as civilians. It had to be over ninety degrees. Humidity—one hundred percent. Cecilia's face had started to slide about fifteen minutes ago, and Fox could feel sweat trickling down her back and neck, but staring into the back of Bubba Peters's truck, Fox saw Cici hug herself and she felt an icy dread.

"You know those deep grooves in the ground at the crime scene, you know, where James Otis was killed?" Wolfe asked.

Fox nodded as her eyebrows drew together, first studying Cecilia's face then Wolfe's. Taking the last step to edge of the truck bed, her gaze followed theirs, and she finally saw the blood-splattered object.

"I think we're looking at the very thing that made those grooves," Wolfe said. Her voice was monotone. Instinctively, she stepped back, taking Cici with her.

Fox copied her, not wanting to contaminate the truck any further. As she did, she blew out a whistle.

"What are you saying?" Cici was stunned.

"I'm saying, this could be the murder weapon, Cici. This could be what we've been looking for."

█ █ █

It wasn't here. He needed to find it. Lives depended on it. Certainly *a* life.

The damned dog. He hadn't meant to kill it, but when the dog had broken free, when it had lunged, he'd had no choice but to protect himself. Then he'd panicked and run. There had been so much noise. And blood.

His head was pounding now, and it felt like he was suffocating. It was such a simple task. *Find it, destroy it.* Without the evidence, there was no way to prove anything. The 911 call had been made with James's own phone. He'd already found the keychain. It was a simple cleanup job, and he couldn't even get that right.

█ █ █

Everything had spiraled out of control. Nothing was as it seemed.

"You don't know me."

It was her only clear thought. Funny thing, since everyone in town believed they knew her so well. But they didn't. They didn't know at all.

Her eyes were swollen from crying, and she knew she couldn't go out in public. She was a wreck, but he would be calling soon.

She wrung her hands then bit at her nails, a habit she had long broken but was taking up again.

If she didn't answer, he might make good on his threats. He had pictures. He had power. He could make her already shitty little life unbearable. Each time she went to him, she made it worse, but she didn't know what else to do. So she went, half zombie, half slave, she went.

CHAPTER THIRTY-THREE

Chief Teague's face darkened as he slammed down the phone. His mood had been foul from the start. At breakfast, his bright, inquisitive, fourteen-year-old daughter had asked him if it was true that he'd gotten the job as Chief of Police due to Affirmative Action.

He'd sputtered over his coffee then laughed. "Who told you that?"

It was something she'd just heard, she said.

Initially, he explained what Affirmative Action was; how it came about and how, in principle, it was supposed to work. He'd pointed out that there were certainly cases of people hired for a job they were not qualified for, but he was also quick to point out, there were plenty of whites who also held positions they did not deserve. In his case, he was more than happy to list his education and experience. He dared anyone to question his place as Chief of Police.

She'd seemed satisfied, but having to defend himself first thing had soured his morning.

It had also been a reminder that his leadership was in question. The James Otis case was about to bust wide open. Three white men were to be arrested on charges of capital murder in his small town. The same men who had allegedly dragged a Mexican migrant worker almost to death. Alleged because the Mexican—*What was his name? Garcia*—Garcia had disappeared, and no one from the Paradise Park or Roy Herdman's crew had been willing to talk, but Fox and Wolfe had uncovered what was believed to be the weapon used in the dragging death of James Otis.

Even before the find, he'd felt it. It was something they didn't teach in law enforcement or at the academy, but a good cop knew. Call it the full moon, changing of seasons—whatever the reasons—there were certain times of the year when human beings lost their minds. He'd been feeling it for some time, and he knew there would be no stopping it.

Chief Teague had issued one order. "Let's keep this quiet." He wanted to do this quietly and quickly.

The facts were simple. The fiberglass found in Teddy Peters's truck was a missing top to a porta potty. The porta potty was one stolen from Shelby Harrelson's property by Milford East, Willie Strictland, and Roland Wyck. The impressions in the ground at the crime scene matched the grooves and pattern of the fiberglass top. Most damaging, the blood on the fiberglass did belong to James Otis.

Almost immediately, they had cleared Peters from any wrongdoing. Although it was vexing that he'd not contacted the police about the bloody fiberglass, Peters claimed to have found it on the side of the road at dusk and picked it up, thinking that he would alert Ms. Harrelson about his find. He was unaware of any stories of Milford East stealing the porta potties. His defense was that he'd forgotten about it.

Had he been anyone but Teddy Peters, the chief might have been more suspicious, but he was a bit of a social outcast. It was plausible that the Granby grapevine had not reached Peters's ears.

Shelby Harrelson had confirmed that it was, in fact, a piece of one of her porta potties. Unlike the Mexican workers, she was ready and most willing to press charges against East and the boys.

The more charges, the better chance they'll stick.

He could only imagine what a circus this town would become if he let it. Milford East had murdered James Otis. It would spread like a brush fire, sweeping everyone into it if he wasn't careful.

"Chief!" Francis yelled. "You better get over to Griffin's Garage."

"What's going on?" Even as he asked, he moved to his feet and the phone cord caught the Styrofoam cup and spilled coffee all over his desk.

"It's Tasha Williams. Fox called it in. Sounds bad. Sounds like the whole town is out there, but Tasha's out there trying to beat the crap out of Milford East."

He groaned, making a few futile dabs at his desk with a wad of tissues.

"And Shea Griffin's there, too. He's making citizen's arrests!"

"For hell's sakes!" Chief Teague dropped the soggy tissues and made a run for the door. He jerked it open and slammed into Dr. Randy Hirsh. They bounced against one another, hitting stomach to stomach.

"Well, damn, Chief," Doc Hirsh said in his slow, friendly manner. "Looks like I caught you in the middle of somethun."

Chief Teague nodded his head eagerly, wanting to be pleasant but also wanting to get the Doc out of his way. "Well, it's not good," Teague mused, scooting around the Doc. "You okay?" He really didn't have time to hear the answer.

"Good enough," Doc said. "But I need to report a . . . damn, I just hate to even say this, but I need to report some stolen medications."

Teague fumbled with the door for a moment, caught off guard. He turned to assign an officer only to find an empty squad room, and he winced.

On cue, Francis radioed Fox. "Hang on," she instructed Fox.

Teague could hear Fox yelling something back. It was bad. Whatever was happening, it was bad. He licked his lips.

"Stolen?" His eyes darted around again. "What's stolen?" Chief Teague forced himself to slow down and look the Doc in the eyes.

"Yup. I've been thinking somethun was off for a while now. Didn't want to have to own up to it. I hate to think it's any of my people. But I need to report it. You know, in case of an audit or anything."

"Look. Can I . . . can this wait for about an hour? I'll send someone out to your place. Will that be okay?" Chief Teague was almost hopping from foot to foot.

Teague heard Francis attempt an explanation as he ran through the door. "This whole town's about to blow." She radioed back to Fox, "The chief is on his way."

▮▮▮

While every village has its idiot, our town has a posse—our own mini metroplex of morons—and they were all in attendance. I stepped out of the office to find Milford East, Willie Strictland, and Shea Griffin standing side by side at Griffin's Garage. Shea was yelling at what appeared to be no one in particular. Behind them and off to the left was Roland and his father, David. David Wyck was in a shoving match with Terrell Whitehead.

My pace quickened. The last time I'd seen Terrell had been at James's funeral and he'd been *very* angry. It didn't look as if that had changed a bit. Melvin Sparks and Jeff Hanson stood behind Terrell, apparently ready to back that anger up. David Wyck appeared to be protecting his son. Roland seemed to be in some state of shock, his mouth hanging slightly open as he looked around.

When I saw Tasha with Darion still balanced on her hip, I broke into a run. Angela the-skank-whoremonger Wyck was about to come to blows with Tasha. Even from a distance, I could hear Angela screaming the most vile, degrading things. She was calling her every racial slur you could imagine. This deplorable white woman, this piece of complete trash—a person who cheated the government, cheated her townspeople, and cheated her family any chance she got—was calling Tasha Williams names. Bad names. Unjust and cruel names.

I didn't even look when I crossed the street. I ran straight into the mob, ignoring the police as they dragged people off each other. Vaguely, I heard Tina Wolfe yelling commands. I forged ahead with only Tasha and Darion in my sights.

Tears streamed down Tasha's cheeks as Angela screamed at her, and just as I got within arm's reach, Tasha reached out and slapped Angela's face.

More names.

I snatched Darion just in time, and for the briefest of moments, it registered on Tasha's face who had him, and she gave me a tiny, almost relieved smile.

Oh, it's on now!

Say what you will. Call it racist if you want, I don't care. I know what I know. Black girls can fight.

I remembered a time in high school when we'd played a football game about forty miles away. As we had walked back to our cars, some girls had stepped out to voice their issue with us. It had bothered them, apparently, that we were either black *Uncle Toms* or white *wannabes*. Before I'd known it, Tasha had been in the middle of it. It had been the first honest-to-goodness girl fight I'd ever seen, and Tasha had been like a wild tiger—all claws. I'd realized just how stupid the term "cat fight" was because this was not some hair-pulling rout. It had been a full-blown WWF throw down, winner take all. Tasha had done enough damage on her own to get suspended from school and earn the reputation as "Wild Thang" for years to come.

Beefy Angela may have had some forty or fifty pounds on Tasha, but I knew who would win this one. I just didn't want Darion near it.

From the moment I grabbed him, I cradled him up against my chest and began talking—babbling actually. My voice was unnaturally high as I talked about cartoons and what Ella liked and wouldn't he like to see my office, and oh, how I'd missed him. Could I have a hug? Could he say his name for me? My mind was racing as I tried to jig-jag through the crowds and back to my office.

"What is *he* doing here?" I hadn't even noticed Tammi, but there she was, scowling at us behind the front desk.

"Well," I said in a super happy, high-pitched voice. I was a Botox experiment gone bad, my eyebrows at their absolute highest point and frozen there. "His momma is otherwise disposed soooo . . . we thought we would come in here and . . . peekaboo."

A brilliant, megawatt smile that consisted of all three teeth illuminated Darion's face, and he gave a low, infectious giggle.

Tammi opened her mouth, all prepped to give her expert opinion, when LeAnn flung the front door open. "My stars! You wouldn't believe . . . oh!" She let out a squeal, throwing one hand to the side of her face. "They're arresting Milford East and Willie Strictland and Roland Wyck for murder!"

"What?" Tammi's mouth fell open.

"Oh, it's crazy. The boys aren't fighting it, but David Wyck's gone plumb insane. He's screaming at everyone, and Shea Griffin was tryin' to quiet him, but then he threw him up against the side of the tires like he was going to arrest him and . . ." She made another indiscernible noise. "Tasha Williams is beating up Angela Wyck. Oh my! They're rolling around on the ground!"

I didn't know if Darion could actually process that Mommy was rolling around on the ground, but I knew that people just didn't give enough credit to little kids.

"Peekaboo!" I said, speaking loudly but happily. Darion had looked at the door, watching LeAnn with concerned eyes but snapped his attention back to me again, smile in place.

"Rosa Fox is trying to . . . oh dear Lord! She was trying to pull Tasha off and she got, I don't know, kicked or something."

"What in the blue blazes is going on?" Tammi shot to her feet and scurried herself around the desk. "Thia, you should be down there."

"Can't."

"They're arresting Ford and 'em." Vicky Jackson ran through the back of the office, having come in from the back parking lot. "Tammi, Tammi!"

"Peeka-*who*?"

Grin.

"Peeka-*you*!"

Vicky looked confused when she saw me sitting at my desk, playing with Darion Otis, but she kept on going, a human train chugging through the office, headed straight for the front door. "Look it! Look it! The Mexicans heard about it and came in. Look, they're here to see Ford and 'em get arrested!" She sounded beside herself.

"Who is that?" Tammi asked excitedly, and I could see her bobbing and weaving around on the front walk, trying to see through the melee of people and squad cars. "That's Hector Lopez. Oh, he's always hated Ford!" she exclaimed as though Hector had somehow arranged all this.

"Uh-oh," I frowned at Darion. "Did you . . ." I sniffed, and he looked slightly worried ". . . did you . . . Oh no!"

More giggles.

"Peekaboo! Not peeka-*pooh*!" I contorted my face, and Darion chortled with certain delight.

"Oh! Tasha just punched Angela in the face! My word!"

"Yay!" I clapped Darion's little hands together. "Mommy's fighting evil!"

"Thia!"

"Yay! Mommy's fighting evil!" I said again in a low, almost

inaudible whisper.

"Thia! You need to come out here!" Tammi was all a dither. There was no way she was going to go down there and be in the mix of such riffraff, but she wanted the story.

"Don't worry!" My voice rose a little more than I meant to allow it, and I gave another reassuring smile to Darion. "I'll—"

I'm not sure which I heard first—the crash or the three of them, as they stood gawking at the riot, scream.

CHAPTER THIRTY-FOUR

She was off. That was the best way to put it. She could walk, talk, drive, all that. She wasn't tired. She wasn't wired. She wasn't dizzy or stoned. She was just . . . off.

When her father had asked her to do this job, she hadn't been particularly thrilled about it, but she hadn't minded either. Mrs. Vargus was good people, not like some of the others.

She and Mrs. Vargus had a lot in common, truth be told. They'd both been given a raw deal in the family department. Both had been the victims of abuse, abandoned by their mothers in one fashion or another, and both had been forced to play nice and pretend like their life was okay when, in reality, it stank. What she'd liked most about Mrs. Vargus, however, was she'd been a virtual shut-in. Monica was willing to wager Mrs. Vargus hadn't known much about her past, and that gave Monica a freedom she'd rarely felt with anyone else.

People were polite enough. They had to be. The good father was pastor of the main church in town. It was important that he keep his flock in good standing. In return, it was important to his flock that he liked them. Politics. Everything was politics. But Mrs. Vargus seemed to be a person who avoided such things. She was what she was, and Monica respected that. She did not, however, respect Johnny Vargus, making it all the worse that he chose to ride with them this day.

She decided that was why she was off. She didn't like having him sitting next to her. The abuser. Just the way he took the front seat, never asking his wife or opening her car door as she climbed into the back seat. She wasn't a partner to him but an extension. There was a subtle difference, and Monica felt very uneasy around him. With Johnny Vargus in the car, there was complete silence, and it had been that way the entire drive into town.

"What in the world?" Mrs. Vargus asked, leaning forward in her seat. She pointed to be sure everyone saw what she saw. But there was no missing it.

Monica saw Chief Teague first. In fact, she saw what looked to be all the police, along with Travis Miles, Jared Durham, Shea Griffin, and David Wyck going nuts. Milford East looked like he was being handcuffed, and there were what seemed to be half a dozen other fights. She recognized some of the Paradise Park residents who came into town from time to time, and Terrell Whitehead was rolling around with someone. It seemed as though all the storekeepers were standing outside their venues, watching.

Then she saw him. He was rushing toward the scene. He was rushing in to save the day. She was surprised, yet not at all surprised, to see him. She hadn't formulated a thought beyond that when everything went black.

▉ ▉ ▉

By the time Wolfe and Fox arrived on the scene, complete madness had overtaken Granby. While Frankie Larson was able to deal with the victims, Fox was given an assessment of what happened by a number of witnesses.

Monica was unconscious. The air bag had deployed, bruising her chest and shoulders. It looked as if it may have also bounced her off the headrest and knocked her head against the driver's side window. The glass had given to the impact, shattering around the door.

At first glance, it appeared as though Johnny Vargus was dead. He'd been pinned between the crushed dashboard of Monica Tyree's car and Travis Miles's pickup. Miles had had some fence posts in the back of his truck—posts that ran right through the car, almost shredding it in half. It was hard to know what the damage actually was. Several men tugged at Johnny's car door, trying to get to him, to see if he was still alive. Someone else had yelled to call the firehouse; they were going to need the Jaws of Life to get Johnny out. The urgency increased when the old man moaned.

In the midst of the hysteria and utter confusion, Gail Vargus simply unbuckled her seat belt, opened her door, and stepped out. For a moment, everyone ceased to move. Open mouths, blank stares, disbelief, and astonishment ruled. Then she collapsed into the arms of Terrell Whitehead.

There was plenty of speculation regarding the accident with Monica at the wheel.

She's probably stoned.

That one's no good.

Why would anyone get in a car with her? She's just an accident waiting to happen.

In the midst of screaming sirens, pushing and shoving for directions on how to get Johnny out, taking care of Ms. Vargus, and tending to Monica Tyree, Fox took a quick breath as the police department got a crude but brief reprieve from the mob fight. Suddenly, the citizens of this small town were working together. Even David Wyck was over by the accident, working to get Johnny Vargus free.

"Get 'em out of here," Chief Teague ordered.

By the time Fox and Wolfe had processed their prisoners, both women were drenched in sweat. Between the heat and impromptu wrestling match in the middle of Main Street, they'd had themselves quite a workout.

Rain, someone had said on more than one occasion, would be nice. They were in the middle of a drought that just made everything seem that much hotter and more stifling.

"We're innocent," Ford shouted from the jail.

"Ah, shut up!" Wolfe yelled back, removing her uniform top.

She'd been warned about disrobing in the middle of the station house, but she didn't care, and on this day, Fox was in full agreement. It was too damned hot to abide by rules. In fact, Fox joined her partner and slipped her shirt over the back of her chair to dry and peeled out of her chest protector. Both women inhaled with satisfaction.

"Oh, so much better. I can breathe," Wolfe said. Her white T-shirt clung to her body, soaked in sweat.

"But we're innocent! You've got the wrong—"

"Shut up, Ford!" Wolfe yelled back. "I'll bet we lost five pounds each. That was intense."

"Yeah, I'm okay with not doin' that again anytime soon," Fox said, not looking up. She was already busy typing up the reports. Even as she prepared her thoughts, she chuckled. "Heck of a day, wouldn't you say?" She decided to prepare citations in order of the seriousness of the fights. Tasha Williams would be tops.

"Heck of a *week*," Wolfe said, taking a seat, and plopping her feet on top of her desk, one leg over the other.

Fox pecked out the name Tasha Williams.

Tasha had been in her house when the phone rang.

The police are arresting Milford East for the murder of James Otis.

It was all she'd heard. According to Tasha, she'd grabbed her baby and run into town. A rage she'd never known welled up inside of her. She had told Fox that while she was sure Milford East had killed James, hearing of his arrest had nearly driven her crazy.

As though Milford somehow sensed that Fox was typing up a report that included him, he yelled again from the jail cell, and Wolfe screamed, "Shuddup!" from her seat and then turned back to Fox, grinning.

"Hell, he's big enough to pull a cart and shit in the streets, and about that smart, too, but who knew what a big mouth he had?"

Fox laughed, nodded, and continued to type.

Without thought, without plan, Tasha had gone to see ol' Ford be arrested. In honor of James, she had wanted to see it. But when she'd gotten there and had seen people arguing with the police, when she'd heard Milford make some smart remark about James, she'd snapped.

She told Fox that if she'd ever questioned whether James's attack was racially motivated, now she knew. The way Milford responded, as though James was somehow less than Ford East, brought her to an enraged frenzy, and then she was in the middle of it. She wanted to tear out his hair, and that of Willie and Roland. Next thing she knew, the biggest piece of trash, Angela Wyck, was in her face. Screaming.

Fox's fingers paused over the keys, thinking about Tasha. She'd actively disobeyed a police command to stand down. In fact, many could argue that Tasha had incited much of the rioting and possibly caused the accident with Monica Tyree.

". . . are you even listening to me?" Wolfe suddenly asked.

Fox looked up startled. "Huh?"

"Crap. You're not even—"

"We didn't do it. We weren't even there!" Willie Strictland chimed in to the wails of protests from the jail. Their voices bounced and echoed down the hallway into the main room.

Fitz and Hatch walked into the station looking sweaty and exhausted. Like Wolfe and Fox, they instantly began to peel off clothing.

"You boys shut up in there before I send Fitzie in to do a cavity search." Wolfie looked over her shoulder, spinning in her seat. Her grin was huge. "Fitz, when was the last time you did one of 'em? I'll let you start with Milford. You'll lose your entire arm. Shit, we may never see you again." She cackled and slapped her own knee.

Fox went back to her report.

Mercifully, Thia had appeared in the middle of all the chaos. At first, Fox had groaned. Last thing she'd wanted was to have the press nosing in and taking pictures, but Thia had a way about her that Fox had always genuinely liked. Instead of acting like a reporter, she'd snatched Darion Otis from Tasha's arms. And a good thing, too, since it hadn't been two seconds before she and Angela Wyck were rolling around on the ground.

The professional in Fox knew that only trouble could brew from that situation. She wouldn't be the least bit surprised if Angela Wyck sued Tasha Williams for assault. It hadn't mattered that Angela had it coming. Unfortunately, Tasha was the first to strike, and Fox had seen it.

Still, she had so enjoyed watching that white girl get her butt beat.

"You ask Frankie Larson. He knows! He'll vouch for us!" Ford continued to yell from the cell.

"Geez!" Wolfe rolled her eyes, and more to herself than anyone else, she said, "So, how was your week? Well . . . let's see. Sandy Riley shot Teddy Peters, who just happened to have a murder weapon in his truck, but he didn't think it prudent to tell anyone about it. Um, a riot broke out in the middle of Main Street, and Monica Tyree, possibly high on drugs, nearly killed two passengers. Not to mention that we now have to listen to the loudest, most annoying—"

Fox glanced up, intrigued, as Wolfe's diatribe died mid rant. She watched as Tina scanned the contents of her desk. A large manila envelope was perched against her phone. The name Officer Wolfe scrawled across it in heavy black magic marker.

"What the hell is this?" Wolfe picked up the envelope.

Fox watched both Hatch and Fitz exchange glances, smirk, and busy themselves.

No one even remotely pulled off the subtle non-stare as Wolfe opened the envelope and read. Her mouth dropped open, eyebrows shot up.

"What in the hell . . ." She was up on her feet, slamming her seat against the desk. She spun a few circles, as though she were looking for just the right person to ask or vent to.

Fox glanced over to Hatch and Fitz again. Both were smiling. Whatever it was, they were in on it. Fox reached out to her partner, making the *Gimme* gesture with her fingers, but Wolfe was on a rampage.

"What is it?" Fitz asked with feigned worry.

For a moment, Wolfe narrowed her eyes at him. "You know about this?" She waved the papers in her hand, and he pretended to protect himself.

Again, Fox reached out for the envelope.

"You ask Frankie Larson!" It was Roland Wyck who cried out this time. "Ask him. We weren't even there. We got nothing to do with James's murder."

"Shut up!" Wolfe screamed up at the ceiling just as Chief Teague entered with his trademark cowboy swagger—the lone sheriff, pushing through both doors.

His chiefly presence always changed the aura in the room, but Wolfe didn't appear to care. Or notice. Fox braced herself. Teague opened his mouth, as if to ask, then closed it. He knew.

"You know about this? Did you do this, Chief?" Wolfe turned to Teague as if demanding the punch line to this joke. "Sensitivity class?" She almost laughed.

Fox watched Teague and counted silently to ten. She could feel the tension rising from everyone, but her only mission now was to keep Wolfe in check. Fox began to move around her desk toward Wolfe. Teague held up a hand and Fox halted.

"Tina," he said, as if the use of her first name might calm her. "Look. I got three people in the hospital right now—"

"I know. And I'm sorry about that. But—"

"I'd never hurt James. I liked the guy. I never had a problem with the guy. I swear," Roland yelled again.

"Shut up!" Wolfe almost screeched. "Shut up or I swear, I'll come back there and make you wish you'd shut up!"

Chief Teague wagged a finger at her. "Now, see. That's the kind of thing I'm worried about, Wolfie. You can't go around threatening to shoot people or their goats. You can't . . ." He sighed. "You can't threaten prisoners and—" He looked her up and down. "Where is your uniform?

Instinctively, Hatch, Fitz, and Fox all shrank back.

Wolfie turned to her partner and waved the letter she held. "Sensitivity classes. I'm officially required to take *sensitivity classes*. You believe this? Me? Sensitivity classes."

Fox opened her mouth but nothing came out.

This was, everyone knew, long overdue. Ever since she'd thrown a flashlight at Carol Dickson at the Fourth of July parade and made her fall off the float, Ms. Dickson had had it out for Officer Wolfe. She'd made a complaint every chance she'd gotten. Wolfie wasn't helping her own cause, and last week, when she told Ms. Dickson that it was good that she'd taken her sweet time crossing the street and held everyone up because, *we don't want you breakin' a sweat and shedding a pound or two. We like you just the way you are.* That had been the last nail in the coffin.

Fox had warned her. Fox had warned her repeatedly.

"I've got but three things to say to you, Wolfe." Chief Teague found his official voice and it boomed across the room.

No one moved. Smiles faded.

"One. This is not open for discussion. You like your job and wanna keep it, you go to these sensitivity classes. It won't kill you." Wolfe opened her mouth to say something but Teague was fast to shoot up a finger and silence her. His glare seemed to dare her to speak. "Two. Put your uniform on. No one else comes in here and strips. A uniform is to be worn while on duty for a reason. We're all hot. Put it on. And three—"

Wolfe held up her hand, ignoring the fact that everyone else was standing around in sweaty shirtsleeves, too. "Wait," she said, looking back toward the jail cells. "Wait a minute." Hand still held high, she looked at her partner. "Why would we ask Frankie Larson?"

"What?" Fox asked, not following. Fox looked back and forth between Teague and Wolfe.

"Frankie Larson. They keep yelling at us to talk to Frankie, that Frankie can verify that they weren't there on Larson's property when James was killed. How would Frankie Larson know where they were? And," Wolfe let her hand drop, stood, and headed back toward the jail, "what would Frankie Larson know about James's death?"

All eyes watched as Wolfe disappeared down the corridor, headed back to Milford East, Willie Strictland, and Roland Wyck.

"And three . . ." Chief Teague counted off on his fingers, speaking to everyone except the one person he was talking to. "We need for you to follow the rules and be part of the team because we can't afford to lose you. You're a good cop. A little wild, a little temperamental, a little hard to manage, but you're a good cop."

CHAPTER THIRTY-FIVE

Our big date was delayed a few hours following the town brawl and the time it took for Frankie to process his patients at the hospital. It had given me just enough of the day to take care of Darion, get him dropped off with Tasha's mother, and get Ella picked up before we met back up. It was then that Frankie appeared with one rule *No phones.*

What a world we live in that the mere thought of no phones sent me into a near panic.

I protested. "But what if something happens with Ella?"

"Okay. You can leave it in the car, but no phones in the park," Frankie said, and I found it rather romantic until the real reason came out., "Besides, I lost mine at the wreck so it's only fair."

Somewhere between pulling victims from the crash and dodging fights, Frankie had dropped his phone and couldn't find it. "It's only fair." He grinned, and I agreed.

Granby Memorial Park, which by any other standards would have been called a throwback to the 1950s, was the only park in town. We didn't have fancy playground equipment with bright colors, wide plastic slides, or wood chips surrounding all landing surfaces. We didn't have the ever-popular wood frames with mock castles, ships, and trains.

We had one narrow, ten-foot slide, from which a kid could easily fall over the side. However, in the history of the park, no kid was ever dopey enough to do it, or if he was, no parent was dopey enough to complain about his kid being dopey enough to do so.

We had chain swings with rubber seats and one swing set with pipes for arms that went around rather than back and forth. A larger person could really whip a little kid around, and if their little fingers lost their grip, a body could be flung into the neighboring trees. But again, no one ever had.

The landing surfaces consisted of something called grass . . . oh, and dirt, too. Even the drinking fountain was a relic—an old stone statue with a huge, wide bowl as the catchall for the water. It didn't work, but it didn't matter. It was cool looking.

"Somebody ought to get that thing working again," I said lazily, pointing to the fountain.

"Hmm, sounds like a job for the mighty pen. You could do an article, stir up public interest." He sat up and looked so innocently at me, blinking his eyes in a mock flutter. "Pretend I'm the first person in the park you see. Interview me, interview me!"

I laughed.

Lying next to Frankie Larson on the grass, picking the green blades, watching Ella nap in the shade of the old trees, and talking about our nutty neighbors, Granby felt wonderful.

"So, she's okay?" he asked about Ms. Riley.

"Yeah. I went over this morning to talk to her. She seems distracted. She knows Mr. Peters is going to be okay, but she's a little gun-shy. No pun intended."

He laughed anyway. "I'd still watch myself. I think she's a little out there," he said, and I nodded.

"Don't I know it? I've already told Momma not to let Ella play outside in the front. It just makes me a little nervous. For all I know, she's out in her backyard right now, practicing with her nunchucks or throwing knives."

Ms. Riley had been warned by both Officer Fox and Chief Teague against discharging firearms in town and said she'd be arrested if she did it again, but they didn't know how much she hated that little gray squirrel.

"I think she's pretty harmless," he said absentmindedly. It was a lazy day, and for Frankie, a well-deserved day off. "I mean, unless you're a gray squirrel or Bubba."

"You've been putting in some serious overtime lately," I said.

For a moment neither of us spoke, and I wondered if he was thinking about James as well. Since playing peekaboo with Darion, James had been on my mind a lot. I dreamed about his megawatt smile. However toothless, Darion had his daddy's grin, and it both comforted and saddened me.

"I've been putting in some serious miles, overtime, you name it."

I looked at Ella and watched a small bead of sweat begin to trickle down the side of her face. She scrunched up her face from time to time, stirring from her dreams. She'd be waking soon.

"So, what do you think's going on?" I asked as I rolled onto my back and stared up at the clouds.

"What do ya mean?" Frankie followed my move, and we lay there, shoulder to shoulder.

"When we were in school, nothing ever happened. I mean nothing. Now, it seems like the whole town is going nuts," I said.

"Maybe nothing this big, but there was always stuff going on. We were just too young to know or care about it."

I shrugged, unconvinced.

"You remember when Principal Baxter was busted for screwing around with Ms. Thayer?" He laughed. "Or, when it was first discovered that Monica Tyree was a pothead and all those rumors that there was a drug dealer here in town? Hell, that one even had the police jumping. Judge McKinley was leading the pack."

"Oh, yeah!"

I did remember that one. It had been a big deal. And yet a decade later, everyone, myself included, had forgotten how McKinley had carried on with a court reporter in chambers. There had been plenty of scandalous affairs back then but none this violent, and I said as much.

Frankie sat up, folding his arms around his legs. He sighed. "Yeah. I don't know what to say about that. It does seem like things are getting worse or crazier or something. You know, Monica was high. Stoned. It's crazy, man. Here you think she's all better. Then this."

"How's Ms. Vargus doing?" I asked. It was hard to care too much about Mr. Vargus. I'd known him since I was a kid. He was mean and scary even back then.

"I don't even know how she stood up." He shook his head at the memory of it. "She's got a broken hip. We think she saw it coming and tried to brace her feet against the back seat. Both wrists are broken, so she'll be laid up for a while."

"And Mr. Vargus?"

"Last I heard—two broken legs, broken nose, jaw, and enough bruises and cuts to hurt like hell. From what I hear, he's not exactly been a joy to work with."

"It's weird to think that if there hadn't been that big brouhaha in the middle of the street, she might have been okay. She might have driven Mr. and Mrs. Vargus to the church, and no one would have ever been the wiser."

Frankie shrugged.

"But . . ." I just couldn't shake James from my mind. "It just seems like everything bad happening right now, everyone getting shot, it all has to do with James."

"Oh no. Not again. You promised . . ." Frankie gave me a nudge.

He was right. When he'd asked me to go to the park with Ella, I had promised no interviews, no interrogations, and no tirades about what was happening in town. Frankie didn't know what I knew, though.

"I know, I know," I whined playfully. "But it is. I mean, I can't help it. And . . ." I tried to decide just how much to share with him. Frankie looked slightly disgusted. I didn't want him thinking that I was going on and on just for the sake of a story. "I've been getting calls," I said.

"What do you mean? What kind of calls?"

"Tips. A woman." I gnawed the side of my nail as I automatically started flipping through the list of names and faces in my mind. "Someone I know. I *know* I know her. But I just can't—"

"What? What is she saying to you?" Frankie was sitting straight up now, almost leaning into me.

I was still trying to piece together some of the things she'd said to me. There it was. I *did* know the voice. I gasped.

"What?" He took a hold of my elbow, shaking it slightly, almost commanding that I focus and look at him. "What is it?"

"The voice. It's Monica Tyree." I could have laughed out loud with relief. It had been driving me crazy. "All this time. I *knew* I knew the voice! It's Monica."

"But what did she say? What's she been tipping you off about?" He gave my elbow another little jiggle, refocusing me.

I looked at him, wondering how in the world Monica was connected to what happened to James. For a brief, sickening instant, I remembered all those rumors about drug activities. At the time, we'd all blown it off. There was no way James Otis was involved in drugs. For those of us who knew him, we knew that was a ridiculous scenario.

Ella moved, crying out against the heat, and I knew, the very act of waking up.

I started to move toward her, but Frankie stopped me.

He couldn't stand the suspense. Initially, when he grabbed my arm, it surprised me, but he'd smiled so sweetly. He looked like a little boy, wide-eyed and eager to learn some important news about his birthday surprise.

"What did she tell you?" he asked.

▌▌▌

"Where the hell is Frankie Larson? It's not like this is the big city!"

Fox watched as Wolfe ranted and paced around their cruiser.

They'd put out feelers everywhere and no one seemed to know where Frankie Larson was. She'd called *The Recorder*, hoping to find him, only to learn that Frankie had picked up Thia for a date, also taking the baby along. Where they went, no one seemed to know. How long they'd been gone was also uncertain. Cecilia had been at the house and seemed to think Thia left at noon. But both Vicky Jackson and Tammi Whatley were firm on the fact—with some irritation—that Thia had left late morning.

"What story was she working on?" Wolfe had asked just before she hung up. "Really? Like what?" Wolfe turned to Fox and whispered, "She's got some hot new lead on the James murder."

Fox raised her eyebrows and wondered why this was the first they had heard of it.

Wolfe clicked off and relayed the rest of the conversation and together Fox and Wolfe agreed there was no point in pressing, not with Tammi Whatley eavesdropping. They would have to catch Vicky Jackson when she was alone, and Fox made a mental note of finding Vicky later.

▮▮▮

The Internet—the greatest and worst thing for humankind. It was the beast that brought everything to life. Researching late nights in the library had become almost obsolete. Shopping could be done online. Finding old friends and classmates, getting directions, finding phone numbers, and paying bills could all be done without ever standing up, much less leaving the house. But there were other places you could go as well.

The deepest, darkest passages to fantasy and lust were suddenly open. And for men, men like him, the beast that had remained dormant awakened. He'd lusted from afar, watching the children play, but he had never touched. He'd never even talked to one, he'd just watched.

At night, he could replay in his mind how the children moved, jumped around, and play-tackled each other. He could hear their laughter in his ears. One of innocence, purity, and sweetness. Pure sweetness.

Young boys were left alone so often, walking and talking and completely oblivious to the outside world, and it would be so easy. Just the idea of snatching up one so innocent drove him to wondrous, terrifying feelings that later embarrassed him. It wasn't shame that kept him from acting, if the truth be told, it was the fear of being caught.

It was a package deal, small-town living. Everyone knew everyone's business. Everyone was always watching. You could beat your wife, leave your cattle for dead in times of drought, or drive drunk, and people barely batted an eye. But step out of the box, do something considered perverted, and there would be no forgiveness—not with his neighbors, not with the law. And he knew what happened in prison to men who liked little boys.

Occasionally, when he traveled, he'd stop at the adult stores along certain highways, but even then, he'd had to be careful. Most of the material was heterosexual, but if you knew where to look or how to ask, other material could be made available. For a price. Always, more for the price. There was a certain irony there. You paid more money to get it and would pay so much more if caught.

Then the Internet came. With the wonders of bill paying and shopping and browsing came little boys, all eager and willing to talk. They shared pictures and stories, and people could say whatever they wanted to say. Screw nature versus nurture. There were boys who knew by the age of five that they were different. By twelve, they were ready to talk about it, express their feelings, and—he knew—excite other men.

Some sites offered porn where boys were exploited, and he might have felt bad for them, but he'd been so repressed, so pent up, so isolated for so long, the Internet allowed for a great release. But the beast was the beast. Once unleashed, he couldn't stop to think about others. So he'd poured himself into late-night surfing.

God help him but it was the most amazing and frustrating experience of his life. He could remember the first live feed he'd seen. He'd sucked in his breath, frozen. There, sitting in his room, hovering over the computer, with just the light from the screen illuminating the room, he'd laughed out loud.

A young boy, naked. Performing.

He looked around, almost hopeful to find someone there with him to appreciate it all, but there was no one. It was, oddly enough, the same the feeling he had when he'd been a child watching cartoons. He would see something very funny and comment, but finding he was alone, felt disappointment that no one was with him to share the moment.

When he found chat rooms, it changed his world. He could comment. He could share his feelings, and remarkably, he learned that other men felt the same as he did. There were doctors, lawyers, contractors, teachers, and businessmen who spoke openly. Reality was skewed, and he loved it. He'd even attended some chats where the topic was safety—how not to get caught. How to avoid traps and cons. He knew that as long as he didn't meet anyone in person, he could continue to watch young boys online. He could interact.

Interaction.

His downfall.

Daniel. A boy of twelve. He was young and sweet and naïve. His parents were divorced, his mother distraught and distracted, his father gone. His older sister had gone off to college, so Daniel had befriended the Internet. There, he confessed, he discovered how much he loved attention. He loved getting notes from strangers. At first, it hadn't mattered that they were notes from men, then he realized he liked that they were men.

Initially, their conversations had been relatively innocent. They talked sports, pets, cars, clothes, and television shows. They talked about music and food, and then, little by little, they shared about each other and soon discovered they had a lot in common. Not age, not education and career, not even geographic location, but they felt the same insecurities and the same feelings of uncertainties. It was so easy to forget that Daniel was just twelve.

One might argue that the abundance of pictures of Daniel could and should have reminded him of Daniel's tender age. Instead, they excited him. Daniel sent a picture of himself, leaning back against a tree, his bare chest pale and underdeveloped. His hands were folded behind his head, and he smiled into the camera with a certain seduction. There was one of him in a soccer uniform, one of him petting a puppy, and there was one of him leaning over, shirtless, to take a sip from a garden hose, his mouth open, eager, and ready to take it all in. He looked into the camera, unsmiling, with the eyes of a twenty-year-old man. But it was the picture of Daniel leaning against the tree that he loved most.

CHAPTER THIRTY-SIX

"Die," she whispered, leaning over Monica Tyree's bed. "Why don't you just die."

Monica Tyree had slipped in and out of consciousness since the accident, crying out in pain from injuries the hospital staff couldn't identify. Nothing had been broken, and while a laceration to her head had required fourteen stitches along her hairline, all other injuries had been minor due to the drugs that had been coursing through her system. At the scene of the accident, Monica's injuries had looked worse than those of Mr. or Mrs. Vargus due to all the blood.

Officer Fitz had stated it best. "It was like a rag doll and two china bowls in the car."

The doctors and Pastor Tyree were shocked by the high dosages required to keep Monica pain free. Her body's need for a fix had grown to frightening proportions, and it was decided by the doctors and Pastor Tyree that Monica would remain hospitalized, strapped down, until she could be made clean again.

The problem was the talking, the screaming—a furious unleashing of spiteful, nasty rantings about her hometown, her father, her life, her addiction. She was talking too much and telling too many names. For the most part, Pastor Tyree sat vigil by her side, shushing her more than anything else. He fooled no one. He was more embarrassed than distressed. He was more angry than heartbroken. Only when Monica slept did he leave to shower and to tend to the church.

That was all the opportunity she needed to creep into Monica's room.

"It would make so many people happy if you just croaked," she whispered into Monica's ear. "Die. Just . . . stop breathing," she hissed.

Monica drew in another deep breath.

"Not even your father would miss you," the woman said. She reached for the pillow but hesitated.

"Tell me something I don't know." Monica sighed, her eyes still closed.

The woman gasped.

Monica's eyes fluttered open, struggling against the low but constant dose of morphine. They were weaning her off the drug slowly, but it was hell—shakes, nausea and sweeping feelings of insanity rolling in and out. "But then again, if I died, where would that leave you?"

The woman's mouth fell open.

"You know, I've been meaning to put all this in writing, you know, God forbid, in case something happened to me. I've been talking to Thia. You know, Thia? Up at *The Recorder*? I ought to write up everything and seal it up in an envelope with something like, 'Read in case something should happen to me.' " Monica laughed at the thought. "Yeah, that's what I ought to do. That way the world—well, okay, the town—could know what its sons and daughters have been up to."

"Bitch."

"Well, now," Monica smiled again, "that's not very nice. No one is making you do what you do."

The other woman laughed. "Not making me? Are you kidding?"

"You're just part of the puzzle. That's all. In exchange for my silence." She could tell the other woman was not amused and stood staring at Monica for several seconds. "Come untie me," Monica said.

"Can't."

"Wrong answer." Monica shook her head, her serious expression seemed to worry the other woman.

"You know what I mean. They know I'm in here. If I loosen your straps . . ." She ran her fingers nervously through her hair and Monica studied her face for a moment.

"No, I guess you can't. But you can do something else."

"No," the other woman said. "I can't do this anymore—"

"Oh, I don't think you're in any position to say 'no' to me." Monica looked up and down the other woman's frame. "In fact, I'd say you've got too much on the line."

"I'm going to get caught!"

"Not my problem." Monica shrugged.

"You're never going to stop, are you?" the woman asked, and Monica chuckled. The woman's face flushed bright red as she reached for the pillow once more. "This has to stop!" She moved in, raising her arms when the door opened behind her. She dropped her arms to her sides. "Pastor Tyree."

"Good to see you," he said, nodding, but his eyes revealed his true thoughts. He couldn't imagine why anyone would come to see his friendless daughter.

"Do give Thia my regards," Monica called out as the woman slipped from the room. "Tell her I'll call her soon."

"What was Amber Hirsh doing here?" Pastor Tyree turned to ask his daughter.

▌▌▌

On the other side of town where no one really knew about James Otis or his case, José Moreno was distracted. His reputation as a mechanic had grown, so now they came to him. From time to time, he'd get a call about someone being broken down. In fact, that was how he'd come to work on that truck. He'd seen the blood and he'd pieced the rest of it together. Still, it wasn't his place, he'd decided. He had too much to lose, so he had vowed to stay quiet.

When he returned home that night covered in mud, he showered, threw on a clean white T-shirt and boxers, and climbed into bed with his beautiful, young wife. He studied her perfect frame for what seemed hours while his mind raced. Inside of her grew a baby. His baby.

The plan had been for José, his sister, and mother to join José's brother, Javier, in Texas when there was enough money. The attack on his wife, Sonja, had changed everything. With the approval of family members, the young lovers had set off into the night on a trip that he had all but banished from his memory. He knew Sonja still remembered, but they never spoke of it. What he did remember were the promises he'd made along the journey.

He'd promised her security. He'd promised to be faithful to her, never to hurt her, and to give her babies. He had sworn on his life to be the very best husband and father. After seven grueling months, he'd done everything promised. He found his brother; he bought her a home, married her, and put a baby inside of her. He would protect her at all costs.

While James Otis's death was unfortunate, it had nothing to do with him, and he saw no reason to get involved and risk losing everything. His involvement would not bring James Otis back. He didn't dislike police, but he did not trust them. They had the power to destroy his world. So he remained as respectful and as far away from them as possible. He needed to care only for what was his—his wife and child.

In fact, he had hoped it would all go away. If he didn't talk about it, didn't think about it, didn't share anything he knew or saw, maybe it would all go away. And so he continued with his work and kept to his own business. Each passing day since James Otis's death gave José a sense of relief. As though it were on a calendar, every day that passed was one day further away from problems, and José was content to not talk or think about any of it.

Terrell Whitehead had other ideas.

José stood, wiping his hands on an oil rag, and poked his head from around the hood of the car.

Terrell Whitehead was standing with his back to José, but talking to everyone within earshot. "Yo, man. I'm tellin' ya. I been down there. They got 'em locked up, but nothing's happening."

Everyone was there, and typically, the music would be on, the regulars taking their shots with the horseshoes, talking in their native tongue, smoking and drinking, and talking about their women, work, and politics back home. Instead, they listened as Terrell, who had spent three nights in jail for assault and battery, regaled them with stories of Milford

East, Willie Strictland, and Roland Wyck.

"I'm telling ya, a brother gets killed and Garcia about gets his head ripped off. We know who did it. We know it was them. We all know that!" There were nods while he spoke to the crowd. "But they gonna get off. You watch. They gonna get off."

There was a chorus of mumbling. Someone said something that was quickly translated into English for Terrell.

"That's right. If the cops ain't gonna do something about it, we should. James gets dragged to death, and they put on a good show like they care until all the press goes away. Then don't nobody want to talk about it."

José watched as the group got more and more animated, all thanks in part to the empty beer cans littered around his garbage can. Among the group was a relative of Luis Rodriquez who had just appeared in recent days. Such was the life with migrant workers. People appeared and disappeared without a trace, if they so chose. José didn't know much about the young man but had known he didn't trust him and had said as much to Sonja.

José liked Terrell—a little loud for José's liking, but he was funny, always clowning around and ragging on someone. He was also a live wire. He was always talking about the injustices of being a black man, talking smack about the politics of Mexico, and had comments about the brown skin man versus the black man. Yet José never saw Terrell work. Not once. He always had cash, but never had a blister. To make matters worse, José knew who was responsible.

The decision was made before he'd headed down the driveway.

"We'll go find 'em ourselves," someone said. More nods.

"All you'll find is trouble, my friends," José warned, but no one listened.

"Are they out?" another asked.

José looked around for Javier, wishing that his older brother was there to reason with these young men, but they were all focused on Terrell Whitehead.

"Are they out?" Terrell laughed. "Shit, they made bail before I did!"

CHAPTER THIRTY-SEVEN

Chief Teague groaned, hung up the phone, and let his head fall into his hands. The whole damned world was falling apart, and it was starting with Granby. He couldn't even remember the last time he'd read the national and international news. He had no idea what was going on outside the insanity of Granby.

He hit the speaker button to his intercom. "Francis. Find me Wolfe and Fox."

"They're out, Chief! What's going on?"

"That was Sandy Riley. She's hysterical." He sighed and rocked back into his chair. He did not need this. "Apparently, we've got some practical jokers," he said.

"Jokers?"

"Someone strung up a bunch of stuffed animals, little squirrels, up all over Ms. Riley's tree. She came outside and—"

"Oh no!" Francis's voice crackled over the intercom.

She was laughing, and Chief Teague sighed. "Yeah. 'Oh no.' " Suddenly, he had a mental picture of Sandy Riley stepping out onto her porch to find stuffed squirrels, swaying in the wind, strung up by their little squirrel necks. Each one with a pecan taped into a furry little paw.

This is going to push that batty woman right over the edge.

"Last check, Wolfe and Fox had gone over to the Vargus farm to secure things and make sure their goats are okay. You want me to find Fitz and Hatch?"

Chief Teague moved around his desk and took four long strides so that he could stand in his doorway and face Francis. As predicted, she was suppressing a grin. He looked around the office for a moment and then sighed. "No. I'll do this myself. Hell, if it's not goats, it's squirrels. What is it with this town?"

Francis broke into a laugh, the sound echoing in the empty office as the doors swung back and forth. The faint ring of the phone followed him out of the building.

▮ ▮ ▮

Amber Hirsh is a whore.

She'd heard it said many times, had even become numb to it, but had never said it to herself.

It wasn't cruel, unfair, or untrue. She *was* a whore, and it had to stop. She was pregnant now—with Cody's baby. While he was in trouble more often than not, so was she. Maybe that was why she identified with him. She loved Cody, and she'd screwed enough guys to know the difference between love, like, infatuation, and flat out desire.

Absentmindedly, her hand touched her belly. This was her chance to do things right—to start over and maybe become a role model for her baby. Aside from living in a miserably small town, she had it all, right? He father was liked and respected, and as the town veterinarian, he'd achieved personal as well as professional success. It seemed reasonable that his only child would have it all as well, but it didn't work that way.

When she'd learned she was pregnant, she thought it would be the chance to make everything right. She could stop being a whore. She could stop the cycle of stealing. She could make her father proud.

Instead of being proud to learn he was going to be a grandfather, he'd sighed and left the room. It had completely deflated her. The same man who got excited about cows and horses giving birth had had nothing to say about his own grandchild. She could imagine what he'd say when he learned she'd been the one stealing from his medical supplies, that she'd been the one who gave Monica Tyree the drugs that had caused the accident and almost killed people. She had to stop it; she had to stop it all.

She fell back into her seat and stared out at the park.

What was she going to do? How was she going to stop all this? If she didn't bring more drugs to Monica, she would tell. She couldn't let her father know what was going on, she couldn't let Cody know what she'd been doing. And while she couldn't believe her father would press charges, what if it was beyond his control? What if the police stepped in and arrested her? What if she went to prison? Lost her baby? She would lose her father, Cody, the baby, and all her friends forever. She'd tried to be so bad for so long, being good was exhausting. How was she ever going to undo all the wrong she'd done?

She rubbed her eyes, trying hard to make the mental images go away.

A noise startled her and she looked across the field to see two figures on the ground, rolling and laughing. She almost smiled.

Well, well, well . . .

She would not have put those two together. But as Frankie rolled on top of Thia, pinning and tickling her, it was clear they were. Just a few feet from them was Thia's sleeping baby, and Amber felt a trickle of envy.

Thia knew how Amber felt. Amber rubbed her stomach again and really considered that. Thia *would* understand. From everything she'd heard, Thia had hated Granby, and while she'd never been considered a whore by any means, she'd been wild and had almost killed herself trying to get out. But she got pregnant, came back home, and everything was perfect. To hear people talk, Thia was one of the most well-liked people in town. Her baby, Lily, had given her new life.

Without thinking, Amber opened her car door. Not only would Thia understand, but she could do something about it. She was one of the few people who genuinely cared about the James Otis murder and Amber had something to share.

You scratch my back, I'll scratch yours.

As she walked, she practiced what she would say to Thia. She and Theresa Franks had never been friends. She'd been a freshman when

Thia was a senior. All she knew of Thia was hearsay, but she felt as though she knew her since there had been plenty to hear. While the same could be said of Thia's knowledge of her, she was pretty sure as much as she admired the rebellious Thia, the college-educated Thia looked down on her.

Amber had something of value to say, however. She'd seen what she'd seen. She knew something not even the police knew, and she was certain Thia would be interested.

When she saw the trio head into the woods, all holding hands, she decided she needed to get Thia alone. She couldn't talk in front of Frankie.

Her cell phone rang.

"Hello?"

"Amber!"

"Dad?"

"Girl! Where are you?" he asked.

She could tell that something was very wrong. "I'm, uh, out runnin' some errands. Everything okay?"

"No. It's not okay. I got Brian Neilson up here with his dogs and a lame heifer. I don't and won't have time for anything else. I need you to get on up to the Vargus place and help 'em with the goats."

"The Vargus place? Well, what's going on up there?" She couldn't help but sound irritated. The very last thing she wanted to do was go up there and wrestle with some goats.

"They got their heads stuck again. And they need their shots."

Amber had spent far too many of her teenage years wrestling goats too stupid to keep their heads out of the fence lines. More than once, she'd secretly wished they'd just die. Boer goats were the worst with their horns, and she was convinced the Varguses' Boer goats were the dumbest on account of the inbreeding. Old Man Vargus had always been too damned cheap to realize he should have brought in new lines.

For a moment, Amber said nothing and she heard her father sigh.

"You won't have to do anything but give 'em their shots. Tina Wolfe's up there. She'll hold 'em, but you better hurry. Knowing her, she'll lose her temper and shoot 'em all. Now, hurry up. I've got no time right now."

No *good-bye.* No *thanks, honey.* He just clicked off and left her staring at her phone.

She didn't bother talking to him when she went into the clinic. She picked up the shots already marked and labeled, nodded to a few people in the lobby, and headed back out to the Vargus place.

Her cell phone rang again, jerking her from the thoughts of exactly how she'd landed in the middle of this nightmare to begin with. She frowned at the phone and tossed it over to the passenger seat. It was him.

A smile crept across her lips despite her mood. There, at the end of the driveway, was Officer Rosa Fox, perched on the hood of her cruiser, laughing. Beyond Fox was Officer Tina Wolfe—renowned goat hater—standing on top of a flatbed trailer, holding a shovel in her hands, and poking at the Varguses' billy goat, Buzz.

Buzz was the single meanest billy Amber had ever known. Mr. Vargus would sit out back, presumably after having a fight with Mrs. Vargus, get drunk, and throw cans at his goats, but for whatever reason, Buzz liked Vargus. Two mean old men. And in the spirit of old man Vargus, who was still in the hospital, Buzz had taken on Wolfe.

Amber put the car in park and sat watching the show for a few moments longer, laughing out loud.

"Any time you want to step in!" Wolfe yelled over her shoulder toward her partner.

Poke. Poke.

Amber climbed out of her car and wandered over toward Fox. "How long she been out there pokin' at that goat?" she asked.

"Couldn't say." Fox smiled. Buzz lowered his head and butted against the back of the shovel each time she jabbed it at him.

"You know, the more she does that," Amber said, "the more it just agitates the goat."

"I know." Fox smiled.

"Well, don'tcha think we should, you know, warn her?" Amber watched Wolfe as Buzz appeared to become more aggressive.

"In a minute." Amber looked at Fox and saw that she was clearly enjoying the show. "Just a few more."

Poke. Poke.

"And where have you been?" Wolfe snapped at Amber. For a moment, Amber was taken aback. "I'm doing your job."

Poke. Poke

"I wouldn't do my job like that," Amber said.

Fox laughed, and Wolfe narrowed her eyes for a moment.

"Yeah, well, all I know is I should be out looking for Frankie Larson, but instead I'm here—"

"Frankie Larson's at Granby Park."

"What? Fantastic. You hear that, you piece of crap!"

Poke. Poke.

"You know," Amber said, moving toward the fence. "That only makes things worse."

"Right! Like I'm gonna put this down!" Wolfe shrieked as Buzz came in again.

He moved forward, putting his front feet on the trailer. Amber saw the trembling of muscles as they bunched in his hindquarters and knew he was going to jump up onto the trailer.

"Okay," Fox said. "Game time over." She moved toward the gate.

"Really? Can I shoot him?" Wolfe asked.

Poke. Poke.

"The problem is," Amber said. "You're between him and his herd."

"What?"

Buzz jumped up on the trailer, and Wolfe released a slew of curse words. If it was possible that goats sensed when someone did not like them, Wolfe radiated that negative *goat-hater* aura.

"I know it doesn't look that way to you"—Amber pointed beyond Wolfe to the herd behind her—"but to him, you've placed yourself between him and his herd. This is very aggressive behavior on your part." She smiled. "So, with that shovel, you're fighting for his herd."

With a graceful flick of her wrist, Officer Fox released the night baton she carried at her hip. It extended to almost two feet. Passing the trailer, she moved closer to Buzz's herd which caused him to scuttle off the trailer, bleat, and trot over toward her.

Working in a counterclockwise motion, Fox backed up until Buzz stood firmly between the women and the herd. He stood stoically for a moment, his long beard flowing in the slight breeze, his heavy head swinging back and forth, assessing the situation. He let out a huff and meandered back to his herd.

"It's hotter 'n hell out here!" Wolfe raised her hands to the skies. "And once again, I'm outside in full uniform, goat wrangling. God! What have I done? In what former life was I a goat herder because here's the news bulletin: I'm not anymore! I don't herd cattle! I don't herd chickens. I don't herd goats!"

"You shouldn't talk to God like that," Fox said, and she winked at Amber.

"And we still got two damned goats with their damned heads stuck in the damned fence! We need to be talking to Frankie Larson, Rosa! Why are we out here? We need to be talking to Frankie, but instead we have to go free those damned . . ." Wolfe remained atop the trailer, hands still outreached.

"It's okay." Amber shrugged. "Two less to fight with. I can give 'em their shots before we get 'em out." She lifted her medical bag filled with syringes.

Officer Wolfe's eyebrows shot up, then she laughed. "Are you kidding me? We have to give shots to all the goats? Nowhere, and I mean nowhere, in my job description does it say that I have to give shots to goats. Hell, you know I'm still in trouble for *shooting* a goat. But it's okay for me to waste taxpayers' dollars playing vet and *giving* shots."

"You don't have to." Amber frowned. "I have to. I'd appreciate your help seeing as how I'm pregnant, but you don't have to do anything."

"Argh! Dammit!" Wolfe yelled, and Amber smiled to herself.

For all Wolfe's bluff and bluster, she knew there was no way she was going to allow a pregnant woman—a pregnant girl—to stand out in the scorching heat with a dangerous billy goat on the loose.

"There's way too much damning going on for my comfort. You better move, Amber," Fox said. "If lightning's going to strike, it's going to hit right—" She stopped. Suddenly, a light mist sprayed. It covered the entire trailer, surprising Fox.

Wolfe, still cursing and fussing as she paced around the trailer, stood stock-still. "Is it raining?" The spray had covered her face, arms, and shirt. But there wasn't a cloud in the sky. "Did you feel that? Is it raining?"

Amber and Fox were holding each other up as they doubled over in laughter.

A mature billy goat can spray urine, marking his territory up to fifty feet. Officer Tina Wolfe was officially initiated into the herd. She now belonged to Buzz.

CHAPTER THIRTY-EIGHT

For the second time in less than a week, Chief Teague surveyed a riot on Main Street. It appeared that every young man in Granby was in the middle of the street. He sighed heavily before he stepped out of his cruiser.

Hut Langford had returned to town for the day before he found himself right smack in the middle of a throwdown. Some people cruised neighborhoods hoping to find a garage sale or an old friend, but nothing delighted Hut Langford more than to drive up on a street brawl. He didn't need to know the circumstances or the whys. He just knew he wanted in. At least, this was how Teague saw it. It was classic Hut behavior.

By Hut's own admission, he'd seen over half a dozen Mexicans, all from Paradise Park, alongside Terrell Whitehead and a few other blacks from the east side, and didn't need to know anything else. He had figured they were in town to fight, so he'd cranked the wheel to his truck, slid to a stop, and reached under his seat for a pool stick he carried for such occasions.

When Teague got the call, witnesses said Terrell and one of his buddies were holding Willie Strictland while someone else beat him up. By the time Hut had arrived, Willie seemed to have been unconscious while his body became a human punching bag. All the while, Terrell taunted him, claiming that was what James must have felt before he died. It had been Teague's worst fear. Retaliation.

But Hut had beaten Teague to the scene.

Another call came in while Teague was in transit. Apparently, Milford East had been taken down by a group of Mexicans. Before Teague could arrive to the scene, Francis was talking to him again, this time informing him that the ladies from the newspaper were outside screaming.

When Francis called once more to inform Teague that Hut Langford was in the mix, Teague said, "I know."

From his car, he could see Hut with the pool stick in his hand, choking up on the narrow end, which had the last couple of inches wrapped in tape.

Teague watched helplessly as Hut came up on Terrell, and made a long, powerful swing at the back of Terrell's legs. Terrell folded, going down hard with a yelp. His buddy let go of Willie, who also collapsed to the ground.

Teague was out of the car and calling for backup.

"Man! Whatcha doin?" Terrell looked up at Hut, recognizing him. "This ain't your fight, man. This got nothin' to do with you, Hut!"

"Like hell," Hut said, taking a step back and bringing the pool stick up high over his right shoulder. Although he spoke to Terrell, he never took his eyes off the other two men, and he pointed to one of the men. "I know you." He nodded at the hitter. "Rodriguez. Yeah. I seen you 'round." He took a swing, and Rodriguez jumped back.

Teague yelled, but no one seemed to hear him as Terrell's other buddy lunged, grabbing at Hut's pool stick.

Hut smashed his face with a fist. The guy released the stick and staggered backward. Rodriguez pounced, but Hut took a half-step backward, successfully dodging Rodriguez's heavy swing and brought the stick down on the back of Rodriguez's neck. Rodriguez grunted and crumpled to the ground while Terrell rolled sideways and struggled to his feet.

"You son of a bitch, this ain't got nothing to do with you!" He dove forward, kicking off against the ground. It was a perfect lineman's body tackle. While Hut's stick made impact once again, it didn't seem to faze Terrell as he wrapped his arms around Hut. Both men went down with a heavy thud.

Chief Teague spotted Roland Wyck pinned beneath Oscar Ruiz. Simply put, Wyck was getting the snot beat out of him.

"Hey!" Teague boomed, pointing to Oscar Ruiz. In mid-hit, Ruiz glanced up and froze. "Right now, get off him. Now! Move! Now!" As he pointed, he moved forward aggressively.

Ruiz looked taken aback and the young man slid from Wyck's exhausted body.

"Don't even think about it!" Teague said as Ruiz stood, looking as though he might run. He knew just about every man fighting. To run was absurd, and Ruiz knew it.

"Stop. Right now!" Teague's voice boomed over the bullhorn. "The next man who hits or takes a swing goes to jail! Got it?!"

Silence. One by one, collars were released, chokeholds loosened, fists were withdrawn.

Teague watched as the men let go but refused to back away from whomever they had squared off against. He lowered the bullhorn but asked to no one in particular, "What the hell is going on here?"

"Them Mexicans come into town with Terrell there."

Teague turned around to find Travis Miles leaning back against his truck. Teague had hardly noticed him.

Travis had one foot crossed in front of the other, arms crossed against his chest with his fingers tucked up under his arms, his thumbs poking out. He looked as though he was just leaning back and watching the sun set. He gave a slow grin. "They come up sayin' some nonsense about 'em boys killing James Otis. Ford there mouths off and it was game on," Travis said.

Teague sighed. "Who threw the first punch?" This was all Teague wanted to know.

"Well, now." Travis squinted up at the sky and scratched his head. Again, the movements were slow and easy.

Teague counted to ten to keep from tearing into Travis.

Some thirty feet away, Willie Strictland moaned. Teague saw Officers Hatch and Fitz moving through the crowds, getting people out of the street, and separating the parties.

"I'd have to say it was Ford." He wagged a finger at the captain. "But it would be in self-defense. 'Em Mexicans were coming for a fight." Travis eyed the chief and lowered his voice a little, as though he hated to say what needed to be said. " 'Em black boys, too."

Teague nodded. *Neighbors against neighbors.* This wasn't going away, the displaced hostility and anger, until they solved the case.

He looked around and saw Milford East upright and talking to his attackers. East said something which elicited a soft chuckle from one of the men who had just moments ago had been hitting him. They all nodded in agreement. All appeared to be cooperating with Teague's command.

"You okay?" Teague asked as he approached Willie Strictland.

Willie winced, gingerly touching his eye.

Terrell leaned in and gave a sympathy wince as well. "That's gotta hurt," he said, and Willie managed a smile.

"I had worse."

Teague shook his head, doubling back toward Hatch and Fitz, who were consulting over a notebook. David Wyck and Shea Griffin were bending the officers' ears back but stopped as Teague neared.

"What are you going to do about this?" Wyck Senior poked a finger at Teague. "What the hell are you gonna do about this? 'Em boys came into town and started all this . . ." His arm swept over the street, gesturing wildly, and finally pointing to his son. "Look at my boy! He's bleeding! He didn't do a damned thing."

Teague watched as Roland and Oscar Ruiz stopped talking and looked back at the group.

Roland Wyck frowned. "I'm okay, Dad."

David Wyck would hear nothing of it, shaking his head and pounding his fist into his open hand. "This ain't okay! My boy comes here, comes to work to earn an honest living, and work as an American citizen. He pays his taxes and holds an honest job but can't work because he's—"

"Aw, Dad. Knock it off. It's no big deal," Roland said and struggled to his feet. As he stood, he hit Oscar Ruiz on the shoulder with the back of his hand. "C'mon, Oscar. I'll buy you a cold one."

Oscar turned his head away, still playing hard to get. He was mad and wanted his old school yard friend to know it.

Roland frowned. "Aw, shit, Oscar. You know I got nothin' to do with what happened to James. I'm sorry 'bout it. Just like you. But you know I got nothin' to do with that so, c'mon, let me buy you a drink. You and me. Let's go. No hard feelings."

Ruiz shrugged again and stood up.

In awe, Teague watched as the two young men, tattered and worn from their fight, walked down the street toward the Town Pump for a Coke.

He turned back to David Wyck. "What would you have me do?" Teague asked.

"What should you do? What should you *do*?" Wyck's mouth fell open. "You kiddin' me? You got a bunch of punk thugs who come into town and whoop up on my boy, Ford, and Willie, and you just gonna let 'em walk."

"I don't like it any more than you," Teague said and used his hand to showcase the scene. If he hadn't seen it himself, he wouldn't have believed it. He'd moved to Granby because he wanted to get away from the big city violence. He'd handled more gang-related crime and racially heated fights than he cared to remember, but at no time could he recall the suspects walking off together for a cold drink. "But no one is complaining, and I've got a witness who says Milford East was the first to throw a punch."

David Wyck scowled and muttered under his breath as he walked away.

"What did you say?" Teague leaned forward.

Hatch and Fitz went rigid.

"I said, 'It figures.' "

"And what's that supposed to mean?" Teague's eyes narrowed, his nostrils flared, and his back jerked board straight.

David Wyck was a heavy smoker with an almost permanent hunch from his bowed cough. His box hat was oversized on his small head, and standing next to Teague, he looked like a ridiculous scarecrow.

"It means what it means. I'da figured you'd take sides with 'em coloreds." As if he sensed what Hatch and Fitz were thinking, he puffed up. "That's right. I ain't ashamed, and I ain't afraid to say it. If this had been some white boys beatin' up on some coloreds, you'd be all over it.

You know what I'm talking about, Shea." David Wyck turned to Shea Griffin.

Dreams of working alongside Teague faded rapidly for Shea Griffin, and he paled, his mouth falling open.

"Shit," Wyck hissed and moved away, shaking his head in disgust.

"I, uh, don't . . ." Griffin stuttered.

Teague saved him. In truth, Teague had no interest and no patience for whatever nonsense was to come from Griffin's mouth. "We got lucky today, boys," he said to his men. "But we're running out of time."

" 'Em boys got enough of a history with each other that they don't really want to fight, much less believe one of 'em would hurt another, but . . . Chief's right. We're running out of time." Fitz's assessment made Hatch nod.

"Racial tensions are running high." Hatch turned to survey the street. "They's friends and all, but it's just a matter a time. I'd never figure Terrell Whitehead for coming out like this but—"

His partner finished his thoughts. It was what all the Granby police had been thinking. "He's pissed. He wants to see someone pay for James's death. I guess I don't blame him. And since it's a matter of public opinion that a white boy done it . . ." He just shook his head.

"But I talked to everyone at the party." Shea Griffin wanted to be valuable to the chief. "James didn't have a problem with anyone. Black or white."

For a moment, the four men stood in a circle, saying nothing. Shea Griffin's words rolled around in Teague's head. Black or white. It had been assumed that this had been a hate crime, a white-on-black crime. But what if it hadn't been?

What if it was a black-on-black crime? Or a brown-on-black?

"Damned wet-backs," someone from the crowd murmured.

Chief Teague's thoughts mixed and mashed as he worked through the details they had thus far. He turned back toward where Willie Strictland had gone down.

Willie had hobbled back to Griffin's Garage with Terrell Whitehead chattering away at him. What they were talking about, Teague could not be sure, but the conversation seemed amiable.

Hut Langford, however, was not making friends with the Rodriguez kid. While everyone else had made a certain peace with his attacker or victim, Langford and Rodriguez looked as though they might go at it again.

Teague pointed his chin toward the two. "What have we got here?" he asked.

"Hut Langford, brandishing a weapon," Hatch said, liking the possibilities of running Hut Langford in.

Teague shook his head. He was less interested in Hut than the Mexican kid. *Brown-on-black.* He pointed to the new guy in town, Rodriquez's cousin.

"What do we know about that one right there?"

CHAPTER THIRTY-NINE

"Johnny Vargus passed on," Pastor Tyree said.

Had it be anyone but the Pastor, I might have sneered. I never cared for that expression. Passed on. Passed over. I got the meaning, but in the case of Johnny Vargus, I had to wonder.

"Really? You think so?"

I was met with silence. Surprise, more likely.

"I'm sorry?" Pastor Tyree asked.

"You think a guy like that really goes to Heaven?" I saw the heads of Vicky, Tammi, and LeAnn crane over in my direction.

Someone died!

I could feel the collective breath being held. They were just minutes away from getting the firsthand poop that would begin the Granby grapevine. How exciting.

I managed my words carefully, not letting on who had just died. It was killing them, and if I played my cards right, one might drop dead right in front of me. What I wanted to ask was what the death of Johnny Vargus meant for Monica Tyree. She was up to her eyeballs in legal trouble before. I cut eyes to the side, watching the sharks circle my desk.

"That's not for us to judge, Thia." His tone was practiced and patient.

The pastor had had a tough go of things. As a favor to Ms. Vargus, he was calling in the obituary.

How does that even work?

His daughter kills the man, and he calls in the obituary, makes the arrangements, and comforts the widow. How strange that must have been. *Well, since my daughter killed your husband, would you like for me to make the arrangements for you?*

"He was a churchgoing man . . ."

While the pastor gave the expected party line speech, I watched as Tammi leaned so hard onto the desk that I feared it might cave in on us all.

Religion is a funny thing. In principle, it's perfect. Have faith. Practice and believe in the words of your God or Prophet or Allah, and experience inner peace, for the world will most assuredly be a better place with the even better promise of a heavenly afterlife.

People go and mess it all up. They go and get married in a church, before a priest or minister. Swear to do right by their Lord and—bam! Cheat. They cheat on each other, beat each other up, swear, drink, smoke, look at porn, do porn, and all those other things one is not supposed to do when they've sworn to honor their religion.

In the case of Johnny Vargus, I didn't know if he looked at porn, but he did all the other things. It was hard not to judge whether or not I thought he ought to go to heaven. Boy, that would be some gig. What I wouldn't give to be the guy who got to determine who got past the pearly gates.

Oh, Hut. I'm sorry, but you're nothing but a gun-running, two-bit criminal with a nasty disposition and a horrible habit of dropping your pants every time you see a halfway decent looking female. You can't come in. You'll scare all the children.

Ah, Angela Wyck. No, sorry. Nope. We don't allow insurance scammers here. See, here in Heaven, we'd like to keep our clouds pure and free of filth and scum. You rob from your neighbors, cheat, and steal, yet have the audacity to judge others for doing the same thing. You are one nasty chick and a potential poster child for venereal disease. Please exit to the right.

Milford "Big Man" East. We've got a quota here for fathering stupid, inbred children. As you can't seem to contain yourself, we just can't let you in. Besides, your ridiculous and embarrassing notion that fart noises are funny at your age prevents us from allowing you in. You're too stupid.

Why, if it isn't Tammi Whatley. Well, you do go to church every Sunday and give to charity. You sing in the choir and have never taken a drink of devil's water in your life. Okay, we will let you in. But you have to stay over on the cloud with people of color. You can babysit all the little niglets while the others tell stories of overcoming obstacles, discrimination, and how they managed to not kill someone such as yourself and instead, chose the righteous path to love their neighbor and forgive.

I smiled to myself, liking that thought very much.

Tammi rapped on my desk with her knuckles then thrust out both hands impatiently. The international sign for "Well?"

"Well," I said, skimming my notes for all the pertinent information, "I'll make sure this gets in the paper. And I'm sorry." I was. Not for Mr. Vargus, not even for Mrs. Vargus. It was about time she lived life as something other than a punching bag. But I felt sorry for the pastor.

By the time I hung up, Tammi was reading my notes, upside down. She no sooner deciphered my scribble than she blurted out, "Well, the old bastard Johnny Vargus just died."

"No!" said Vicky, leaning forward in her seat.

"Yup. Died this morning, 10 o'clock. Heart failure." She stiffened, looking back to her friends. "Not that anyone cares."

"He was a rotten person," Vicky echoed.

"I'm sure Gail won't miss him. I'll bet she's secretly happy," LeAnn said, and for a moment, all three women nodded at this.

"Well, one less. That's all I have to say." Tammi smiled and sashayed across the room.

"Tammi Whatley!" Vicky pretended to be shocked. "I can't believe you just said that."

"What? You know it's true. One less dirty Mexican beating up women and causing trouble." For effect, she looked around the room, daring each one of us to protest that statement.

While I was no fan of Mr. Vargus, I did wonder out loud. "He was

Mexican?" It didn't make Tammi's statement any more or less appalling. I just wondered.

She shrugged. "Mexican, Cuban. Same damned thing."

I choked with laughter. "I dare you to go to a LULAC meeting and say that." I smiled wryly.

She frowned at me. "What's that?"

"Never mind." I sighed, returning to my work. I had several messages on my desk, and I began to thumb through them. "I don't see you going to one any time soon." I missed whatever quizzical or cynical look Tammi might have thrown my way when I noticed that Amber Hirsh had called.

"You know, I was talking to Shea Griffin the other day," Tammi broadcast as I picked up the receiver to call Amber. "He was telling me how his business is suffering because of all the business that Mexican boy, what's his name, José, has been taking, working on over there at his place in Paradise Park."

The others clucked their tongues.

"And I'll tell you another thing. I wouldn't put it past them to steal the parts or wreck people's cars or cut tires up just to get more business."

"Oh, you don't think that." LeAnn made an attempt at reason.

"Don't I?"

Woo-woo. Tammi, the freight train was roaring into the station.

She put a hand against her breast, playing with the string of pearls draped around her neck. That would be the same string of pearls she made sure everyone knew was insured for three thousand dollars and the same string Miranda McGhee said she bought over at Sam's in Waco. "You know how Mexicans are." Tammi did a little twirl around the office, letting us all see the seriousness of her statement. She, Tammi Whatley, was as serious as a heart attack. "They all stick together and do anything they can to undermine us all, take our money, and laugh at us behind our backs."

She strutted over toward the front counter and leaned against it, checking out her manicured nails and basking in the sudden light of attention.

"Even my own son." She and LeAnn nodded, already aware of this story. Hell, she'd probably been forced to hear it ten times over. "He got his tailgate stolen, and where do you think he went first? To that José fella's place. Said he could get it cheaper there. Well, gee, I wonder why?" Sarcasm dripped from her voice. She jabbed a finger toward Vicky. "Why, just the other day—Vicky, you remember this. We were . . . where were we? Oh, yes, we were at the Town Pump getting something to drink when those little Mexican kids came in the store. You saw how they worked. One distracted Henry at the register while two other little shits, excuse my French, tried to sneak out. That's just how those Mexicans operate."

"Did you report this?" Officer Fox asked.

If life really were like the movies, at that precise moment, there would have been a beam of light shining down on both Rosa Fox and Tammi Whatley. The rest of us would have faded into darkness while the audience could watch Tammi die a thousand deaths. Rosa Fox would have been elevated to a heavenly state while Tammi Whatley melted into a puddle of ooze.

I smiled.

Tina Wolfe smiled. Arms folded across her chest, one leg kicked out casually in front of the other, Wolfe did her cool-cop lean against the doorjamb while Officer Fox tilted her head, as if confused. But the most brilliant and comical part of their whole grand entrance was *what* Fox was actually doing. With her right arm outstretched, Fox extended the baton in her hand. The same baton that held the bell trapped over the door, so presumably, when Wolfe pushed it open, Fox had caught its *ting-ting,* allowing them to enter in silence. I wondered how many times they had done this before, and I could barely contain a laugh.

"I don't remember hearing a call on this. When did this happen?"

"Well . . . I . . . it wasn't that big of a . . ." Tammi's face flushed brighter with the start of each new sentence.

"Oh, go on." Wolfe's voice boomed across the office. "What does it matter, right? Ol' Fox here is most likely related to 'em little rugrats anyway. Like you say, they cover for one another. She probably birthed 'em, right, Foxie? Just how many kids do you have right now? Twelve? Fourteen?" Wolfe looked over at me and winked. "She just pops 'em out like Little Debbie cakes. One after another. Little brown goodies of delight."

Tammi's mouth actually fell open.

Fox withdrew her baton and the bell jingled. It was the only sound in the office.

Bravo, Fox! Bravo!

"I'm serious. Mexican women can have up to thirty children. It has something to do with all the salsa they eat. I read it on the Internet."

For a moment, no one spoke. No one moved.

"Little brown goodies of delight?" Fox asked, turning to face her partner, and they both broke out into laughter, each equally entertained by Wolfe's constant nonsense.

Wolfe tried to straighten up and feign seriousness. "Yeah, what's wrong with that? You're nice and brown and sweet and yummy. I have often said that I would eat you up if I could." Wolfe cackled and slapped her knee. "Oh, wait. That wasn't me! That was Fitz!" More howls.

Fox and I exchanged glances. Despite myself, I could feel a smile spreading across my lips while Tammi, LeAnn, and Vicky were stunned into stony expressions.

"I can't believe you just said that," Fox said.

"What? Oh, you know he likes you."

"Would you shut up?" Fox asked, her voice singing with amusement.

"*What?* Oh, shit! Are you going to write me up now?" Wolfe turned to me. "If I get one more write up, I am in big trouble." She shrugged. "I'm starting my sensitivity training next week."

"I . . ." Tammi sputtered again, still not able to jump on board with anything being said.

"So." Wolfe scowled at me, all traces of humor gone. "Where have you been? Girl, we've been looking for you all day."

"Me?"

"Yes, you."

Fox lost interest in Tammi and rounded the counter. She lifted a leg, twisted at the hip, and sat sidesaddle on my desk. While Wolfe grilled me, Fox leaned forward, reading all the notes on my desk.

"Well," I said, trying to ignore the fact that Fox was invading my privacy. "I took Ella and we went to the park with . . ." I paused for a moment, very much not wanting to revisit the whole *I'm-dating-Frankie* with Tammi and company. "I went to the park, dropped her off home with my mom, and came here. Why?"

"Well, you're a popular girl," Fox said, holding up three different messages from Amber Hirsh.

"It comes with the job." I reached forward, taking the notes from Fox's hand.

"You seen Frankie Larson lately?" Wolfe asked.

"Or know why Amber Hirsh wants to talk to you so badly?" Fox asked, now reading notes from my phone call with Pastor Tyree. "Huh. Johnny Vargus died."

"He was pretty bad off," Wolfe said to no one in particular.

"Now that's curious." Fox continued thumbing through my things.

I'd always liked Officer Fox, but I was beginning to get annoyed.

"Why would Monica Tyree be calling you?"

I could feel Tammi and the others lean forward.

"When was the last time you saw Frankie Larson?" Wolfe asked, a pit bull determined to get her answer.

Wolfe and Fox didn't have a good cop/bad cop routine. They lulled you in with utter silliness and then distracted you by moving in seventeen different directions.

"I like that strand, Ms. Whatley." Wolfe looked across the room toward Tammi Whatley and pointed toward her pearl necklace. "Bought my grandma one just like it. Got it at Sam's for a hundred." She winked.

Tammi croaked, sounding more like a frog than a woman.

"Didn't you go to the park with Frankie and your daughter today?" Wolfe turned back to me.

I felt as though I couldn't keep up. When did this come back to me? "Well, yeah, how did you—"

"Amber Hirsh told us, which is curious she should know. Did you tell anyone you were meeting Frankie at the park?" Wolfe's pace never slowed as she asked her questions.

"And why would Monica Tyree be calling you? From the hospital where Johnny Vargus just died, no less?" Fox didn't ask me that question; she asked Wolfe.

CHAPTER FORTY

Amber picked up the phone on the third ring. There was no escaping this any longer.

"I'm not . . . I can't see you anymore," she said without any greeting.

"You will. You don't have a choice." He stated it as fact. His voice was loud and commanding.

Away from him, out of his reach, she could be braver, and she shook her head at the phone as he spoke. "Not anymore. I told you, I'm pregnant. I can't . . . I just can't do this anymore. It's not good for me or the baby." She wanted to tell him that she was in love with Cody Kyle, but understood that this would only bring more misery upon Cody.

"I won't hurt the baby." His voice softened.

She shook her head at the phone again, saying nothing.

"Amber, I need you."

"You don't need me." She laughed. "You need a whore. That's what you need."

"I need *you*, Amber. It's you and only you."

"No, you just need someone to get your rocks off with!" Amber's voice rose. She was finally putting her foot down, and this time, she swore nothing, but nothing, would change the outcome. She was done with him. She had to have her freedom.

"Amber, please, honey. Don't make me have to play rough. I don't want to hurt you, you know that, but I will if I have to."

"You don't have to do anything!" Her voice trembled.

"We have an arrangement. Have you forgotten that? I've kept my end. I've always kept my end. If you leave me, other people will get hurt." This was his promise. His voice was deep, powerful, and threatening.

"Like your wife," Amber said. She'd tried this route before—months before—and received a slap across the face and an onslaught of verbal threats and promises of what would happen to both her and Cody if she talked. "What would she do if she found out about me?"

"That would never happen, now would it?" His voice sounded more like a growl. "Come see me. We need to talk this out in person. I don't like this over the phone."

"It's over." Amber found a surge of power and wondered if he was getting paranoid. *Good. Let him be paranoid.* "Don't call me again."

"Amber, don't do this. I don't want to, but I will destroy you, Cody, your baby, your father, anyone connected with you if you leave me—"

"I'm going to the press," Amber blurted out. Silence roared in her cell phone. "Hello?"

"Where are you?" he asked, and his voice sounded so menacing, Amber looked anxiously around, afraid that he might be nearby, watching.

"Did you hear what I said?" she asked again.

She'd been sitting in her car, outside the county courthouse, as safe a place as any—to park in full view of the police department, the fire department, and all the county agents. She'd parked beneath a large oak tree, taking one of the few precious shaded spots in town. Still, sweat rolled down her back and the sides of her face, partly she knew from the heat but also from fear.

"I'm on my way to meet Theresa Franks from the paper. I'm going to tell her everything," Amber said, still looking around. "I mean it. I can't live like this anymore. I won't live like this anymore." She hung up the phone.

∎ ∎ ∎

"Whatever Monica's got to say, she won't say with you two staring at her," I told them.

Officers Fox and Wolfe had invited me to step outside *The Recorder*, and we were talking on the sidewalk while Tammi Whatley, Vicky Jackson, and LeAnn Ricks pressed their faces to the glass on the inside, desperate to hear anything newsworthy.

"Why do you suppose she's calling you?" Wolfe asked.

"I don't know but I'm pretty sure she's the one who's been leaving me tips on who might have killed James."

"She sober?" Fox asked, and I just shrugged. I had no way of really knowing.

"You think it's legit?" Wolfe folded her arms across her chest.

"No, not really. It's been pretty weird, vague things, but I got nothing else. I might as well go see her and find out what she's got to say. No more games," I said.

"You talk to Frankie Larson about where he was the night that James was killed?" Wolfe asked in a way that surprised me. I couldn't believe they would be thinking Frankie could have anything to do with any of what had happened.

"He was working. I believe he was the first to respond on the scene when the 911 came in . . ." That wasn't the way I meant it. Wolfe looked at me in that way she does when she thinks she's got a hold of some good information. "You're way off if you think Frankie had something to do with James's death. Way off."

"Could be you're too close to this right now," Wolfe said, and again, I made a face at her.

"Or you're just way off."

"Or it might be that your judgment is a bit skewed because you've got a good-looking guy who doesn't seem to care that you're a single mother, and now that you've been working this murder angle, he's always around, able to pick up any new bits of information that come your way."

The whole time we were talking, I noticed that Fox was just staring at the ground. Hands on hips, she was letting Wolfe go off the way she does from time to time, and Fox didn't seem to want any of it. "It could be that he was first on the scene because he was already on the scene. He used James's cell phone to call it in then ditched it later when no one was around. Could be that he had some deep resentment against James Otis . . ."

"*Or*," I said, correcting her, "it could be that you'll never solve this case because you'll be too busy with your sensitivity classes."

"Ha!" Fox snorted. She gave me a wink, reached for her partner's arm, and gave it a hard yank. "C'mon, Sherlock, let's go find Mr. Larson and see what he's got to say. Let Thia go see Monica. You'll call us as soon as you've talked to her, right?"

I gave a nod and started back in, my head swirling from what Wolfe had said, or more importantly, implied. As I opened the door to *The Recorder* and braced myself for what lay ahead, I looked back just in time to see Fox smack Wolfe's arm.

Thank you, Fox.

"Hey!" My gratitude was short lived as I heard Fox berate Wolfe. "You beat all, you know it? What's to stop her from calling Frankie right now and telling him everything you just said?"

"That's fine by me. Makes him more jumpy."

I paused at the door and thought about yelling back to them. They couldn't honestly think Frankie could be involved. *Seriously?* I could feel my blood pressure rising. There was no way Frankie was involved. *No way.*

"Did you have to make the remark about being a single mom?" Fox asked as Wolfe tossed her the keys over the top of the car.

"Hey!"

"You had that sensitivity class remark coming. Oh, but I liked that 'I got the same strand for my grandma' remark." Fox snickered out loud. "That was a good one."

"You like that? I thought about saying I'd gotten 'em for like fifty bucks, but I didn't want the old cow to pass out. I don't wanna do CPR on anything that bloated and pasty."

I felt myself starting to smile. As wrong as I knew they were about Frankie, I was still entertained by their Frick and Frack routine. Granby's own comedy duo. Before they slid into their car, Wolfe looked up, first at me and then to the bay window.

Tammi, Vicky, and LeAnn were still plastered there, watching. "Look at 'em. Granby's finest." And she gave a little wave to the ladies with her middle finger.

"Tina!" Fox yelled when she saw the middle finger wave and I had to laugh. "Can you ever go one day without pissing someone off?"

"That would be a negative, my little brown goodie of delight."

▮ ▮ ▮

Monica decided that before she talked to Thia, she needed to come clean with her father. With a nurse in attendance, Monica had been allowed to make calls. It had seemed only fitting that someone overhear the conversation that she'd had with the good father.

She'd heard it said again and again. You have to hit rock bottom before you climb back up. She'd thought she'd hit it when she was forced to live with her father, when she became known as the town druggie, when she'd gone sober only to return to more recreational drugs, including drugs for animals. Everything after that had felt like a punishment, but she'd accepted it, believing that it was all part of her healing process.

She'd been in denial. She wasn't sober. She wasn't clean. She wasn't on the road to recovery. Her life was as screwed up as it had ever been, with no signs of getting better. The accident had made that all clear. Now she'd killed someone.

She didn't know what her future held, and if anyone else knew, they weren't willing to say. With each new hour of the day, she expected Chief Teague to walk in and arrest her.

She'd killed a man.

He hadn't been a nice man, but he'd been a living and breathing person, who she'd killed. She could have killed Mrs. Vargus. What a horrible irony that on an errand for the church, she'd taken a life. Criminally.

She'd killed a man.

It was the one thing that resonated in her head: Monica Tyree killed a man while high.

Worse, she couldn't remember how it all happened. She couldn't

278

remember why she'd crashed into the back of Travis Miles's pickup. She remembered hearing something about a fight in the street. Again, it hardly mattered.

She'd killed a man.

She played games before, calling Thia Franks with clues for reasons now unclear to her. Perhaps it was part of her denial, ready to rat someone else out while pretending she didn't have a problem. Until the accident, it was easy to make excuses. *No one is innocent in Granby. You scratch my back, I scratch yours.* But things had changed. She understood that now and no longer wanted to be part of the chain.

She'd killed a man.

Before she'd screwed up her college career and the remote possibility of becoming a veterinarian and working with Dr. Hirsh, an irony she let pass, she remembered just one short story she'd read from a contemporary American writers class. It was the story of a man who went off to work one day and was killed. Friends came around to break the news to the wife, who had a bad heart. The woman sat in her room, staring out the window. To everyone else, she appeared to be in shock and grieving, but what they didn't know was that the wife heard the birds chirping, the chimes ringing in the breeze, the rustling of leaves, and she thought about freedom and the new life she might have. They mistook her faraway looks for dismay and hopelessness. As she was coming down the stairs to assure her sister and her friend that she was okay, who should walk in but the husband. It had been a case of mistaken identity. The wife was so shocked, realizing that her freedom, hopes, and dreams were dashed, that her heart gave out, and she died. The doctor said that the shock and sheer power of happiness had killed her. The truth was she died of a broken heart.

Funny that Monica would remember that one story, and she remembered what had struck her most at the time when she'd read the story—how much it would suck to have it written on her tombstone that she died of a happy heart. Even in death, she'd never had a voice. Monica understood that.

Johnny Vargus was dead. Monica Tyree had seen to that. He wasn't coming back. Would Mrs. Vargus die of a happy heart? There was never any telling how people would or could react to something, and she thought about what might be put on Vargus's tombstone. HERE LIES A

KNOWN WIFE BEATER. Or would Mrs. Vargus play it safe? They all said BELOVED HUSBAND, didn't they?

What would her own tombstone read? DRUG ADDICT? KILLER?

She'd killed a man.

Then it came to her. She would begin with her own father—the pastor. She believed he was the source of all her troubles. Maybe he would be the end.

She would confess to him how she'd learned the vilest things about members of the community and had used that information against them. How the prestigious Judge McKinley had been screwing Amber Hirsh since she was legally an adult. How he cried crocodile tears to the good Father over his obsession with her, how she'd been both young and easily intimidated, and he'd used her criminal activities against her to make her his play toy.

But Judge McKinley wasn't the only man in town who liked sweet, young things. Someone else did, too, only he swung the other way. And while he never actually touched, he did plenty of looking.

Monica remembered huddling outside the good pastor's office, angry with her father, shaking from withdrawal, and listening to Granby's own legal genius Jared Durham confess his addiction to child porn, specifically, young boys. Her aches and her pains had been all but forgotten as she laughed, careful not to move too much, breathe too loudly, and had listened to the confession of all confessions. It had only been two days prior that the asshole had played hardball with her in his own office.

"I'm sorry, Ms. Tyree," Jared Durham said. "My hands are tied. You've created a mess that can't be swept under any rug. You'll probably do time for possession on this one."

Oh, how she'd hated him. He hadn't even tried to hear her story, to understand her situation. So it had been sweet frickin' justice when she'd sauntered into his office, plopped down in a chair, hoisted her feet up on to his desk, and asked, "So, you like little boys, do you?"

It was priceless. His mouth fell open. He blustered, turned red-faced, and teared up, begging for her silence. He would do anything—*anything*—to keep her quiet.

"Let me see what I can do." And he proceeded to bust his rear end keeping Monica out of jail.

She would have to tell her father what she'd done. She had to come clean with how she'd used his office—his confessional—for her own personal gains.

How the setup had been too sweet when Monica sidled up beside Amber Hirsh at the Town Pump while she was buying a pack of cigarettes and a cold one.

"So, I hear you're banging the judge. Do you call him Your Honor when you do it?"

She had begged, pleaded, and cried for Monica's silence. Amber Hirsh, the queen bee, the homecoming bitch who'd never give the time of day to the likes of Monica Tyree was eating out of her hand, buying drugs off Hut's friends, and most recently, breaking into her own father's medical cabinets to supply Monica with what she needed.

She'd killed a man.

It took that to see that she'd become everything everyone said about her. No excuses, no denial, no more self-pity. She was what she was—a drug addict wanting to come clean, and to do so, she would have to tell it all.

CHAPTER FORTY-ONE

Officers Wolfe and Fox had been sitting at the entrance of Larson Farms, staring in disbelief, when the call came in.

Jake Larson greeted them at the front gate, looking every bit like Frankie's father. He was tall and tan with thick, beefy arms and legs, a toothy, white smile, and a boy-next-door look that had somehow stayed with him through his fiftieth birthday.

"Whad'ya think?" Jake Larson spread his arms wide, grinning like a fool. Behind him was a life-size concrete bovine, painted red, white, and blue in stars and stripes. The stars decorated the cow's shoulders, neck, and head while its hindquarters were a striped red and white. Above the concrete statue was a welcoming sign:

LARSON FARMS: UDDERLY AMERICAN.

"Uh," Wolfe said.

"Wow." Fox shook her head, eyes wide, eyebrows raised. "Wow-ee."

"You gals are the first to see it. It's a beaut, idn't it?" Larson beamed.

"Uh." Wolfe looked the cow up and down.

"It's something," Fox said.

When the radio called to them, both pounced and wrestled for the speaker. Wolfie won, forcing Fox to turn once again to the giant star-spangled cow. "Wow," she said again.

"I saw this baby and knew I had to have it." Larson continued to beam.

"Who wouldn't?" Fox murmured, still in disbelief.

"We're on it," Wolfe said back to dispatch, pricking Fox's ears. The tone of Wolfe's voice was urgent. "C'mon, Fox. We gotta go." She turned to Larson. "Jake, we been tryin' to track down your boy all day. You know where he is?"

"Ain't seen him. Hey, everything okay?" he asked.

"You see him, you let him know we've been looking for him. Got a couple of questions for him. No big deal." She patted the car to let Fox know it was time to go. As they pulled away, Wolfe found her words. "Just so I know where we stand, Jake." She pointed to the cow. "Is this supposed to be funny or serious?"

Jake's rounded shoulders slumped.

Serious.

"That's a fine looking cow you've got there, Jake," Wolfe gave a wave as they pulled away.

"You just can't contain yourself, can you?" Fox peeked over at Wolfe.

"He painted his cow with stars and stripes, for crying out loud," Wolfie said, clearly justification for asking.

"So? You had to ask if it was a joke? You just couldn't let it go?"

"It's a star-spangled cow." They rode in silence for a moment. "A star-spangled cow, Foxie. And that sign! Did you see that sign? Udderly American. Shit, I was afraid to touch it for fear it might open its concrete mouth and start singing *Cows Bless America.*"

"You know what I think?" Fox snorted, shaking her head. "I think you want to be the bad guy of the police department. Oooh, look out everyone! Here's comes Wolfie. She's got fangs!" Fox made snarly faces at Wolfe.

"Pay attention to the road, smartass," Wolfe said, pointing the way. "Head to the courthouse."

"Courthouse?"

"Jared Durham got liquored up and hung himself."

By Granby standards, a large crowd had gathered around the courthouse square, across the street from Durham's office. From their car, they could see Chief Teague towering over John Cobbins, the town coroner, and Travis Miles. Teague's notebook was out as he scribbled notes, periodically nodding at Miles.

"Dang!" was all Fox could say as the two made their way through the crowd.

"What say, Wolfie?" someone asked.

She shook her head, refusing comment of any sort.

"He hang himself? That true, Wolfie?" another called.

"I heard he confessed to the murder of James Otis then kilt hisself."

Fox felt Wolfe stop in her tracks before she actually saw it. She knew that voice, and it irritated her to no end. Clara Getz was the town big mouth, possibly bigger, and certainly more irritating, than Tammi Whatley, which was no small feat. There was no way her partner was going to let this pass.

"Now, Clara, you don't know any such thing, and you dang sure didn't hear it from anyone officiating this scene, so don't go spoutin' off stuff that you don't know about!"

Clara Getz drew in a breath, her face going red.

She was the picture of the retired farm wife—short, stout, rosy cheeks, hair too short and too home-permed. The theme of today's wardrobe was just as it was most days for Clara Getz. Roosters. Clara loved roosters.

"Let it go," Fox said in a low, warning tone.

"Well, shit, I just can't—"

"Well, if y'all were doing your jobs, then I don't guess we'd have to stand out here and speculate," Clara yelled, getting a few approvals from the crowd.

"Aw, shut up, Clara!"

"You can't talk to me that way. I pay your salary!" Clara screamed back at Wolfe. More smiles and then nods began to spread through the crowds.

Wolfe's face reddened. "Hell, Clara, if you'd just pay your parking tickets, we'd be mighty obliged. Your outstanding tickets might just cover the chief's salary!"

"Wolfe!" Chief Teague yelled across the courtyard.

"Chief Teague!" Clara Getz called to him. "You hear that? I want to file a complaint! You hear how she talked to me?"

"Aw, shut up, Clara," Fox snapped and Wolfe smiled. Fox threw her finger in Wolfe's face. "You shut up, too."

▮ ▮ ▮

At approximately eleven twenty in the morning, after making five phone calls, Jared Durham drained the whiskey bottle from his desk drawer, lassoed a rope around the cross beams of his office, knotted the rope around his neck, climbed onto his desk, and either jumped or stepped off to his death. Everyone who saw Durham's dangling body noted how the desk was right next to his body. At any time, he could have put his feet back on the desk and saved himself. The self-restraint or utter despair that kept him from doing so made it all the sadder.

Fox had responded to a few suicides over the years and most scenes had that "no turning back" feel. Once the person had slit the wrists, kicked over the chair, pulled the trigger, or swallowed the pills, all was lost. But the desk had been right next to him, beckoning him to lift a leg back on. One foot on the desk would have brought air back to the lungs.

Fox marveled at this for a moment. It was hard to imagine.

"So, we know that he made five outgoing calls. We know what calls came in, right before he, you know, took the big step?" Wolfe asked.

"Yup. Monica Tyree," Chief Teague said, perching on the edge of the desk.

Inside the small office, it was suddenly more cramped, hotter than Fox could ever remember. She knew Wolfe had to be miserable. She also knew neither of them had ever been a fan of Durham's. He was a weasel. She'd developed a keen sense about people, and the vibe from Durham had always been that of someone hiding something. Still, she didn't like everyone milling around his office, talking casually as though he'd been but a blip on the radar of life.

In each corner of the small office, there were at least three different conversations going on; one between Travis Miles and Officer Fritz, another between Tammi Whatley—who had managed to maneuver herself into the doorway, nosing about—and anyone who would listen to her, and finally, the coroner with his tape recorder, murmuring secrets to himself for later notes and peering into the half-opened body bag. This was the part of her job she didn't care for. Durham was dead, and it was all business.

"What'd she want?" Fox asked, but Teague shrugged.

A small trickle of sweat beaded its way down the side of his face. "Easy enough to find out, I'd imagine. Monica's been pretty forthcoming these days," Teague said. "What I'm most curious about is who he called right before he killed himself."

"Who'd he call?" Wolfe asked.

The chief knew and seemed to be carefully processing the information. "Four people—possible clients—and his sister."

"Is Jessie talking? Do we know what he said to her?" Fox wondered out loud. It had been Travis Miles and not Jessie who found him first.

"Nope. Left a message. Jessie wasn't in her office," Teague said, and both Fox and Wolfe drew in a collective breath.

That had to be a hell of a message. *Hey, while you were out I decided to kill myself.*

Wolfe scratched the side of her head and sat next to Teague on the desk, kicking one booted foot over the other. She crossed her arms and sighed.

"Imagine hearing that message," Fox mumbled.

It would be a message that would haunt Jessie for the rest of her life. How Jared thought his sister would find peace with that, Fox couldn't understand, and she peeked at Wolfe.

Wolfe, like Fox, took suicides very personally. There was never closure with a case like this, and she pushed away the memory of a young father shooting his face off, only to be found by his son.

"So, who else did he call?" Wolfe asked. "Who are the clients? And how do we know who Durham called?"

"Well, now, I say clients but we haven't confirmed that just yet. Can't seem to find the paperwork for three of 'em. But Mr. Durham very helpfully left us a to-do list."

Fox and Wolfe raised their eyebrows in unison.

A to-do list before suicide?

"Okay, I'll bite," Wolfe said. "Who are they and how do we know he called 'em?"

"He checked off their names." Teague raised a small piece of paper, already bagged for evidence.

Wolfe extended her hand, encouraging Teague to come clean with the names.

"Marla Dodson." Teague counted off on his fingers.

"Yeah, I remember he was covering that case. Marla stole some money from the video place, right?" Fox asked, and Teague nodded.

"Ryan Whatley, Manny Lopez, and Frankie Larson."

Wolfe and Fox looked at each other.

"Funny how that boy's name keeps coming up," Fox said.

Teague shook his head and frowned, letting them know he was lost. "Manny?" he asked.

"Frankie Larson," Wolfe said.

Fox nodded then frowned. "Who's Manny?"

"Someone I've been interested in." Teague inspected the list of names again. "Was at the fight we had in the middle of the street, new kid in town. He's a brawler, a nephew or somethin' like that to Hector Lopez." Teague drew in a deep breath and shoved away from the desk. "He is a person of interest." He looked back and forth between Fox and Wolfe. "And Frankie Larson?"

"Also a person of interest," Wolfe told him and Teague nodded.

"What about Ryan Whatley? What's Durham want with the Whatley kid?" Fox made a *gimme* motion with her fingers, and Teague handed over the evidence bag.

Inside, both Fox and Wolfe could see the names Teague had listed printed out by Durham's hand. The names of Marla Dodson, Ryan Whatley, Manny Lopez, and Frankie Larson each had a line through the name. Only Jessie Durham's name appeared unmarked.

Teague looked over his shoulder toward the body bag and sighed heavily. He stuck a finger in his ear and scratched at it, an unconscious maneuver he used when he was unhappy about something. Without another word, he headed toward the door, moving tentatively toward Tammi Whatley.

"Couldn't tell you . . . but maybe Ms. Whatley here could. Evenin', Ms. Whatley." Teague ducked his head and slipped on by, leaving Wolfe and Fox to battle out who would take on the queen of Granby.

"Rock-paper-scissors," Wolfie said, and Fox groaned.

CHAPTER FORTY-TWO

Rosa Fox was beyond annoyed.

Tina Wolfe cheated at rock-paper-scissors. What was worse, Fox knew going into the juvenile fisted, scissored, or flat-handed game that no matter how hard she watched, her partner would cheat her ass off.

With the final paper symbol Wolfe threw to her own rock-shaped fist, Wolfe let out a howl and slugged her in her arm, laughing. She said, "Good luck with that old hag," and sauntered out the door.

Tammi Whatley's fat mouth was moving, but it was hard to concentrate. It was obvious that because Fox was the one asking, Mrs. Whatley was carefully monitoring her closed-minded, bigoted, piggish little statements, thereby interrupting the normal flow of her brain waves, and rendering her more stupid than usual. To Tammi Whatley, Fox was a Mexican first, cop second.

"I don't know why he called Ryan, but you need to be talking to that Manny boy," Whatley said.

"Yes, ma'am, we will. But we need to ask Ryan a few questions as well. If you could tell me where he is, that would be helpful."

This is pointless.

Tammi Whatley couldn't conceptualize that perhaps the Granby Police Department would like to speak to everyone on the list. In Tammi Whatley's mind, the Mexican needed to be looked into. And she said as much. Repeatedly.

"You know, he deals in stolen car parts," Whatley said. "I bet this is somehow about stolen cars—maybe an entire carjacking ring. Maybe that's the connection here to poor James Otis's death."

Fox studied the woman's face for a moment. The word *poor* was so affected, Fox could feel her jaw muscles clinch and jump.

"That would be the only reason Jared Durham would talk to Ryan. You know he had his tailgate stolen? You can bet Jared found out about it through his own investigation. He found out that Manny had stolen car parts, including Ryan's tailgate and was going to tell him about it." Her gaze drifted away for a moment then the light bulb clicked. "Are you sure this was suicide and not some cover-up?" She leaned in, whispering. "A cover-up for murder?" Her eyes grew wide.

"The report I have is that it's been ruled a suicide. And the questions we have for Ryan are routine. Do you know—"

"I just don't know why you aren't talking to that Manny boy. Aren't you concerned about him?"

Behind Tammi Whatley, Fox spied Wolfe outside, milling around one of the old pecan trees spared from construction during the "Renovate Old Town" project.

Almost a decade ago, Tammi Whatley and Vicky Jackson had spearheaded a project to beautify the town square, placing wrought iron benches around historic trees and flowered hanging baskets from old-fashioned lampposts. Historic meant it was believed the trees were over two hundred years old, but no hard scientific evidence existed to support this claim. Tammi Whatley had said so, and in the eyes of Granby's finest, this was enough. In the eyes of the Ladies Club, the beautification project was a huge success. To the Granby Police Department, every iron bench, every hanging fern on every antique lamppost, and every flowerpot represented the new cruiser and Taser equipment they would not get.

Periodically, Wolfe would pause, wave at her partner, and grin broadly. Finally, when Wolfe had decided Fox was taking too long, she mimicked just how she'd beaten Fox, slowly repeating how her paper had taken Fox's rock. Rather joyously, she showed her partner how she'd cheated.

Tammi Whatley's voice whined on.

Fox watched with agitation, yet—despite herself—growing humor as Wolfe threw what would have appeared to be scissors—something that would be crushed by Fox's rock, Wolfe then turned her hand over at the last minute, allowing herself just enough time to turn that scissor into a flat hand—paper.

Fox scowled.

Wolfe beamed.

The final insult, but classic Wolfie style, was her silent victory dance. She made 'V' symbols with her fingers and strutted circles like a banty rooster, stopping briefly to answer a question from Norman Myer, then continued her dance.

It was hard to concentrate on Tammi Whatley, who continued her claims that it was the Mexicans who needed talking to, not innocent, upstanding members of the community. Fox thanked her for her time and begged off.

"You threw me to the sharks," Fox grumbled when she joined Wolfe.

"Aw, it's good for you." There was no hiding the humor in her voice. Wolfe had her most fun when she was picking at her partner.

"You know, she came damned close to implying that maybe I don't want to talk to the Paradise Park community because I'm *one of them*," she said, giving a mock whisper to the *one of them* part.

"You are one of them," Wolfe said, chiding her, a smile growing to great proportions. "Come on . . . you know you are. Come on . . ."

They parted around the cruiser, Fox instinctively moving to the driver's seat, Wolfe to the passenger side.

"So, where's Ryan?" Wolfe asked, almost serious.

"Wouldn't say. Or couldn't. And what do you mean, it's good for me? How in the hell is talking to Tammi Whatley good for anyone?"

"All right, so we'll check out their house and the Town Pump. He hangs out there a lot. If not, we'll go over to Paradise Park—you know, to *your people*. He's having work done on his truck for the missing tailgate; maybe he's there."

"My people?"

"Your peeps. You're their homegirl." She settled into her seat, smiling to herself. The heat inside the car was stifling and Wolfe leaned forward, flipping the AC gauge to full blast. All the vents, save the far left vent on the driver's side, were tilted toward the passenger. Wolfe. "Let's roll, homey."

"You're not my homegirl." Fox scowled at her partner. "You're a cheat. And quit cranking up the air even before the motor gets going. It drains power. Just wait two damned minutes. Can you do that?"

"No! It's hot! Mexico hot! See, that's why you don't notice it. You and your peeps," she said, already chuckling.

Fox reduced the AC to the lowest notch and threw the car in reverse. Wolfe leaned forward again, putting it back to high, and made a fist, threatening to hit Fox.

"Fine. When this car dies, I'm blaming it on you," Fox said, pulling out of the square and turning toward Willow Pines, the wealthiest housing development in Granby. In truth, it was one street with just fourteen homes, but more land had been earmarked for future building, no doubt reflecting the homeowners' hopes that more wealthy people would settle into Granby. It wasn't likely. It was a bigger vexation that the development, such as it was, was named Willow Pines. There were no pines. There were no willow trees. There were no trees, period.

The heat was rising from the asphalt, making everything slightly blurry. The call of the Town Pump was too powerful since the Pump set its refrigerators a good ten degrees lower than any other retailer. This time of year, if you reached far enough into the back of the coolers, a cola forming ice could be found. Thus, when you said you wanted "a cold one," Town Pump would be the place to go.

"Let's get a cold one before we do anything else," Wolfe said.

"We see the Whatleys again, you talk. I'm done." Fox threw up her hands, still irritated. As she recalled the conversation, Tammi Whatley had asked her where she was born. *What the hell did that have to do with where her son was or why Jared Durham had taken his own life?* The more she thought on it, the madder she got.

"Foxie, I did it for you." Wolfe smiled, pleased with herself.

"For me." It was more of a statement than a question.

Wolfe waved her arm frantically toward the Town Pump, making

Fox turn into its parking lot. As usual, it was packed. Everyone wanted a cold one. No one was pumping gas.

"It will hone your communications skills when you're forced to interact with a known hater of the brown man," Wolfe said, and Fox laughed outright.

"I cannot believe you." She shook her head and started to say something else but stopped. Instead, she opened her car door, stepped out, and began speaking loudly and fluently in Spanish. Before them was Horrible Hernandez. He was out.

"Man! What's he doing out?" Wolfe asked.

Fox ignored her, focusing on Hernandez, and spoke only to the man, periodically pointing to Wolfe. She was having a little bit of fun with Wolfe, knowing full well Wolfe had no idea what was being said.

Hernandez looked at Wolfe and gave a grave nod. This was a man who did not like the police, did not trust the police—in particular—Wolfe and Fox. Despite his drug-induced state that night, he'd remembered them.

Fox shut the car door and moved closer to Hernandez. As she spoke to him, his eyes shifted back and forth between the two officers.

Fox would make Wolfe wait to hear the details, but she knew that Wolfe had picked up on names she knew, like Jared Durham, Frankie Larson, and Ryan Whatley. When it was his turn to talk, Hernandez had much to say, and again, Wolfe would have to wait for a translation. The more he spoke, the more at ease he appeared, gaining more trust with Fox. Finally, Fox moved over, still speaking to Hernandez, and slapped the shoulder of her partner. Again, he nodded, and Fox leaned in, shook his hand, and bid him farewell.

"Well, what was all that about?" Wolfe asked as they watched him lumber across the street.

Fox gave Wolfe another firm shoulder slap and headed into the Town Pump. "I asked him if he'd seen Frankie or Ryan, asked a few questions about the missing tailgate, and then suggested that he needed to come see you, you know, whenever he has any problems. I told him that despite what he's heard about you, you are in full support of the Paradise Park community and that you will do whatever you can to help them out." She reached for the door, almost laughing.

Wolfe's mouth fell open.

"I did it for you, Wolfie. It will hone your communication with the brown man when you're forced to interact with a man who is a known hater of the white female cop."

CHAPTER FORTY-THREE

"I swear, Ms. Riley," I said, trying to squash the revulsion that was climbing up my throat. "I don't know if this is going to work."

"Well, now, I don't see why not." Ms. Riley huffed, and I heard Momma snicker somewhere behind me.

I was halfway up one of Ms. Riley's stupid prized pecan trees while Momma, Cici, and Ella stood behind me at the fence, hollering out instructions. I was not amused.

"A little lower, Thia." Cici laughed. "I want to see the glare in his eyes so that it hits me as I'm comin' up the walk."

"That's right. Yes! That's what I want." Ms. Riley clapped her hands together. She was overjoyed to have Momma and Cici right there with her, having nary a clue how ridiculous this was.

"Over to the right there, Thia," Momma said in a chirpy voice. "He needs to be even with the other fella on the other side."

"Ms. Riley." I sighed loudly. "This is just . . . well, this is just gross, Ms. Riley."

"Oh, Thia, don't be a snot," Cici called out in mock anger. "If Ms. Riley wants to hang dead squirrels in her tree, well, then I think it's her right."

"It's going to attract . . ." I gagged when I looked down at the squirrel hanging from the rope in my hand. "Oh, geez! Oh, come on, Ms. Riley! It's already attracting flies." I gagged again.

An old rancher's lore said that if you shot and killed rogue coyotes and hung their carcasses from the fence line, it would scare off other coyotes. As much as I hated it, I had to admit I'd gotten used to the sight of dead coyotes hanging on fence posts, gates, and barbed wire. It was the way of the land. When another coyote showed, it either got away, or it got shot at, killed, and hung.

Whether it did or didn't work, Ms. Riley had gotten it into her head that if it was good enough to work for coyotes, then it was good enough to work for squirrels. Specifically, one fat gray squirrel with a scrawny tail. She'd figured if she couldn't shoot him—especially not since Chief Teague had taken away her guns after she shot Bubba—she could damn well scare him away. So she'd gotten two humane traps from the animal control department to use in her scheme. Nobody had cared when she'd asked for them since the department didn't exist, and everyone let their dogs run free, anyway. Herman Luke had quit after he got bit for the umpteenth time, and Dr. Hirsh just laughed and said, "Well, start bitin' back. Hell, Herman, nothin' else seems to be workin'.'"

Within ten hours, Ms. Riley had snared two squirrels, shot them dead with her pellet gun, tied a rope around their necks, and called me to come hang them.

Momma intercepted the call, and with great delight, clapped her hands as soon as she hung up the phone. "Thia! Thia! Come on, girl! Oh, Cici, you gotta come. Ms. Riley's killed two squirrels and wants Thia to string 'em up in her pecan tree to scare off the other squirrels!" She had barely finished her sentence before she was bent forward, slapping the tops of her thighs, and howling with delight.

"No!" Cici snapped, mouth open, smiling like a fool.

"Yes!"

"No!"

"Oh *yes*, and we're going to watch. C'mon, Thia!"

That was when I'd put my foot down, announcing, "I'll be damned if I'm going to climb a tree with a dead squirrel in my hands and tie it to a branch like a Christmas ornament."

But when Momma and Aunt Cici want to see something, they are relentless, and not since the time Cindy Nelson found out that Darrel Nelson was carrying on with her sister and had thrown him out of the house in his underwear did Momma and Cici want to see something so badly.

It had been one of the few times in Granby history we'd had a freezing cold snap. But cold or no cold, when word had traveled that Darrel was running around in his underwear, banging on doors, trying to be let inside, people found reasons to go "to the store," by way of the Nelsons.

Cindy Nelson had called each and every neighbor on the block and said, "Pretty soon here, Darrel's gonna come knockin' on your door, but don't you let him in. He's a cheat, a liar, and has blasphemed God. He'll have to answer to God, so don't you answer your door, you hear?"

Nobody, but nobody, had wanted to cross paths with Cindy Nelson, which had left a pasty, freezing, bare-footed and near naked Darrel Nelson hopping around from yard to yard, swearing to all that was holy that he would surely die. It was a sight.

I gagged again then froze. I was starting to see things. Its beady little eye was looking at me, and I wondered if it was only possums that played dead. It seemed to me that maybe its little leg kicked or something. With one squirrel successfully swinging in the breeze, we were in a debate as to where to hang the other.

What was worse was Ms. Riley wanted to hang it from the perspective of what would be most daunting to another squirrel.

"Maybe if you hunkered down like you were gathering nuts and looked up," Cici said with certain glee. "It might give you a better idea of where you'd like that one to hang."

"Yes," Ms. Riley said, hobbling her way over toward the gate.

"Cici!" I shouted over my shoulder. "Do you mind? We don't need anymore . . ." But it was too late.

She had Ms. Riley hunkering and calculating. Seeing her in the position, wanting so desperately to rid herself of the evil fat gray squirrel, it suddenly seemed perfectly reasonable to hang her dead squirrel in just the right position.

Sometimes it happens that a body gets so involved in what he or she is doing that no matter how insane, it seems reasonable. Then someone comes along and asks that same person what he or she is doing and—

blam!—all reasons melt away.

When you hear yourself say, "I'm hanging dead squirrels" as an answer, there is no reason.

Miranda McGhee pulled up in her little sports car, rolled down the window, tilted up her sunglasses—still chomping away on her gum—and screwed up her face. "What're you doing?"

"I'm hanging up a dead squirrel to frighten away the head pecan-stealing squirrel." I made an executive decision, leaned out on the limb, tied off a knot, and let the rodent swing on his own. Or her own. It didn't seem important at that point. "The idea is to scare off all the neighborhood squirrels." There are some things you can't sugarcoat. I was, in fact, hanging a dead squirrel to ward off other pecan-gathering squirrels.

"Well, hey, Ms. Riley!" Miranda leaned forward a little more, getting a full view of everyone.

She wasn't the least bit surprised to learn that a Duke graduate, mother, and talented up-and-coming reporter was up her neighbor's tree, hanging dead squirrels.

I crawled rather ungracefully down the tree, managing to scrape my inner thighs on the unforgiving bark as I lost my grip and slid down. I winced. Rubbing the scratches, I looked back at the tree to inspect my handiwork. Two dead squirrels.

Miranda eyed the tree then looked back at Momma, Cici, and Ella. She didn't care too much for Cici, which is the reason, I suppose, she locked in on Ella.

"Well, hey, Lily," Miranda said.

Ella cooed, practicing her best wave.

I stiffened. "Lily?" I glared at Momma.

She smiled sweetly and shrugged. "I can't help it if it's catching on."

Miranda looked confused. "Isn't her name Lily?" she asked.

"No, actually, it's Ella, but . . ." I could feel my frustration rising. "It's only her legal birth name and one that I chose, but really, Momma, don't let that trip you up."

She waved a hand, pooh-poohing me. "Oh, Thia. She just looks like a Lily. I can't help it if she looks like a Lily."

"Lileee!" Ella beamed and Momma clapped.

"Oh, yes! Lily! You are my girl, Lily. Gramma's little angel girl!" Momma bent over and swept Ella into her arms.

"Now, Thia, if I get myself another squirrel, will you come back and hang one on my back tree? I think I ought to scatter them about—"

Cici let out a snort.

"Ms. Riley, I just don't know," I said as politely as possible. "I want to help you out but I really don't like hanging dead squirrels." The insides of my thighs were on fire. I was mad at Momma. I was embarrassed to have been caught hanging dead squirrels.

"Why, Thia, I just don't think a live squirrel would work."

Everyone stopped. A half smile froze on Cici's face. My anger ebbed.

"No, I guess not." I shook my head and pretended to wipe my brow. I peeked at Momma beneath my hand. "Hanging live squirrels would be a bitch."

Everyone but Ms. Riley cracked up. Ms. Riley looked put out.

Miranda inched her car alongside us as we walked back home. "You got some time, Thia? I need to talk to you about something . . . private."

I shrugged and looked to both Momma and Cici. They were busily turning Ella into a miniature of them. They could not have cared less. Only when I climbed into the car did Cici yell, "Bring us a cold one."

We headed off toward the Town Pump while Miranda dropped a bomb on me. She was pregnant and Tom Jackson was the father. Given several facts, I should have seen this coming. She had been carrying on with Tom Jackson for some time. That was widely known. She was also a small-town, Southern girl. Statistically speaking, she was a walking ratio of likelihood to get pregnant. Out of wedlock.

"Out of the frying pan . . ." she mumbled to herself. "Why me?" Miranda shrugged for a moment, poking out her bottom lip. "I'm not some . . . thing, you know. I'm not some piece of throwaway!" Her voice began to crack. "He told me that he loved me!"

Ho boy!

"Maybe he really does," I said. "But Miranda, you can't exactly force him to leave his wife if he doesn't want to."

What I wanted to say was, if I had a penny for every time a man told a woman he loved her just to get in her pants, I'd be buying out Walmart. Or maybe I could buy Walmart and offer their employees full-time positions with great medical packages. I would refuse to buy or sell anything made in China. I could reign as queen, the world over. Queen Thia, doer of good deeds.

Miranda's sharp wail brought me back.

I was Thia—a young, small-town Southern girl who was now a single mother because a married man once told me he loved me.

"He told me that he loved me." There was a quiet rage building in her voice. "He told me that he loved me; now I'm pregnant, and the world is going to know about it."

"Well, what are you going to do?" I had a sinking feeling this was where I came in.

"I want you to do a story about me in the paper."

Um.

Er.

Ah.

"You can do that, right?" She turned to me, looking eager and desperate all at once.

"Well, yes. I mean . . . I can write something up, but it has to fly by the editing staff." I almost choked on those words. I couldn't believe I'd said it myself.

The staff was a gaggle of nosy women—none of whom had a journalism degree—who just wanted to look stories over before they hit print so they could know first. I never once saw Tammi, Vicky, or LeAnn so much as add a comma or correct a word in my work, and much as I'd like to think my work was that tight, I knew better.

"Good." She fell back against her seat, looking satisfied.

"But, I mean . . ." I half laughed. "What's the story? I mean, I can't just write, 'Hey, guess who's pregnant?' There has to be a purpose for a profile, a reason for a story. And even then, Miranda, I can't see Vicky or Tammi letting this one by."

It was the way of a small-town paper. This wasn't the *New York Times*. This was a family rag that ran whatever it wanted to. The people of Granby would never fully realize how much of what they read or learned about in the local news was controlled by a small group of people. If I thought on it, it drove me nuts. So I tried not to.

I did, however, sit thinking about Miranda's situation, and the feelings of my own circumstances came flooding back.

He hadn't just said he loved me, he'd shown it. The way he'd laughed with me, spent time with me, held and caressed me. He'd loved me dearly and in a manner that had made everything around me feel secure and real and beautiful. Even terrible stories on the news had brought me feelings of gratefulness that I had him in my life. In an instant, he'd been gone. I'd been pregnant and he'd been gone.

"They won't let that story run, Miranda," I said. I knew the truth. Tammi and Vicky would never stand by for it.

Ella had deserved better than this. She'd deserved to have a daddy who would throw her up into the air, play and giggle with her, hold and care for her in a way that would make her life seem safe and secure and happy. Cici, Momma, and I had showered Ella with love, but she'd deserved her daddy's love as well.

"You could take out an ad—you know, a birth announcement," I said, not even hearing my own voice. "If I was to go in early, set up the page, maybe they wouldn't bother to look at it."

"Thank you, Thia." Miranda gathered up my hands in hers. I could see her hurt. She'd been lied to, betrayed, and hurt.

"That's Queen Thia to you," I said. Happily, she didn't argue.

CHAPTER FORTY-FOUR

When he'd taken the position as Chief of Police in Granby, Texas, Teague had done more than a little homework. He'd made it his business to know everyone else's. The first thing he'd done was look at the demographics of the town. The town was sixty percent white, twenty percent black, fifteen percent Hispanic, and five percent "other." The only "other" he could think of were the Epsteins, who were Jewish.

As the first black police chief, he'd anticipated a few grumbles, even though he'd hoped to come in colorless. He was the second tallest man in town, second only to Milford East, and he was certainly the darkest. Yet he'd hoped to come in colorless and quietly take command. He knew the history, revenues, and taxes. He knew about the school board, city council, founding families, and the high school's sports records. He'd taken the local paper, read about wedding announcements and the community theatre, which was comprised of just four dedicated women. He studied the names of individual citizens, arrest records, and members of his department. And to this day, he would have said with great confidence that he knew his town well. Now, he could only sit in a daze. He didn't know anything.

Francis gave a small knock on the doorjamb to his office and then leaned upon it. She had no intention of coming into the office. It was her standard hello.

"You look like you're about broke down." She offered a smile, and he studied her for a moment.

Francis was another one. Until today, he thought he knew all there was to know about her. Late sixties, been with the department for almost fifty years. Her daddy had been sheriff back in the day when just a sheriff and a deputy patrolled the Granby streets. Later, she'd married a deputy and acted as office clerk. Her father and husband had both died in office, and Teague suspected she would do the same. Never remarried, never had kids. Liked dogs, disliked cats, adored children, and disliked any sweets being brought into the departments because *fire ants can smell doughnuts from the pits of hell and'll bring all their damned relatives for a feast!* She was too thin, her hair too big, her lipstick too bright, but she was perfect. She knew every person, every phone number, every address, and every lineage in Granby.

I am, Francis. That, I am.

He tried to smile, but it was no use. "You know," he said. "I just realized that I have no idea what goes on in this town."

Francis howled with delight. "It's a small town, honey. You can know ever'thing about ever'body and still not know anything that's goin' on."

Teague smiled, poking a finger in his ear and scratching.

She watched him for a moment and chuckled. "What is it, Chief?"

"It's the craziest thing, Francis." And he laid out the series of conversations throughout the afternoon that would offer an education about his neighbors he would have never believed.

Jared Durham's suicide had been as simple as making one phone call.

Monica Tyree set off a chain reaction that no one could have expected. As Tyree lay in recovery contemplating her addiction and the horrible fact that it had caused a death, she decided she had to come clean with everyone, starting with her lawyer.

Without hesitation or remorse, Monica told Teague of her blackmailing ways. Angry and sick, she'd listened to people confess their sins; she'd taken notes, and made random phone calls to various citizens. Some were hateful pranks. Others were used in blackmail.

Without hesitation or remorse, she relayed to Teague that she'd learned how Judge McKinley liked young women. Scouring websites and magazines, he stopped focusing on work. The more he saw, the more he wanted. Monica knew only that the judge was blackmailing a young woman into having sex with him; she didn't know *who* for the longest time.

What she did know was that while she faced new charges of possession of marijuana, Jared Durham dropped the mother of them all in his confessions. He, too, was a porn king, but his preference was much younger and very male.

Monica quickly let Durham know she knew about his sexual preferences. She'd also laid out her demands. That was when Durham's bossy, ever-present sister came into play. To keep Monica's case off the docket, Jessie worked overtime, and in her quest to keep the name Tyree off the radar, she made a late-night discovery.

Amber Hirsh was a frequent visitor to Judge McKinley's chambers.

The girl and her idiot boyfriend had been caught with illegal arms, and while the prospect of going to a women's prison was terrifying for Amber, the prospect of Daddy finding out was even worse. Amber threw herself at his mercy and McKinley couldn't see straight. The perversion worked well for Jessie and Jared Durham and it worked for Monica.

Again, without hesitation and without remorse, Monica told Teague how she'd tried to get clean and couldn't. So, in her time of need, she'd put further demands on Durham, his sister, and as Monica later learned, Amber. She was the perfect supplier. When Amber began to resist, it was Jessie who tightened the screws, whoring her out to the judge, and threatening Amber that she had pictures of their affair.

The game had changed again when, out on a late-night run to her father's animal pharmacy, Amber spotted another of Jared's clients with James Otis the night he died. Jessie's frustrations heightened when Monica discovered her supplier's identity and cut out the middleman.

To Teague's disappointment, Monica had not known the identity of that man.

Stoned, Monica had crashed into Travis Miles's truck, ultimately killing Johnny Vargus, and the game had changed yet again. Suddenly,

Monica had wanted to come clean. Literally and figuratively. She'd told Jared she was coming clean, and in her quest to do so, she planned to tell Thia Franks everything that had been going on in Granby and who, she believed, shared in her responsibility for the death of Johnny Vargus.

"That would include telling Thia how Monica had been blackmailing Jared."

"Good grief," Francis said. "How is Johnny's death Jared's fault?"

"Addicts never take full responsibility," Teague said. "Even when the obvious is staring them full in the face, it's still always someone else's fault, or in this case, shared blame. The way Monica sees it, if Jessie and Jared hadn't been supplying her with drugs, she wouldn't have killed ol' Johnny. And if Jared hadn't been a pedophile, none of this would have happened."

"So everyone goes down." Francis pondered the information. "Wow, imagine that phone call."

They did.

A few phone calls later, Jared Durham had committed suicide.

"You think Monica shares responsibility in Jared's death?" Francis asked, but Teague just laughed.

"Honestly, I don't know what to think. Hard to feel sorry for a pedophile. The man was a perv, Francis. You know what they say, the only good perv is a dead perv."

"So, what's his connection to the other phone calls? I get his call to Marla Dodson. He'd invested in her land, was going to buy it. I guess before he kilt hisself, he needed to . . ."

"Not what you think," Teague said. "Jared Durham had locked out Travis Miles from owning that land. He and Travis had been going 'round and 'round over this since Clyde died. He turned the land over to Jessie. He once told Travis he'd die before he let him have his hands on the land. He did one better. Before he died, he clinched the deal between Jessie and Marla." He shrugged.

Francis's eyes widened as Teague revealed the truth behind the relationship between Travis Miles and Jared Durham. Francis's mouth fell open.

Travis Miles wasn't interested in the ladies. And while they'd had an on-again, off-again relationship, Jared Durham wasn't interested in anyone Travis's age.

"Travis Miles?" Francis finally caught her breath. He is a good ol' boy. A redneck. A gun-toting, NRA card-carrying, tobacco-chewing bubba. "Travis is . . . gay?"

It was a shocker.

"Then what did Jared want with the other three phone calls?" Francis asked. "Manny Lopez, Frankie Larson, and Ryan Whatley. What could he . . . good heavens!" Teague nodded as Francis sorted through the new information. "You don't think they're . . . do you?"

"You know, a lot of people thought the world of Durham when he first settled in Granby. I wasn't here then, but from what I heard, he did a lot of volunteer work," Teague said.

"That's right."

"Including little league baseball with the local boys . . ." Teague drew a heavy breath.

"You really think those three boys could be . . . gay?" Francis swallowed hard.

Teague eyed her.

Travis Miles wasn't the only gun-toting, NRA card-carrying bubba in town. Francis was the stereotypical southern Baptist woman. The very idea of there being gay people in her small town could very well drive her to madness. For Francis, this simply meant there wasn't enough praying going on.

He raised his eyebrows. "Or they're his victims."

Even in Granby.

CHAPTER FORTY-FIVE

Monica had made another call she hadn't told the chief about. She knew. She'd known all about it and his involvement, but as a victim herself, she'd wanted him to know she wouldn't tell. There was something he'd needed to know, however.

Amber Hirsh was another problem. She also knew.

"How do you know?" There was panic in his voice.

"She came to me, talkin' crazy. She'd been blackmailed by Jessie Durham," Monica said. "You know, she was doin' Judge McKinley."

A quick, shocked bellow of a laugh was the only reply.

"Yeah, go figure. So, she'd been gettin' stuff for me, to shut me up and keep me happy so that I didn't say what I knew about Jared . . . you know about all that, right?"

What do I . . . do I admit . . . should I deny . . . "Yeah, I knew."

"Okay, so, this is all just you scratch my back, I scratch yours until . . . you know, with Johnny Vargus."

I've got nothing.

"I gotta own up, you know. I got to do what's right. I killed a man. I mean, I know I'm not the only one responsible here, but I'm in it as much as all the others. So, you know, I told Chief Teague about where I was gettin' the stuff. Amber's name comes up, and she's freaked because, I don't know, I guess she thinks she could be charged. Distribution of illegal substances or some shit like that. So, she's thinking that she can give information about what happened with James Otis. You know, dig herself out from under."

Shit.

"You still there?"

"Yes," he murmured into the phone. He could feel himself hyperventilating. "What . . . what information would she . . . could she give?" He needed to know.

"Well, she saw you guys together the night James was killed. She knows you're the last person to be with him."

"Who else knows?" he asked.

"You, me, Jared. He's dead. Amber. Maybe Thia."

"Thia?"

"Yeah. She went to talk to Thia. I guess I'm not the only person trying to clean house, huh? Just thought you should know." Monica hung up, leaving him paralyzed with fear. *What am I going to do? Oh, God, what am I going to do?*

He had no recollection of even how he'd gotten to *The Recorder* or what he would do or say when he saw Theresa Franks. He just knew he had to get to her. Reason with her, distract her, dissuade her. Something.

It was coming back. That feeling of suffocation. It was coming back strong—as strong as it had been when he was a kid. As strong as when Jared Durham had first laid hands on him. He felt revulsion shudder through him.

Many children of abuse blocked out the actual memories of abuse. He'd read many accounts of how a child of abuse would suddenly awake to the memory. Other children of abuse lived in a shadow of guilt and burden, unable to commit to relationships or fully function in life. Many turned to some sort of addiction as a coping mechanism for what had been done to them. Self-medicated. Still others would repeat the cycle, do unto others . . .

He was aware of the memories. He could even identify the exact date when it first happened. He'd been eleven years old, and he'd just hit his first homerun. It was the most exciting moment of his life. All his friends and family were there. Everyone who loved him was there, within reach, yet so far removed. They never knew.

The pitch was perfect. Outside and low. Just how he liked it.

Coach Durham had told him to expect it. He'd been watching the pitcher for much of the afternoon and realized the kid seemed to be pitching in a cycle. Next up: low and on the outside.

Everything was perfect. The sun was behind him and in the pitcher's face. He was on his home turf, and the ball would be coming in low and on the outside. Two runs down in the bottom of the last inning. The stage was set.

He waited. The first pitch was indeed low and on the outside, but he waited anyway. The next one would be the same. He stepped off, re-gripped the bat, and took a deep breath. He could hear everyone cheering. He could hear his teammates and the coach. He stepped up, exhaled, and let it fly.

The connection felt perfect. It was solid, heavy, fluid. And like in the movie, every second was in slow motion. He dropped the bat on the follow-through and took off. He could see Trevor Matthews push off first with Pastor Tyree standing to the side as first base coach.

He was waving his arms in huge circular motions. "Go! Go! Go!"

Out of the corner of his eye, he could see James Otis shoving off second base. The chase was on. All of the outfielders dropped back, running after a ball that was headed for the woods.

His cleats dug in, and he ran as he'd never run before. He'd hit a homerun. He was sure of it, but his heart pounded. *Get home! Get home!*

His legs pounded into the earth, making longer strides than he'd ever known. Trevor had rounded second, headed for third, and a roar could be heard from the stands. James had made it home. They just needed one more to tie!

He rounded second, headed for third, and could see Willie Strictland standing against the fence line, jumping up and down, and screaming. Another roar as Trevor made it home. As he rounded third, he could see them all now. The entire team jostled around the home plate area while the ump fought them back, yelling behind him. Coach Durham struggled with the boys to keep them clear of the plate. He dug in, his legs aching, his heart ready to explode with exhaustion and excitement.

He hit the plate, watched the ump make the sign for a homerun, and he was mobbed. His ears swelled with joyous vibrations from the cheers. He squeezed his eyes shut and listened to the noises, felt the hard thumps and pounding on his body by overenthusiastic teammates.

It was the single most exciting moment of his life.

As he sat down on the bench, breathing heavily and smiling so hard his cheeks hurt, Coach Durham sat down next to him. As his teammates celebrated on the field, he sat blissfully content. Then he felt it. His thigh.

Coach murmured something about being proud of him. "I knew it! I told you. Low and on the outside. See what happens when you listen to your coach. I know. I know." And his hand slipped up to the very highest part of his leg, to his athletic cup.

It felt so wrong.

His heart slowed. His brain slowed.

Coach's hand slid up and down for a moment, and he panicked, wanting it to stop. Goosebumps raced up and down his arms and legs when the coach leaned close to whisper in his ear.

"Just you and me, kid."

If his voice was meant to sound soothing, it wasn't.

He tried to stand, hoping to join in the celebration with the rest of his team, but Coach Durham's outside leg trapped him so that he was pressed against the inside of Coach's thigh.

Everyone was gathered at the plate and all he wanted was to join them.

As the coach stood, his left hand reached down as though he were going to pat his athlete's bottom. In the excitement, no one would have noticed, let alone thought anything of it. But the coach's hand was moving too slowly, pressing too hard as he caressed the boy.

Bewildered. Confused. He finally broke free and ran toward the rest of his team. The team seemed to open up and swallow him inside as they chanted.

He accepted congratulatory pat after congratulatory pat; his mind was humming.

What had happened? What was that all about?

Coaches exchanged handshakes, parents did the ceremonious victory tunnel for both teams to run through, and baseball moms distributed drinks and cupcakes—and he decided it was nothing. It must not have been as bad or weird as he thought. And he'd gone home happy.

Until it happened again. And again with growing feelings of confusion, dread, true unhappiness. It happened in public, for all the world to see, yet no one reacted, so he didn't know what to do. The problem must be his as no one else seemed to care. Everyone loved Coach Durham—his mother, his father ... the mere mention of Durham's name and most parents would coo on cue.

Isn't he wonderful?

So good with kids!

A natural with kids.

But the touching increased. The whispers, sideways glances, and winks.

He tried to speak out to his father but was shut down. Quitting baseball was not an option.

He'd ridden in his father's truck into town then pulled his bike from the bed and rode over to the Town Pump to buy a cold Gatorade. He'd milled around, looking at certain magazines until Mr. Smith kicked him out. Reluctantly, he headed toward the baseball fields.

He arrived early, and rather than head to the dugout, fearful he would be trapped alone with Coach Durham, he laid down his bike and sauntered over toward the swings, which were partially hidden in a cluster of trees. The trees offered cool shade but also the perfect cover. He sat in a swing, unscrewed the Gatorade cap, and sipped. He froze, drink halfway to his mouth. His mouth was still open as he watched. James Otis and Coach Durham both exited the park's bathroom, and he knew. He saw the way he moved, the way his head hung, the way he lingered behind Coach Durham as they moved toward the dugout, and he knew. He knew.

The lone bike lying on its side and James looked around. They read each other's expressions perfectly. It was an instant bond, a kindred spirit not to be shared with anyone else. He knew. He knew what James was thinking and feeling.

How could it be so wrong when everyone thought that Coach was so great?

What was wrong that this should be happening? And how could they ever tell anyone? There was no way that anyone could understand this. It had been a living nightmare that could not be stopped, understood, or justified.

He jerked to a halt when he realized how quickly he was moving. Both his head and heart were pounding.

There, in the giant bay window of *The Recorder*, he could see Thia at her desk, with Darion James bouncing on her knee. He could hear Thia laughing, occasionally dipping in to blow sloppy, loud kisses against Darion's neck and shoulders. Each time, Darion's head dipped back, letting out a gleeful giggle.

It was unsettling how much he looked like James.

His heart sank.

Of all the times. Tasha Williams had brought Darion to visit Thia. His eyes flashed toward Tasha. She stood, smiling, her head tilted to one side, as she watched the love of her life giggle and carry on. He noted that she looked happy.

He'd tried to go see her after James died. He'd wanted to wrap his arms around her and tell her how very sorry he was, but he couldn't. He couldn't bring himself to get that close. Not after what he'd done.

Suddenly, he felt exposed. He looked up and down the street for a moment then ducked out of sight. He would have to get her when she was alone.

CHAPTER FORTY-SIX

Rosa Fox groaned, remembering the very last words spoken by Chief Teague.

Use discretion.

According to the chief, Travis Miles, ever determined to get his hands on the Dodson property, had appeared again on the doorstep of Marla Dodson. Not knowing what else to do, Dodson had called Jessie Durham. Jessie, still in the midst of her brother's sudden death and being named executrix of Jared's will, had called Chief Teague, screaming something about her constitutional rights and legal ownership of the property.

The task was simple—remove Travis Miles, calm the grieving woman.

Fox knew it was never that simple.

Jessie Durham was screaming hysterically, holding a hunting rifle in her hands while Travis Miles held his ground.

"This is mine!" he yelled. "It's owed me."

"You get out of here, Travis, I mean it!" Jessie yelled back. "You see there." She pointed to Fox and Wolfe as they climbed out of their cruiser. "I've called the police. You don't have a right to be here."

Travis wheeled around. "I have a right! This was supposed to be *my* land! I'd worked out a deal with Clyde. Clyde and Jared. This was supposed to be mine, and Clyde wanted it that way!" He was nearly frantic.

"Go home, Travis!" Jessie bellowed, still clutching her rifle.

"Okay, now," Wolfe said, holding a hand out toward Jessie. "Why don't you just give me that first before we start talking."

"No!" Jessie demanded. "I want him off the land!"

"Whoa! That's fine. That's fine." Wolfe edged closer. "And I'll see to it, but first, let me have the gun, Jessie."

"I ain't goin' anywhere!" Travis stonewalled.

"I just want everyone to go away," Marla chirped from a nearby tree.

Both Fox and Wolfe had missed her. Partially hidden, she looked tiny and frail. Fox moved over toward Marla.

"I ain't leaving here until I get what's mine," Travis said.

"Officer Wolfe, I want you to arrest this man for trespassing!" Jessie waved a hand at Wolfe, and the butt of the gun made a circle around the group.

"Holy shit! Jessie, give me the damned gun before I have to shoot you. How's that? I'm not talking to anyone, and I'll arrest everyone, including Miss Meek over there, unless you put down that damned gun!" Wolfe's voice roared over everyone.

Jessie stopped, considering her rifle for the first time. Her shoulders slumped. "Fine. Take it. But don't let him near me!"

Travis rolled his eyes. "Like I'd touch you." He practically spat the words out.

Fox watched the scene from the distance as Wolfe moved like a cat, reaching in, taking the rifle, and easing back to set it near the cruiser.

"Oh, right," Jessie said. "I forget. You just like to touch men!"

"What?" Wolfe reeled back, a smile spreading to a wide grin.

"Bitch!" he hissed.

"Oh, I think we know who the bitch is here." She laughed at him. It was a hateful, unhappy laugh.

Travis lunged at her with Wolfe wedged between the two.

Again, Fox found herself watching the Tina Wolfe Show. Wolfe gave a definitive shove to Travis, catching him off balance, and got the upper hand. With one graceful wrist snap, her baton was out and released to its full extension, and she tapped it threateningly against her own leg.

"I will break a kneecap, so help me God," she said.

Everyone drew a deep breath.

The smile returned to Wolfe's lips. "No shit? You gay?" Her eyes twinkled.

Travis scowled.

"Hell, yes, he's gay. Gayer than a kite! I don't know what kind of relationship he had with Clyde Dodson..." Jessie clearly had no problems sharing the details.

"Are kites gay?" Wolfe looked over her shoulder to her partner.

Fox shrugged.

"... but I know that Jared owns this land. Or did. He willed it to me for me to do what I see fit. It's all legal. You can see for yourself."

"That's bullshit!"

"That's the law, jackass!" Jessie said.

"Do you have the papers?" Fox asked from her fence post.

Marla continued to peer out at everyone.

"Yes, right here!" Jessie withdrew a white envelope from her back pocket, and Fox sauntered over, reaching out for the paper work.

Travis began to sputter. "Well, I don't care! I know what I was promised."

"I don't care what was promised between the sheets," Jessie said with particular venom. "I own this land."

"Looks legal, Travis." Fox spoke in a calming tone, hoping to bring tensions down.

Travis stroked his hair, and though quiet, he was agitated. For a moment, no one spoke.

Apparently, Jessie could no longer take the suspense. "So, you gonna leave or what?"

"I'm entitled to get my things, then." He looked at Wolfe. "Can't I at least get my things?"

"Sounds reasonable," Wolfe said, eyeing Jessie.

"He doesn't have anything! There isn't one thing here that's his. He just wants to—"

"I've got things here, Jessie. Like it or not, Jared and I invested in some things together." Travis took a threatening step toward Jessie, and Wolfe quickly moved between them, tapping her baton against her leg.

"What've you got, Travis? What's yours?" She put up a hand in a halting motion.

"I've got—"

"You've got nothing!"

"I've got things!"

"You just want to poke around and see what you can find. You've got nothing."

"He just wants to poke around." Wolfie snickered and jabbed a finger at Fox. She turned to Travis. "You've done enough pokin', Travis!"

"You shut up, ya bull dyke."

" 'Bull dyke'?" Wolfe cackled and turned to Fox. "Do I look like a bull dyke to you?"

"People do say you look like Anne Murray." Fox shrugged.

"Is she gay?" Wolfe folded her arms, wondering out loud.

"Not that it matters," Fox said.

"Not that it matters," Wolfe echoed then turned back to the speechless trio. "I don't know what else to do. I washed my wig, brushed my fangs." She fluffed her short hair and flashed her best smile. "But it's never good enough."

"Shut up!" Jessie screamed. "Are you going to do something, or do I have to call the chief?"

"I got a right to look in the barn and get some of my things!" Travis raised his voice to be heard over Jessie's.

"You don't have—"

"I have a right!"

"Ladies, ladies . . ." Wolfe pushed Travis away from Jessie with her baton.

Enraged, Travis lashed out and connected with a heavy right hook squarely on Wolfe's chin. Wolfe staggered back, landing hard on her bottom.

Fox gasped but recovered quickly, moving in on Travis. In one fluid motion, Fox had her baton out and delivered a debilitating whack to the back of Travis's knee. He crumpled like a rag doll. Fox was on him, knee in the middle of his back, wrangling one arm and then another into her cuffs.

"That was a jackass thing to do, Travis. Now you're under arrest for striking an officer."

Wolfe popped up and shook off disorientation. "What the hell . . ."

"Geez! Are you okay?" Fox asked then burst into laughter. "Shit, I'm sorry. But . . ." She stifled a snicker as she led a limping Travis Miles into the back of the cruiser. "You went down like a cement block."

"Yes, that was very funny." Wolfe weaved around a bit. "Hilarious." She rubbed her chin, making *E* and *O* movements with her mouth, testing her mouth and jaw muscles. With Travis in the cruiser, Wolfe looked at her partner.

"Let's cruise on over to the barn and take a quick look. That is, iffen you don' mind, Jessie."

Jessie opened her mouth in protest then shrugged and waved them on. "I don't care. Just you make sure you lock him up. I'm filing charges for trespassing, and I'm a witness to him assaulting you, Tina."

Wolfe glared at Travis through the glass of the cruiser. "Now you see what you've gone and done? I was gonna defend you, Travis. I was on your side. Hell, I don't care if you're gay or what. But you went and hit me, and now I've got *her* on my side. Now I'm gonna have to tell some gay jokes."

"I wouldn't do that, Ms. Murray," Fox said.

"Shut up, Fox!"

The barn was just as Clyde Dodson had left it the day he got kicked in the head by his prized horse. However, the saddles, the pads, and much of the tack had been eaten away by rodents.

"You ever think about gettin' a cat?" Wolfe asked over her shoulder as Marla and Jessie made their way into the mouth of the barn.

"It ran away the day Clyde died," Marla said pitifully and Wolfe shot a look to Fox.

They didn't know what they were looking for—or why, for that matter—but Travis Miles had made such a fuss about the barn, it seemed the thing to do. Standing in the midst of old farming equipment, rusted pipes and tools, old leathers, and a junk pile in the middle of the large barn, there didn't appear to be anything of any use.

"See?" Jessie was being helpful, yet defiant. "There's nothing!"

Wolfe and Fox both turned to leave when Wolfe stopped in her tracks, squinting at the shadowed pile. Something had caught her eye.

"You got any light in here?" she asked Marla.

Robotically, Marla leaned over and hit a hidden light switch. One lone bulb, hanging from a wire in the middle of the barn, illuminated everything, shining over the pile of junk in the middle of the barn floor.

"Hello. What's this?" Wolfe asked, pulling out her baton again. She flicked it open to its full length and used it to push away at an oddly shaped object.

Fox leaned forward to examine it without touching. "Looks like . . . another section of an outhouse." She squinted then looked curiously over her shoulder to her partner. "Covered in blood."

"Why do we keep finding these scattered around town?" Wolfe asked, though she was already working on the answer.

"Curious that this appears to go along with what we found in Bubba Peters's truck," Fox said.

"And then his garage was broken into." Wolfe turned to her partner.

"And his dog was killed." Fox and Wolfe were in sync.

"It appears these porta potties are very popular." Wolfe turned to look at Jessie. "Any reason you can think of that this would be stored in the barn that used to belong to your brother?"

Jessie balked. "This has nothing to do with Jared! This is . . . this must be what Travis was trying to get at so bad! You need to talk to him. You need to talk to Travis!"

"Oh, we will," Wolfe said as they headed back out of the barn. "Trust me. We will."

CHAPTER FORTY-SEVEN

"What have you done?" Tammi Whatley demanded as she entered *The Recorder*. She aimed straight for my desk, eyes blazing.

"What did I do?" I asked.

I knew exactly what I'd done. I'd helped Miranda exact her revenge, but I'd also legally run an ad, as a legitimate paper is supposed to do.

I was careful not to use names, merely stating the fact that Miranda McGhee, proprietor of Blink of an I, was proud to announce her pregnancy. Money went to the paper. I made the deadline. I could not be accused of breaking up a marriage that was already broken, and as a scorned woman, I was pleased to do the aforementioned.

"You ran this ad!" She dropped the current issue of *The Recorder* on my desk, poking violently at the ad. "Do you know what you've done?" she asked incredulously. "Do you have any idea?"

"I ran an ad," I said, oh so innocently. "Miranda's really proud about it." I smiled back to Darion James. He was a heavy chunk of a boy—every bit his father's son. He was bright-eyed and gorgeous.

"What's so wrong about that?" Tasha entered from the bathroom hallway and Tammi whirled, noting someone else in the office for the first time.

"Oh, hello, Tasha." Tammi tried to recover. Too late. Her look said it all. She did not like Tasha. More importantly, she did not *approve* of Tasha. "Is there something I can do for you?"

"No." Tasha smiled back, giving a one-shoulder shrug. "I was just leaving."

Tammi gave a satisfied nod and moved around the counter, waiting for Tasha to go. Her eyes bored holes into all three of us.

Suddenly, I wondered where Vicky was. Vicky was usually just three steps behind Tammi. Obviously, she'd seen the ad and was in hiding. I couldn't decide why, since everyone already knew Tom Jackson didn't have a faithful bone in his body. He was always on the hunt. News that he'd impregnated someone wasn't news.

The bell to the door chimed as LeAnn blew in, shooting death rays at me. She opened her mouth to say something but pulled up short at the sight of Tasha. She stopped, stared, and then made a huffing noise.

"You sure it's okay to leave?" Tasha asked, drawing her eyebrows together with concern.

I knew Tasha wanted to get out of there. She disliked them as much as they disliked her. I blew another slobbery kiss into Darion's sweet shoulder and smiled at his mother.

"Yeah, Momma'll be here any sec," I said and waved her off.

She gave a mischievous grin, looking over her shoulder toward both Tammi and LeAnn. "Okay then. Have fun."

As her hand fell on the door handle, Tammi spoke out. "Where are you going? Aren't you taking that—"

Tasha froze and turned. "That . . . what?"

Her eyes were blazing. Her mouth turned upright, making her look more catlike than human. She was daring Tammi Whatley, for once in her life, to have the nerve to say the word. Just say the word. Out loud to someone other than her little cronies.

"The baby." Tammi gave a little tug to her dress and cleared her throat as Tasha stared at her a second longer.

"Darion"—she never broke eye contact as she enunciated his name—"is in very good hands. Not that it's any of your business." She spoke each word so carefully, so slowly, and so distinctly, I feared she might leap across the counter and strangle Tammi Whatley.

Now that would be news.

No one moved for a moment. Finally, Tasha turned to me once more. "Call if you have any problems."

I nodded, and Tasha eased on out, glaring back through the window at Tammi as she disappeared down the street.

The two women muttered under their breath while I snarfled on Darion a little more. His giggle was contagious.

"Thia! Do you have any idea what you've done?" LeAnn broke the silence.

Again, I looked innocent.

"You've destroyed . . . you . . . ugh! I can't believe you would run an ad announcing that slut's pregnancy!"

"Slut? You mean Miranda McGhee?" My eyebrows shot up.

"Yes, and I do mean slut. Do you know what you've done?"

I shook my head. I couldn't wait to hear what I'd done.

"She trapped Tom! She lured him into her shop! Seduced him! Got herself pregnant when he refused to leave Vicky! And now you've pretty much confirmed that to the entire town. Vicky is . . . poor Vicky is so mortified, why, she can't even show her face."

I bounced Darion on my knee for a moment. "Wow, that's news to me," I said rather breathlessly. "I had no idea . . . although . . . I mean, it's pretty hard to imagine that she *forced* Tom to have sex with her. Seems to me—"

"Oh, you know exactly what we're talking about, here!" LeAnn looked at me. "Miranda is a slut. Just like all the women of today. No one gets married anymore, everyone runs around, spreading their legs—"

I raised my eyebrows.

"Just like that . . . baby." Tammi pointed to Darion.

Instantly, I felt the hairs on the back of my neck rise. I started to push the chair back, ready for whatever they were going to throw at Darion and me.

Oh, bring it on you fat, big-mouthed, hypocritical—

The door chimed.

What a sight it must have been as Momma and Cici strolled in, pleased as punch with themselves. We must have looked like a pack of she-wolves, baring teeth and ready to draw blood.

Momma entered first, holding the door open for the stroller Cici was pushing. I had to laugh. Both Momma and Ella wore huge floppy hats. Ella had white sunblock covering the whole of her nose. All three wore flip-flops, loose-fitting T-shirts, and capris. The stroller was loaded down with drinks, munchies, toys, books, diapers, wipes, a blanket, and a first aid kit.

"Where are you going?" I was still laughing, but Momma was surveying the crowd.

It didn't matter how old I was. She sensed it. Someone was messing with her baby. As she and Tammi Whatley already had a history—and not a pleasant one—I tensed again.

"What's going on here?" she asked.

Enter Cici. She and LeAnn were old buddies.

After several cuss words and her own personal struggle to manhandle the eight hundred pound stroller into the office, she charged over to LeAnn, doing the whole kiss-kiss greeting.

Momma eyed Tammi warily.

"Girls! I have news!" Cici clapped her hands together. "I'm getting married."

My mouth fell open.

"Yes sir! I'm getting married. This Saturday."

I'm not sure, but I think my mouth fell open even more.

"Cici!" LeAnn gasped then laughed. "To who?"

"Teddy Peters." She beamed.

"Bubba?" Tammi Whatley laughed. "The trash man?"

"Why, Cici." LeAnn circled around the counter and gave Cici a hug. "I'm so happy for you. I declare, I never thought you would ever settle down . . . with Teddy Peters. Will wonders never cease."

"He's the—"

LeAnn shut her down with a rare, bold glare that Tammi would no doubt be paying back.

"Yup. This Saturday. Hell, I figured there's no sense waiting. Once I decide to do something, I bull right in." Cici let out an infectious whoop.

Darion stirred in my arms and snapped me out of my fly-catching trance.

"This Saturday?" I asked. Cici's eyes were twinkling. I hadn't seen her look so happy or vibrant since I didn't know when. And I found myself smiling along with her. It was crazy. Insane. *À la* Cici.

"And Lily will be our flower girl." Momma clasped her hands together. "And maybe we'll have to find a job for young Darion." She leaned over toward me, her hands outstretched for Darion.

"Girls, there is so much to do," Cici said.

"Well, maybe you don't need to—" I was wondering about the play date with Ella and Darion.

"Oh, no you don't. We've been looking forward to this!" Momma said.

"Well, what can I do to help?" LeAnn asked Cici.

"Oh, my gosh! There's just . . . well, we need to run something in the paper. You could do that," she said. Somewhere, I was sure I heard Tammi make a smart remark about me running an advertisement. "I've got Arlene Myers making up the menu . . ." LeAnn, Momma, Cici, Darion, and Ella all stepped out into the street.

I fell back into my seat, deflated as only Cici can deflate a person.

"Why does your mother call your child by another name?" Tammi asked.

"She just does." I sighed, already not liking where this was leading. Before any more could be said about it, LeAnn saved me. Or, so I'd thought.

"Well, it doesn't seem very respectful," Tammi said.

"Can you believe it?" LeAnn burst into the office, laughing. "Bubba Peters. This Saturday." No sooner had Cici left her sight, LeAnn was back to being Tammi's mindless sidekick again. While she was careful with her words with me sitting so near, we all knew what was being said.

I began to pack up my things for the day. I dared anyone to say anything about my leaving.

Tammi had no interest in being tactful. "Trash!" she mumbled, causing LeAnn to glance over at me. "Oh, can you imagine how dreadful it's going to be?"

"Tammi!" LeAnn gasped and her cheeks flushed pink.

"They'll probably serve pigs in a blanket and salsa." She laughed at this image. "Pure white trash. It's going to be a white trash wedding."

I stood up.

Tammi Whatley was the essence of trash, but she was such an ignorant snob, she had no idea how repugnant she was. She couldn't see that she was all flash, no substance. She couldn't see how hypocritical she was. For all her church functions, all her Bible meetings, and Sunday school classes, she was probably the most unloving, undeserving person in town. *Do unto your neighbors . . .* please! She didn't even know what that meant.

"You couldn't pay me to go to something like that." She laughed.

I opened my mouth to speak when she said it.

As I said before, one word can change everything you know. Or think you know. One word can play so powerfully on the mind that it can change life as you know it. One word. For the second time in my life, I heard it.

It shocked me and rocked me out of my way of thinking. Previously, I had believed I needed to stay quiet for the greater good of keeping my job. Somehow, with the disappointment of leaving Duke, I'd decided I needed to just accept certain things as they were. By coming home again, I'd adopted a "roll over and take it" attitude. Until she said that word, that is.

". . . can you imagine?" She continued to laugh. "Cici's going to marry a trash man and use that little niglet in her wedding!"

Here's the thing. I may have spent the better part of my youth sure that by getting as far away as possible from Granby, my problems would all go away. The first time I'd gotten into serious trouble, I'd run straight home. To Granby. Into the arms of Momma and Cici, my friends, and neighbors. My problems didn't go away; they simply changed.

I realized that I loved my town.

Finally, I found my words. I had always hoped I would say something eloquent, something razor-sharp, perhaps followed by some wise quote in a situation like this. It would have been great if I could have waxed philosophical and stormed out, letting the door slam behind me, but there was every reason to believe it would have been wasted on the likes of Tammi Whatley. Instead, I said, "I used to think the problem was this town. It's not Granby. It's you. You're an embarrassment," and I walked out.

I was done.

CHAPTER FORTY-EIGHT

It was a liberation that was short lived. I made it around to the back of the building where I'd parked next to the dumpster when he popped out at me.

I gasped, scaring him more than he scared me. I saw him jump then run a hand through his hair, trying to regain his composure.

He looked distressed.

"Where are you going?" he asked.

"I'm . . ." I almost laughed. "Excuse me?"

"I mean . . . have you talked to Amber Hirsh?" he blurted out, and I cocked my head at him. He was acting peculiar.

"Yeah," I said, studying him. "Why?"

He sighed, his shoulders slumping. "Then you know."

I stood still and watched. *Journalism 101: Never tip your hand.*

"Have you . . . written anything? You know, about all this?" He was fishing.

So was I. "I like to get all the facts," I said, trying to figure him out. I'd always liked him. A lot. I hadn't thought there were any secrets, let alone walls between us, but something about his demeanor was different.

It was something that told me to be quick on my feet. I shrugged my shoulders. "We'll see. I'm not exactly a favorite in the office right now."

He grimaced. "I can't let you do it," he said, sounding more desperate.

"Do what?" I asked, deciding that I was done with the games. I hadn't the foggiest notion what he was talking about.

"Write about it, investigate it." His voice began to rise. "Whatever it is you do to unearth facts and past histories. I can't let you!" He grabbed my wrist as I was digging for my keys, causing me to drop my purse.

"Ow! What are you doing?" I asked. I wasn't scared. I was too stunned. "What are you talking about? What's the matter with you?!" I was more angry than frightened.

He released my arm and sank back. "You don't know." He put his hands up to his face, rubbing his temples. I watched in stunned silence as he paced back and forth, talking to himself. "But you will know. Pretty soon, you'll know and so will everyone else. What am I going to do? What am I going to do?"

"Hey!" I stepped forward, attempting to reach out to him, but he reeled back.

He looked insane, and for a moment, he seemed as if he might hit me. Then again, maybe he feared I would hit him. I'd never seen him in such a state. I opened my mouth when I heard a *woop-woop* sound. A police siren.

"Boy!" Officer Wolfe stepped out of her cruiser, one hand on the car door, the other on her holster. "You are hard to get a hold of."

"I don't want to talk to you!" Ryan Whatley yelled at her, panicked.

"Whoa!" She snapped her head back. "What'd I do?" Wolfe looked hurt.

"Words gettin' around," Fox said as she stepped from the cruiser. "No one wants to talk to you." She made a face at Wolfe then smiled at me. "She cheats at rock-paper-scissors."

Ryan seemed to have no humor. He jerked on my arm. "C'mon, Thia. We were just leaving." He began pushing me into my car, trying to open the door and shove me at the same time.

"Hey!" I cried out. I was rapidly leaving a state of concern and entering the land of straight-up annoyed.

"Hey! Ho! Ryan, buddy . . ." Wolfe said, moving closer. One hand was still on her holster, edging closer to her baton, the other held out. It looked as if she was trying to pacify him. "I just want to ask you a few questions. No big deal."

"No! I don't want to talk. I don't want to . . ." He suddenly sounded exhausted. "I just want to leave. I just want to get out of here! But . . ." His hand motions were exaggerated. "If you'd done you job, if you'd found my freakin' tailgate, I would have been out of here. But no!" He was almost yelling. He looked wild-eyed. Frantic. Then he started to laugh. "You couldn't even find a tailgate when we all know who did it. The damned Mexicans!"

He spat out the word Mexicans with certain venom, and for the first time, I saw Tammi Whatley's boy.

"I hate this town! I hate . . . God! I just wanted to get out of here, but Mom wouldn't let me leave until I had the F-ing tailgate done."

We all stared in shocked silence at this familiar face with the mouth of a stranger.

"But you couldn't do that, could you? It was just too much to ask that you might find one simple tailgate. Everyone in town knows it was Luis Rodriguez's cousin who stole it. He's a damned wetback! Straight over. And this is the way he makes his living!"

"Ryan!" I said in surprise.

"But I guess you and your Mexican partner here don't feel the need to go into Paradise Park, do you?" He shot a look of defiance at Fox.

While Fox showed no expression, Wolfe erupted. "Look, kid, I don't know what the hell your problem is—" She stepped forward just as he took a swing at her. Wolfe saw it coming, ducked back, and countered with a swift blow to Ryan's gut with the butt of her baton.

A loud *whoosh* erupted from him, and he sagged like a doll to the ground.

What just happened?

"Assaulting an officer," Fox said, moving in. As she pulled him to his feet to turn him around, he feebly attempted to wrench free from her grip.

Still winded, his effort was in vain, but he managed to speak between the gasps. "Get . . . your filthy . . . hands . . . off me."

"Oh, shut up! Damn, he's just like his mom." Wolfe threw on the cuffs.

"Shut up! You don't know anything about my mom," Ryan said, still coughing.

While they wrangled Ryan back to the cruiser, I stood paralyzed. I couldn't believe what I just saw. I couldn't believe what I just heard. Ryan Whatley—possibly one of the most mild-mannered boys I'd ever known—a raging bigot. Assaulting an officer. Over . . . what? I hadn't a clue.

"Why is everyone always taking a swing at me?" Wolfe muttered as they climbed into their vehicle.

"I told you. It's because you cheat."

▌▌▌

Two hours and forty minutes later, I was sharing a drink with Tina Wolfe and Rosa Fox at the Town Pump and shaking my head in disbelief. It was over. Everything was over, and it was nowhere near the reason or motive I'd guessed had caused James Otis's death. Even as Rosa and Tina laid it out for me, I wondered how Tasha would take the news. How could someone—*anyone*—come to grips with this kind of a crime? Accident?

No, definitely a crime.

Ryan Whatley, his parents, and now some highfalutin lawyer from Houston were calling it an accident. Ryan covered his tracks, withheld information from James's family and from the police, but more than that was the revealing of his true self. The way he spoke. The venom in his voice. He'd admitted that he would have gone back to Texas Tech if his tailgate hadn't been stolen. Oh, the irony that he believed everything had happened because of a Mexican.

How would Tasha ever come to terms with this? I shook my head, nursing a cold coke.

"At least we know it wasn't a hate crime," Tina said.

"Wasn't it?" I looked up.

Rosa was already nodding. She understood.

"No," Wolfe said. "They were friends. James and Ryan were friends."

"A friend he was so ashamed of, he couldn't be seen with in public," Rosa pointed out. "A friend who, when killed, he couldn't even come forward and admit that they'd been hanging out. Who knows, maybe . . ."

"But it was more than just his skin color." Of this, I was sure. "The Whatleys looked at James as, I don't know, someone who was limited in his potential because of his family, economic status, and color. If Tammi had known that her precious son was spending his time with locals, she would have come unglued. That's what all this is about. Mommy dearest."

Tina shook her head.

For a moment, the three of us stood by the counter, watching trucks and cars roar up and down Main but saying nothing.

Granby had been turned upside down. We'd made national news. We'd had street brawls, threats, and the most damaging of speculations about our own neighbors. In the end, James Otis had not been the victim of some white supremacist group. He'd been a victim of molestation and deceit.

▌▌▌

As Ryan Whatley unraveled in the station house, speaking to Officers Fitz and Hatch, he confessed his connection with Jared Durham. Travis knew nothing of the bloody porta potty piece in the barn. He'd just wanted what was his. It had been Jared, in his quest to retrieve any and all evidence linked to Ryan, who had killed Bubba's dog, Brutus, and stashed the porta potty piece. It was the least he could do for Ryan. It was the least he could do for James. At least, this was how Ryan saw it. When he'd gone to Jared for help, he'd called in all the chips.

Both Ryan and James had been molested. How many other boys had also been victims, Ryan hadn't known. But he'd known about James.

For two seasons, they did not speak to each other about anything other than baseball. They met at the fields for practice and games. They didn't speak at school or anywhere else. After Ryan told his parents about the molestations, his relationship with James was triggered. It developed out of necessity.

Rather than contact the police or get their child into some kind of therapy, the Whatleys moved into denial. Scandal was devastating to any thriving small-town business. And so, he was never to speak ill of the coach, never speak of any inappropriate touching or nightmares.

As a safety precaution, Mrs. Whatley began to attend every practice and game. She watched, appraised, analyzed, approved, and scrutinized every movement her boy made from that moment on. Whatever problems he was having could be fixed in the home, so she guided his view of the world and the way things should be.

He found someone who understood what he was feeling each time he attended practice and took direction from the monster. James Otis knew. James internalized as well, and they became brothers, of a sort. They shared a bond that no one else understood. Not their preachers. Not their parents. Not Tasha.

They stole away as often as they could, often fishing for hours on end but never speaking. They didn't need to. It almost became a problem in high school when Tasha was sure James was stepping out with another girl. She went wild with rage, but James still never revealed who he was with. Their kinship was sacred.

After graduation, they exchanged a few phone calls, but it was awkward. They were best together, in silence, doing something of no real consequence. Fishing. Riding with a cold drink. Listening to music. Taking comfort in each other's presence. Each was a reminder to the other that he was a survivor. Nothing else needed to be said.

On the night James was killed, Ryan had done something unusual. He'd gotten James a gift in celebration of his graduation.

Ryan attended James's party and hung back, watching the ridiculous boxing match until James told Tasha he'd be right back, making some noise about getting ice.

How could James have known he would never come back?

"Hey, man!" James laughed in surprise as Ryan handed him a box with a large white bow on top. "You get me a ring?"

Even in the darkness of the cab, Ryan saw James's wide smile light up. Ryan pulled to the right out of habit, or perhaps as part of their ritual, and headed out to Larson's Farm. It was a place they frequented, unbeknownst to Mr. Larson. It was quiet and hidden by trees. There, the two could fish for hours in Larson's stocked pond without ever being seen.

He pulled into the brush and cut the lights. A car cruised by, and both friends slid down for cover.

"Amber Hirsh," Ryan said and they both joked about the kind of girl you did and did *not* want to hook up with.

Amber was a definite *no, thanks!*

"You gotta good thing with Tasha," Ryan said, and James nodded then jiggled the box at Ryan.

"What is it?" James asked, squinting at the single piece of paper he withdrew from the box.

"It's not for you." Ryan smiled. "It's for Darion."

"No kiddin'?" James's eyebrows shot up in happy surprise, and instantly, Ryan knew he'd made the right decision. There wasn't anything James wanted for himself. It was always all about Tasha and Darion. "What is it?" He squinted again.

"A savings bond. Five hundred dollars."

"Damn!"

"It's just . . . you know, something for your boy's future." Ryan was almost embarrassed, but he knew it was the best thing to give James.

"Man!" James laughed again. "I don't know what to say. Thanks, man. Wow. I can't believe you did this." In a surprise move, he leaned over and hugged Ryan.

It was a hard, heartfelt hug that Ryan was ill-prepared for. The instant they disconnected, neither knew what to do with themselves.

A noise in the distance offered a distraction, and both men turned their attention to it instead.

Before them, in the moonlight, they saw them: Milford East, Willie Strictland, and Roland Wyck. They were performing a Granby ritual. Hell, it was the pastime of any small town. Trucks, ropes, open pastures, and anything to ski atop of made for great fun.

"What a bunch of jackasses," Ryan said, but both men laughed while Roland Wyck cowboyed behind the truck, riding some kind of saucer.

Time slipped away as they laughed about how Milford East only ever drove the truck, no doubt understanding that his standing atop anything would just plow four foot ditches into the ground. Willie and Roland skied up and down the back pasture. When, at last, they drove out Larson's gate entrance, James and Ryan rolled forward, curious about the disk left behind.

"It's the top to a shitter." Ryan laughed out loud.

They both knew what was coming next. They had to have their try at the ride. With a rope in his tool chest, it took just minutes to concoct the same rig Milford East had. It was James's night, so Ryan had relinquished and let him go first.

Fastening his feet to the lip of the lid, James made two successful passes. He hooted and hollered, bending and flexing as the lid hit divots in the dirt. He was an expert.

Then Ryan saw James's left knee buckle and he began to slow. An old football injury. But as he slowed, James waved him on, wanting Ryan to pick up speed once more. Or so Ryan thought.

It all happened so quickly. Ryan would never be sure of what exactly transpired. James went down on his knees, and Ryan believed it was an intentional move. Perhaps to protect his knees, or—typical James—to test new moves. As he moved down, the lid hit another divot and the rope slackened as James jolted forward. From his rear view mirror, James looked as if he was praying, hunched forward.

Then came the snap of the rope.

James's body flipped and contorted. Ryan saw it. He saw it fully. The rope was wrapped around James's neck. Somehow when they'd lurched forward, he'd become entangled. Another bump, another divot, another flip. Even as Ryan slammed on the brakes, it was too late.

The truck slid forward as the brakes locked. Dust blanketed everything for a moment, and Ryan swatted desperately at the air as he ran back.

Oh, God!

Blood. Blood was everywhere.

He ran to James but halted inches from his body–the anguished look on James's face, the rope sawed more than halfway through his neck, the crumpled body.

Oh God!

Ryan staggered back and choked out James's name.

No answer. There would never be an answer to that name again.

He felt a sob crawl up his throat.

Oh God!

He turned and ran. It was all he could think to do.

Get help. Call someone. Get help.

Even as he thought it, he knew it was too late. He slammed the truck door shut and lurched forward again, only to feel a horrific snap and tug on the truck.

Oh sweet Jesus!

The rope.

Sobbing and screaming, he threw the truck into park, fell out onto the ground, then staggered back to James's body.

The rope had all but gone through, and Ryan cried out. Bordering hysteria, he paced back and forth a moment longer, then he remembered his knife and sawed through the rope before peeling out once more.

His heart was pounding. His heart was broken. He was numb and every fiber of his being was screaming all at the same time. He was quite sure he was going insane at that moment.

Help. Help. Get help.

James's cell phone was lying on the seat, and he snatched it up, dialing 911.

When he heard a voice, he didn't know why but he reacted. He wiped the phone against his shirt and tossed it out the window. Impulsively, he picked up the savings bond and card and shoved them inside his shirt pocket. He drove wildly, blindly, for as long as he could. He could feel himself hyperventilating. Desperate, crazed, he pulled over. He ran. He ran and ran. He ran until he fell exhausted to the ground. He rocked back and forth, sobbing as anguish and horror spilled from him.

Slowly, reason and survival flowed back to him. He'd done what he could. He called for help. But there was no help. James was beyond dead. He was mangled. Destroyed.

He'd died having a blast.

Over and over again, he told himself that James died as he lived—on the edge. He focused on the memory of James, one arm waving in the air, a smile that could light up New York City, riding the lid like a cowboy.

Only James had handled the end of the rope. Only James had touched the lid. The cell phone was James's, wiped down and tossed out. No one saw them leave together. He was safe. No one needed to know about this.

In true Whatley fashion, Ryan gathered himself. He sniffed and stood. He smoothed his clothes out, wiped his eyes, and took a long, deep breath. There was nothing to tie him to James. No one ever need know. God help him. No one ever need know.

He looked around, trying to get his bearings. He was somewhere outside Paradise Park, along the roadside, some four or five miles from town. As he walked back to his truck, he thought about his alibi, where he might have been tonight, who he saw, what he did. But he halted when he saw his truck. There were shadowy figures surrounding his truck. One of the men had his hands pressed up against the driver's window, peering inside. Ryan felt a knot form in his throat. This was all he needed.

He stood stock still as he watched them move around to the back of the truck. In fluent Spanish, one of the men directed the two others to help him remove Ryan's tailgate. His feelings about this theft were mixed. James was dead. But he didn't need any witnesses to his truck being out at this hour on this side of town.

Was there blood on the tailgate?

He stood motionless, trying to decide what to do. He'd expected the men to jack his truck. When they all jumped back into their own vehicle, content with just Ryan's tailgate, he melted back into the brush along the road and watched as the man who stole his tailgate drove by.

Manny Rodriguez.

Manny Rodriquez and his sticky fingers had changed the game forever.

CHAPTER FORTY-NINE

"This entire wedding cost two hundred twelve dollars and eighty-four cents," Momma boasted.

"It did not!" Arlene Myers said in dismay.

"It did. I've got the receipts here in my purse to prove it."

With that, word got around very quickly. Indeed, this was the wedding of all weddings and something to make Granby proud.

We'd gone to the Dollar Store to get all the white plates, linens, sporks, and fake champagne glasses. Cici already owned a beautiful white dress she'd once planned on wearing to an opera up in Houston but never got to go on account of a mass exodus from New Orleans when a terrible hurricane destroyed much of the city a while back. Aunt Cici had also gotten out the word that she did not want gifts, although she was registered at both Target and Victoria's Secret for some, as she called it, "Ooh-la-la" items, but that she hoped everyone in attendance would bring flowers. Either white or red roses and carnations.

"We don't need anything," Cici said, unwittingly unleashing renewed tension between Officer Wolfe and Cici.

"True enough," Wolfe retorted. " 'Sides, whatever you might need, ol' Bubba there can just pick it up along the side of the road."

It was a seemingly innocent joke that landed Wolfe with traffic duty, as per Cici's personal request from the all too obliging chief.

The wedding took place on the steps of the courthouse. It was the perfect place for a majestic backdrop. After they said, "I do," Cici and Teddy moved down the steps and into the beautiful town square, which was covered in white lace bunting and flowers supplied by the Ladies Club of Granby.

It was an interesting thing to see the rats fleeing the sinking ship as news of the Whatleys' political views and the deeds of their son were played out in the press. And not, I might add, by me. LeAnn Ricks tried her hand at her first story in the paper. She'd been delicate and diplomatic, a promise she'd made to Tammi, but she'd wet her whistle and seen firsthand how difficult it is to withhold information.

Word was that Tammi was not at all pleased with the article, and relations between the women had cooled considerably. Whether Vicky Jackson was too wrapped up in her highly public separation from Tom, or if she really wanted to distance herself from the Whatley scandal, remained to be seen. Not only had she crawled out of her hole, she'd headed up the Radosa/Peters wedding preparations, and she'd been instrumental in flower and lace placement around the courtyard.

Shelby Harrelson had gone over the top, which she always did for celebrations, and had arranged for a horse-drawn carriage—complete with a gorgeous white horse supplied by Chester Kennedy—to take the newlyweds from the courthouse to their honeymoon suite at the Limestone Inn.

Momma and I had been assured that fainting spells were not contagious and Chester's horse was in no way going to faint like his goats.

And while I'd been a bit worried about where her squirrel-killing hands had been of late, Ms. Riley supplied an amazing three-tier wedding cake. I had to squash images of little dead squirrel bodies dangling from cords outside Ms. Riley's kitchen window, their little squirrel hairs wafting into the open window as the cakes cooled on racks from her little toaster oven. Suddenly, I had this horrible vision of her using a little Easy Bake Oven to cook squirrel parts. Some things, I decided, were best left alone.

Everyone was there and everyone, it seemed, had some part in the wedding, including the gorgeous Frankie Larson, who acted as my date. Pastor Tyree led the service and as cheers mounted when Mr. Peters, a.k.a. Uncle Bubba, leaned in to kiss Cici, it felt as though all of Granby was a family. Once more.

Uncle Bubba had asked his good friends, Javier Moreno and Hector Lopez, to play at the wedding, and as Cici and Bubba descended the stairs, the full-fledged, Texas-proud mariachi band swung into action. The entire square came alive with delightful sounds, smells, color, and long overdue goodwill.

There were certain outcasts. Judge McKinley, Amber Hirsh, Hut Langford, Cody Kyle, Jessie Durham, Monica Tyree, and Ryan Whatley would be answering to a new community behind bars. If they were lucky, some might serve community service, but it was unlikely it would be in Granby.

Tom Jackson was serving his own sentence, but it was one that deserved to be public. He'd tried to play with two women and got burned.

I watched as Vicky Jackson took to the center of the square, twirling and dancing to the band with Pastor Tyree while Tom sat a distance away, looking uncomfortable and miserable. I didn't know what Miranda would do but planned on stopping by to admire more turquoise and tell her the story of another young woman I knew who got pregnant.

Frankie gave me a soft nudge and directed my gaze out toward the center, where everyone was dancing.

I instantly smiled at the sight of Tasha dancing with both Darion and Ella in her arms. She looked across the courtyard to me and beamed—megawatt smile.

She knew now. She knew how and why James had died. And, amazingly, had taken it better than most. She understood. It was all she said. She understood. I realized that was all she ever really wanted—to understand why. She was moving forward, just as James would have wanted.

"She sure is pretty," Frankie said, letting his arm slide away from my back and took a hold of my hand.

"Which one?" I asked.

"Well, both, but in particular, Ella." He gave Ella a little wave and she struggled to get down from Tasha's arms.

To anyone else, the move might have seemed unspectacular. To me, it was quite the opposite. Ella loved Frankie, and he, her. It moved my heart in ways I couldn't express. It filled me with something I felt I was lacking with my own father.

Tasha set Ella down, and Ella padded her way through the crowd to my open arms. Before I could get her, Frankie snatched her up in his.

"Phank-ie! Momma!" she cooed. "El-la." She pointed to herself.

"Yes!" I laughed with approval and then scanned the area to find Momma but found she was already staring at me.

"You relinquish?" I teased her.

"Not at all." Momma winked at me. I could feel it coming. Somehow, I was going to be embarrassed. "I merely changed my way of thinking."

Move along. Let's just move along.

But Frankie bit. "How's that?"

"Ella is a beautiful name. A beautiful name for a beautiful child," Momma said, but I knew that was for the benefit of Ella's sweet ears. "But I can still have Lily."

Somewhere behind us, we heard someone call out to Cici and Bubba. "For all the money you saved, you should have sprung for air conditioning!"

Someone else called, "Pastor Tyree, can't you talk to God about this heat?"

Even in the shade of the trees, the heat was stifling and about to get hotter.

"I've been watching you two." Momma continued her own reign of terror.

Run away! Flee!

"Tell me, Frankie, what do you think about the name Lily?"

"Wow." Frankie laughed and pretended to tug at his collar. "It really is hot out here, isn't it?" But his smile was warm and wide, and he made no moves to go anywhere. He winked at me. "I like the name Lily a lot. Or, little Frankie."

Momma clapped her hands with delight just as a breeze picked up.

In typical Granby fashion, clouds rolled in, moving down Main

Street like a locomotive and showering a very thirsty town. The bursts of *oohs* and *ahhs* came from the drought-weary residents of Granby as pellets of rain bounced off the pavement, against our bodies, and the overly sunbaked earth, yet not one person made a move to leave. As the storm moved in, the band played on, and we danced through the night. I knew then it was good that I'd left. It was so good that I'd left because I'd needed reminding that you can go home again. You really can.

EPILOGUE

"Right here." Tina Wolfe patted her right hip, her hand hovering over her pistol. "I got a bullet for ya right here, Ms. Vargus."

"Tina Marie!" Ms. Vargus snapped, and Wolfe cringed at having her christened name called out for all the free world to hear. "I am moving as fast as I can. If you're in such a damned hurry, go on in. I'm perfectly capable of opening a door for—"

"Ugh!" Wolfe cried out, impatiently tapping her foot and looking around.

With two completed, yet unsuccessful, sensitivity training classes under her belt, Chief Teague had been in a quandary as to what he should do with Officer Tina Wolfe.

She continued to harass the residents of Paradise Park, as well as senior citizens she believed too old to drive, anyone with a fancy new car, and all males under the age of twenty. She embarrassed the department last Halloween when, after being pelted once too many times by flying candy during the parade, she stopped the entire procession and refused to let anyone drive until all candy was put away. She shot Ms. Riley's squirrel carcass out of a tree, citing it to be a health code violation, and used an official car to escort Thia Larson to the hospital when Thia was in labor with the Larsons' baby, Lily Marie—named for both Ms. Franks and Officer Tina Marie Wolfe.

It had been a kind gesture but hadn't overridden the fact that Officer

Wolfe had been leading Mickey Kennedy's funeral procession when she'd decided to fly down Highway 547 with a pregnant woman in her cruiser. Worse, she'd left Officer Fox to fend for herself.

Yet everyone loved Wolfe.

On a personal level, Chief Teague liked her. On a professional level, she drove him to near madness. She stripped each time she came into the station house, complaining loudly about heat and sweat. She was slow to write up reports and even slower to take commands. She was his dark horse.

A community service, of sorts, was the solution he searched for—more specifically, Mrs. Gail Vargus. Three times a week, it was Officer Wolfe's duty to check up on, transport, and run errands with Ms. Vargus.

"No errand too grand, no errand too small," he'd told Wolfe. "Just shut up and do it."

To everyone's surprise, though she denied it vehemently, Wolfe liked the old woman. She complained miserably about Buzz, the goat, and how long it took Mrs. Vargus to get from point A to point B, yet she spoke of Mrs. Vargus constantly. And for the first time in Granby history, Officer Wolfe had met someone who wasn't the least bit frightened of her. Even better, she called Wolfe "Tina Marie" and lived to talk about it.

"If you could actually lift up your feet, rather than shuffling, you might gain another couple of minutes in your stride," Wolfe said, tapping the door of the Town Pump.

"Just go inside." Ms. Vargus waved her on. "I don't need—"

They were interrupted by the honking of a car and revving of a loud engine. Wolfe stepped back out onto the pavement and squinted down Main. Coming on fast and loud was a sports car she did not recognize. It was flashy, red, expensive, and did not belong in Granby.

As it roared on by, Wolfe was shocked to see its driver. Angela Wyck.

"Son of a bitch!" Wolfe shouted, almost dropping the door.

"I beg your pardon?" Mrs. Vargus looked shocked.

"You see that?" Wolfe could hardly contain herself. "You see that?"

"No! I didn't see anything. I was too busy—"

"I'll be damned! She got it! She actually got it!"

While the charges of assault had been dropped against Tasha

Williams, Angela Wyck moved on to a more profitable payday. When a large peanut butter company recalled a batch of bad butter, it took Angela no time at all to be found doubled over in the emergency room while dialing a good lawyer.

"Who? What on earth are you talking about?" Mrs. Vargus asked, looking far too late. The roar, the car, and Angela Wyck were gone.

"C'mon!" Wolfe leapt in front of Mrs. Vargus, rerouting her.

"Good heavens! What are you doing?"

"You didn't see that? That white trash! That piece of trash got herself a new car at the expense of us! Of us!" She turned Mrs. Vargus, giving her little nudges and pushes against her back.

"Stop it! Tina Marie! You're going to knock me down."

But Wolfe was too busy running to her car, opening the passenger door for Mrs. Vargus, and darting back again to the curb. "C'mon! C'mon! We have to go after her! C'mon . . . ugh!" She looked to the high heavens.

"I don't know why I should have—"

"C'mon . . ." Wolfe whirled her arms in big circles. "Let's move, move, move." She moved behind Mrs. Vargus again, giving helpful nudges toward the car. She resisted, moving more slowly. "This ain't just about you and me, Ms. Vargus. This is for peanut butter lovers everywhere!"

"Peanu—"

"I got a bullet, Ms. Vargus, and I'll shoot at your feet. I swear I will!"

THE END

ABOUT THE AUTHOR

Alexandra Allred's writing career began through, of all things, bobsled. Allred made the first ever U.S. Women's Bobsled team, where she won the gold medal for the U.S. Nationals, was named *Athlete of the Year* by the United States Olympic Committee and served as a role model for the International Olympic Committee for pregnant athletes. She then wrote for *Sports Illustrated* about life as a professional female football player, later penning the award-winning **Atta Girl! A Celebration of Women in Sport** (Wish Publishing, 2002), test drove the Volvo Gravity Car, and began adventure writing for national publications and blogging for NBC's Olympic coverage.

Allred turned to fiction after hearing one word. "Niglet." A social commentary on racism and hypocrisy, Allred released **White Trash** and soon after, **Damaged Goods**, now headed for the silver screen. The award-winning author then teamed up with documentary filmmaker Mark Birnbaum for the short film, **Swingman,**

Allred was nominated to the White House Champion of Change for Public Health and, in 2016, launched Pas Fitness, a fitness venture for the special needs populations. Allred is the author of more than 20 books, hundreds of articles for national journals, magazines, and newspapers, and continues to speak before the EPA, US Senate, House of Representatives, medical, educational and fitness forums.

www.ingramcontent.com/pod-product-compliance
Lightning Source LLC
Chambersburg PA
CBHW070745190726
48292CB00002B/427